"You're [illegible] smooth voice as low as his own. "Go away! You don't belong here."

"You don't own the pond. I'll take off my clothes and join you."

"Don't bother removing them. Just jump in over there." She indicated a spot several yards to one side. "Now get off my clothes!"

"You'll have to come get them," he said slyly, eying ripples that concealed the lower half of her body.

"Very well then, I will," she said with a determined nod. "Now get off my clothes."

Benadek was still grinning when she jerked her knee up to his chin, and barely changed his expression when he came to rest flat on his back. He tasted blood. She spun full circle, her hard, bare foot catching him first alongside his head, stunning him, then again in his ribs, knocking the wind from him. He made it to his hands and knees before her deadly foot landed across his buttocks and sent him sprawling again.

"Now will you go away, you disgusting child?"

Speechless, humiliated, Benadek stumbled toward camp. He heard her say "Oh, damn! Now I'm all dirty again," and heard the splash as she dove back into the water.

SIMPLY HUMAN

L. WARREN DOUGLAS

For Sue

SIMPLY HUMAN

This is a work of fiction. All the characters and events portrayed in this book are fictional, and any resemblance to real people or incidents is purely coincidental.

A Baen Books Original

Baen Publishing Enterprises
P.O. Box 1403
Riverdale, NY 10471
www.baen.com

ISBN: 0-671-57882-0

Cover art by John Monteleone

First printing, August 2000

Distributed by Simon & Schuster
1230 Avenue of the Americas
New York, NY 10020

Production by Windhaven Press, Auburn, NH
Printed in the United States of America

PROLOGUE
The Dry Hills, Earth

Sweat-soaked, caked with bitter salt-dust, the wizened brown man peered out from the dead rocks at a scene straight from his guiltiest childhood vision of Hell.

Snarling hounds as big as ponies milled about the narrow defile, slashing at each other and their masters with finger-sized teeth. Their sparse, coarse hair left dirty gray skin exposed, and failed to hide fresh, gaping wounds. The whole pack had gone mad.

Horny claws left raking tracks in the soft sandstone. The hellhounds shook their massive heads, blinked saucer-sized ocher eyes and twitched their long, ratlike noses as the old man's powdery fire-dust seared their nasal membranes. They howled like canine banshees. They ran in circles and backed across their own tracks as if desperately avoiding swarms of invisible bees.

Unable to identify the source of their excruciating pain, they fell upon each other blindly; great fangs tore patchy fur, grimy skin, and dark red flesh. Gobbets of blood-flecked foam dangled from their jaws and flew through the air as they twisted and spun madly about, oblivious to their hideous wounds and to their hidden quarry.

The old man allowed himself an almost-silent chuckle that was drowned in the howls and snarls of his erstwhile pursuers. He held up a tiny leather bag, gave its drawstring a decisive tug, and tucked it away in his sorcerer's robe. His eyes returned to the bloody carnage beyond.

The dogs' masters, huge men with identical shocks of white-blond, curly hair, waded among the beasts swinging short clubs and heavy chains, their black leather jerkins and trousers impervious to teeth and claws. Sweat thickened with alkaline dust glistened on their almost-identical faces. The hidden man noted with satisfaction that they were reeling with heat and fatigue. A baleful red sun, desert-hot even late in the day, beat down from a dust-laden sky, casting crimson shadows over a rust and ocher and black landscape unrelieved by a single growing thing.

The oldster was not pleased they had holstered handguns—lasers, judging by the powerpacks slung over their buttocks. Forcing his ancient knees to be steady, he rose to his feet and began the arduous climb to the safety of the heights above the ravine.

Atop the gully, the oldster paused to catch his breath and to reflect. Two thousand years, more or less, and at times like this it seemed like nothing had really changed. Two thousand years after the Fall of Man there were still dogs, and leather-clad cops—honches, they were called now. Their wide belts still sagged with leather packets. They were still a-jingle with chains, their garments studded liberally with silver bosses, their calf-height boots strapped and buckled. He recognized them for what they were: shiny, timeless tools of intimidation and threat. Even after two thousand unsuccessful years, those cops were still chasing the last black man on Earth.

Never mind that the steely-eyed Aryan types were only half-men spliced together from the genes of military policemen and second-rate TV stars who looked good in uniform—any uniform, from a Roman centurion's or a Nazi SS colonel's to an NYPD sergeant's. They were still cops.

Never mind that the polymorphic, mutated hounds had brains twice the size of an Alsatian's. They were still dogs.

The odds were not much worse than they'd been in Detroit or LA. Those eight honches and all their relatives were identical in mind as well as physiognomy, with none of the quirks or sparks of creativity that had made real cops dangerous. What would fool one would fool all the others, and with two millennia of practice, the old man had learned all the tricks.

Even the hounds were not perfect. They resulted from the chemical mutagens that had poisoned the planet, not from careful design, and were cancer-ridden from the day they were whelped. Their hides were ulcerated by desert sunlight and irritated by salty dust, and their clever brains never had time to learn enough to make them truly deadly. Most lived only two or three years, and none reached five. While the rest of the world, plants and animals alike, was recovering from the PCBs and DDTs and polyfluorinated this'n that, the honches' unimaginative breeding programs had preserved their hounds' imperfections along with their great size and their brains.

Rising stiffly to his feet, the oldster shook the dust from his faded robe. The mystic symbols adorning it were as old as mankind, and were interspersed with benzene rings, flowchart conventions, and microcircuitry diagrams. Only an educated man would have recognized any of them, and there had been none on Earth for over a thousand years. He wrapped the robe over his all-weather Everlon® utility suit, and strode off in search of his mules.

Memo:

Kaledrin—something's wrong with this output. This is no classic myth. Who is this old man? What in the name of Sapience is a "honch?" Have you been playing games with the biocybes' input again?

(Saphooth, Head Archivist,
Project MYTHIC)

Memo:

Patience, Your Intellect. This is preliminary stuff. Abrovid says that the biocybes are self-calibrating quasi-organic computers. They need more input, more myths, before they develop the proper algorithms.

(Kaledrin, Senior Editor)

The mules had not strayed far from where he'd hobbled them. One was saddled, and the other bore battered leather trunks, one on each side. One was four-legged, the other, eight. They had discovered a rare clump of rock-thistle in a shady crevice, and were deftly pulling fat, succulent flowers from the prickly bush with their pink lip-tendrils.

His old brown hands stroked the saddle mule's cheek. Some ways off now, down in the rocky defile, the hellhounds' harsh baying waned. The old man was unworried, secure among the rocks many man-heights above the trail. His mules stood rested, ready for a long night's work.

A heavy staff crafted of twisted blue beech leaned on a jutting outcrop. Both ends were bronze-shod—the base a scarred cap and the top a sphere the size of a small apple.

"Well enough, old ass," he murmured, peering over his mount's shoulder and down his back trail, "the devil-dogs'll recover soon enough. It's getting dark and we must make tracks. Are you rested enough?"

<Rested?> the beast replied querulously. Its voice was as smooth as the old man's, with no trace of mulish bray. <I carried your sharp-boned carcass for hours, and rested for mere minutes—don't be an ass, yourself. But I'm not ready to be dog-meat. I'm rested enough.> The mule's words came forth without visible movement of its lips and their dangling tendrils. It stood motionless, no shine of superior intelligence in its huge, brown eyes.

<Quit bickering,> said the pack mule, continuing to chew its mouthful of coarse weed even as it spoke. <The honches have eyes to follow our trail, not pepper-filled noses.>

"Don't talk with your mouth full," the mules' owner said. "Nevertheless, your point's well taken. Your hoofprints will stand out even by moonlight. We'll have to lose them in the rocks above."

For all their conversational abilities, the two mules responded no differently than their less verbose ordinary brethren to the old man's attempts to get them moving. Several blows and curses later the trio were on their way up a narrow trail among dry, broken boulders. The hounds' uproar diminished further. Still, the mules' hoofprints stood out clearly in the dusty soil.

"Here's a vantage point," the oldster said, "high enough so they won't see us." The defile was a line of blackness among the rocks, impenetrable to human eyes. The old man swore mildly, fiddled with a tiny bump on his staff, and mumbled an incantation. The landscape took on an eerie reddish glow quite in contrast with the sickly moonlight.

"Seven," he whispered. "Where's the eighth?" The red glow intensified. "Ah! There! He's off the trail, cutting in front of us"

<Oh, no!> The exclamation came from the direction of the saddled mule. <You want us to go over the top, don't you?>

<With both these trunks on my back?> came from the other beast. <Impossible!>

"Not impossible. You'll prance over those rocks like goats, with my help," their owner said.

<He's going to use his staff,> the saddle mule said, dully resigned.

<Not again!> the other replied. <I'm still queasy from the last time he played that trick. Goats, hah!>

"You'll do it," the old man countered. "That pepper will wear off. Those hounds'll be no happier for their new scabs and sores."

<Shut up, old man. Wind up your silly staff, and waft us over the hills.>

"It doesn't wind up, you ass. It's a magic staff."

<Magic, shmagic,> said the mule. <I could put your magic in my left ear.>

"It's a big ear, you being a mule."

<S'what I said. Wind it up.>

"Hmmph!"

The old man peered down the hillside a last time. "They're still on our trail. Six behind us, one cutting ahead, and one staying with the dogs."

There was a route through the rocky, shattered countryside besides the obvious trail—a narrow, difficult side path over clean, soil-free rock. The honches would follow it, never dreaming that man and mules had gone straight up the steep hillside.

He hefted his staff. "If I remember how to do this . . . the honches, ahead and behind, will get the worst of it . . . and you fellows'll feel like colts again." He mumbled another incantation and followed it with, "C'mon, mules, giddyup!"

Both beasts responded without further prompting. Like goats they took to the heights, finding footholds where none seemed to exist. Even laden with trunks and elderly rider, they seemed to float over small obstacles and climbed easily over larger ones. Below, the honches responded to the spell differently: they moved slowly, without swagger, plodding like fat old men.

The mules reached the top of the ridge. The oldster peered backwards one last time. The six exhausted honches and the one who had tried to cut the quarry off met in mid-defile, and concluded what the oldster had wished: that he and his mules had taken the side trail.

<Well!> his mule exclaimed. <It worked.>

"Of course it did. You doubted my sorcery?"

<Sorcery, shmorcery! A mere cone of deflection between us and the Earth's core, a minor reduction in local gravitation here and an equally minor increase over there. Any horse's arse with the proper gimmickry could do it. Just don't forget to recharge the batteries this time—square of the distance, isn't it? If those honches got everything we didn't, that staff's about shot, right now.>

"Don't tell me my business. It's a clear sky—tomorrow'll be sunny. I'll have all the power I need by noon."

<S'what you said the last time, old man.>

By dawn's first gray glow they were plodding down the northern slope over short, verdant grass. Songfrogs hopped out of their path, chirping merrily, and flying snakes circled about them, bright, iridescent colors flashing off their tiny multiple wings. The air was full of humming, whistling, and nattering creatures, each celebrating the return of day. The bleak lands were behind them.

The old man was less cheery than his surroundings warranted. <What ails you, old fellow?> his mule demanded. <We lost them, didn't we? And there's a city only a half-day's walk, all downhill.>

"I hope they give up once they're sure they've lost our trail," he replied. "There's a pure-human camp that way. I'd forgotten about it, or I'd never have steered them that way."

"Whuff!" the mule snorted, in an entirely different, definitely more mulish, voice than before.

"You're right," the man replied, "they'll turn before then. After all, they'll be eager for a night in town, too. We're lucky Vilbursiton is large—they'll never find us there."

<What will *we* find there?> asked the mule.

"Who knows? Perhaps a stable with good oats for you, a warm room and a bottle for me. Then we'll do magic tricks to fool the yokels, write letters for others, and of course there'll be a temple needing reprogramming and repair—there's always that," the old man's voice grated bitterly. "A thousand years and fifty thousand temples . . . and I've barely begun the task."

<Bury your self-pity, old fraud!> his saddle mule scolded mildly. <You're only responsible for half a continent. Let the other magicians worry about the rest of the world.>

"If there are others," he muttered peevishly. "Old Yasha hasn't reported in for five hundred years—since the last satlink failed."

<Neither have you, Archie,> the mule replied. <After all, the satellites weren't built to work a thousand years overtime.>

"Neither was I," the old man said, shaking his head sadly. "Neither was I."

INTERLUDE
The Great School, Midicor IV

Saphooth, head archivist of the MYTHIC* Project, slapped the hard-copy binder on Kaledrin's worktable. "What's *that* supposed to be?" he growled. "The biocybes were instructed to translate old myths, not create nonsensical stories." His skinny anthro-form digit pressed itself white on the printout.

Kaledrin grimaced. No one not an anachronism himself used hard copy in this day and age. "I'm sorry if the output displeases you, Estimable One," he said aloud, failing to suppress a snide overtone. "The biocybes' instructions were given exactly as specified, and the source-tales were read into their memory from the earliest and most reliable documents—also exactly as directed." Careful, K, he warned himself. Old fool he may be, but still he's your employer. Taking a deep breath, he said "If this 'Archie' is truly Achibol the Sorcerer, the next batch of output will tell us. Perhaps he's merely a minor character dredged from obscurity by whatever sophisticated new algorithms the biocybes have created for themselves."

"Perhaps so. I fail to understand how such programs, intended to clarify ancient tales, present instead new enigmas. 'Honches,' for example. From what forgotten legend do they spring?"

"I don't know, Perceptive One. We've given the biocybes millions of ancient words to digest, from so many worlds. Speculation is premature. This entry is, after all, a 'Prologue.' The next output batch may arrive tomorrow." Kaledrin leaned back on his nether tentacles, his breath whistling evenly from wide-open spiracles, the perfect picture of a relaxed and calm human being. "Surely," he said smoothly, "we can both suppress our . . . curiosity . . . for another day?"

Saphooth spun about on his two bony shanks. "Twenty million neuro-creds," he muttered as the door

---

* MYTHIC: an acronym in Sengrawlish, an ancient tongue read only by Saphooth and a scattering of other scholars. Roughly translated as "Glorious Seeking of Truffloids among the Roots of the Ancestral Tree."

irised open before him, "and we get nonsense." He departed abruptly.

"Well?" Kaledrin said, seemingly addressing the musty air of his small office, "Do you see what he's like, now?"

"A crotchety old soul, indeed," replied a second voice, from behind a stack of dusty data-cubes that contained the entire history of the planet Obolost, from its primal mud to the glory of its gleaming interstellar fleets (now themselves dust for several millennia). "But you told him the truth." The speaker arose with a rattle of chitinous exoskeletal plates. Like Kaledrin, the second man affected the utilitarian, arthro-molluscoid form indigenous to this world, Midicor IV.

"You're the systems operator, Abrovid," Kaledrin retorted. "Why *doesn't* the tale bear closer resemblance to what we put *into* the computers?"

"Stop thinking of the biocybes as computers," Abrovid said. "They're class-A self-programming, organic-matrix artificial intelligences. Linked together, they're a synergistic quantum leap beyond their individual selves. We may never know exactly how they think, or why they've chosen to give us output in the form they have. If you don't like what they're producing, you'll have to change the parameters they're ordered to work within—or Saphooth will. For now, why not follow your own advice—wait and see what they give us tomorrow, or the next day?"

Abrovid rose to full height, motational tentacles curled like helical springs, and glided to the door. A shaft of sunlight fell on him as it opened. "A lovely day for a man to sun himself along the river," he said, but Kaledrin did not reply.

"Dictation!" Abrovid heard the scholar command his personal AI terminal, buried somewhere amid the clutter and dust of his lair. "Editor's Introduction."

The first Tome of Achibol the Scrivener, Sorcerer and Ancient Man.
Editor's Introduction

Achibol. His name reverberates down the corridors of prehistory, the primal character in a thousand mythologies. He is Achibol the God, who led the first men from their animal state to true humanity; he is also the Trickster whose attempts to conquer the universe always fail, instead freeing humanity from its planetary prisons and giving it the stars.

In some cultures, Achibol is a savior, in others an elfin spirit. Among the Moldabi he is a molt-sprite who trades gold tenday-pieces for infants' outgrown skins. The Yarbandrum stuff effigies of him with addlewort and dreamdust, and dance in the smoke of his burning, For a tenday they adopt shapes and semblances glimpsed in their hallucinations, all the while vilifying Achibol, father of lies.

Achibol myths are as varied as the somatoforms of those who tell them. Crustacean watermen of Scyllis people their tales with arachnoid and simian demons. Among the arachnoids of the Inner Arm, heroes are eight- or twelve-legged and villains are simian or crustacean or . . . but you, whatever your chosen form, have surely observed this.

The single unifying thread of the myths is the struggle to *become*, to attain mastery of bodily form, whatever one's planetary ancestry. All human evolution converges toward that ability, that sets us apart from lesser lifeforms. But it is the nature of ancestral forms to reject such innovations, and many myths develop to express that primordial conflict.

Does the uniformity of mythic cycles point

toward a single origin-world for all humanity, paleontological evidence to the contrary? Several persistent cults continue to believe so, and we hope that MYTHIC's revelations will put paid to such nonsense for once and for all. But these myths have been studied for millennia, you protest. What new insights can there be, after all this time?

Biocybernetic computers have their roots in prehistory. What is new is the application of the total resources of the Midicor biocybes to a single problem in literary analysis. Consider: there are 58,000 worlds with physically distinct sentients who share the ability to shift between shapes suitable on different worlds (and to interbreed freely). There are approximately 58,000 related origin-myths, the Achibol tales, whose universality suggests that they emerged early in human prehistory, during the "interstellar threshold stage" of each race's development.

The biocybes of Midicor IV are capable of holding the sum of human knowledge in their tumorlike memory masses. They have databases of all known languages, current and antique, extensive collections of myths, legends, and apocryphal tales from scores of worlds, and billions of terabytes of histories, planetary biologies, and astrophysical compendia.

Use of the Midicor IV facilities by linguists, mythologists, and historians is not new, but the methodology of this experiment is. The experimenters combed the archives of several thousands of planets for variants of the Achibol tales, regardless of literary or historic worth. Apocryphal tales were not rejected, nor were outright works of fiction.* All the data are being entered in the biocybes' memories.

---

* Fictional works input were clearly identified as such.

No parameters have been set; no criteria have been stated, no algorithms specified. The biocybes' sole instruction is to compile a single version of the Achibol tales that is internally consistent, makes maximum use of the data, contradicts no sound scientific evidence on record, and that has the highest probability of being a factual account of actual historic events. Thus this first episode, this Prologue, is not a direct translation of one mythic sequence but a synthesis of many, each passage reconciled for consistency of form, style, and content by the most sophisticated artificial minds in the galaxy. Without human preconditions, the story you will read is their own interpretation, derived from the most complete data ever assembled.

The biocybes' processes are holographic—or intuitive. Secondary programs written by men and lesser cybernetic minds provide a reliability check on the biocybes themselves, but their function is strictly hindsight—they cannot duplicate what the biocybes do.

The interactive nature of the biocybes' research has amusing side effects: each time new mythic fragments are introduced, they are analyzed for consistency not only with the developing narrative, but with previously rejected data as well. The effect is a story that shifts subtly with each new input, as if the whole narrative were a fisherman's net, hexagons tied so that the slightest tug causes every other to change. It has been impossible to pin down the exact origin of particular changes.

Thus the tale you are about to read may change between this issuance and the next. As yet, the differences are so minor as to be unnoticeable, but the possibility exists that the next newly discovered myth from some backwater world* may initiate changes that ripple like a stiff breeze through the entire net. The truth of the whole, and of our human origins, will not be known until the last myth has been input.

(Kaledrin, Senior Editor)

---

* Research in distant places is not cheap, nor is the biocybes' time. Every credit given will help us bring out newer, more accurate versions of the tale, and . . . within the next decade, we hope . . . a sequel to the story you are about to read.

For ten neurocredits you will receive a handsome certificate and a discount on a bound collector's volume of the biocybes' output.

For a hundred neurocredits, you will receive an invitation to the prepublication ceremony and banquet here on Midicor IV (transportation not included), the wall certificate, and a year's membership in the Universal Museum Association.

A donation of a thousand neurocredits will bring all the above, plus *each chapter of the biocybes' output, with commentaries by scholars, direct to your home or office terminal, within hours after the biocybes release it.*

BOOK ONE:

Myths from the Scattered Worlds

CHAPTER ONE,

wherein the Pure Boy invades the Sorcerer's sanctum and is given a task.

Though placed near the beginning of the narrative, this chapter was among the last to be input. It derives mostly from recent inputs of Sarbadathan fourth-wife tales, which give it its unique character. Sarbadathan irreverence has been thoroughly incorporated herein.

Since Sarbadathan tales are mostly thinly veiled justification for that cruel rite they call the "crucible of minds," only the account of Benadek's striving to enter Achibol's domain is included here.

(Kaledrin, Senior Editor)

An urchin tugged at the old man's trousers, desperately working to remove them before his victim awakened from his winy stupor—but one shaggy eyebrow already twitched like a caterpillar with hiccoughs, and a drooping eyelid struggled to open, to discover the reason behind the breeze cooling his exposed genitals.

And what genitals! "If I had even the half of this old sot's meat . . . " young Benadek marveled . . .

<If you had old Achibol's sausage, you'd be limp as a pudding and no prettier than you are now, ignoramus.>

"Huh? Whozere? Who said that?" Benadek's quick rat-eyes combed the crannied alley for the source of the resonant voice. The passageway was as empty as when he'd first arrived. The old man was still out, his eyes glued shut with road dust and sweat. Benadek tugged harder, determined to get the fancy trousers over those fine leather shoes.

<Why bother with those gaudy pantaloons, child? Get the shoes, first. Or better yet, take that shiny coin. Surely you didn't overlook it?>

Benadek was not fooled. The voice was real. But where was the speaker? No one should care if an old drunk woke up with his balls in the breeze. The urchin surveyed the alley again. There were no hiding places, but Benadek's search turned up details hitherto unnoticed: next to a nailed-shut door was a bronze-shod staff, twisted wood that resembled a muscular arm. Crumpled on the dirt was a faded cloth embroidered with odd symbols.

A sorcerer's robe! The urchin's beady eyes darted about. Sure enough, there in the shadow of the boarded-over doorway was a tall hat painted with the same symbols. Why had he not seen that before? Sorcery! Benadek had not survived back-alley life without being observant. But if the stuff had spells on it, how could he see it? And there! A shiny gold tenday piece, not even dusty. Only magic could have made him miss that.

Caution warred with greed. He stretched out a grimy hand, his earlier objectives abandoned.

<That's it, boy! Take the coin. Run away and leave old Achibol to his slumber.>

Benadek's hand jumped back as if the coin were red-hot. Again his beady rat-eyes combed the alley. Again, he saw nothing but staff, robe, hat, and the old wino with his pants down.

Complex emotions flowed crossed his mobile face. An urchin is by nature avaricious, quick to seize the least opportunity for gain: a loose-tied pouch that jingles, a hasp whose rivets are loose, a door left ajar—the stuff of prosperity, or at least of a meal or two. But such opportunities don't include disembodied voices or magically appearing coins.

The trembling in Benadek's limbs was a physical reflection of mental oscillations between warring impulses to snatch the coin and run, to ignore it and run, or to freeze like a frightened nutstealer.

His hand crept outward, beckoned by the prize that glittered atop the alley dust. His eyes darted from the old drunk to the coin, to the niches, crannies and shadows. His nose twitched like a crack-rat's; he lacked only long whiskers to make the semblance exact. His hand approached its goal. He imagined he felt heat from the rich, fiery disk.

<Wait!> The voice came from directly overhead. He stiffened into renewed immobility, a ledgebird caught in the open square. His eyes rolled upward, but they saw only his own eyebrows. <The old fart needs help. You've been paid—now get him to his feet.>

Paid? A familiar word, but not in this context: payment came after an errand was run, a message delivered. Who would give a copper minute-bit for his services, in advance? The oddity of the notion kept him from running away. He was also less than sure that the voice would not follow him, even as he ran.

Urchinhood demands flexibility: no two opportunities are the same. Routine activity leads to habit, and habit to getting caught. Benadek had never been caught. He made his decision: the voice had not harmed him; it had told him to take the coin. In one quick motion he snatched it from the dirt and turned to dart back to the relative safety of the street beyond.

He never made it. The street was not there! He faced a brick wall as solid, old, and dirty as the rest of the narrow way. With sinking heart, he turned slowly, his empty gut knotted around a lump of black coal: fear. Sorcerers trapped unwary boys and turned them into beasts of burden, dooming them to lives of servitude as mules or dogs or . . .

For all his slight stature, Benadek was no coward. "Well, old man? Is this your best trick? Show me a dragon, not a beat-up wall. Show me a dragon, or let me go on my way. I could have slit your drunken throat, you know, but I didn't. You owe me."

He turned to face his captor. The robe was no longer on the ground. It was on the sorcerer, who stood facing him, staff in hand, tall pointed hat on his head so that he towered over the slight figure before him.

"Never fear, rat-child. The wall can be removed as easily as it was built. As for dragons—dream them yourself. I have trouble with simple things like talking mules. I put the wall there to stop you, else you would have left without your coin."

Benadek's fist squeezed tighter over his prize, over the golden tenday piece that . . . was no longer there. His eyes darted from his empty palm to the gleam between the sorcerer's finger and thumb. "You see? You would have forgotten it." With a careless gesture, the old man tossed the glittering disk in Benadek's direction. The boy caught it, and in the same motion backed up against the wall. He backed up one step and two, then three. In the corners of his eyes he saw the ends of the alley walls, and beneath his feet felt the cobble paving of the street.

The wall was gone! He spun about and ran as he'd never run before. Behind him, he heard a low chuckle that carried further than such a quiet sound should have. With several blocks between him and the alley, he still imagined he could hear it.

Achibol the Scrivener, sorcerer and fortuneteller, charlatan extraordinary, continued to chuckle as he made his way from the alley to his commodious room in the old stone inn. Once, in a time lost to all but memory, he too had been an urchin, a tiny brown face in the ghetto of a huge city, a brown face among other brown and tan and black ones, surrounded by a greater metropolis of well-scrubbed pink, yellow, and white. He sprawled in his lumpy chair, and sighed. It was not good to remember the old days, he reminded himself. Still, in an ancient, forgotten dialect, he murmured an idle paraphrase:

"Ain't no Jim Crow heah no mo',
Ah don't got' sit on de flo'.
No mo' sign say 'Sit in back,'
'Cause dey ain't no streetcar, ain't no track.

"Ain't no Jim Crow any mo',
Dis ain't nineteen fifty-fo',
Ain't no Jim Crow Ah kin see,
Cause dey ain't no nigguhs lef' 'cep' me."

<When you gonna learn you can't sing, old man?> his footstool said.

<Same day he learns he ain't Huddie Ledbetter, either!> said his robe from its peg by the door.

"I wonder where that boy is now?" Achibol murmured as he dozed off.

✧ ✧ ✧

Benadek was at that moment emerging from a gape in the rubble of a collapsed mill-house, a secret place for occasions when he did not dare risk being pursued to his more comfortable regular hideaway. He'd stashed a tin of crackers there, and a water-bottle, but had touched neither.

He had, however, not been idle. Even running away, his mind had worked something like this: "I wish I knew magic! I'd never have to run and hide again. Poots would see me with my bright clothes and my gold, and they'd lift their skirts! Benadek the Magician! Benadek the Great Sorcerer, to whom the stones whisper their secrets!"

Ignoble dreams—but don't great endeavors start with small fantasies, with base desires? Is not Art transmuted Lust, and have not the greatest bards scrawled doggerel love poems to impress objects of desire?

Benadek climbed from his hidey-hole with one goal in mind: find the old man and throw himself at his feet. Benadek, the wizard's apprentice. Benadek, assistant to the great Whatsisname. Benadek, colleague of warlocks and tamer of demons. Benadek . . .

He had an opener ready: "Sir," he would say, "I'm back to perform your service. I'm sorry I ran, before—your skill and your demon voice terrified me but I, Benadek, will be your apprentice, your good right hand. My wage? Merely throw me the odd tenday piece when my purse grows light, and I'll bend all effort in your behalf. I'll utter the spells you teach me, to save your own throat from strain, and will taste the fine meals you surely demand, so no evil dose passes your lips . . ." Firing his resolve with such thoughts, Benadek the Urchin strode toward the alley whence he had emerged in terror only hours before.

Expectedly, the magician was no longer there, and no voices spoke from the stones, wood, and tile. Nor were there tracks in the dust. Magic, he determined, not knowing that it had rained while he hid, laying the dust and washing the cobbles.

There was only one inn in the neighborhood, surrounded by a wall twice Benadek's height. From a thief's apprentice, he knew it contained not only dwelling rooms but an alehouse with four porches and a stable for thirty steeds. Against the stable leaned an enormous haystack, its top just below the enceinte wall.

A guard stood at the gate—a honch of menacing demeanor. Blue leather failed to hide rippling muscles. His clothing was a-jingle with chains and shiny buttons, and his belt sagged from the weight of a nutwood club and a sword. Benadek was loath to approach him.

Further along the wall a chokefire vine had established itself. The inn's proprietor, unwilling to touch a noxious plant which bled acid sap when jostled, that filled the air with lung-burning fumes when seriously disturbed, had let it grow. After all, it was no help to a wall-scaler. But Benadek was no average thief. He picked up a broken laundry-pole and probed the thick vine. His eyes burned, but most of the fumes rose straight up. He poked and prodded until he had jostled every branch. Beads of milky sap formed on twigs and leaves. The main branches and stems remained uncontaminated.

It was the work of a moment to slip into a greengrocer's shed to steal a pair of sharp scissors—the screws holding the door's hasp were loose. Benadek had dined on the vendor's produce before.

He clipped twigs and leaves from low branches, letting them fall to the ground. A second tier of foliage and a third followed. In short order, Benadek stripped the thick vine as high as he could reach, and hardly caught a whiff of acid vapor from the exhausted plant.

Gritting his teeth against the possibility of stray drops of acid on the stems, he pulled himself as high onto the vine as he could without touching his head to the foliage above or his hands to the stubbed branch-ends, which wept copiously. From one side of the vine he trimmed the other, dodging deadly falling leaves. He shifted to the cleared side and clipped an arm's length more. Finally, he raised himself to the next level and began cutting again, one side and then the other, ascending the chokefire vine, then climbing atop the wall. He dropped safely into the haystack.

Unfortunately, he had little view from his hiding place. He would have to wander about, looking for the magician, and risk being apprehended and the guard called.

No one was in the courtyard. No one sat at the porch tables either. Should he enter the common room? Benadek sank into the shadow of a well house to think. If he had a message, and the name of someone to deliver it to . . . Did he know the name of anyone who might be here? Some prominent citizen, perhaps? No, the inn staff would be alert for such deception. He was not the first boy to enter under false pretenses, but he was determined to be one who got away with it. Minutes passed, and by the time he caught the first glimmer of possibility, he had been seen!

A fat, common fellow approached—a cook, by his once-white apron and the great cleaver dangling in one hamlike hand. "Here then, youngster!" the cook bellowed. "Come forward or I'll call the guard."

What had the sorcerer said? Had he spoken his name? Reluctantly, Benadek obeyed, trying all the while to remember.

"A message, good cook! I have a message for a gentleman here."

"So you all say," the cook said, shaking his head.

His jowls flapped back and forth. "And who're you seeking? The lord mayor? The constable? I can find *him* quite promptly."

"The magician," Benadek squeaked as the fat man lifted him by his ear. "Ow! Please! Let me down! I have to see him. It's very important." The name. What was the name? It had sounded like a sneeze! Achoo . . . Achoob . . . "Achoobowl! I have a message for Achoobowl! Ow! Let me go." The cook relented slightly, allowing Benadek to dance on his toes.

"And what, tell me, does he look like?"

"He's skinny and wears a pointy hat. His skin's the color of an old saddle. Ow! That hurts. Let me down."

"You won't try to run away? You can outrun me, but be sure you can't outrun Pretty Face here." He held the meat knife so close to Benadek's nose that his eyes crossed. "And if you did, Hammer—that's the guard, Hammer—would catch you anyway. You wouldn't want that!"

"I won't run! I have to give my message to Master Achoobowl."

"Then I'll take you to him. You'd better pray he's pleased with what you have to say." He led Benadek up the steps to the dining porch, still pinching his ear. He kicked open the double-hinged door, and dragged him into the common room.

Benadek's eyes adjusted rapidly, and he spied the magician at a far table. "There he is, master cook! That's Achoobowl. Please let me go."

The sorcerer, hearing his name, turned and looked directly at the boy. "Ah, there! Cook, what are you doing to the lad? I've been expecting him."

An expression of surprise crossed the fat man's face. Reluctantly, he let go of Benadek's ear. The urchin gamely resisted the urge to spit on his oppressor. But what luck! He had not mistaken the surprise on the sorcerer's visage, but the old man had rallied immediately, and covered for him! Why?

"Now boy," Achibol said mildly when Benadek came close, "have you come to apologize for your sudden departure? It wasn't necessary, you know."

"Master, I owe you a service. I've come to pay my debt, or to return your coin."

"Ah, but you already did that. Don't you remember?" The sorcerer pulled a gold tenday piece from his sleeve. "See? I have it here."

Astounded, Benadek reached into his crotch-pocket for his own coin, but it was gone. Was the one the old brown man tossed from hand to hand his? How could that be?

"Master, is it the same coin? Can it be?"

"One and the same, boy. You disbelieve? Here, take it again." He tossed it to Benadek, who again caught it and held it tightly, only to feel it fade from his fingers like cool steam and to reappear in the sorcerer's palm moments later. "See?" Achibol said with a dry chuckle. "It's a magic coin, boy. You can have it, but you can't keep it. That's the way of all gold, isn't it? But is that all you wanted? To set matters right between us? If so, you may go now, with your conscience at rest."

"Master, I want to serve you," Benadek blurted, all his fine speeches fled like mist before a breeze. "Will you have me?"

"I don't need a servant."

"An apprentice, Master. I want to be your apprentice." Now that he'd said it, Benadek was amazed at his temerity. The sorcerer could call up demons to press his robe and fairies to polish his boots. Why would he need a boy? He hung his head.

Achibol did not disabuse him. "What makes you think I need an apprentice? Men like me live a thousand years, even forever. Why would I want to share anything, let alone a thousand years, with a mortal?"

The old fellow inflated his skinny chest. "I've had

apprentices before—bright boys who've come oh-so-well recommended, with fat, jingling purses to pay for their keep and their training. I've seen them come—and go. Yes, go! Tender ones slunk off home, unable to withstand this old owl's hooting. Impatient smart ones, all hot to learn a few of my tricks, were unwilling to sweep mule droppings or carry water. You see?" He shook his head, his ancient, wrinkled face now a caricature of sadness. Benadek was hard put to keep up with his mercurial shifts in mood.

"Worst of all," the sorcerer continued, "were the dedicated ones—the little boys who wanted nothing but to learn my lore and perform my chores, who in spite of my temperament and my tongue came to love me. Yes, those tested me most sorely of all. Why, you ask? Because they grew up, and went their own ways, as is natural for boys. Then, having spent their natural span toadying for townmasters, priests, and wealthy old boffins, they died."

Did a tear glitter on the brown leathery cheek? Benadek kept his eyes respectfully downcast. The sorcerer's voice dropped to a mumble. "There's no future for my apprentices, boy. Would you wait for me to die, to inherit my books and potions and tools? Can you wait a thousand years, or two or three? I've watched faithful boys grow old and die, waiting and serving me. And even worse . . . oh, so much worse . . ."

Pulling himself out of his lachrymose slump, the old man met the boy's eyes. "See what you've done, boy? Spoiled my meal and my evening. I need no more of this—and no apprentice." As he reached for his wineglass, his still-blurred eyes caused him to misjudge, and he knocked it over. A flash of anger lit his eyes.

"I'm sorry, Master," Benadek murmured. "It was a foolish hope. With your permission, I'll leave now."

"Hmm. Where will you go?"

"Back to the warrens, where I live. If I can get past the guard on the gate."

"Ah, yes. The redoubtable Hammer. Has he set his sights on you, then?"

"I entered by a different gate."

"There is no other, boy." Achibol grinned. His bright brown eyes gleamed among nut-brown crinkles and folds. "You're not only bold, but clever and resourceful. Perhaps I can arrange for you to pass the gate, earn a less elusive coin, and do me a service as well. Would that please you?"

Benadek's hopes rose again. If he performed the service well, perhaps Achibol would reconsider, or at least retain him for such tasks in the future. "I'm at your service, Master Achoobowl."

"Then take this token to the temple priest. Tell him it's an offering from Achibol the Charlatan, who will visit his brothers in supernatural knowledge on the morrow." Achibol carelessly tossed the same (was it the same?) gold coin to the boy. "Mind you, make sure the message is delivered just as I have spoken it."

Benadek repeated the message to Achibol's satisfaction. The old man called for paper, and wrote a brief note requiring all to pass his messenger through without delay, and signed it with a grand flourish. He waved Benadek away.

The urchin approached the guard, his note at arms length. Hammer squinted intensely at it. Recognizing Achibol's distinctive rune, he allowed the boy to pass, all the while creasing his brow and wondering whether he himself had let Benadek in. But that was impossible. For all their social faults, honches' memories were perfect, a record of laws, infractions, and crimes, faces of officials, criminals, and ordinary citizens. He would have remembered the boy. Only long after Benadek had disappeared in the darkness of a narrow passage did he satisfy himself that the boy must have passed by his counterpart on the earlier watch.

INTERLUDE
The Great School, Midicor IV

Kaledrin shook his head. "The old man *is* Achibol! Saphooth will have my career for this!"

"Why?" Abrovid asked. "You don't control the biocybes' output."

"Can't you see? This Achibol is an *anthro-form* like Saphooth."

"So what? Lots of people choose that form. It's handy for climbing ladders. Why, on some planets, people are even born like that."

"Saphooth was," Kaledrin said darkly, "and he'll die that way too. He's an immutable."

"Really?" Abrovid's eyestalks stiffened in morbid interest. "You mean he can't *change*? He's stuck in that somatotype? Is it a disease?" He shuddered, and tucked his manipulator-tendrils safely behind protective chitin.

"Of course not," Kaledrin chided him. "There are hundreds just like him—stuck for life in one form or another—on every inhabited planet."

"Hundreds—among how many billions on Midicor IV alone?" Abrovid whistled derisively. "No wonder he's disagreeable. But why should he blame *you*? I don't see the connection."

"Because *all* the characters in this 'translation' or fantasy or whatever it's turned into—except those stupid 'mules'—seem to be two-legged, bilaterally symmetrical anthro-forms, just like Saphooth, and he'll never believe this entire tale isn't a ghastly jape at his expense," Kaledrin moaned. "I may as well start packing right now."

Kaledrin need not have worried. At that very moment Saphooth held a printout of Chapter One on his lap, and was chuckling contentedly. He obviously saw something in the tale that Kaledrin missed. "Benadek, Father of Humanity, indeed! The little bastard." He grinned. "I wonder when Chapter Two will be done?"

* Autochthonous: originally applied to gods "sprung from the earth," the word has come to refer to anything that has evolved on or otherwise originates upon a planet, and was not brought there from elsewhere.

CHAPTER TWO,

in which Benadek enters a foul Temple and confronts the Demon within. He gains Forbidden Knowledge, but is judged yet unready for his great Purpose.

Most chapter headings in this volume are taken unchanged from the orthodox Ksentos Venimentum text, long considered the most complete and reliable rendering of the Achibol legend. The KV is a derivative story based on ancient, perhaps autochthonous * tales. Use of the well-known KV headings is this editor's whim. Their archaic flavor provides piquant contrast to the biocybes' contemporary style, and highlights the changed emphases of the new text.

The Demon incident exemplifies this. Schoolchildren know it as the climax of the Battle for the Temple, but herein it is only the passing, fearful fantasy of a child; it emerges, is dealt with in short order, and is dismissed forever. Forbidden Knowledge, contrastingly, has been demystified, presented as oddly distorted "science," plausible-sounding, only slightly at odds with what we know.

(Kaledrin, Senior Editor)

The temple. Benadek alone, as far as he knew, had never been in a temple. Everyone else paid visits. Travelers made detours in order to call at a temple. Regular visits, every month or so, were the rule.

Rites of passage took place there: boys became cozies, honches, or boffins, and girls* became poots, and fertile. Old folks and sick ones died in the temples—or at least were never seen to leave.

Once, Benadek had worried that he would remain always a boy, lacking whatever magic the temple performed, but his fears had been groundless. His body hair arrived on schedule, and his libido grew strong—uncomfortably so, for no poot would submit to one as ugly as he. Perhaps that was the temple's magic—to gift boys with whatever it was that made poots like them. Surely, temple magic made muscular honches or smart, edgy boffins out of some boys, and plain, stolid cozies out of the rest. But he, Benadek, who had never been "templed," was neither fish nor fowl, and did not belong.

---

* The biocybes have left two mysterious words untranslated: "woman" (plural "women") and "girl" (plural girls). These sometimes seem to be used as synonyms for "poot," with "girl" applied to the immature form, "woman" to the adult, but they cannot be exact synonyms. What ineffable, untranslatable difference do they imply? We must wait and see. Perhaps future chapters will reveal their secrets.

Many times, after humiliating rejection by one poot or another, Benadek had come close to giving in. He'd come as far as the temple's courtyard gate, but people died in there. As his father had died.

Benadek pushed such thoughts away. He'd forced himself to forget all but the bare fact of his father's death, but this much he remembered: the temple had killed him. And old Klert, who had suffered from nearsightedness and headaches—he'd gone to the priests for a cure, and had never come out. Even young Jigbo, frightened when he discovered the stub of an extra finger on his right hand, had gone to the priests, and was never seen again. Benadek had neither headaches nor extra fingers, nor was he nearsighted—but neither had been his father. No, he had determined to stay well away from the priests and their lair.

Now he had a problem: how could he deliver Achibol's message without going inside? The sorcerer would discover if he lied and pocketed the gold piece, and that would put paid to his hope for a career. Not that Achibol had made any promises, Benadek reminded himself, but he had not really said "no," either—at least not directly.

Benadek thought long and hard. Could he skirt around his instructions? Achibol would not fault him if he delivered the message in a different way—perhaps he'd never even know about Benadek's improvisation.

The boy scurried down the street to a scribe's kiosk, devising a stratagem en route. "Sir scribe!" he called out, "I delivered the six chickens to your room."

"Chickens?" The boffin, skinny and sharp-faced like all his kind, set down the pen he had been sharpening. "You mistake me for another, boy."

"Don't you live over the Broken Axle? I've seen you there. At any rate, I brought the chickens, and spread papers from your table about, to protect your clean floor from their droppings."

"My papers! My letters!" Grasping his purse, the scribe dashed off to rescue his labor from the imaginary chickens. He left pen, ink-pot, and blank sheets that fluttered to the ground with the breeze of his exit. Benadek hid them in his shirt. Mission accomplished, he strode jauntily away.

Benadek believed himself the only urchin who could read and write. He had vague memories of the mother who had lovingly taught him, but memories of that part of his life were vague, shut out to damp the pain of his losses. But he had not forgotten his letters.

In the quiet dimness of the crawl space beneath a tailor shop he drew forth a dogeared book of ABC's. Referring to it for the correct shapes of certain letters, he scribed Achibol's words on his stolen paper:

> THIS IZ THE OFRING OF ACUBOL THE CARLATIN WHU WIL VIZIT HIZ BRUTHERZ IN SUPERNACURAL NOLEGE ON THE MARO. SINED, ACUBOL.

He wrapped the gold tenday coin in the note, folding the corners so it would not come apart, and set off for the temple.

Outside the courtyard wall, Benadek waited and listened. On occasion he'd noticed that, where a warehouse across from the temple leaned outward, voices from inside the wall bounced off the smooth stone and were directed downward to the street. He would know if chattering priests passed on the other side of the wall.

Sure enough, he had not waited two fingers of daylight when voices seemed to issue from the blank stone above. For a moment he was distracted: had the voice in the alley been Achibol himself, somehow casting his voice to reflect from those walls? But Achibol's mouth had not moved, and the voice had been clear, not muddled with echoes.

He remembered his reason for being there, and tossed the paper-wrapped coin over the wall. Muffled, echo-distorted voices told him his delivery had been found. Satisfied that he had fulfilled the spirit of his task, he turned once more toward the inn.

Assured that his message and offering had been delivered, Achibol bought Benadek a meal the likes of which he had never imagined—tiny fowl stuffed with chopped nuts and dried fruits, vegetables lightly fried in sweet oil, a slab of meat, red in the center and crisp around the edges, so tender that he hardly had to chew it, and finally, a bowl of creamy stuff so cold it made his teeth hurt but tasted of fresh raspberries! With each course, Achibol urged upon him a fresh, tiny glass of tart wine, a different flavor each time.

Later, when the sorcerer led him to his room above, Benadek was so full of food and wine that he could hardly have cared if the old man had taken advantage of him (some urchins earned coins that way), but Achibol tucked him in a bed, muttering the while about children who took advantage of foolish old men.

"But he can read," Achibol had marveled again and again, "and even write, after a fashion!" Benadek was vaguely aware that he had, after his fourth or fifth glass of wine, told Achibol how he had delivered the coin and message.

Having seen the boy to bed, the mage unlocked his two heavily built trunks, then spent an hour or so poring over a heavy tome from one trunk and a map from the other. But the wine he had imbibed affected his concentration, and he laid his head on his arms for a short rest. He slept more soundly than he'd expected—surely more soundly than he would have, had he known Benadek was awake.

With a youngster's resiliency and an urchin's

instincts, the lad threw off the wine fumes and quelled the fatigue that had incapacitated him. In a glance, he took in the sleeping sorcerer, the guttering wick, and the open trunks. He slipped silently from the bed. The trunks had locks, he reasoned, and must therefore contain things of value that warranted his inspection.

Benadek did not intend to steal from the man who he hoped would take him on, but it was impossible to ignore the trunks. The habits of his short lifetime were grounded in one basic precept: survive. Survival meant never overlooking potential gain. He peeked in the first trunk. Books. Books and wooden racks of tiny bottles strapped with canvas and buckles. The books' lettering was a strange script, unreadable. Perhaps someday . . . Perhaps the bottles were love-potions he could use to his own advantage, but how could he tell? He could make nothing of their labels.

The second trunk held instruments of unfamiliar design, and tiny packets that must contain things of value. There were clothes, and beneath those . . . He insinuated a hand beneath folded fabric, and was rewarded by something slick and cool, of irregular shape, heavy, but not as dense as metal. Just then the dying light went out.

Benadek held the object in moonlight from the window. He gasped. With shaking hands he replaced it. He shut the trunk lid and slipped the padlock through its hasp, but did not snap it shut. Perhaps the mage would not notice anything amiss. He retreated to the bed.

From under his coverlet he peered across the room, every sense honed. When nothing happened after an undefined but interminable time, Benadek dozed. He awoke in a state of confused panic, then dozed again. Finally, he slept, but not without frightening dreams of what he'd held in his hand.

Death. He had held death, and stared into its dark,

empty eye sockets. He had held the cool, heavy skull of a man. The mage's familiar, to be called up and refleshed at the sorcerer's command? Had Benadek known human anatomy he would have seen that the cranium was not ordinary. With a little knowledge he might have suspected it was that of a demon. With a little more, that it was human, but incredibly old. Had the light been better, and had he turned the ancient calvarium over, he might have seen tiny white-painted lettering:

H. Sapiens neanderthalensis
104598
MUSEE de l'HOMME
Paris, Fr

Had he possessed the ability to peer beyond the veil of time itself, he might have seen what part that same ancient skull would play, in one possible future, in saving him from a fate far worse than mere death could ever be.

In the morning, Benadek was treated to a repast only slightly less impressive than supper had been. He ate eggs whipped with cream, deftly cooked in butter until they were light as air; he tasted crisp sliverings of roast meat from the proprietor's dinner table, refried and hot; with stern urging from Achibol, he drank a bitter, hot, black brew that the sorcerer insisted would make him preternaturally awake and alert. Philosophically, Benadek drank it, though he shuddered with each sip. Everything could not be wonderful—and it was, after all, a magic potion, not really a drink.

"Well, isn't it time we were on our way?" Achibol asked, suddenly impatient. "The morning gets no younger." We? Benadek wondered, hardly able to believe his good fortune. Was he to stay on? He dared not broach the subject, afraid of breaking the delicate spell of hope. "The temple, boy, the temple. I—or rather, you—promised I'd pay them a call."

Benadek was ecstatic at the chance of further employment (and soft beds and delicious food and fine, tart wines), but deeply concerned that he would not be able to avoid entering the temple itself, the very place from which his father had emerged, screaming and clawing at his body as if invisible fire . . . No! He would not think about that. Not now, not ever! Numbly he followed Achibol through the dusty streets.

The sorcerer strode up to the temple gate and struck the bell with unseemly vigor. A dark-robed figure arrived immediately, a silhouette with a drawn, white face. "Open for Achibol the Charlatan, colleague. I wish to pay my respects to your superiors."

"In one sense," the priest replied dryly, "all men are my colleagues. In the same sense, hardly stretching the reasoning, the fleas and lice that infest your shabby garments are colleagues as well, for in their own way they glorify the spirits with their tiny lives. In that sense, I accept your affiliation with my order. You and your tiny colleagues may enter. But my superiors can't be troubled by the importunements of semiliterates and late-risers."

"Semi . . . See what you've done, boy?" Achibol said. "Your poor scribbling has cost us our converse with the high priest. And a great loss it is." He stepped through the opening gate. "Even among the poor, uneducated clergy of underprivileged towns like this, even in such tatty, run-down edifices, occasional bits of wit and wisdom can be gleaned, if only by the bleak example the priests set, illustrating the fate of laziness and sloth in the schoolroom.

"Very well then," he said to the priest, whose white face had turned fiery, "since your own masters have shut themselves in the latrine without rags or papers,

I'll be content merely to experience the temple's rite. Move aside."

Surprisingly, the priest did so, and Achibol strode in with Benadek close upon his heels. The boy tried hard not to gape, his terror masked by confidence in Achibol, but priests had been known to seek out those who avoided the temple rite, and Benadek had carefully maintained his position as a dirty-faced urchin interchangeable with other boys. He hoped the priest would assume that he had come into town with Achibol, and had performed the rite—whatever it was—in another place.

Achibol seemed to know his way, and the priest did not follow. There was much to gape at. The temple anteroom had been cold and stony, dingy with time and neglect, but the inner corridor walls were smooth and jointless, and the ceiling glowed with cold, white light. The floor looked ground from a uniform mass of pebbly rock, cracked in a few places, but otherwise shiny and perfect. The last door they passed through was metal. Iron-bound doors were common on better houses and shops, but how could a smith have hammered a single piece of iron so flat and smooth?

This final room had metal boxes with tiny windows that pulsed and glowed with pure shades of monochromatic light: cerise, cyan, emerald, and amber. A few had larger windows, where numbers and letters scrolled down, or wavy, jagged lines cavorted. Only Achibol's calm, unruffled presence kept Benadek from bolting. He sensed an evil presence, but that could have been only active imagination.

"Now, boy, we have work to do." Achibol swung his robe from his shoulders and spread it flat on the floor. He removed an array of shiny tools from pockets in his undergarment, a form-fitting black suit of leather unlike any Benadek had ever seen. Surprises and mysteries multiplied. Who is the magician—or what? What is this forbidding place? Why are we here? Surely, this is not the temple where dutiful citizens make monthly pilgrimage. Was this what those who disappeared saw, before they vanished forever? Was a room like this the last place his father had seen? He shuddered uncontrollably, expecting priests or demons at any time.

"Don't gape, boy," Achibol scolded. "Bring me that toolbox—the gray one by the door. I can't do all this myself, or we'll miss dinner." The sorcerer's voice should have brought priests scurrying, Benadek thought. He looked meaningfully at the door.

"Don't worry about the priests, boy. They are enjoying a rest. None will disturb us while I fix this damnable machine."

Machine? But machines are noisy, dirty things of wood and iron that leak and spit black oil. Benadek's concept of "machine" broadened immediately.

"Rest, Master?" he asked. "Why are they tired? It's still morning."

"Magic, boy. The magic of my talisman and that coin you delivered yesterday. They'll sleep—or at least stand motionless and oblivious—until I am ready to leave, and be none the wiser for the time that has passed—if, that is, we hurry, so the discrepancy is not too great. Now get the toolbox."

Benadek fetched it, then watched the sorcerer open first one box, and then another. He connected colored strings to shiny knobs in the toolbox, and stretched them to points within the innards of first one box, then another, punctuating his actions with muttered exclamations and sighs. "It's a wonder this system's stayed on-line as long as it has, with only oafish priests to care for it. There was a dead roach on that circuit board! A roach, mind you. If not for me, every temple in the land would be spewing toadstools instead of simples."

"What are simples, Master?" Benadek asked as he handed the oldster a "screwdriver."

"Simples are people like you and those priests—poots, honches, ordinary cozies like the innkeeper and cook, boffins, and a rare pattum or so."

Benadek had never known there was a collective term like "simples". People were just people. There were poots—the female of the human species, desirable to every male past puberty but interested in nothing more than cooking and raising babies (unless it were making more babies.) A delicious shudder ran from Benadek's groin to his extremities.

Cozies were ordinary males with common jobs and tastes, and faces much alike but for age and attitude. Benadek suspected he was a cozy, but he was not old enough to know for sure. He was smart, so maybe he was destined to become a boffin, like the scribe or the lord mayor. He was absolutely sure that his further development would not make him a honch, for honches, of all people—all "simples," he corrected himself—were cruel and domineering even as children, and progressed by matters of degree to full, burly adulthood. Of pattums, he knew nothing, except that poots threatened uncooperative infants by saying, "The pattum'll get you."

"And you, Master? What sort are you? A boffin?"

Achibol laughed. He bellowed, and slapped his skinny thighs. "I'm sorry, boy," he said when he'd recovered. "I'm not a simple."

Benadek suddenly saw the sorcerer in a different light. What, if not a person, was he? A demon! The being Benadek had hoped to apprentice himself to was not a man, but a denizen of the black depths, come to devour and destroy! No wonder he had fed Benadek—he was fattening him like a poot fattens a hen!

The boy backed slowly until the door was cold and hard against his back. His hand groped for the handle.

"What's wrong, boy?" the demon demanded, with

a leer that Benadek would have interpreted minutes earlier as a puzzled frown. "What's eating you?"

The phrase was unfortunate. With a shrill cry Benadek turned and clawed the door, breaking fingernails and tearing skin from his fingertips. Achibol, concerned, grasped him by the shoulder, and the boy collapsed in a dead faint.

He awoke in the old man's arms, staring into his brown, leering face. "Are you going to eat me now?" he asked in a quavering falsetto.

"Eat you? Whatever for?" Achibol asked, genuinely surprised. "In a thousand years, I've never eaten anyone—though, when I was younger, there were women I wouldn't have passed up, had they been shorter of leg, and I longer." It was a joke, Benadek realized. He was not about to be eaten. Not right then. But what was a "woman*," anyway? Achibol questioned him further, and gradually came to understand what had terrified the boy.

"I'm not a simple, boy, but I'm still a man, not a demon. Some of my kind call themselves 'pure-humans' or 'true humans', and consider all others to be 'simples.' Actually, we're all humans, and the 'pure' ones are no more pure than the rest. They are less . . . less *simple*. It's a matter of genetic makeup." Benadek watched the blinking, winking lights that flickered across the sorcerer's dark face.

"Once," Achibol explained, "there were really 'pure' humans, with a full complement of human genes. You know what genes are, boy? Of course you don't. But no matter—listen, and you'll learn. The world was different then. There were no song-snakes in the

---

* In this instance, "woman" seems not to apply to a human female, but to a wild creature Achibol considers edible. Or is this an indirect reference to the myth "Benadek and the Cannibals of Orkenor," which has been input but is otherwise ignored by the biocybes?

trees, no liver-beasts in forest pools, and no simples. There were millions of different kinds of creatures, all neatly divided into species, so that all of a species were much the same. 'Dogs' had four legs and fur, snakes had no legs and scales. There were no six- or eight-legged dogs, and no snakes with feathers.

"Humans made machines to do everything for them—wash their clothes, cook their meals—and dirtied the world with machine by-products—PCBs, PBBs, mercury, dioxin, acids of every kind, and finally DFK and compound X. Some chemicals were mutagenic; in combination with the deadly sunlight of an atmosphere stripped of its protective ozone, they caused species to change. Most changes were lethal, but some creatures survived, to pass on their changes."

Benadek understood only a fourth part of what Achibol said, but was heartened by the magician's assumption that there would be further opportunities for him to listen and sort out the unfamiliar words. His fear faded. A demon would not have explained anything.

"Humans," Achibol continued, sorting through his odd tools, "either died or changed. None were pleased, because they believed they were created in the image of a god, and to be different was a terrible thing.

"The poisons and mutagens were long-lasting, and the atmospheric degradation wasn't reversible in their lifetimes or their children's children's. A thousand years would have to pass before the human genetic code would be safe from meaningless change. But in a mere hundred years their race would be dead, or changed beyond recognition.

"Boy! Hand me my talisman—the small gray box with the buttons. Ah! Good, you're learning something.

"Desperate proposals were made. Suggestions that

humanity migrate to orbital habitats were dismissed—the hazards in space outweighed those at home. Living in sealed caves for a thousand years was an unhealthy solution, and for only a few; sterilization or extermination of the new, changed humans was rejected too, because the mutation rate threatened to match exactly the birthrate.

"In desperation geneticists, molecular biologists, eugenicists, and other scientists developed a plan to simplify the human genome to the point where it could be recorded in the memories of computers like these that surround us here. The simplified codes would be inserted in fertilized human eggs and implanted in host wombs where they would develop, eventually to be born as the first of the new, simplified human race.

"The advantages of the plan were many: first, the simpler code, though just as vulnerable to change as the old natural one, was more easily read by machines. As each 'simple' human had four copies of their streamlined code, it was easy for the machines to tell when a copy had mutated. Cell samples could be taken from children before puberty, and those with defective genes—genes that did not fit the established template—could be painlessly sterilized.

"Second, 'defective' pregnancies could be aborted, and females implanted with standardized fertile eggs even if their own genetic capabilities had been altered by the mutagenic environment.

"But less than a millionth of the world's population could be so treated. The rest had to be sterilized, or left to die of their own genetic flaws. It was necessary to automate the process, because a reduced population could not keep up the science, technology, and culture of a system that had evolved to serve—and to be served by—billions. The poor remnants of humanity couldn't maintain the computerized laboratories that would preserve them. Those had to be reliable enough to maintain themselves for a thousand years.

"The engineers built such automated genetic laboratories in heavily protected installations, each able to grow and implant standardized embryos in suitable human subjects, or to sterilize 'flawed' ones. No human needed to enter the labs except as a subject.

"The system worked, as far as it went. But when a thousand years was up and the danger was past, real human genotypes had to be reintroduced into the world. Until then, those would exist only as information in computer memory, but would be reconstituted, and implanted into the wombs of simplified human females. The changelings would, in a matter of generations, reassume their proper place, and the last 'simples' would be sterilized or euthanized. For that to happen, the laboratories had to know when the time was right.

"They were programmed to record the deviance of every genotype they examined. Such information was sent, via satellite links, to a central storehouse deep in a mountain burrow. The central computer would signal the laboratories when the level of deviations dropped below a predetermined point, and command them to instigate the full-human regeneration program. It should have worked, too."

Achibol began putting away his tools. "Time passes, boy. The priests will suspect something is wrong. They've lost half an hour from their miserable lives, as it is. Pick up those screwdrivers."

"Master? Will you finish the tale later?"

"Finish? It isn't over yet. How can I, a mere charlatan and an old man, finish it? Must I perform heroic labors to bring on the new age? How do you suggest I go about that?"

"I only wish to know. I understood what you said only in small measure, but my head burns with the desire to comprehend."

"Good! Such burning is the beginning of wisdom. Knowing how little one understands is the spur to discovery. Later, then, when we're out of here." He draped his robe over his leathery suit. "Come. We must awaken the priests." He flourished the worn metal rectangle with tiny tiles on its face. Minuscule black numbers and letters marched incessantly across it. "My magic talisman controls the coin. When we approach the final door, I'll deactivate the sleep function.

"Boy?" Achibol asked, as an afterthought. "Do you crave templing? I'll wait while the rite is performed."

"Oh no, Master," Benadek replied, almost too abruptly, "I feel no need."

"Very well then, let us be gone."

They returned to the inn with Benadek still safely untempled, and Achibol went to his room. He seemed to have forgotten the boy, who followed, painfully reminded of his tenuous hold on his new profession.

In the corner chamber with cool, whitewashed walls and glass doors opening onto sunny balconies, there was little sign of Achibol's occupancy except for his trunks. The mage withdrew a book with covers of the same material as his under-suit. Its leaves were smooth and white, like no paper Benadek had seen.

Achibol made tiny, neat entries with a cylindrical pen that needed no ink-pot. *Magic—or is the ink held inside that fat shaft?* Even with short exposure to the old man, Benadek's ways of thinking were changing.

With no desire to disturb Achibol at his writing, he sat on grassy matting in a bright sunbeam, and let its warmth lull him to sleep.

Achibol interrupted his doze. "It's time to dine." Benadek had observed that townsmen took meals at sunrise, high noon, and sunset, but urchins ate when there was food in hand, and fasted otherwise. But regularity freed a portion of his mind from constantly thinking about food. He had time to think upon his new experiences, and to catnap as well.

Their noon meal was cold meat sliced thin, on slabs of black bread drizzled with rich, spicy red sauce.

"Can you tell me more of the world that was, Master? My mind still burns."

Surprised, as if he had forgotten Benadek's presence, Achibol set down his mug of cool ale. "Of course, boy. Where was I? What were we talking of?"

"I asked you why I am a simple, while you are not. And you were going to tell me why the plan to bring back real humans failed."

"So I was—and both are related. The plan failed because the scientists were sure that the increasing mutation rates would kill off those who were not simplified. With four copies of every essential gene, 'simples' could take much more damage without dying for want of an enzyme or an amino acid, you see. But there were too many humans, back then. The survival rate of the 'pure-humans' didn't have to be high to insure that a few kept on breeding.

"Their population has never been large. Most live in small villages, or isolated families. But they mix with simples all too often, and that's where the plan failed.

"To explain this, I must tell you of another of the planners' clever tricks: they needed a way to assure that simples would visit the laboratories periodically, to be checked against the standard genetic templates, so they omitted the genes for a particular neurotransmitter hormone and an associated polypeptide—substances the body needs. Without them, simples become irrational, depressed, and eventually go mad and die. The only sources of what they need are the laboratories. Are you getting this?"

"I think so, Master. Are templates the same as temples?"

"Ah! You're perspicacious, boy. The 'temples' are

buildings put up by unscrupulous priests—boffins—to bilk the population of their coins. That's a tradition far older than temples, planners, or plan. The true templates are inside the machines themselves, and are mere memories of the patterns that make up men. But as the machines house the templates, and the laboratories house the machines, so the 'temples' grew up on the laboratory sites, often covering them entirely, as has been done here.

"To continue, simples come to the temples, and thus to the laboratories, when they sicken, are brought by relatives if they become irrational, or by honches—city guards and the like—if they are wild or mad. Those occasional pure-humans who drift into the towns are eventually 'templed' too. And that's the greatest problem of all."

"Why? Do they suffer the same lack as simples?"

"The priests suffer always from a lack of cool, shiny gold, so their honch minions bring all strangers to the temples. Failing that, if the pure-humans become disagreeable or seem odd (and don't all foreigners seem so, at times?) then their neighbors force them. Too, when they hear of the benefits of templing, they're often convinced to go on their own."

"What happens to them?"

"Can't you see, boy? Have you been daydreaming? The machines read their strange genetic codes, and pronounce them defective, and they are destroyed. And there the problems begin."

Benadek's head filled with horrid images of his father writhing and screaming. He shuddered, but Achibol had not noticed, and was still talking.

". . . the tallies of mutated versus normal 'templings' are sent to the central processing facility. The computer considers all the counts of flawed genes—mutant 'true human' ones—and puts off the day when the original human genotypes will be reconstituted. This has happened again and again." He shook his head sadly, then fixed Benadek with a bright, reptilian stare. "Do you know how long it's been since the world has been free of mutagens? Almost a thousand years! It's been *two thousand years* since the plan was effectuated, and there will never be an end to it, I fear."

"Can't something be done, Master?"

"I try, of course, but then, I'm only one man, and the world is large."

"What do you do?"

"I reprogram 'temples' to erase readings outside simples' parameters, so the mutation counts stay low, where they belong." Seeing Benadek's blank look, he rephrased the statement: "I cast spells on them."

"How did you learn so much, Master? Who was your teacher?"

"I had many teachers. They've been dust for ages. I'm a tool of men and women who opposed the planners, set in motion long ago and still running on my own inertia." He shook his head sadly and then, annoyed that Benadek had seen his lapse into self-pity, snapped at him. "Enough questions, boy. I can't spend all day entertaining you. Run off and play."

"Can't I stay, Master? I won't be in the way." Though hurt by the sudden dismissal, Benadek was determined not to be thrust aside. "Your shoes are dusty. I'll clean and oil them."

"Enough, I said! Find someone else to bother! And the same goes for tomorrow, and the next day. I have no more time to waste on foolish boys." He got to his feet and stalked off to the stairway. Benadek, hopes crushed, slowly trudged through the gate into the narrow street that led, eventually, to his cold burrow and a crust of stale bread.

INTERLUDE
The Great School, Midicor IV

"Exalted Wisdom! I didn't expect you so soon." Kaledrin's dry, unpolished chitin rattled like ill-tuned castanets. "You've read the second chapter?"

"Indeed!" Saphooth responded, his two-eyed face expressionless despite its evocative wrinkles and creases, his beaky breathing-bulge unflared and still.

"What quirks of simian evolution does such odd physiognomy represent?" Kaledrin wondered, not for the first time. Three breathing orifices, two which function as chemosensors as well, and the third a toothy ingestor and communicator—and gods know what else. How crude! How inefficient! "What do you think of the tale, so far?" he asked, not without trepidation: MYTHIC had been his idea, and while Saphooth would bask in the glories of its success, failure would fall upon Kaledrin alone.

"Intriguing," Saphooth mused dryly. "A melange of myth and pseudoscience that might credit an imaginative schoolchild . . . but a scholarly work?" His blue-gray light-sensors flashed reflected sunlight from beneath bushy, pileous over-shades. "This is, after all, your project," he reminded Kaledrin ominously. "What do you think?"

"I'd rather not speculate, Cognizant One. The tale is evolving. What makes little sense now may be clarified further on."

"Indeed," Kaledrin silently complained even as Saphooth departed, wearing an expression he suspected was self-satisfied, even smug, "it evolves, and I have no more idea than he what it will become—my guarantee of tenure in the Great School, or a monster that will consume me.

"Dictation!" he snapped at his resident AI. "Introduction to Chapter Three." He did not want to work any more, but it was too early to leave. The sunwallows would not even be warm, this early in the day.

CHAPTER THREE:

How the boy Benadek's search for the meaning of life leads him to forsake fleshly pleasures for an apprentice's posting.

Honches, dogs, mules . . . now poots. The mythical bestiary grows. Are such creatures mere beasts, unable to *become*, or are they humans? Their forms—common simian types—are akin to Achibol's and Benadek's, but is something lacking? Are they ancestral archetypes, perceived to lack some critical spark that kindles the human fire?

(Kaledrin, Senior Editor)

Benadek's return to his old life was harder than before. Achibol had showed him what life *could* be—not just enormous, delicious meals or clean, well-kept surroundings, nor the ale and wine that Achibol bought so freely. It took the boy a while to decide what he missed most: the hope that he could become, through listening and learning, more than just an older urchin, then later a cozy doing odd jobs for minute-coins, and finally a useless oldster, ready for a final templing.

Achibol's dismissal was so abrupt. Just when he'd begun to believe he was a real apprentice, with direction and purpose, all had fallen apart.

He moped about the town the following day, passing by the inn several times, and by the alley where he'd first encountered the sorcerer. Peer as he might through the gate, and into the recesses of the alley, and into shops and stalls in the bazaar, he saw no tall, pointed hat, no gaudy robe, and no brown face.

By the end of the day, having exhausted his store of self-pity, he decided that he would not be thrust away without a fight. Achibol had told him not to bother him: "not tomorrow nor the day after." But "tomorrow" was almost over. Another day, and he'd return to the sorcerer as if nothing were wrong. He'd fight for what he wanted. He did not know how, but there had to be a way.

He sat in his burrow and tried to sleep, but speculations, visions of success and failure, swirled and entwined before his closed eyelids. Finally, he gave up.

"A poot," he decided. "I'll find a poot, and forget the old codger."

Benadek never had luck with poots. Females found his slight body and ratty eyes unappealing, and rejected, with catcalls and laughter, his most determined efforts to seduce them. Still, with the optimism of youth, he continued to pursue.

After all, the attraction to poots was the one thing all the kinds of male people had in common. Whether cozies, (ordinary illiterate laborers and tradesmen all), or unstable, fidgety, intelligent boffins, or sullen, tough, methodical honches, they all wanted poots, and poots reciprocated their desires—so why not him? He too was male, and though he wasn't old enough to tell whether he'd be a boffin or a cozy when he grew up (he couldn't even imagine becoming a surly honch), he was old enough to burn with desire. Somewhere out there was a poot who felt similarly toward him . . .

This night turned out no differently than most. The first unescorted poot he approached, a pretty one with impressive hips and thighs, ignored his soft-spoken greeting, swung into an open doorway, and slammed the door in Benadek's face. The second, a slender brunette, laughed outright and made obscene suggestions that in no way implied her participation. Benadek faded into the deep shadows.

Frustrated and indignant, he returned to his burrow and dug up his pitiful hoard of coppers, hiding them in his clothing.

He walked down the river road then. As he left the central town, the size and solidity of the buildings decreased. More were wood, fewer stone, and the road between them grew wider, even grassy in spots. Courtyards became small farmyards confining four- and eight-legged wool-beasts. Some had spiralling horns that swept backward the length of their bodies; others displayed branched horns, or none at all. They blatted their dislike of him, a stranger, and he walked swiftly past. His destination? The house of Agby, a poot of advanced years who, he'd been told, might accept a copper or two in exchange for her acquiescence.

Her house was marked by an ancient brass bedstead, long turned entirely green in the weather, atop the roof ridge. What if she were with someone? What if she were really old and ugly? What if she laughed at him? He did not think he could stand that—to be laughed at by even the lowest of all the poots. The young and pretty ones . . . he was used to that.

Agby's door swung open. She came out on the arm of a brutal city guard whose reputation Benadek knew. His trousers were still unbuttoned. Agby hung on his arm, cackling. She ran ancient spotted hands up the honch's arm, and wheedled "Wasn't that worth a little tip?"

The honch saw Benadek. "What are you staring at, boy?"

Benadek saw the poot's sunken eyes in a face that looked to be one solid bruise, and said, "I've come to the wrong place." He backed away, then turned as he reached the street. Even several buildings away, he could hear the honch laughing at him.

"At least I still have my money. Tomorrow I'll buy a fat sweet roll and some fried meat." The thought of such a meal, with a cup of spice-bark tea, helped him sleep, for the imagined tastes and aromas drove out bleak thoughts and optimism alike.

When morning came, the thought of sacrificing his meager assets for a mere breakfast had less appeal. He settled for crusts left out for a neighbor's chickens. Though he could have snatched one of the birds as well, Benadek was careful to behave in this, his own neighborhood. His claim on his burrow was tenuous, and if a hue and cry should go up, even over someone else's folly, he could lose it to thief-hunters who would burn his blankets and kick down his dirt walls.

The day promised to drag on and on. Purposeless, he wandered squares and marketplaces, never spending too long in any one—urchins were always suspect whether they pilfered or not, and guards acted first, and invented incidents to sustain their arrests as they needed them.

Before midday his perambulations took him by the inn, where he saw six strange honches in black leather, bedecked with trail gear and strange weapons. When he saw the objects of their interest, his heart sank: they surrounded two mules, one carrying the leather trunks from Achibol's chamber. His dismay was multiplied when two more honches exited the inn, propelling a protesting and expostulating Achibol between them.

The honches surely bore his hoped-for master no good will. That was an unhappy circumstance, not likely to cheer the magician or make him receptive to the importunements of a skinny urchin.

Achibol should be able to use his spells and magic to free himself, but he seemed to be doing no such thing. He fumed and jerked in his captors' grasps like any cranky boffin, helplessly. *Is he a fraud? Why doesn't he destroy his persecutors?*

What grieved Benadek most was that Achibol had been leaving without him—the laden mules told the tale. Affecting an air of nonchalance, he strode by within the mage's sight. The honches did not notice him, but Achibol's voice rose above the city sounds . . .

"I've decided to teach you what you wish to know," he said abruptly. "To enter the inner temple, you must find the talisman with five and twenty keys." He directed his voice past the honches. Benadek understood: he saw the sorcerer's talisman hanging from a thong on the riding mule's saddle, and lifted it free. Achibol's fleeting grin rewarded him. He slipped back, still within earshot, and pretended to doze against a water trough on the far side of the street.

"The keys, used in the proper order, will open the inner temple doors. But any one of them, used in improper order, could destroy you and all you strive for!" The speech was clearly intended for Benadek, not the honches, but Achibol was at pains to conceal that from his dusty leather-clad captors.

"Wait!" one honch grated. "A scribe has been summoned." Even as he spoke, an eighth honch came around the corner dragging the boffin Benadek had victimized before.

Achibol sneered. "Are you ready, now?"

"Tell us how you enter the temples," snarled the honch leader.

"You heard my warning: touch only those keys I tell you."

"I heard that, old man. Scribe! Note down that caution."

"The first key will be marked with four crossed lines, the second with a star." Benadek peered at the talisman, and found two buttons so marked. He extended a finger and cautiously touched [#], and then [*].

"Keep this simple, now," the honch cautioned.

"Would you have me miss a step? You'd end up lost in eternal night. Listen well, and hope your scribe does too." The honch, chastened, leaned a bit less closely. "The next key will be marked with an upright cross. Touch it once, and then once again."

Benadek saw a button marked [x]. No, an upright cross! He touched the [+] key twice. Blue letters on a white ground began marching across the tiny window over the keypad:

```
REDIRECT OUTPUT: READY.
ENTER INSTRUCTION SEQUENCE.
```

Achibol risked a glance in Benadek's direction. The boy nodded slightly. "Find the keys numbered one, three, nine, and two, and touch them in that exact order. Scribe! Have you written that?" The scribe, his brow furrowed in concentration, nodded even as he scratched at his paper. "Make sure of it," Achibol stressed, "for should one of these guardians be inundated in demon-fire that burns forever, or turns inside out with his bowels to the breeze, those who survive will fetch you to correct your error."

The scribe paled. "The numbers, good master. Say them again." Achibol repeated them. Benadek tapped the sequence: [1] [3] [9] [2], and nodded again. The numbers appeared in the window, after the message already there.

"The next sign has the form of a bent arrow which points leftward . . ."

"A moment, old man! Just how will we know left from right? Won't it depend on how the key is held?"

"These are no ordinary keys." Achibol sniffed. "You'll know."

"Perhaps we'll keep you here, old fraud, until we enter a temple or two, and your words prove out."

Benadek touched the key. Numbers scrolled too rapidly to distinguish individually. The talisman emitted a chirp. A surreptitious glance told him that no one but Achibol had noted it. The magician allowed himself a faint grin. Benadek saw that the scrolling numbers were gone, replaced with another cryptic message:

```
INTERFACE: NERVESYNC MODULE 4:
           ENGAGED.
CAUTION:   PROJECTOR IS WITHIN
           ACTIVE RANGE OF
           CONTROL UNIT. IS
           OPERATOR SHIELDED?
           1: ABORT 2: PROCEED
           3: DELAYED ACTIVATION
```

Benadek did not understand the message in its entirety, but its urgency did not escape him. He raised a questioning eyebrow toward Achibol. The old man looked at him and said, "You must delay your progress then, for guardian spirits of sleep will seek freedom, and you stand in their path. Remove yourself from the vicinity of the keys for a time."

"How long? How will we know it's safe to return? And how far must we go? Try no tricks or clever words, old man. You alone will suffer for them."

"When the '3' is touched, walk away at an ordinary pace. Forty such paces, and you'll be safe. As soon as you've gone the distance, you may return at once."

Both the honch and Benadek nodded. Benadek touched the [3] key, and walked away. He fought a strong impulse to run, and another to look back over his shoulder. He counted off thirty paces, then lost track and started over.

He crept back along the path of his flight. To his amazement, the honches were all prone, and the scribe as well, his paper fluttering away. "Here, Master. Your talisman. I know I was not to return to your service until the morrow, but sensing the urgency of your situation, I disobeyed. I'll accept whatever punishment you command, Master—but consider that my disobedience was out of loyalty to you. I am, after all, your bound apprentice"

"Punishment? Nonsense, boy. Apprentice? Did I say that? Never mind. Such things will sort themselves out. But now, we must go. They'll not sleep forever. Here. Help me mount this mule. The stubborn beast sidles away as I approach."

<Foolish old men who feed loyal mules only straw deserve such treatment,> the mule muttered. Benadek, after all that he'd seen in his new master's service, was hardly startled by the beast's speaking.

"Shall I mount behind you, Master?" he asked. "Or is my place with the pack mule?"

<Your place is with both feet on the ground and your nose in our dust,> snorted the saddle mule.

"Master?" Benadek questioned plaintively, putting on his best beggar's face.

"Ignore this surly mismatched horse. Ride behind me in the saddle."

Benadek sprung over the mule's hindquarters and grasped Achibol by the waist. He was happy to ride so, where his face could not be seen, for his gleeful grins alternated with grim, fearful looks into the future ahead. Perhaps it was only the stress of the day, and not a premonition, but he was convinced that his association with Achibol would not be easy, and that honches might be the least fearsome dangers he would face.

INTERLUDE
The Great School, Midicor IV

Kaledrin was uncomfortable with his boss's lack of visible reaction. Saphooth had hardly shown himself outside his office in weeks, unusual in one whose habitual prying tormented those who worked for him. This whole project, which Kaledrin had hoped would lead to his own name engraved over the gate of the Great School's tenured-faculty residence, was moving in unforeseen directions.

The tone of letters and comments in the simulnet were noncommittal or downright negative. Kaledrin all too easily pictured himself, a year or three older, as an impoverished data-collector on some sunless world, exchanging his photosensitive chitin for wooly fur and his carefully tuned energy-tapping antennae for a rude protein-engine of a body, running on the heat and ferment of decaying, half-chewed meat. He shuddered, rattling his chitin. Perhaps he was only tired. Too much work, too much energy expended, and no time to spread his radiation-absorbing body-plates beneath the bright, white rays of the star Midicor, the local sun. He should not work so hard, he scolded himself, nor live entirely on energy supplements in this dark, academic womb.

He considered the latest submission from the biocybes: Chapter Four. Fringe cultists would consider it sacrilegious. With Saphooth refusing to communicate, he would have to send it for publication under his name alone. But that was not all bad—if the biocybes explained themselves in future chapters, and if the project gained the respect of highly placed academics, then his, Kaledrin's, name would stand alone on several chapters, And if future chapters degenerated from inexplicable to ridiculous?

"Dictation!" Kaledrin ordered, words forming in his mind even as the office AI readied itself for voice input.

CHAPTER FOUR,

or how a sorcerer's spell gains Benadek a young and desirable bedmate.

Variations on this episode are found from one edge of the galaxy to the other. They are treated as everything from lessons in cleanliness to homilies on the rewards of conformity and social integration.

In the biocybes' version, Achibol steps handily between his traditional guises—disciplinarian, moralist, teacher, and trickster. Benadek dances between condescension toward the poot, Sylfie (for which Achibol punishes him), and desire for her (and in the role of Trickster, the sorcerer abets him).

One is impressed with the foreignness of this new context. Old elements are missing, and new are left unexplained. Take Sylfie. What, exactly, is her handicap? Why does Benadek treat her first as a lesser being, then as the object of his desire? If she is dissatisfied with her role, why does she not simply change it, change herself, *becoming* what she wishes to be?

Perhaps the confusion lies less with the biocybes' shadow-characters, enacting their drama against the black backdrop of forgotten times, than with our own cultural biases. Do we force significant reality on simple allegorical tales where none in fact exists? Perhaps as this project progresses, our perceptions will have to change.

(Kaledrin, Senior Editor)

Bassidon town was not much, to Benadek's city-bred eye—a half-dozen streets like wheel spokes, lined with unpainted wood shacks and barns. The village center was a hexagonal marketplace with merchants' tents huddled forlornly at one side.

"Is this it, Master?" the boy asked, sneering. "Can we gather an hour's worth of coin here in a week?"

"Appearances, boy! Appearances. Bassidon's folk will part with their coin when they see our offerings. Unload now, and set up for business. Right here will do nicely."

Benadek dug Achibol's fine silky tent from its trunk. Like the merchants' shelters it was faded, but otherwise there was no resemblance. Benadek set no stakes and strung no cords. Instead, he manipulated the keys of Achibol's talisman, and the tent lifted itself. It stretched like a baggy leech filling with blood, and in minutes stood tall, a domed shelter in deep blue and bright violet, painted with oversized palm prints and the magician's usual runes.

It was almost sunset, and there would be no business tonight. "Shall we find the temple, boy? With that out of the way, we'll do nothing tomorrow but read palms, flash arcane lights, and collect coin."

Benadek demurred. There was a tavern on the road

they'd come in on. He'd heard music and poots' laughter. He suggested dinner and something to wet his dry throat.

"Work first," Achibol insisted. "No fuzzy heads or clumsy fingers should tinker with delicate things. Except poots, of course. That's where your thoughts are, I'll wager."

He would have won the bet. Benadek's thoughts seldom strayed far from poots. But considering his earlier experiences—from quiet failure to having a chamberpot dumped on him from a window—he was depressingly willing to consider such thoughts utter fantasy.

How many temples had they visited since they'd left the honches sprawled in front of the inn? Four? No, five. Benadek had the routine down pat. He went to the door—no gate and courtyard in this poor place—and hammered. A priest opened it, and he laid the magical coin in the pale, outstretched palm. "My master, Achibol the wise, gives this," he said, "and will visit moments hence." The priest took the coin, and shut the door. No words were wasted on the scruffy child.

Achibol arrived soon after. "Wait," he said, forestalling Benadek's knock. "Let him carry it to the almsbowl in the sanctum first. It's effect will spread evenly, then. No priests must waken while we're inside."

Benadek was bored with the whole business. Temple visits were the low points of their arrival in a town. Who would have thought it? For all his erstwhile fear, he had nothing but bored contempt for temples and their machines. Achibol did all the tinkering, and he merely handed his master the proper tools. He knew their names, now: number two star-drive screwdriver, ratchet, socket wrench, jumpers, alligator clips. Even the talisman had a special name—"universal interface"—and Achibol's staff was a "multipurpose distribution nexus"; only its blue beech shaft, like twisted musculature, was just plain wood. Temples, tinkering, and gadgets were no longer fun.

He had a hard time accepting that temples were foremost in his master's mind and that fortunetelling, scribery, and magic shows served only to earn money for food and drink, and a spot at the inn. And not even that, in Bassidon! There was only a dirty roadhouse with a privy needing a good dose of lime. They would sleep in the tent, where they'd gain no small new companions to ride in their clothes.

The temple adjustments took little time. There were no roaches or crickets in its workings, no corrosion on its circuit boards. Achibol connected his talisman, then tapped keys in a careful but habitual manner. He called up images on several "screens" and perused them, then nodded and began stowing his tools. "This one was easy," he muttered. "No damn stone fortress around it blocking the air ducts and solar collectors. Half the city temples have been on backup power for a coon's age—and this coon doesn't age much." He snorted and chuckled noisily at his obscure joke. Benadek, accustomed to his master's madness, smiled politely.

"Aren't you in need of templing, boy? When was the last time you had your genes read?"

"Oh no, Master. I . . . I took care of that a few stops back. Abbro, was it? No, I think it was Vank—the town on the river. You remember, don't you?"

Achibol remembered nothing. There was nothing to remember. Achibol gave his apprentice a searching stare. "Well," he said. "At any rate, I think I'll stay here a while, and engage in stimulating repartee with the good clerics when they awaken. Leave the door ajar when you go out." Benadek made his exit quickly, before his master could change his mind. The tavern awaited.

Three drinks and as many rejections later, Benadek

trudged dispiritedly into the marketplace. He was hardly tipsy.

When he saw a shadow move across the fabric of the tent, backlit by Achibol's strange fuelless lamp within, he paused to observe. His master had cautioned him to beware of curiosity-seekers who might be in league with his honch enemies. Achibol steadfastly refused to explain *why* they were enemies, but to an urchin, almost all adults were, and honches the most dangerous. Achibol did not consider honches who guarded gates or patrolled muddy streets at midnight as his foes. He feared roving bands without ostensible purpose—"military" honches. "Military," Benadek decided, meant the same as "mad dog."

This shadow was no honch. It was a poot. She walked around the tent, engrossed in its symbols. Benadek was captivated by her pert fanny and the blond gleam of her hair. She can't be much older than I am, he thought.

"What are you looking at?" he asked when he was only a pace from her. Her shoulders jerked convulsively and she swung around, her face a mask of fear.

"Hey! I'm sorry I frightened you. Don't run away."

"I didn't hear you," she said. Her voice, too, was pretty—a soft contralto. "Is this your tent?"

"It is. What interests you so?"

"These markings—they're like letters, but they aren't. What are they for?"

"They're magical runes. But how do you know they aren't letters? You can't read."

"I can too! I taught myself how, from my father's books."

Benadek's indulgent smile showed his disbelief.

"I can!" she insisted. "Find something written, and I'll show you."

Benadek drew forth a small practice-tablet Achibol had given him. He could write on it, and the tap of a tile imbedded in its surface would erase what he'd written. If he wanted to keep the result of his effort, tapping another tile stored a memory of his scratchings somewhere inside where he could recall it. There were fifteen touch-tiles, but he'd mastered only the three.

He scrawled three words in the cursive style Achibol was teaching him, and handed the device to the poot. His smug smile grew wider as he saw her forehead wrinkle in puzzlement, as her eyes narrowed with her effort to draw meaning from the sinuous traces.

"That's not writing!" she exclaimed angrily, thrusting the tablet away

"It is too. Admit it—you can't read." He cleared the tablet.

"There aren't any letters, only worm-wiggles." She snatched the pad from him, and painstakingly drew two connected lines, and then a straight one. "There! Those are letters. See?" She had drawn a capital V and an I.

"What letters are they, then?" he teased.

"What do you mean? They're letters, that's all."

"You don't know what they're called? If you don't know that, you can't read them."

"You're stupid! Letters are only little things. Words have names, but they're all longer than that, except a few like 'it.' "

Benadek took the stylus and, while she still clung to the tablet, printed what he had written before, this time in capitals. He raised his eyebrow with practiced cynicism—a look that Achibol claimed would earn him whippings from a less tolerant master. "Read that."

Again she concentrated, lips forming first one syllable and then the next. At the third syllable, she threw down the pad. "That's not true!" she said as tears welled up in her eyes. "I won't say that." She stalked stiffly away.

Regretfully and angrily, Benadek watched the

shifting of her slim hips and the jiggle of her behind as she departed. Regretfully, because she was leaving. Angrily, because she was the first poot who had ever said more than a dozen words to him, and he'd driven her away. What galled him most of all was that he'd done it for no cause. She *could* read. He'd watched her lips as she'd picked her way through his three short words. "POOTS CANT READ," he'd written.*

He thought about following her, but by then she had disappeared in the moonless darkness. "Shit!" he said loudly. "Shit, shit!"

"Is that how you treat them all, boy?" How long had Achibol been listening? "No wonder you're as horny as a goat."

"That's not how it is!" he protested. "Everybody knows poots can't read. All they're good for is . . . is . . ."

"Who's stupid? Poots, you say? Pots and kettles, lad! With 'magic' all around, can't you accept a little human magic?" He shook his head disdainfully. "No one took the drive out of simples' genes, boy—only most of the abilities." He sniffed scornfully. "You witnessed a human miracle, first hand, and all you can say is 'Poots can't read.' She couldn't read well, poor thing. Not like you. But she isn't going to grow up a boffin either. Somehow she has surpassed the inborn limitations an evil creator gave her—a miracle, I say. And you? You mock her and drive her away in tears, her supreme accomplishment defiled." Achibol was truly angry, his brown face yellower than tentlight could account for, the whites of his eyes round and large.

---

* The differing capabilities of honches, poots, cozies, and so on seem to imply a minimax specialization, each type only as aggressive, smart, strong, or quick as their allotted positions require. Does this portray overspecialization and an evolutionary dead end—or a planetary population on the verge of *becoming*?

"Inside, boy!" the sorcerer commanded. Benadek scuttled past him. Then, observing Achibol loosening his belt, he wished he had run away instead. It was a master's right to whip his apprentice, but Benadek had never considered it happening to him. He'd come to terms with the perils of being turned into a toad or a goat, or being afflicted with boils, but a whipping? He was too old for such punishment.

He was not too old to howl like a child as his master's heavy belt caught him across the buttocks. He howled no less exuberantly with the last stroke than the first—perhaps louder, for he had no idea how many times Achibol intended to shellack him, and if his agony sounded sufficiently intense, perhaps his master would be sooner satisfied. . . .

"It's human to strive, boy," Achibol said when Benadek's yells diminished to sniffles. "We climb as high as we can—even those without legs struggle to attain the heights of their dreams. Laugh at the efforts of others at your own soul's peril."

"What's a soul, Master?" Benadek whispered. Achibol would never punish him for asking questions, though he might for *not* doing so. . . .

"It's what makes you and me—and that poor poot—better than mules or dogs," Achibol said sadly. "It's what makes you human."

In spite of his stinging buttocks, Benadek sat with his chin on his knees, his face on his folded arms. His shoulders shook as he wept with a pain not physical.

"What is it, lad?" Achibol asked, putting a large, bony brown hand on his shoulder. "Why do you weep?"

"I'm not sure I *am* human, Master. Poots treat me like I'm a dog or a mule. If I'm human, why don't they want to do . . . human things with me?"

"If you treat them all like . . ."

"Master, I don't! This time I was just turning the

tables on one of them. Mostly I try to act just like a cozy would, but they laugh and slam doors on my nose, or dump chamberpots on me."

"Hmm. I suspect now that you're never going to be a cozy, so why act like one? You're my apprentice. Act like that."

"How?"

"I've neglected your training, haven't I? To say 'act like me' would be foolish, for I don't want that. One Achibol is enough." He chuckled.

"First, you need new clothes—those urchin's rags will hardly do. There's a long-forgotten ritual for just such occasions as this. It dates back to Old Human times."

Benadek perked up, pain or no pain. Was Achibol going to show him some real magic?

"We'll need water, boy. Lots of it, and hot, too. Puff up the horse trough and let's begin." Benadek fetched a parcel from the trunk, and pressed a tab. Like the tent, it swelled, forming an oval vessel as long as Benadek himself. A bucket of similar construction lay inside it.

The village well was on the far side of the square. "Why is it," he muttered, "that even real magic means only more hard work for *me*?" Fifteen trips later, the trough was full. Achibol stuck the base of his staff in it, and murmured an incantation.

"What did you say, Master? If I'm to learn this magic, I should know."

"I said only 'I hope the water doesn't short out my staff.' "

"Oh." Benadek observed steam rising from the water, which had been cold when he'd brought it in. Obviously, the sorcerer was not about to give up all his secrets at once.

Achibol sprinkled thick green syrup in the water and swished the staff to mix it. The fresh odor of piny forests rose. "Now—off with your clothes. Get in."

"In the magic potion? It's hot!"

"The hotter the better. Duck under and soak your hair, too."

"Yeeow! It's too hot!"

"Did you think sorcery would be easy? Your difficulties have only begun. Under! All the way under."

It was not too bad, once he was all the way in. Even his sore behind felt better for it.

"Now this!" Achibol said, holding a rounded block like white lard. "Rub this in your hair, and over your face."

"Yuk! It's greasy," Benadek said, but he obeyed.

"Keep your eyes shut, or they'll burn."

Mixed with the water on his skin, the lardy stuff became slick, and smelled of spices and springtime. "All over!" Achibol commanded. "Now stand up. You must be cleansed of Earth's essences if you would be master of the air." Benadek did not understand why Achibol found that funny.

The sorcerer scrubbed Benadek from head to toe with a stiff brush, eliciting loud complaints, and darkening the water considerably. "Under again, boy," he said, "and we'll see if this has made a difference." Benadek complied gladly, hoping his ordeal was nearing its end.

Achibol expressed approval of the new, considerably lighter, Benadek. "Now we'll see if poots will find you more to their liking," he said.

"What is that stuff you used on me called, Master?" the boy asked as he towelled himself dry. "And the ritual—does it have a name?"

"It's called soap," Achibol snorted, "and as for the ceremony, you just had your first bath. Now," he continued with a flourish of his dark, bony hands, "I don't know that this is necessary—or that your difficulties with poots are anything more than abysmal lack of sensitivity to the feelings of others, but in case we haven't done enough, I'm going to guarantee you'll find a companion tonight."

He rummaged in his trunk and produced a glass vial. "Here! Androsterone Five. Just the thing for a night on the town."

"What is it?"

"A rare and wondrous extract. From the balls and brain of a great boar."

"Yuk!"

"Would a sow think so? Or a poot? Don't deride what you don't understand. Put a dab of this on a dentist's chair, and not a woman in town would have an unfilled cavity." He snorted at his obscure joke. Using the glass dropper attached to the vial's lid, he dabbed Benadek's chest with odorless fluid.

"What's a dentist?" Benadek dutifully queried.

"Don't ask. In fact, pray heartily you never find out."

Benadek filed "dentist" in the part of his mind where he kept a list of Achibol's demons: Cop; Racist; Politician. And now, Dentist.

Achibol shook out a gaudy shirt and handed it to Benadek. It came to his knees. Then he proffered two black lumps. "I've only one pair of these fits-all army-surplus boots left. Treat them carefully." The boots, seemingly much too small even for Benadek's narrow feet, stretched easily over them. Once in place they felt neither tight nor uncomfortable, though hard as iron to the touch.

The final embellishment was a gold-colored link belt that Benadek thought too light for metal. "An alloy of lithium," Achibol explained. "It's very rare." Cinched around Benadek's waist, the belt turned the oversized shirt into a smaller version of Achibol's own sorcerer's robe.

"Now, Master," Benadek said, proudly glancing down at his finery, "I'm going poot hunting." He strode toward the door, hard-soled boots lending him a decisive, confident stride.

"Wait! Where will you go?" Achibol demanded. "Will you command the first female you see into an alley and be done with it? Did I do all this for you to waste it in a few sordid minutes?"

"What then, Master?" Benadek asked him, truly puzzled. Was there more to be desired than he'd imagined?

"What of the pretty young girl* you so grievously wronged? The one who can read? Don't you owe her an apology?"

"How can I find her? There are hundreds of doors on this street."

"Her name is Sylfie. She lives upstairs, at the sign of the Gray Bird, a featherbed and pillow shop. She's alone and sad, and might welcome your gentle comfort—but compassion, boy! Remember whose apprentice you are. I am Achibol, who gives delight, laughter, and hope, not a butcher or honch."

"I understand, Master. I'll do as you say." Benadek turned again to the exit, afraid Achibol might think of more admonitions, and that his imagined pleasure would become yet more constrained.

When the boy had gone, Achibol shook his head ruefully. <Will you never learn, old fool?> his staff demanded. <What have you loosed upon womanhood?>

"The boy is not what he seems," Achibol replied. "If his pheromones are really different, as I suspect, he'll never find happiness in a poot's bed without help."

<Whoremonger!> the steaming tub called him.

<Yes! A nasty old man, indeed. For all your kindly intentions.> That, from his trunk.

"Just wait, all of you!" Achibol muttered. "It will become clear, or it won't. Just wait and see."

---

* See preceding notes re: "woman" and "girl."

✧ ✧ ✧

Benadek had no trouble finding the Gray Bird. The sign was newly painted, an arm's span across. In an upper window, a candle flame waxed and waned as someone moved about. He was not ready to knock on the staircase door. Was he afraid, now that his moment was purportedly at hand? What was to fear?

That question brought a torrent of answers: Achibol was not above playing nasty tricks—in the name of learning, of course. Or his master's magic might fail him—the old man was not perfect—and Benadek might actually be outside the door of some honch who would beat him. He leaned on a pillar in the shadows across the street.

But fate intervened. He heard the upstairs sash open. A face, a white-clad body, leaned out into the moonlight. It *was* her! Her sand-blond hair gleamed silver. She looked first one way up the street, then the other. Was she expecting someone at this time of night?

Benadek tensed to move deeper into shadow or to step forward and announce himself. The decision which was taken from his hands.

"You in the shadows! Are you a thief? Come forth or I'll set the bell to ringing!"

"I'm no thief! I'm Benadek, apprentice to the great sorcerer, Achibol. I'm here to apologize. I tarried only to collect my thoughts."

"As well you might!" she snapped. "You might apologize as well for skulking and spying, instead of coming straight to the door."

"Let me in, so we don't wake the neighborhood, and I'll apologize for that too."

"Why don't I fear you?" she mused. "But very well, I'll be down in a moment." He heard her light footsteps on the wooden steps, then the rattle of an ancient lock.

"You're different," she said immediately. "I hardly know you."

"I'm dressed as befits my rank and position," Benadek said glibly, "not in the anonymous garb I affect for lesser occasions."

"There's more to the difference than clothing," she observed astutely. "But never mind. Come upstairs."

The ascent was the high point of Benadek's life, or so he believed. His eyes followed her pert behind from a vantage point only a foot or two away, and he studied the flash of her slim ankles and delicate feet. He had never seen such pretty legs, such a firm . . . He almost fell as his foot reached up for a step that was not there. They had arrived.

The room, lit by a candle on a small wood table, was not what Benadek had expected. It was lined with shelves, and on the shelves were . . . books. Leather-clad books and cloth-covered ones, titles in colors that contrasted with dark leather or yellowed cloth. But his desire to examine them would have to wait.

"I came to apologize," he said, "and to explain why I acted as I did."

"Explain later," she murmured, moving close.

"I was special before," he insisted. "Reading made me different from the other urchins. And you—I wasn't special anymore, you see?"

"I'm sorry," she said, unbuttoning him, running her hands over his chest as his shirt fell open.

"I'm supposed to be sorry, not you! Learning to read is special. I was jealous and selfish. Forgive me."

"If I haven't forgiven you, why am I taking your clothing off?"

Benadek, for once, had nothing further to say—and much, so very much, to learn.

CHAPTER FIVE,

wherein a Demon's spell is averted, and intimations of distant Evil are revealed.

An erotic Celambese mystery play provides the raw material for the first part of this chapter, and a martial chant from Sarbadathian schismatics for the second.

The complete biocybernetic rendition of the Celambese portion of the tale contained thirty nights of sexual acrobatics, pared down by this text's human editors to a hint here and a kiss there.

No moral qualms lie at the root of such censorship: in fact, several of our "censors" are connoisseurs of literary erotica upon whose expert advice more than thirty thousand words of the text were cut.* Consider that both participants are bipedal forms of rigid inflexibility and that all possible variations of "who does what, and with which, and to whom" are limited to a few orifices, a quasi-rigid zygopositor, and four five-digit manipulators. What wonder that discriminating connoisseurs found themselves bored by Benadek's couplings?

Intimations of distant Evil . . . on Sarbadath VII, this tale is propaganda, justification for planetary war; herein one finds only foreboding and muted fear. One begins to suspect that the Biocybes have developed a talent for suspense.

(Kaledrin, Senior Editor)

INTERLUDE
The Great School, Midicor IV

"I'll bet Saphooth wasn't bored with it." Abrovid snickered.

"Are you kidding? You know who those 'several' censors were? Saphooth, Saphooth, and—after he put the pressure on—me. I thought some of that stuff was pretty good, myself."

"I wonder if Androsterone is for real," Abrovid said pensively.

Light of pale morning washed across Benadek's eyelids but, for an eternity, he decided not to open them,

---

* The biocybes' complete text is available to scholars at a nominal charge; but seekers of novel erotica beware: it isn't worth it. Recall Achibol's words in Chapter 4, suggesting that "Androsterone Five" was not a love potion, but merely a remedy for some deficiency innate in Benadek.

not to admit whatever reality lay beyond. He savored the soft bedclothes, finding no lingering trace of tent material or mule dung, but instead the sweet freshness of female youth. Only when he had assured himself that he was indeed in a poot's bedroom and that the wondrous events of the night now past had indeed occurred did he open his eyes.

There had been other times when he had awakened to such scents, such sensations, but he adamantly refused to remember that he had once had a mother—and that his father must have loved her in such ways. He thrust those thoughts aside, leaving only warmth and diffuse contentment.

Sylfie entered with a tray of sweet rolls and a pitcher of fruit-water from the vendor whose cries even now entered the room through a distant window. Dressed in a light woolen shift, she was every bit as lovely as he remembered her by candle flame and diffuse moonlight. She sat on the edge of the bed, and offered him food. His eyes never left hers. She then poured him a drink.

"I never asked your name," he said. "I'm Benadek."

"I know. You told me that. I'm Sylfie."

"Did you say all this was your father's?" Benadek asked.

"It was. He's dead now. All this will be gone soon."

"I'm sorry. How did he die?"

"He was old."

"He went to the temple?"

"To die? No, he died here. With me. I buried him secretly, under the house, or the magistrate would have confiscated everything."

"And now? What will you do? What about his books?"

"Everything's been sold. I have some coins hidden away. I can get along for a while."

"It's funny that you knew your father, isn't it?" From what Achibol had told him, most fathers were no more than recreated sperm in the temples' banks; only rarely were natural conceptions left alone to fruition; mothers—poots—were all that counted.

"He was with my mother when she bore me, and he kept me here after she died," she said sharply. "Should I call him 'uncle?' "

"I meant only that my friends knew no fathers," he replied. "I'm sorry."

The words came easily, Benadek noticed without surprise. A certain edge had worn off, a touchiness he'd not even noticed before, but which had, he now realized, pervaded his every thought and action. There was a clarity to his thinking, like the surface of a pond no longer disturbed by the tiniest ripple, wherein he could see not only a clear reflection of his own face but the waterlogged twigs and pebbles and minnows that lay beyond . . .

"We apologize too much, you and I," Sylfie murmured.

"Then no more of it. We must assume no harm is meant by each other's words." Dismissing the topic, he raised another. "Can't you keep his books, and become a scribe, since you can read?"

"A scribe? Would you buy a goat to do a horse's work? Has there ever been a poot who was anything but a poot? Impossible. No one would come to me—look at you! What chance did I have?" She shook her head sadly. "And besides, I'm not clever like you."

Benadek politely disagreed, but her objections were valid, even if she were not stupid. "Where will you go? Will you live alone?"

"For a while, at least. When the money runs out, perhaps I'll find a man—but the skinner and a temple honch are my only suitors at present. One stinks of blood and the other would beat me. There's an underpriest who would have me, but he's pale as a corpse, and has nowhere to house me except the temple stable. I'll not raise babies there."

"Then come with us!" Benadek blurted. "My master needs a lovely assistant like you. The rubes will love you."

"Rubes?"

" 'Respected customers,' my master says. We read their futures, and put on exhibitions of magical things. You'd be perfect for that . . . a pretty girl to draw their eyes."

"Has he said as much?"

"Well . . . not in so many words, but he'll love you. Shall we ask him?"

Sylfie reluctantly agreed. When they approached the tent, she hung back, motioning Benadek to go in alone.

"Well, boy!" Achibol huffed as Benadek entered. "My magic persisted until noon? I surpassed myself! I've been telling fortunes unaccompanied since sunup—and postponed our performance twice. Come! To work!"

"Master? I have a request."

"Are you a fool, boy? Ask me later, when our purse is full."

At that moment Sylfie, who had heard all through the tent wall, peered inside. "Never mind. I can see it won't work." She attempted to withdraw, but Achibol stayed her with an imperious gesture.

"Wait! What is this?" He stared first at her, then at Benadek, who assumed his meekest posture and expression.

"Master, this poor poot's home is about to be taken from her, and we need a pretty face to enliven our magic show. You yourself said as much."

"I did?" Achibol raised his bushy eyebrow and glowered at the poot. "How does a mere apprentice remember his master's words better than the master himself? Or is it that, as I suspect, my magic potion

---

* See preceding notes re. "woman" and "girl."

still endures?" He eyed Sylfie. "Go outdoors, young woman *," he ordered, "and don't eavesdrop . . . but remain close at hand, where I can call you."

He turned on Benadek. "Do you think it will last as long as you have balls—that the vial will be ever full? Indeed, boy, you complicate my elementary life. I find myself first with an apprentice, now with a comely stagehand, and what next? Babies to dandle? What of our clandestine work—our visits to the temples? Dare we share our labors with someone who'll follow our path a while, and leave?"

"Never, Master! She'll remain with me always!"

"Always to you, and always to one who has lived a thousand years and more, may not be the same." He shook his head. "Magic is ephemeral, no longer-lasting than the potion drops in my flasks. When the last drops are gone and the spell wanes, what then?" He shook his head ruefully. "As a matter of fact, what if you tire of her? Will you cast her by the wayside?"

"Perhaps the magic is in *us*, master, not spells and potions. Even if not, I can only do what I can, because I'd sorely regret losing her so soon after I found her."

"You're twice the fool, boy! But call her in here."

"It's settled, then? She can stay?"

"Am I an old fool? Do I take in urchins who importune me and strut visions of grandeur before me? Am I a sucker for a winsome face and a pair of pretty legs? Of course she can stay. Can she cook? Is that too much to hope for?"

"I'm sure she can, Master," Benadek blurted as he rushed for the open doorway.

Sylfie could cook. Her pretty legs provided distraction for sharp-eyed critics of magical shows. She developed a sense of when to show a bit more leg, an inch more shapely bosom, when Achibol attempted a trick that depended less upon gadgetry than innate talent.

On the road, day followed day much as before Sylfie joined them, with certain differences: Benadek took catnaps now where before he might have read or gone swimming, for he got less sleep at night. He and his bedmate slept away from the fire that warmed Achibol's old bones, lest they disturb him with their pleasures; they often emerged from their comforters with snuffly noses and leaves and morning dew in their hair. When opportunity presented, they explored the joys of their differences amid wayside ferns, beside chilly creeks, and half-submerged in warm, sunlit ponds. Endless days, uncounted nights . . . until the reactions of their bodies were familiar and comfortable, predictable and even routine.

But it was not all bliss . . . Stronger loves than theirs have foundered over differences, and different they were. No blame attached to Sylfie; within the limits imposed by streamlined, fourfold redundant genes, she attempted to be part of Benadek's life and of the lessons his master taught; but esoteric concepts glittered in her mind like shiny fish darting forth into clear water, then glided away into the reeds just as swiftly—slippery and ungraspable.

Benadek gave Sylfie the magical writing tablet. She spent long evening hours practicing her hard-earned writing skills. For a while, her ability seemed to increase, but there was a threshold she could not pass. As she learned new things, old ones faded, as if her mind were a vessel of limited capacity that had to be emptied a bit before it could be refilled. That was frustrating for the boy, whose own mind was a vessel of seemingly unlimited volume. But even when his interest in teaching her waned, she practiced indefatigably.

More than limitations of genetically engineered intellect worked against her; she knew, as Benadek refused to know, that all things had their time, and a time of ending would come, whether then or down a long road.

She wished to keep that parting sweet, so she did not enquire what they did in the temples. Secrets were secrets, and the less she heard of them, the less discomfort she would cause her companions when the day came for her departure. She took to walking with the mules while Achibol and his pupil strode ahead. Benadek was content with that; he was frustrated with her inability to comprehend things he absorbed with ease. Achibol curbed his apprentice's sharp tongue as best he could, but he was not in their bed at night nor did he share all their daytime moments. It was better that Benadek be with her only when his mind was upon what she was truly able to give him.

Cor Absiddy was a village much like the last dozen—a flat spot in rough country, a clearing in the forest, a dry stretch amid marshy expanses. It had, as all towns did, a temple. Perhaps it would be more correct to say that the temple, as temples did, had gathered about itself a town.

They unloaded their goods in the muddy square. Sylfie had been wan and restless for several turns of the sun, and it did not surprise Achibol when she asked to accompany him to the temple. They left Benadek to set up camp in the marketplace.

When an hour passed and they had not returned, Benadek went looking for them. He was not anxious, only annoyed, and when he spied a voluptuous poot of middle years, he followed her for a minute or two, admiring her ample posterior. When her quick glances turned to glares, he discontinued his pursuit, but not until he had gone beyond his destination, the temple. Thus he approached it from the other side, and he heard sounds of a commotion around the corner. Ever cautious, he peered around it with an eye for possible routes of escape.

His urchin's experience paid off, for there against the wall was a scene that, in broad scope, was straight from his past: Achibol in the massive grip of a black-clad honch, struggling and expostulating. The honch held one of the weapons Benadek's master had called "lasers." But the scene was not exactly the same as that other time: there were no mules, and Sylfie was slumped against the temple wall with her clothes all dusty and awry, a dark spot at the corner of her mouth—dirt, or blood?

Benadek's rage gave way to preternatural calm, and he saw more details. Achibol's robe was torn, exposing his black under-suit, and the tools he usually kept there were scattered on the cobble pavement. The "talisman" was there too, beneath the honch's boot toe. Benadek had seen that coarse, scarred face before—in Vilbursiton. The honch knew firsthand what Achibol's magic could do, and had come prepared for it.

"Cease struggling, old fraud," he said. "You'll not reach your toy. Yes—I know how you took us before. It was the boy, wasn't it? The rat-faced one? But this time, I have your nasty trinket, and the boy is not here."

"Why didn't it work?" Achibol demanded.

"My hat, sorcerer! Don't you like my new hat?" Benadek saw it then, even as did his master—a fine metallic mesh that covered his skull down to his ears and eyebrows.

"A Faraday cage!" Achibol exclaimed. "You've nullified my device. How did you know to do it?"

Confident of his mastery of the situation, the honch responded easily. "*My* master is as clever as you are, fraud."

"Who is your master? Are you taking us to him? Or will you kill us alongside the Valstock road?"

The question alerted Benadek. Achibol was pumping his captor for a destination! Did he know Benadek was there, behind a crooked wooden staircase, or was he merely hoping?

"Valstock? My master isn't in Valstock." Honches, Benadek observed not for the first time, were not too smart.

Valstock road was a hundred paces away, the way Benadek had come. Only one other road led out of the town—the way they'd come in. Thus the honch and his captives must go around the temple. Benadek backed up the way he'd come.

The honch ordered Sylfie to pick up the scattered tools and carry them slung in her skirt. He let Achibol go, but kept the laser pointed at him. The useless talisman and the staff went to Sylfie, who was having difficulty with her burden. Or was she? Benadek had never seen her be so clumsy before. He hoped that she and Achibol were intentionally stalling the honch. There might be time to get around in front of their path, and find a way to free them.

Once they were in the square where he'd set up the tent, it would be too late. Only the narrow streets and alleys provided close cover for what he hoped to do. That depended on whether the "talisman" was still activated.

His eyes scanned the second stories of the buildings he passed, noting balconies, low roofs and ledges. None seemed right.

There! A projecting sign reached over the narrow way. He jumped, and pulled himself up on the side opposite the trio's approach. He reached out and down. No! He was too high! But there was no time to find another ambush spot. It was the sign, or nothing. Desperately, he scanned the entire street, not knowing exactly what he sought.

There—a broom on the balcony of a shuttered

room only a short jump from his perch. He stretched for it, but his arms were too short. He heard the honch's booming laugh and Achibol's scratchy complaints: they were almost upon him! He launched himself from the sign to the balcony, and the broom was in his grasp, slippery with blood—he'd left skin on the rough, rusty iron balcony rail. Miraculously, his jump had made little noise.

He snapped the broomstick across his knee, near the straw end. It was a splintery break, no good for stabbing. That narrowed his options: he would have to lift the mesh hat from the honch's head as he passed under the sign.

Only when it was too late did he realize the flaw in his plan: if the talisman were on, Sylfie would not be walking. She had no mesh protection. Everything depended on whether Achibol was alert enough to take the device from Sylfie and turn it on as soon as the mesh was lifted from the honch's head.

He heard them approach. Hiding on the far side of the sign, he swung it slightly. There was no breeze—would the honch notice it?

He did not. But Achibol did. The old man's expostulations shifted immediately to cries for the gods, the unknown, unknowable gods, to send him a sign. A sign!

There was no time left—they were passing under him. First Sylfie, close by the sorcerer, then the honch, laser in hand. Benadek stretched his broken broomstick and lashed out at the mesh. He missed. Again he reached out. The honch swatted at his ear, thinking it an insect, but the mesh caught in the splayed broomstick fibers, and Benadek lifted it away. Overbalanced, he fell. Even as he dropped, he could see that he'd failed. The honch was turning angrily toward him, the deadly muzzle of his weapon swinging into line.

He came back to consciousness slowly. There was no feeling in his limbs. At first he thought himself tightly bound, or that his neck was broken. He smelled Sylfie's light scent.

"I'm sorry," he muttered. Sylfie was holding his head in her arms. He knew it was her, though his eyes were swollen shut. "I tried to save us."

"Benadek, you did save us! Open your eyes." He did. There was Achibol, talisman and staff in hand, and there, sprawled unblinking and motionless, was the honch. The talisman, not his fall, had knocked Benadek out. The talisman, in Achibol's hands.

"Don't sleep now, boy. We must hurry. My little toy is running down, and we must be gone."

"What about him?" Benadek asked, kicking the rigid honch's ribs.

"Stop that! We'll leave him. There won't be time to pack. We'll just take the mules and go."

"And leave the tent? The chests?" Benadek shook his head emphatically. "Let's kill him."

"A life for a tent?"

Benadek forestalled Achibol's morality lecture. "A headache, then!" he exclaimed, and levelled a sharp kick at the honch's head. Even under the waning influence of the talisman, his expression changed from restrained and uncomprehending to the blankness of oblivion. "There. Let's get the tent and be gone." He took Sylfie by the hand and strode off toward the marketplace.

"How did he find you, Master?" Benadek asked later. It was almost dawn. Bright Vega and the wide summer triangle had risen high overhead and were already swinging northwestward and down. There was no dawn glow to mute its brightness yet, but soon . . .

"He awaited us inside the temple."

"How did he know you'd come?"

"I don't think he did. I suspect he'd stationed himself there on the off chance of my arrival."

"That seems unlikely," Benadek mused. "From Lothamby, last week, we could have gone west into the Fallogun hills, or taken a river-barge, or even crossed the Sera range. What was the chance that we'd come this way?"

"I suspect there are honches in the temples of Fallogun, too, and in the downriver towns, even the mountain hospices. That frightens me for many reasons."

"I'd think one's enough. What reasons?"

"Besides curtailing my work and the usefulness of my handiest tool, I fear this concerted effort is too well organized for ordinary honches. First the lasers, then their determined pursuit when I lost them before Vilbursiton, now Faraday cage hair-nets and an organized blockade of the temples. All to catch me—not to kill, but to bring me before some unknown honchmaster."

"Who?"

"I have my suspicions, boy. There have been times long past when honches gathered into great armies under the sway of . . . but never mind. We'll know when we know."

"I fail to understand *why* we've been singled out."

"The temples," Achibol replied. "Our repairs and reprogramming are undesirable to someone. Again, I have glimmers of suspicion, but nothing to back them. But tomorrow is upon us, and we must be far off the usual trails before daylight. We'll discuss means of accomplishing our tasks in spite of this setback as we progress. Perhaps a side-trip, an unpredicted change in our routine, is in order. There too, I have ideas . . ."

INTERLUDE
The Great School, Midicor IV

"You never told me if my program modifications helped—getting the biocybes to define their 'primary sources,' I mean." Abrovid fondled the furry quadrupedal creature that rode with him everywhere upon his back or tucked beneath a loose-held chitin-plate. He called it his 'biocybernetic interface.' Kaledrin was not sure if he was joking.

"Of course I have . . . haven't I? You've seen my chapter introductions, where I use the data, and the reference lists we send out to the data-net subscribers." Kaledrin had submerged himself in the biocybes' "translations." Perhaps he had been remiss. "Your help has been invaluable. Without clear source references, scholars would laugh at us. Even Saphooth appreciates what you've done."

"I should hope so," Abrovid said, mollified. "Especially considering the way he acted at first, as if the odd things the 'cybes were turning out were *my* fault." He grinned. "He's certainly changed his tune, hasn't he?"

"That he has," Kaledrin agreed. "You'd almost think he believes this tale we're creating."

"Creating? Is that what you think, Kal? Don't you believe in your own work any more?"

"I don't know what I think. I suppose I 'believe' the biocybes have either sorted out a tale representing one planet's prehistory, or have synthesized one that applies generally to all the human lines. Old Saphooth's fallen in love with this 'human' Achibol, who's just like him—two-legged, and stuck that way. He and I have been at odds for so long I automatically swing to the opposite point of view. I've even come to like that little shell-parasite Benadek, in spite of his attitude problem." Kaledrin raised the latest data-cube from the biocybes in his hand. It glittered in the waning sunlight. "Especially after what happens to him here."

"Really? I haven't seen it yet. May I?"

CHAPTER SIX,

in which Benadek's nightmare yields a strange truth that sets him apart from all others.

This episode is found in the mythologies of the Pharsees of the Esbaahn Cluster and the Brassad subcultures of the Sarsan Reach. Both include it within larger, dissimilar bodies of myth.

Lacking intermediary occurrences in space and time, the two versions have been cited by one-world proponents as evidence for prehistoric migrations from a common origin-world, but there is still doubt about the tale's provenance. The Brassad myths are older by a thousand years, and the episode's "fit"—the number and sequence of commonly repeated elements between it and the larger body of works—is superior to that of the Pharsee mythology, wherein it may represent a late inclusion.

The Pharsees treat their version as a moral fable—only the pure in heart can peer into the world of dreams and spirits, but they risk the sickness of understanding too much. Considering the Pharsee's reclusive nature, and their refusal to join in galactic politics, it is hardly irresponsible to discount their interpretations of the story.

Obviously, Benadek is "special," as the story implies. We, millennia in his future, assume it if only because his myths have endured. But so have other archetypal figures. Is there some deeper meaning in this new, internally consistent story? Where do "pure-humans" and "simples" fit in our cultural histories, our moral fables? The relevant question is not why Benadek is special to us, but why he was special to Achibol and Sylfie.

Chapter Six reveals one secret, but this editor suspects it reflects only the primitive belief of incipient humans in their own uniqueness and, for us, represents a yearning for simpler days when one world was the center of our universe, and sun and stars revolved around it.

(Kaledrin, Senior Editor)

The temple wall loomed. There was Achibol, silent in the honch's grasp, perhaps dead. Sylfie slumped against the wall. There was blood on her face, and her head was cocked unnaturally sideways.

The small, round eye of a laser pistol stared at Benadek, unblinking, unmoved by the screams all around, screams that made his eardrums flutter like diving june bugs. Screams of mothers, women; man-screams, father-bellows—rage and pain, agony and despair, underlain by hoarse honch-laughter. Then the sounds attenuated to moans and dying mutters and, somewhere near, woman-voices crying.

"Boy! Awaken!" It was Achibol.

"Benadek—it's a dream. Please wake up," Sylfie pleaded. "You're safe now."

Benadek forced his eyelids apart. Dawn-sounds filled his ears. Achibol's face filled his field of vision. "That was quite a dream, boy. Are you awake now?"

"Master. I dreamed . . . but it's gone now." Only the byproducts of the nightmare remained: cooling sweat on his clothing, the aftermath of adrenaline making his gut knot and his hands tremble.

"Do you remember anything?"

"I'm sorry, Master. It's gone. It always is." Sylfie was holding his hand to still his trembling. Their mutual grip was hot, sweat-slick.

The sorcerer ignored her, and pressed on. "Such violent dreams. So powerful, yet so soon gone. No trace remains?"

"None, Master."

"This is not new, is it? Not the first such terrifying, unrememberable dream?" There was no doubt in his voice.

"No. Not the first time. I never remember them."

"When did they start? Do you remember that?"

"I've had them as long as I can remember. Years? Yes, years."

Slowly, Achibol wormed answers from him. Benadek remembered nothing of how he came to be in Vilbursiton, how he became an urchin among other urchins. His life began in those dirty streets, five years or so before.

"Do you want to know?"

"Will I remember the dreams then, even waking?"

"Can you face them, otherwise? They're child-dreams, and you're mostly a man. You've hidden some monstrous agony your child-mind couldn't face. But the dreams will keep coming until you do. No good comes of pain held so close. The question is, are you now strong enough to withstand that which drove your entire childhood into hiding in the back alleys of your mind? Will you?"

Benadek did not answer immediately. The dreams plagued him, and he had no past. He remembered only . . . his father. His father, the connecting link between the after and the unremembered before. Sylfie squeezed his hand. Achibol peered closely. "I'll try," the boy said.

Achibol got to his feet. Benadek heard, rather than saw, as he rummaged within his trunk. He returned with a tiny glass cup of clear fluid. "Drink this," he commanded. Seeing Benadek's hesitation, he explained. "A potion to help you relax. The real work of recalling your life, the 'magic,' if you will, will be your own. I'll assist, and guide you. Now lean back and be comfortable."

Handing Benadek the cup, he flourished a blue-glass bauble on a frayed string, and swung it in front of the boy's face. "Watch this. Relax. Feel your body becoming loose, heavy . . ." Benadek was familiar with the routine. He'd watched his master mesmerize rubes, curing hives, impotence, and unnatural cravings.

For a moment he dozed, but soon became freshly aware of Achibol's voice. "The man with you. Who is he? Who is the man?"

"My father." The words were not Benadek's, but someone else's, a younger someone using his mouth, his lungs and breath. Once the voice began speaking, it did not stop. Achibol injected short questions periodically, but the voice needed little prompting.

Short, crooked rows of summer corn march across Benadek's mind—small, weak plants, but tall to a little boy. There are lamp-lit memories, too: his mother's face, animated, reading and storytelling. Somewhere, a more mature Benadek fights not to leave those safe, halcyon times, before the mountains and the cold.

"It is late fall," the unwelcome voice prompts him. "The corn is in. Where is your father?"

Fire! The little corncrib, their pitiful harvest, is burning. Flames lash its hand-split slats, weaving in and out, consuming. A horrid face looms up, grinning, with big, flat teeth. "Honches!" someone yells. Honch-hands pick him up. His screams and his mother's commingle. She claws the honch, who throws Benno away.

He is being carried, and the horizon goes up and down with his bobbing head. He sees tracks in the snow.

"In the snow? When is this? Where are you going?"

"The mountains. They're big and gray and cold, but the honches won't follow us there."

"Who is 'us,' Benno? Who is with you?"

"Mama."

Who else? Where is Papa?"

"Hunting."

The mountains grew taller every day, Benadek remembered. He was always hungry, always cold. Then there was a tiny house of stones, with a pine-branch roof and a raggedy blanket door. Sometimes, at first, it was warm inside, when the snow blew deep around it. Later, it was always cold.

Game is scarce. We're too high up, Papa says. The rocks and scrub shelter only goats and eagles. Papa has to go down into the trees to hunt. Mama is sick from cold. Wood is scarce—twigs scarcely worth the effort to dig from the snow. Mama reads to me. I show her letters and words I know. Outside, the wind howls.

Now our food is gone. Mama gives me leather to chew, but I mustn't swallow it. Mama is very quiet. I crawl under the fur with her to get warm, but

Mama is cold too. She puts her arms around me. "Good-bye," she says, not "good night."

Mama is holding me. I have to get up or I'll wet us, but she won't let go. Wake up, Mama. I can't wake her. I wet myself, and for a few minutes I am warm.

Papa is here. He picks me up. Mama is sleeping yet. Papa is quiet, so he won't wake her. He is crying. "We have to go, son," Papa says. "I'll take you to a town, where you'll be warm." He wraps me in the blanket. Mama will be cold, with nothing over her. Papa says she isn't cold anymore. "Now we must go. You must have warmth, and food. You are very sick."

"Bring Mama! Mama's hungry too."

"Mama's gone, Benno. Now it's just the two of us."

"No! Mama's in there. Wake her up."

"Mama wants me to take you where there's food and a warm place." Papa was still crying.

"I'll say good-bye to her," I told him. He let me go. Mama wouldn't talk to me. I think I fell asleep again. Papa carried me away.

"The temple. Tell me about the temple."

"I don't like the temple. The temple is bad."

"Why is it bad?"

Father at the temple gate, and he peering from behind a rain barrel? No, that was later. Before that, there was a house with many rooms to get lost in. Other faces stared from doorways, frowning at crying little boys.

"Did you just arrive there?"

No. Been there a long time. Papa says, "Not much longer, son. Come spring, you'll be on your own."

"Did he go away?"

Papa coughs blood. His skin is papery and gray, and his bones stick out. "I'm going to the temple," Papa says. "These simple folk go there to be healed. The honches there don't know me. I'm dying, like your mother. Maybe the temple can fix me up. I have to risk it, boy."

"Then the temple? You went with him?"

The big wood door. Waiting outside for Papa. The sun goes two hands across the sky. Then Papa comes out. He's crying real loud. The temple hurt him. Papa kicks and bump-bumps his head all bloody. I say, "Papa stop it," and his eyes go funny and he gets all gray. The honches laugh.

"Enough!" another voice said angrily. "No more!"

"Mama?"

"No. Sylfie."

Sylfie? In bits and pieces, Benadek's memory returned. He opened his eyes. Sylfie's face filled his field of vision, upside down. A distance away, Achibol's eyes were like black coals, angry. But not at him.

Achibol rummaged in his trunk. "Drink this, boy," Achibol commanded, proffering him a tiny glass with a trumpet-flared rim. "It will make you sleep—real sleep."

Later, when he awakened, Achibol asked him if he remembered it all, now. Benadek nodded. His face was pale and drawn, and he looked older. There was another thing there, too: rage. Silent, deadly rage.

"I remember."

"Do you know what it means?"

"I think so."

"Tell me," Achibol pressed.

"I'm a pure-human. I'm not a boffin."

"What else?"

"I was right to stay away from the temples. They would have killed me, too."

"In all likelihood they would have, had you gone there. Anything else?"

Benadek shook his head. "Nothing."

Hearing the edge in Benadek's voice, the old man desisted. "Never mind, then. There's time enough later. Can you walk? No? Then I'll help you onto the mule."

When they'd been moving for several hours, Benadek felt recovered from his ordeal. It was all in his head anyway. Why should he feel so weak? He must never be weak again. There was too much to be done.

"Master? What does it mean to be a pure-human?" he asked as he walked beside Achibol again.

"For me? Or for you?"

"Is there a difference? Aren't I like you?"

"You have the same number of chromosomes, and a full complement of genes instead of simples' multiple redundancies—but we're of different stock to begin with, and there will be other . . . differences . . . too. Successful mutations that didn't kill your ancestors, or you."

"What differences?"

"I can't know unless they reveal themselves. But I will be watching closely for clues—there may still be danger to you. Have you remembered any more about your father? How he differed from simples? That might help."

Benadek shrugged. "He was smarter, I think."

"Your mother?"

"She was funny. I used to laugh at her story-faces . . .

"What were those?"

"Bears and squirrels, things like that. She made faces when she told stories. When she was being a frog, she made her face like one."

"Truly? Could she turn green, too?" Benadek's flush warned Achibol he was treading on dangerous ground. "I'm not mocking you, boy. I need to know exactly what your parents were, for your sake. Did she turn green? Did she grow squirrel hair on her face?"

"Of course not! They were just faces. She was still

Mama. You're sure you're not teasing me? Can pure-humans do such things?" What, he asked himself, can pure-humans do? What tricks and talents might I have that will prove useful to me?

"There are many stories, and few facts. They—and you—are special, though. We must discover in what ways."

That was good enough for Benadek, for the time. To be special and to be wanted. He would ignore the rest for now, and let his present and past selves merge. He knew what he had to do. How he would accomplish it could wait. His parents' deaths were now fresh as yesterday, the price of his long respite from grief. At least he had Achibol to talk with, and Sylfie to comfort him. Sylfie. She smells like Mama. They'd make camp soon, he hoped. Achibol would sleep by the fire. He looked back at Sylfie. He was really looking forward to darkness, for the first time in days.

BOOK TWO:

Myths from the Central Suns

INTERLUDE
The Great School, Midicor IV

"What do you think of Chapter Seven?" Saphooth asked, eying Kaledrin from orbs shaded to obscurity beneath bushy white eyebrows. How conscious I've become, Kaledrin reflected, of the nuances of simian-form expressions. They're so much more complex—and at the same time more transparent—than my own hard-shelled reserve. It's Benadek's fault, I suppose, and Achibol's. I read of "smiles" and "frowns," and I seek analogues in Saphooth's face. "I think," he said aloud, "that the tale will bring us both to grief."

"How so?" Saphooth queried.

"The tale, as the Biocybes tell it, is too 'real.' People cease to think of it as a construct of programming, myth, and artificial minds, and take it seriously. I've read letters from simulnet subscribers who want to know where 'Earth' is, and whether all humans descend from simians. Some letters are from scientists who should know better than to ignore the evidence against a single origin-world."

Saphooth nodded. "I've answered several such letters myself," he said. "You must admit, the tale seems to lead in that direction." He raised shoulders and eyebrows simultaneously—a *shrug*, Kaledrin translated. "And though the one-world theory has been ignored in recent years, the biocybes' acceptance lends it credence. After all, they've taken all the evidence into account."

"'Ignored?'" Kaledrin blurted. "'Theory?' The one-world myth has been thoroughly debunked. Only primitives and cultists cling to it in the face of clear paleontological evidence to the contrary. The prospect of this project supporting such nonsense terrifies me." Saphooth's blase attitude terrified him even more. "Is it possible you're more than just a *physical* anachronism, Saphooth? Can a man in your position still believe a planet is flat, or that the universe revolves around it?"

---

* The name Sufawlsidak, for example, often shortened to Sufawlz, is common throughout the Inner Galaxy where it is a common noun for *school* or *hospital*.

CHAPTER SEVEN

This short chapter has no counterpart in any orthodox mythology, and thus no classical heading. It seems to have been fabricated from petty details. * It is our editorial guess that it will function solely as a transition to succeeding chapters.

Myths of Achibol portray him as demon and tempter, mage, even god. There are two distinct traditions, and their common use of Achibol's name is explained as a late imposition of a dominant culture upon an autochthonous mythology. The source-lists for this chapter show that the biocybes have joined them in this narrative. Future chapters, we suspect, will be drawn mostly from that larger body of works available from the worlds nearer the galactic core.

(Kaledrin, Senior Editor)

Achibol was uncomfortable with his own thoughts. Benadek had changed. Not, admitted the old man, necessarily for the worst. He seemed to have lost a certain childish heat, and to have gained an air of clear-eyed rationality. The boy was no longer the puppy who had joined him in Vilbursiton. And that bothered him.

The sorcerer had sworn time and again over the course of his centuries that he would not succumb to any more puppies. Their lives were too short—or his own too long—and he was inclined to become distracted by grief at old dogs' passing. But he had done it again, he reluctantly admitted. Benadek's "crush" on him had not been as one-sided as he'd pretended, though he had tried gruffly to keep a safe distance between himself and the boy. Oh, yes. From the first he'd tried to push him away, as much for the boy's own good as for his own peace of mind, but circumstances had intervened.

Now Benadek had changed. Achibol sensed a new hardness, a determination. Gaining his past anew, had the lad also gained a future? Achibol laughed. He was worrying like a schoolgirl. Would the "new" Benadek still find meaning in his apprenticeship, or would he seek goals of his own, now that he was free of his self-inflicted amnesia? Enough! Give the lad time. He'll either see it through, and give me a few more years of his company, or he won't, and neither way will I be less the old fool.

"Master? What now?" Benadek's words were no different than they might have been before, but their delivery differed subtly. He wanted to know, so he asked without subservience.

"We'll go on, I suppose. Is there aught we should do?"

"Just that? Exactly as before?"

Achibol read unease in the boy's voice. "Well . . . not exactly. You have much to learn—things I can't teach you by myself."

"If *you* can't, who can?"

Despite Benadek's new maturity, it was obvious to

the sorcerer that the boy still considered him highly, and he was pleased. "There's a place where you can learn what you must. It's near an abandoned city called Sufawlsidak, north of here."

"A school? I've never been to a school."

"It was a hospital and a laboratory, among other things. An experimental lab. Now it's a graveyard of frozen memories." Benadek, used to his master's enigmatic utterances, altered his expression only slightly to signify his perplexity.

"There are machines that teach, and drugs distilled from the recollections of men. Partaking of such enchantments one can gain knowledge that others spent their lifetimes accumulating, without the years of effort they expended. You'd be a surgeon? A flier of aircraft? A mage? A single dose, and you'll grasp all that one of the finest minds remembered."

Benadek's eyes lit up at the prospect of even more knowledge than Achibol possessed. He tried to imagine vast other fields of learning, and failed. "Have you done it, Master?"

"Have I gained all my pinches and tidbits in that manner, you mean? Or have I given my own memories over to a frozen flask?" He chortled. "I've done neither. Nor would I want to. The process may seem simple, but it won't be easy on you. But then, there'll never be an easy way for you."

Sensing a trap, Benadek proceeded carefully. "Is there something wrong with the spells and potions—the frozen memories?"

"Not to my knowledge. One difficulty is a moral one. When the machines render a brain's contents into a jar, the donor dies. Thus for every dose of secondhand experience you take, a man's life was consumed. Half-portions have no effect, and once thawed, the potion cannot be returned to its vial. How many lives can a man justify taking, thus? The burden of one alone, it seems to me, is as much as a decent fellow could bear."

Benadek's momentary confusion rapidly evaporated. After all, he was a pragmatist. Wisdom—and the power it gave—was not to be lightly spurned, no matter the weight of it. A lifetime's journey without the toll of years ordinarily demanded was treasure indeed. Achibol's reservations were cause for care, but on balance would weigh lightly enough on his apprentice's slender shoulders.

"Is there another consideration, Master?"

"Yes. It is this: to know a thing is not the same as having it in your bones. I know tricks, but I am no Houdini, no Blackstone or Merlin. I am still Achibol, a charlatan and no more."

"Then what good is it, Master? If such knowledge can't be used, why take it?"

"You don't attend my words precisely, boy. What do you have in your very soul? What deep talent and craving consumes you? If what you take fits what you are, and if you use it before it fades like the glow of last night's wine, then it's yours to keep—and your incessant questions lead me to suspect you will retain enough to warrant sacrificing a minor historian, at the very least."

Achibol doesn't know everything, the boy reflected. A historian? There's more worth knowing than dead rulers and ancient countries. How can he even guess how much I want to know, or how much my bones will hold? And these memories are already dead, so what guilt will I bear for bringing them to life once more?

Benadek's mood was broken by Sylfie's arrival with their breakfasts. In spite of their passion the night before, by daylight she seemed distant, treating him with the same reserve she did Achibol, but without the daughterly fondness she showed his master.

"What's wrong?" he asked when they were packed.

"Nothing. I'm just not used to your being so different."

"I haven't changed. It's just that I remember everything now. You should be happy for me."

"I'm glad you remember. It's just . . . just that . . ."

"Boy! Come here," Achibol called. "Kick this mule's belly for me. The beast is puffing himself up again." Sylfie looked relieved.

"You should leave well enough alone, boy," the sorcerer said. "Some things don't bear talking about."

"She should be happy for me."

"What of *her* gratification?" Realizing that Benadek had no idea of what he meant, he continued cheerlessly. "You're a pure-human. She is a poot. Not only is the disparity between you greater even than she feared, but her own prime function cannot be fulfilled—with you. Be grateful for every moment she remains with us, for she cannot linger indefinitely."

"What do you mean?" True, Sylfie's life with him was nothing to celebrate—bedding at the side of the road, walking or riding all day long, but didn't she love him too?

"Babies, boy," Achibol exclaimed. "You can give her none."

Babies! The thought had never crossed Benadek's mind. What did he want with babies? The connection between infants—tiny, noisy, smelly—and his customary nightly pleasures was indistinct. He knew, of course, but it did not bear thinking about. An uneasy feeling crept upon him. "Is something wrong with me?"

"Is something wrong with a horse that mates with a deer?" The old man snorted disdainfully. "What about a bird and a fish?"

"We're not horses or . . . Oh! I'm a pure-human, and she isn't. But can't the temples do something about her? There are poots who have babes without men."

"The temples sometimes implant embryos in empty wombs," Achibol agreed, "but that depends upon the population balances they record as local simples pass through them, not upon a poot's desire. Should a healthy female appear at the same temple many times without being pregnant, an irreplaceable fertilized egg might be provided for her—but Sylfie only visits temples once. While she remains with us, she'll remain indefinitely unfulfilled."

"Must she have babies?"

"Must you ingest food, quaff wine, and excrete? Denied all that, what would you be? Dead. Were you content with your sex life before I intervened? Would you be so again? Some things are beyond rational control."

"What must I do, Master?" Benadek quietly asked. "How can I make her happy again?"

"You can let her go. You can let her know that you understand, and that you care enough to release her."

"But I want her! I don't want her to go."

"You want. You don't want. Are your petty desires what we've been examining? I remember otherwise."

"I'm sorry, Master. But I love her. I do want her to be happy."

"I know, boy," Achibol sighed. "And I know how hard it will be on you, when the time comes. But you will mend, as will she. She, with a babe in her arms, you in some other manner." His old, dark eyes bored intensely into Benadek's. "I know what it's like to lose someone. I also remember what it's like to survive it." Benadek believed him.

"On another subject," the old man said, "I've been thinking of a pure-human camp not far off our route to Sufawlsidak. I may have inadvertently steered that troop of honches there, before you and I met in Vilbursiton."

"What would honches do?" Benadek asked.

"In the past, they've raided camps and killed the

inhabitants. I'm sorry—is it too soon to remind you . . ."

"No. My memories are fresh, but old too. I can live with them."

Achibol nodded approvingly. "On other occasions, less killing was done, and captives were taken—to the temples, I presume, which would be no less fatal to pure-humans in the long run."

"Why can't they just let the . . . let us pure-humans . . . alone?"

"Honches were bred, or created, to be the controlling arm of their creators, and to maintain civil order among the simples. Those you've seen in the towns have been of the lesser breed. Most honches experience restlessness and dissatisfaction in adolescence, and wander far from their birthplaces. Some merely settle in different towns, but others find their way into free-roving military units, remnants of their creators' armed forces. Those who hunt pure-humans, and who pursue me, are the latter sort.

"As to why they hunt—their ancestors were programmed to do so, and the programming is reinforced by their standing orders—a relict of the planners' last attempts to salvage their failing plan. When they discovered that not all pure-humans were dying they feared that surviving full-spectrum humans would wreck their program."

"But that was the plan's goal, wasn't it? Pure-human survivors? Why didn't the planners help instead?"

"Their goal was not the survival of 'twisted mutants,' boy, but the eventual restoration of their own kind of humanity." His eyes narrowed to shiny black beads almost hidden in crumpled brown leather. "I don't believe there are 'simples' with brown hides like mine—nor are the genes of my kind stored in the computer records with those of the paler races. The brown and yellow peoples of the earth—the stock to which most of humanity belonged—were, in the terminal moments of the ancient's reign, deemed unfit to inhabit either the interim world of the simples or that which would follow."

Seldom had Benadek heard his master speak in such sepulchral tones. He had not considered Achibol's brown skin, his odd, puffy white hair and goatee, to be other than sorcerer's affectations, artifice to distinguish him from common folk. The apprentice had even speculated that his master's odd coloring was a result of his long life, that anyone who attained such an age might turn brown and wrinkled like overripe fruit. That Achibol had seen his own folk die, and had lived on, added a new dimension to Benadek's understanding. He had known suffering to surpass Benadek's own.

There was nothing the boy could say, just as he himself would not be comforted by words. Only time could mute such pain—yet Achibol's intensity demonstrated that pain could endure a thousand years.

The mage shrugged off his black mood. "Here is an aspect of plans and programs you might keep in mind, should you ever set any in motion: once begun by individuals, committees, or governments, they acquire lives of their own. The goals of such programs are forgotten, and their means become ends in themselves."

Benadek hardly absorbed his master's cautions, for bitterness had risen in his own throat. It had all been for nothing. The ancients should have dropped their plan once they saw that race survival was assured. Had there been no great plan, perhaps he, or whoever his genes might have represented, might have found a pure-human Sylfie who could go where he went, and Achibol might be grandsire to dozens of small, brown children. There would be no honches, no poots constrained to be lovers, mothers, and housekeepers. What was so special about the ancients?

How could they have raised themselves above the likes of Achibol, or even himself?

With his bitter thoughts came a fresh, new resolve, born of his recent revelation: a goal that surpassed Achibol's puny determination to repair the temples so that in another thousand years or so a sterilized and sanitized humanity might join the pitiful bands of "pure-humans." But he would not discuss that—not yet.

He pulled himself up to his full height—he was almost able, he noted with surprise, to look his master in the eye. "I'm ready to go to Sufawlsidak, and ready to take on the burden of as many frozen lives as I may need, Master. Whether I myself live a thousand years or only a few score, I must do what I can to set things right. My own children, should there ever be any, must not be required to forget their parents or survive their childhoods alone.

"You must teach me all you can even as we go, so I can be ready for this 'school.' I'll be your apprentice yet a while, but what I want to be taught goes beyond your craft, beyond repairing temples and charlatanry. There will come a time when I will be . . . when we will be . . ."

"Partners?" Achibol said, smiling broadly, supplying the very word Benadek did not quite dare utter.

"Yes. Partners. It will come to that."

"I'm sure it will. And none too soon, I foresee."

INTERLUDE
The Great School, Midicor IV

Abrovid squeaked his manipulator-tendrils against the smooth chitin of his mouth-parts, an irritating sound Kaledrin interpreted as amusement. "So the old biped is falling for my pets' stories, eh?" He chuckled. "And do you think that should displease me? Why?"

Kaledrin was exasperated. "Because he's not accepting them on their merit, but for his own twisted reasons. He's crazy, and when people—influential scholars—find out, they'll toss out everything we've begun to accomplish, along with him."

"What's wrong with him?"

"Can't you see? It's his ailment. How it must rankle him, to be fixed in that ridiculous two-legged form, never to sample all the other worlds—the ones that are too hot or too cold, where the air is too thin or too rich. And how smug he acts now, convinced that his bony form is identical to Achibol's, to Benadek's. He's convinced that his is the one, true ancestral image not just of one world's sentients, but of us all. He'll make a fool of himself, and we won't be able to disassociate ourselves."

Kaledrin crossed his eyestalks in negation, picturing his Great School tenure receding further into the mists of improbability, hearing with his mind's ears the rage of a million mutable humans on as many worlds crying for his removal. . . .

CHAPTER EIGHT,

wherein amid death and destruction a new companion is created from barren earth.

Of the ambiguous, ever-changing Teress of myth, only Benadek's suspicions remain. Teress, their new companion, metamorphoses from an autochthonous demon to genuine humanity, masked first by subterranean darkness and then by a homespun veil.

From dirt rose ta-Rossa,
Dust in her eye,
Dust in her mouth;
Keth-Harum, first star of evening,
Beckoned her hence;
Enas-of-Sky's-delight
Brushed soil from her face;
Bhena-d'kha'a of the Circle of Light

Brought her forth with his hand.
From dirt rose ta-Rossa
To light.*

Skirting the issue of human emergence from separate planetary wombs which Teress's legend is usually associated with, the biocybes give no satisfaction to rational scientists or to popularizers of the one-world "theory" (which of course is only a myth unacceptable to thinking minds.) Herein, Benadek's celestial mating with Teress, considered to symbolize formal acceptance into the Community of Worlds, is replaced with an adolescent spat.

A note of caution: conclusions are premature. The biocybes' programming demands only consistency. Though the narrative thus far unfolded is more consistent than the scattered myths from which it derives, truth must be determined by different criteria.

Teress's reaction to Benadek's overtures is puzzling, nonetheless, as is her clear distinction between herself and Sylfie. Contrasted with the warm and lovely poot, Teress is prickly at best, and even Benadek's attraction to her seems autoerotic, while his liaison with Sylfie does not. Too, Sylfie seems human enough, within her particular constraints. On what grounds does Teress consider herself superior?

(Kaledrin, Senior Editor.)

---

* Te'hen birthsong from *Religious Poems and Songs of the Arafan Cluster*, by Kerbol Ruck, unpublished ms., Midicor V Universal Library.

INTERLUDE
The Great School, Midicor IV

"Aren't you the one skirting the issue?" Abrovid asked Kaledrin, his eyestalks and polyps twisting quizzically.

"What do you mean? I thought I was pretty clear about the 'one-world' thing. I'll probably be blacklisted by the fundamentalists for what I wrote," Kaledrin said with a trace of a whine, "and I'm not even a paleontologist or a historian."

"You're not a believer, either," Abrovid responded dryly, "so what do you care?"

"I don't! Damn it all, Ab, this is a *literary* experiment. I'm a mythographer, not a public relations hack. My commentary on the biocybes' text isn't the place for all this stuff. That's why the journals have letter columns. Besides, it's Saphooth's job to deal with the public."

"And he's hardly going to deal with them as you wish, is he? As for journal letters, maybe I can help you come up with something. Where do we start?"

"How about explaining why your damn pets aren't following instructions?"

"You mean, taking into account relevant data, like fossils? Are you sure they aren't?"

"Some help you're going to be."

"Now wait a minute. Lets take a long look at what they're telling us. . . ."

AN OPEN LETTER TO THE *MYTHIC* PROJECT'S SIMULCAST SUBSCRIBERS

Popularizers and theologians have raised the possibility that MYTHIC's biocybernetic compilation of the Achibol myths represents actual historic documentation of a single planet of origin for all humanity. Planetologists, archaeologists, and paleontologists have reacted angrily to these unwarranted conclusions.

With utmost dismay, I find myself in the middle of a controversy that should not even exist. MYTHIC does not purport to be historic or archaeological research. It is no more—and no less—than an experiment in the interpretation of myths, legends and outright fairy tales. And it is unfinished. The novel idea of publishing each chapter directly and selling subscriptions did not come from the project's research staff but from our public relations and financial advisors. While an effective fund-raising device, I am deeply concerned with its effect upon our research. I do not expect all MYTHIC's subscribers to be scientists, but I do hope that all will cultivate scientific reserve, and avoid speculation until the biocybes' complete document is in hand.

Much has been made of the biocybes' apparent disregard for the third of their four directives—to contradict no firmly established evidence. Abrovid Legum, Assistant Programmer at the Biocybernetic Institute, the man most familiar with the biocybes' thought processes, is querying them about the anomaly. We hope that their response will clarify the situation.

I contend that they have not gone against their programming. Because Benadek, Achibol, and Teress are archetypic ancestors in our traditional myths, some of us have assumed that they are so in MYTHIC's production as well. *But at no time have the biocybes specifically stated that the fixed-form bipeds in their narrative are ancestral humans*. To the contrary, honches, poots, boffins, and cozies are "simplified" and not regarded as fully human even by their contemporaries. Possibly, even probably, these "pure-humans" may turn out to be ancestral to one particular line of simianoid humans. Less probably, the biocybes will reveal the entire tale to be a construct without any real historic connections. It is, after all, derived from sources which few of us would accept, in their original forms, as factual. We at MYTHIC limit our speculations to literary ones, and sincerely hope that our subscribers will do the same.

Kaledrin, MYTHIC Project Senior Editor
Department of Galactic Literature,
The Great School, Midicor IV

The croaking water creatures of the forested swamp sounded loud amid the stony crags of ancient buildings. No matter how hard Benadek looked, he had never caught a glimpse of the animals making the sounds, nor had he seen much other life—only stinging flies, and land-leeches that had to be salted from their legs; the dwellers in mossy ground, trees, and green, weed-covered ponds were as elusive as the pure-humans who called the morass home.

For days now he had followed his master's unsure steps among ancient ruins that thrust up from the soggy peat, hunting the pure-human camp. They lived, Achibol said, in "caves," gutted interiors of long-abandoned towers of steel and artificial stone. Miles of ancient streets spread about them, straight paths between pockmarked cliffs higher than the oldest trees, paths now clogged and overgrown, or flooded and impassible. The pure-humans could be a hundred yards away and they'd never be found unless they wanted to be. Why was Achibol so worried that honches would have found the village, if he himself could not, even knowing that it was here?

Young noses were better than old, and the faint, acrid stink that pervaded the lowland mist was the best clue they had to follow. The fire-scent meant either that the pure-humans were near, or that there had been a fire of unusual size. Benadek observed the waxing and waning of the odor as they moved about, and carefully noted the direction of breezes that swept down the ancient streets.

The burning had occurred north and west of them, and there were no diagonal avenues directly to his goal, but before the sun moved two fingers' breadth, the odor was overpowering, and there was no doubt that a disaster of some magnitude had occurred. The old man advanced hesitantly, postponing the moment he dreaded.

"It's not your fault, Master," the boy said as he grasped the sorcerer's skinny arm. "The honches have burned other villages, too. You couldn't have prevented it."

"Perhaps you're right," Achibol said.

"Should we leave the mules with Sylfie?" Benadek asked. "Their harnesses rattle and their hoofs suck and slop in this watery soil."

"If the camp's inhabitants are dead, it won't matter if we're noisy. If not, they'll welcome us. Many in this camp knew me, once."

A sound! Not the croak of tree-fish or the rattle of stiff leaves against scaly hide, but a jingle. Metal-sound. And the rhythmic suck-and-pop of large feet. The listener's pale eyes darted from the still-empty trail below to the cave-mouth surmounting the rubble slope. A tactical dilemma. He must hide until the intruders were in full sight, then decide whether to attack or remain in hiding. Or, he could enter the dark cave and confront his quarry, the most recent pure-human survivor to return and fall into his hands.

The thinker did not shape such thoughts vocally,

as might Achibol or his apprentice; rather, the mental pictures of alternative actions presented themselves simultaneously, as if he viewed a separate image with each mental "eye."

Left: the sound of metal-shod hoofs striking rubble evoked an image of a mule climbing the rise toward his position. Vaguely human shapes accompanying the beast were smoke-wraiths, faint positional images with little informational content or detail. The watcher did not speculate; the densities of the images signified probability, determined by that organic computer that was his analogue of imagination.

Right: a gray silhouette made a dash from the black cave-mouth and slipped away into the wet woods. The image shifted again: a pure-human lurked just inside the cave, a jagged rock in hand, waiting for him. He saw himself darting quickly into the cave, throwing himself forward and rolling before coming erect and knocking the frail mutant over, its stone falling harmlessly.

Left: mules approached. Smoke-wraith figures with clearly defined ears heard the sounds of his motion and paused cautiously. Faint images of unspecified weapons formed in their misty hands.

The images faded. A decision had been made. The flesh-and-blood honch made his dash into the open cave-mouth.

"I heard something," Benadek whispered, raising his hand. The mules, edgy from the stink of dead fires and the thick odor of rotted flesh, skittered as he halted suddenly.

They all heard it then: a muted, muffled shriek, the growls of a forest predator, the clash of metal on stone. Benadek pointed. "It came from that cave." A deep moan confirmed his statement, overlaid with echoes as if the cave were large and open inside.

Achibol's hand on his arm restrained him. "Let us see who emerges before we show ourselves."

"Master, if someone is dying in there . . . Let's make a light."

"Wait. If something dies, something may have killed it. Didn't you hear the beast-sounds?" Benadek had heard the growling and snarling, and subsequently the shrieks. He squatted next to Achibol, and watched, and waited.

The sun continued its slow course above them: one finger, two, three. Then the clack of rubble alerted them. With a scrape and the jingle of metal on stone, a pale hand groped outside the cave, a hand extending from a black leather sleeve.

"Honch!" Achibol breathed. An arm appeared, bare white flesh dark with blood, shredded as if by great claws. A blond head followed, matted with leaves and blood, asymmetrical where an ear had been torn away, dark where an eye socket gaped empty.

"Why doesn't it die?" Benadek whispered.

"That would be poor design in a soldier. Let's see how far it gets."

Such callousness surprised Benadek. He would have succored the honch, or put it out of its misery.

"Let's go," Achibol said getting to his feet. "I have some questions to ask before it dies." Still astounded by his master's unseemly objectiveness, Benadek followed. The honch lay on its side, breathing in shallow pants, stopped by a coil of its own spilled intestine snagged on a stone. The dirt-encrusted organ was stretched tight and thin. The stink of peritoneal gasses was unbearable. Benadek bent to one side and let the contents of his gut fly, spattering his boot toes.

"Report!" Achibol snapped. Honch breeding demonstrated itself: to Benadek's renewed horror, the honch attempted to rise. "As you were!" Achibol snapped. "Report!"

"Sir!" it replied in a surprisingly clear voice.

"Observed mutant camp as ordered. Killed three who returned. A fourth went in the cave."

"What unit? What orders?"

"Garvig's platoon, sir. Standing orders from Jorssh: all platoons to leave guards on mutant nests destroyed. Captives to be tortured for knowledge of Ahh . . . Aachu . . . to be . . ." The honch's breath became a wet burble. It raised its head and slammed it down on the rough rock. Heels drummed on the ground and stones rattled beneath them.

"Achibol," said the sorcerer. "It was trying to say my name. And Jorssh . . . that was hundreds of years ago. Could he still live? *That's* not programmed into the genes of his kind. Did the planners have tricks my own people didn't discover?"

"Master? What does this mean?"

"I'm sorry, boy. I merely thought out loud. Jorssh was . . . or apparently still is, a pattum, an un-simple 'simple' of a special kind."

With lightly veiled sarcasm he never would have dreamed of using before his new accommodation with his master, Benadek said, "Good. A pattum is a jorssh, a jorssh is a pattum, both thus are simples, but neither is simple. I understand fully."

Achibol granted him a thin, penitent grin. "Pattums are honches, of a sort—special-purpose military tools. Technically 'simples,' they are in actuality complex, and more dangerous than ordinary honches."

"I have a hard time imagining anything more dangerous."

"Honches are guards, policemen, or soldiers. They're punctiliously obedient, and capable of concerted action in small groups, but no honch can control more than a squad of his fellows, a safety factor in the designers' plan. Honches can protect and regulate, but cannot make war.

"Honches couldn't be mobilized in organizations large enough to exterminate pure-humans completely.

With powerful pheromones, pattums can command a hundred or a thousand.

"Jorssh is a pattum I encountered several hundred years ago. I nullified his campaign against pure-humans, and thought him long since dead. If this Jorssh is one and the same, he may have found immortality of a kind, though not like my own. But whatever he is, not only our mission is at stake, but our very survival. We must hurry ahead, and hope our destination provides us with the solutions we require."

Benadek gestured with his thumb. "The honch said a pure-human went in there. The beast we heard must have killed him too."

"We don't know the pure-human is dead, or if the beast has another exit."

The sun was only a hand above the taller ruins. "I'll help Sylfie set up camp—not too near any of these cave-holes."

The young people found a dry stretch of ancient paving, and erected the tent. Benadek made fire while Sylfie prepared food. He gathered wood for the night, never venturing out of sight of Achibol on the rubble talus, or Sylfie in front of the tent. He did not like the black cave-eyes peering down, hiding unknown death.

Sylfie took a pot of root-and-squirrel stew to Achibol, and a tall mug of tea. As soon as she'd set down her burden, the mage motioned her away.

"How can he stand it up there?" she asked Benadek. "There are bugs all over that honch's eyes."

"He thinks there's a pure-human in the cave. But wouldn't he have come out by now? Even now some beast could be sneaking . . ."

"Don't say that!" Sylfie exclaimed. "I hope there is a pure-human there."

"Then what clawed up the honch?"

She had no answer. They sat by the fire. Every swamp-sound seemed magnified in the still dusk. The croakers fell silent as they did every evening, and the night-creatures had not yet begun wailing and grunting. Benadek's eyes widened at every crackle of small feet, at the fluttering rush of each falling leaf, the rattle and splash of every nut falling into the green water.

When the cave-mouth's blackness became for a moment less dark, a reddish glow, neither noticed; but on the next sweep of Benadek's patrolling eyes, he saw a dark figure standing by Achibol. A human, not a beast, wearing a full-length cape with a hood that kept its face in shadow. The shadowy figures bent over the corpse, dragged it to the cave-mouth, and rolled it within. Together they came down the slight slope toward the fire. What had happened to the beast? Perhaps the pure-human would explain.

The pure-human answered no questions. "This is Teress," Achibol told them. "She'll accompany us to Sufawlz. Consider her in mourning, and ask her no questions." Benadek peered into the shadows that hid the pure-human's face. His imagination supplied him what his eyes could not: great yellow cat-eyes in a face not human at all. The pure-human turned its head away, as if ashamed.

Achibol took food from their pot, and then led the shrouded figure away from the fire's light. The newcomer would not speak to him or Sylfie, Benadek noted with unease, but conversed with Achibol. No words could be made out. Benadek could not get rid of the impression that the hooded face kept turning to look at him.

When Benadek's head was nodding, Achibol returned silently to the tent, and took a packet from his trunk. He returned to their new traveling companion and shook out a fluffy blanket. The pure-human wrapped itself in the cloth. Benadek saw nothing that proved it was human, or female. He conceded only that it walked upright.

✧ ✧ ✧

In the morning, the apprentice's curiosity was still not assuaged. Each time Benadek pumped himself up to question Teress, Achibol silenced him with a stern look, a shake of his head. When camp was broken, his master walked ahead with the newcomer, leaving Benadek with Sylfie and the mules.

That night, while Benadek and Sylfie arranged their camp, Achibol and Teress still remained apart. When dinner was prepared she joined them, neither speaking nor removing her hood. Try as he might, Benadek got no more than a vague glimpse of her face. Her skin was light and her hair probably dark.

After their meal, the pure-human went down a faint game trail to a creek. She returned within an hour, saying nothing, with nothing to show for her trip.

"She went to bathe," Sylfie stated.

"Or to mate with another monster, a demon or catamount," Benadek replied.

"Don't be silly. What makes you think that?"

"If she's really human, why doesn't she take off her hood?"

"Perhaps that's how pure-humans show grief."

"I'm a pure-human, I grieve, and I don't even own a hood. The beast that rended the honch . . . was her."

"That's stupid," she said without much conviction. She pulled him closer.

The next day passed similarly, and the one after that. They emerged from the swamp into high-ground woods. The distance between trees was greater, and their feet stayed dry except when they crossed streams. The last ancient building was a day behind. Achibol walked with Benadek and Sylfie for a while, letting Teress lead them. "Wait," was all he would say. "In her own time, another day or two . . ."

Benadek was not satisfied. "Tonight, when she goes

to bathe, or whatever, I'm going to find out what she looks like," he told Sylfie.

"I don't think you should. What will you do?"

"We'll camp near water. I'll hide, and see what she does."

"And if she only bathes?"

"Then I'll know if she's human, won't I?"

"Achibol told us to wait. I won't go with you."

"I didn't ask you to, did I?"

Sylfie refused to speak with him after that. Benadek passed up the evening meal, pretending to be ill from berries eaten along the trail. He walked north of their camp, then circled back south, where a small river flowed briskly. A deep pool had formed upstream of an uprooted tree. The impoundment was glass-smooth and barely cool to the touch, an ideal bathing spot. "If she really bathes," Benadek muttered to himself as he settled himself among stream-side willows. He had a view of the entire pond. Teress would have to pass within yards of him, but would never see him. The willows in front were undisturbed, because he'd entered from the other side.

Teress approached the water at about her usual time, pausing frequently to check her back trail and the woodland shadows, as if she had anticipated Benadek's intentions. At the water's edge, she waited again, scanning the far side of the pond almost as if expecting someone—or something. Benadek waited motionless.

Finally, when he thought the cramps in his legs and the stinging bugs sampling the blood of his ankles and face would drive him mad, she threw back her hood, and draped her cape over a low limb.

Benadek stared. She was very human, very female. Her back was to him, so he still had no glimpse of her face, but her waist was slender, her hips sleek. Her hair, when she shook it out, was silky, almost as dark as his own. When she removed her light cotton shift, Benadek unashamedly admired her graceful back and trim, round buttocks, and became uncomfortably aroused.

She stepped gingerly into the water, found it to her liking, and waded deeper, splashing her arms and shoulders. She was lithe where Sylfie was soft, dark where Sylfie was light. Much as he was, he realized with a start. A pure-human. His own kind. For a moment he viewed her as if she were not only his kind but himself, a female version distorted as if reflected in rippling water. His groin ached as he imagined himself joining with her, black hair against black, her slender body against his.

She turned, then launched herself on her back. Benadek glimpsed small, conical breasts. Seeing them rise out of the water, he considered relieving himself right there, something he had not done since Sylfie had come into his life, but the contemplation of slinking back to camp afterward, self-embarrassed and smelling of half-sex, dissuaded him.

His next idea was crazier, but moment by moment seemed more reasonable. She was human and female. She was already naked, alone, and probably feeling the need of comforting. Besides, if he sat on her clothes, what could she do? Run back to camp naked?

Her back was toward him as she swam toward shore. He tossed her shift and cape on the grass, and sat on them.

When her feet dragged in the shallows, she turned, and her darting eyes took in the situation immediately. Cat-eyes, Benadek saw, golden yellow in the late evening light, much like the eyes he'd fantasized, but human-sized and humanly luminous. They were lovely eyes. Her face was prettier than he had imagined, though lit by an angry flush.

"You're sitting on my clothes," she said in a smooth voice as low as his own. "Go away! You don't belong here. Go back to your *poot*." She spat the word "poot" as if she were disgusted with Sylfie and, by extension, with him.

"You don't own the pond. I'll take off my clothes and join you."

"Don't bother removing your clothes. Just jump in over there . . ." she indicated a spot several yards to one side of her ". . . and cool off. Now get off my clothes!"

"You'll have to come get them," he said slyly, eying ripples that concealed the lower half of her body.

"Very well then, I will," she said with a determined nod. Benadek continued to grin as she strode up to him, his eyes level with glistening droplets that adorned the tight curls at the base of her belly. "Now get off my clothes," she repeated sternly.

Benadek raised his arms to grasp the firm buttocks he could no longer see. He was still grinning when she jerked her knee up into his chin, and barely changed his expression when he came to rest flat on his back. He tasted blood. A pale human whirlwind, she spun full circle, her hard, bare foot catching him first alongside his head, stunning him, then again in his ribs, knocking the wind from him. Demoralized and in pain, he made it to his hands and knees before her deadly foot landed across his buttocks and sent him sprawling again.

"Now will you go away, you disgusting child?"

Speechless, humiliated, Benadek stumbled toward camp. He heard her say "Oh, damn! Now I'm all dirty again," and heard the splash as she dove back into the water.

He did not go straight to camp, but lurked in the woods nearby nursing bitten tongue, bruised ribs, and shattered ego.

Full darkness fell. Achibol waited by the fire. Teress was a dark lump beneath her blanket.

Sylfie was not asleep. "Well?"

"She's human," Benadek replied.

"I know that. Pretty, too. She wasn't wearing her cloak when she came back. She seemed angry. What did you do?"

"Me? What do you mean?"

Sylfie shook her head, but did not press him further. She could hear the thickness of his speech, and when she helped him undress, she saw his bruises.

Benadek took her then. He grabbed her roughly, without preliminaries, without even noticing her grimace of pain or the tears that welled up in her eyes. The coupling was brutally quick, and he fell asleep immediately after. Sylfie did not sleep for a long time, if at all.

In the morning Teress, hoodless, joined them for breakfast, bright-eyed, cheery and voluble. She conversed lightly with Achibol, whom she treated like her indulgent uncle, and with Sylfie, to whom she was almost too attentive and sweet. For Benadek, she had not even a glare or a self-satisfied smirk.

Sylfie's eyes were red and puffy, and she avoided Benadek's. Only Achibol noticed him, and the apprentice would gladly have waived that attention. The mage's gaze was as cold as a snake's. He sat between the two females, first squeezing one's knee, then wrapping an arm around the other in a fatherly manner. Benadek was glad to break camp by himself.

That day was, he told himself, the worst of his life. Later, when the pain, embarrassment, and ostracism faded, he would reconsider that, but there was no question he was miserable. He led the mules, and when Sylfie dropped back to walk with him, he sent her away with a wordless shake of his head, and averted eyes.

By noon, Achibol found words for him. They were, the boy was surprised to find out, still heading north to Sufawlsidak. He had assumed that his fall from favor would have caused their route to be changed, that all question of his worthiness for the "school" had been settled, and was dully relieved to discover he still figured in Achibol's plans.

At nightfall, when he sank onto his blanket alone, Sylfie brought her bedding where he lay and refused to move away. She stroked his hair but, getting no response from him, she soon dozed, leaving him wide awake and alone.

In the days that ensued they progressed from timberland to open grass and then into scabbed, rocky hills. Teress still pointedly ignored Benadek, and Achibol walked with her on the narrow, dusty trails. Sylfie lagged behind with the boy, but in spite of their proximity he sensed an expanding void between them. The magical writing-tablet that had given her pleasure, though little gain, remained packed away even in the evenings when she had time on her hands, and she seldom stopped to admire windflowers growing in clefts in the rock, or iridescent flying lizards overhead. She was always red-eyed and haggard in the mornings.

CHAPTER NINE,

wherein Benadek is driven from the House of Healing.

Heated arguments will result from this episode, which focuses upon Benadek, Sylfie, and the temple. The origin of the temples has become a popular topic among mythographers. Do they represent the Pit of Ashemon, or the House of Healing from the Ksentos Venimentum text? Do they derive from the Death Chambers in the Rift Worlds legends?

It is an amusing conceit to reverse the literary scholars' questions, to ask instead, "Did those myths derive from such ancient installations as the temples?" Such speculations have been gaining a following, but this editor cautions the reader against taking them seriously.

(Kaledrin, Senior Editor)

"Why aren't we heading directly north?" Benadek asked. "Your old maps show the way to be clear all the way to this Sigh-oh-icks Fawlz place . . ."

"Soo!" Achibol corrected him. "That's Sioux Falls, boy. Sioux Falls, South Dakota."

"Sufalsidak?"

"Yes. Sioux Falls, Ess dot Dak dot. An abbreviation."

"The ancients had funny ideas about names. Like 'DNA' for 'deoxyribonucleic acid.' "

Achibol snorted, amused. Three days earlier, he had recommenced Benadek's lessons without discussing the boy's blunders. After all, what could he possibly say that Benadek had not punished himself with a hundred times. Sylfie was miserable, and that plagued him, as did Teress's scornful silence. The magician chose not to inform him that Sylfie's depression was less the result of his behavior than of chemical deprivation only a temple visit could cure. He suspected that once they reached a town and a temple, Sylfie would no longer continue with them.

Lacedomon is a pleasant place, he told himself, thinking of the next settlement on their route. The boy won't be happy about her departure, but there's no path to wisdom except through regret.

"Their world was complex, boy. There were discoveries every day, new things calling for names. No one stopped to establish a rational system. They would never have caught up. Ridiculous abbreviations were the least of their worries."

"I see, I think. But my earlier question concerned our route . . ."

"In the two thousand years since the mapmakers died, forests have grown where none were before; acidic bogs cover fertile farmland; the winds have shifted, bringing life to old deserts and creating new ones no less harsh. Roads have vanished more completely than cities, so I've chosen only to avoid the worst bogs, deserts, and swamps. Only one morass can't be avoided. There, I hope to trade our mules for a boat. Here, I'll mark the location on the map."

Lacedomon was a refreshing surprise. Their trail led out of eroded loess hills and bleak rocks to the shore of a lake garlanded with crisp aspen woods. Its waters were turquoise. A hundred years earlier there had been only a rushing stream fed by springs and mountain snow, but a landslide had dammed the river and created a fifty-mile impoundment. The lake's color was fine suspended sediment. It was nonetheless cool and palatable.

The lake and the town near its downstream end had the same name. The town had been only a temple and scattered huts before the lake had filled. Now it was a sparkling array of whitewashed edifices climbing the steep slopes

"The town is new enough to be clean," Achibol said, "and rich enough to remain so. It's the eastern terminus of the mineral trade, and supplies sun-dried fish to the interior. Caravans stop here, so we'll surely find a cool, comfortable suite, and good meals."

They traversed the narrow, stony beach until their way was blocked by fishing boats drawn up on shore. Numerous channels led to fine stone boathouses. A fisherman working the seams of his overturned craft with blunt iron and cotton twine gave them direction to a boat broker.

"Do honches still watch the roads?" the fisherman asked.

"We saw none," Achibol replied cautiously. "What business have they here?"

"They haven't explained," their informant said, "but it's no good for trade. Caravan-masters get no joy from detainment and delay. How'd you come here?"

"Overland," Achibol answered with a vague wave.

"That's why you missed them. They've a watch on

the waterfront and the town gates, but a hundred foreign thugs couldn't block every forest trail. You'll have your fill of them 'fore leaving, though—sure as the sun rises."

"This changes our plans," the sorcerer said when they were again alone. "I have no doubt what these 'foreign thugs' want. We must rid ourselves of these telltale mules."

<Ingrate! Callous fellow!> the lead mule muttered.

"What?" Achibol exclaimed, looking not at the mules, but all around him, genuinely puzzled. He had not thrown his voice.

<All those miles, and his boxes harder than his bony arse, giving me bruises . . . > grumbled the second.

The mage's eyes fixed on Benadek. "I taught you more than I was aware of. When did you first catch on, lad?"

"In Vilbursiton, delivering your coin to the temple, I heard priests' voices rebound from a wall. Since then I watched, and listened."

"I'm pleased. Perhaps you'll amount to something, in spite of your undesirable habits and . . ."

"I hope so, Master," Benadek interrupted, forestalling embarrassing elaborations. "But only if we get out of here. What must we do?"

The mage pondered. "Teress and I will seek out the marine agent. You purchase supplies for a week's passage of the swamp thither." He gestured toward the lake's end where, beyond brush and low trees, the waters dropped through great stone sluices into a forty-mile-wide depression laced with countless small channels, expanses of open water, and braided remnants of earlier channels now overgrown with trees, surfaced with duckweed and lilies. The glimpse afforded by the present lake's higher elevation was threatening. Achibol's maps showed only wide valleys traced with right-angled roads, but the morass looked all trees, with patches of algae-skinned open water.

"It's not as bad as it looks," Achibol reassured him. "There are locks to let boats down, and the water below is clean, for all its greenery. Shallow-drafted smacks traverse it easily, and the river beyond the swamp is swift and stone-free. Our difficulty will be attaining its shelter undiscovered . . ."

"Master Achibol?" Sylfie seldom interrupted like that.

"Yes?"

"With these honches about, may I still go to the temple?"

"You must, girl. They'll not look closely. A poot visiting the temple—what could be more innocent? And we've outdistanced any who might know you."

He turned to Benadek. "Take her there, boy, then shop for our own needs. Buy no sweets or frivolities, be quick, and meet me on this spot before sundown." He waved them away.

In the shadows of a fish-house Teress helped Achibol remove his robe. He turned it inside out. The plain lining was something an ordinary scribe might wear. He withdrew a vial from a pocket and spread pale cream over his face and the backs of his hands. His lightened skin was blotchy, but would have to do. They left the mules outside a well-lit alehouse patronized by fishermen and caravaners. Anyone with designs upon their baggage would think twice, believing them inside. Caravaners always left a watch upon their beasts, but never an obvious one.

The first person they saw as they made their way back among the boats was a sailor, barefoot and in knee pants; the second was a honch in black leather, and so were the third and the fourth. Achibol saw the telltale gleam of wire mesh in each honch's hair. "So many!" He slipped into a long-extinct vernacular:

"This town's wors'n Chicago. If there was a Chicago. No place for a black man. Good thing honches ain't no smarter'n dumb Irish cops."

The floating boats were guarded by honches. He walked further. None of the honches seemed to be patrolling set routes. That made it hard to plan, but increased the chance for gaps in the surveillance.

The boat agent proved avaricious and unscrupulous. There was a boat that would serve, but he named a price well over what they could get for the mules. "Draw up the papers," Achibol said.

"We have no sale yet," the broker protested. "I'll look your beasts over and determine what must be put with them."

Achibol shrugged. "Our goods, for what they are worth, are with the mules. Show us the boat."

The lake constrained city growth to the south. The temple, the center of an erstwhile village, now stood among stone warehouses a mile from the great sluices and boat-locks that gave access to the morass and river downstream. It seemed to Benadek that every third or fourth person was a honch. There in the town proper few wore black, being warehouse guards and city militia, not soldiers of their mysterious enemy.

"I'll only go in for a little while," Sylfie reassured him. "Everything will be better then, you'll see." Benadek was not comforted. He could not go with her. The coin and talisman were no protection any more. They slunk up side streets until they were in sight of the temple gate—and two black-clad honches. His grip on Sylfie's arm tightened. "You can't go in there! Not past them."

"Master Achibol said they won't know me—and they wouldn't dare deny townspeople their temple." She tugged against his restraint.

"No! Wait. Let me think."

"There's nothing to think about. Let me go!" She

jerked loose and began to run. Benadek snatched at her blouse. It tore, but held long enough to spin her around facing him.

A small object clattered on the cobbles of the temple square—the magical writing tablet that Sylfie loved.

Benadek gaped, understanding. "You weren't going to come back! You were going to leave us."

"I can't stay. I love you, but if I go with you, I'll die a little each day. Let me go."

His eyes caught movement across the square—he and Sylfie were no longer in the shadows. The honches had seen her run and him give chase, and were coming to investigate.

"It's too late! They've seen us." He tugged on her arm.

"You go. They don't want me.

"They'll guess where the tablet came from, and make you talk." The honches stepped up their pace. "We have to run *now*!" He pulled. She stumbled and began to cry. The honches, convinced that something was indeed amiss, gave chase. Benadek dragged Sylfie around a corner and out of sight.

It was too late for her to go back, almost too late to escape. They darted into one narrow alley, then another, avoiding airy courtyards and squares, sticking close to the sides of buildings. They worked their way from the temple into a hillside district, until they were satisfied there was no pursuit.

"I can go back later," Sylfie said with downcast eyes, her face still wet with tears that had not stopped flowing as they ran. "Tonight there'll be new guards."

Benadek shook his head regretfully. "They'll have found the tablet by now. You'll have to wait until the next town."

"I'll hide for a day, or two. I'll dye my hair."

"Can't you wait another week? We'll be through the swamp, and you'll be safe. And I'm sorry. I shouldn't have stopped you. I know what you have to do."

"I understand. It took you by surprise—when you saw the tablet. I shouldn't have taken it. It's no good to me. I'm no more skilled than I ever was, but I wanted it to remember . . . to remember you and Master Achibol by." She blinked away still more tears. Benadek's own vision blurred. He reached for her, and she came into his arms.

"We'll have a little more time," she murmured into his shoulder. "But I hope you won't wish I'd already gone."

He assured her he'd never wish that. Neither could have known how wrong he was, nor that only a few days later he would wish he'd died rather than stopped her from entering the temple. But right then, they were reprieved from the loneliness that neither could deny would follow their parting.

They sought out a neighborhood market where merchants still braved the late-afternoon sun, and bought foods that would keep well on a boat. They walked slowly, shouldering their purchases and other, less visible burdens.

Achibol was surprised to see Sylfie. "What happened?"

Benadek made it sound as if the fallen tablet had been the start of their problems, not a result of his actions. Sylfie did not contradict him, but the mage drew her aside "You can hide until we're safely away," he said. "Then even if they force you to tell them everything . . ."

"I don't feel sick yet, Master Achibol. How long before you next expect to pass a temple?"

"A week. Two. I won't risk you, girl."

"Let me decide. I'm coming with you."

The mage, hearing something, stood with his head cocked. Sylfie welcomed the distraction. She allowed herself to wince at the sharp pain that spread from her gut to her chest. "My pain. My choice," she murmured. She had to make sure Benadek was on the right track. If she stayed behind, she would never know. Besides, maybe they would really make it to a temple in time.

"Listen!" Achibol commanded. They heard shouts and angry cries, the brays and snorts of mules, and the clatter of iron-shod hooves. "The honches gather at the gates, and at the locks to the lower waterways," he said, gesturing in the directions of the commotion. "There, the boat-seller is attempting to control his new mules. Soon he'll discover the sandburrs I tucked under their harnesses, and he'll find his purse a bit light besides." The sorcerer grinned and tossed a gold tenday piece from hand to hand. "I'd not give this wayward coin to an honest merchant, but he planned to inform the honches. Teress is at our new boat. Let's hurry."

"But Master, if they're watching the locks, how will we get through? We can't sail up and down the lake waiting for them to forget about us."

"We'll portage around the locks," Achibol told him, "and slip away into the swamps." He gave Benadek no opportunity to question him further.

When Teress saw that Sylfie was still with them, she scowled and turned to Benadek. "You stupid, selfish little bug . . ." but Achibol waved her to silence. "Later," he said, "when we're well away."

By dusk, a light fog gathered on the water. "The honches must be emplaced now, awaiting us," Achibol remarked, "and the broker will have visited them. He'll lead them here. We must get out on the lake."

"It's not dark," Teress said, peering through the crack in a slatted shutter.

"Once we're a hundred yards out, we'll be in the fog and safe, for the night. As Benadek pointed out earlier, there's nowhere for us to go, except back and forth in the water. They hold the locks."

"Then what's the point? Maybe we should just sneak back into the woods again, mules or no mules."

"No, there's another way, but we must navigate that first hundred yards to safety."

Benadek got no small satisfaction from his observation that Teress was less inured to Achibol's roundabout ways than he was. He, though unfamiliar with boats, carefully followed his master's soft instructions on readying the craft. Teress, in her anxious frustration, bruised her hand readying the mast to be raised, then bumped her head on the companion top.

The boathouse doors opened outward onto the short channel. It was easy for Benadek and Teress to swing them apart and guide the craft out. Achibol and Sylfie strained to raise the short mast on its pivot. Benadek swore softly when the hull's heavy rub-rail caught his knee, then regretted it when he heard Teress's snicker. Sylfie slid the mast-pin home and tapped the wedges tight just as the bow cleared the channel end. Benadek and Teress pushed hard, and jumped aboard just as they ran out of paving at the lake's edge. They were so far unnoticed.

"Up sail," Achibol whispered. He and Sylfie pulled the halyard, and the tan sail rose with the faintest chuckle of wooden sheaves, the smallest scraping of sail hoops on the mast. "A good boat," the mage commented, "and well-maintained. I almost regret foisting my rambling coin upon its seller. But then," he reconsidered, "he no more intended us to keep the boat than I did him the coin."

There was the barest ghost of a breeze, not enough to fill the sail, but because it moved them outward from Lacedomon, in a direction that suited the mage's unspoken plan, he did not order them to break out the long sweeps strapped to the coamings. The town was soon lost in the fog.

"Climb the mast, boy," Achibol said mildly, "and tell me if you can see over this soup." Benadek scrambled to obey. "Quietly, quietly. Sound carries over water." Benadek nodded, and removed his boots, the better to use the sail hoops as a ladder.

At first uneasy, he was enthralled with the view from on high. At the height of the spreaders the fog attenuated, and with his feet firmly upon them his head was in clear night air. The moon cast a white glow across the puffy white blanket. There were clear patches of dark water near its middle.

"What do you see?" His master's words came muffled from below.

"I can see the upper town behind us, and something dark ahead on the left."

"Can you make out the sluices? Our destination lies on their far side. Face forward, and guide me with your words."

Benadek complied. The low point where the shore disappeared was only a few degrees off the boat's present course. Achibol allowed for the leeway the shallow craft would make, and headed not quite directly for the presumed sluices. With the boom full out on the port side, the wake was reassuringly straight. Benadek remained above, whispering occasional corrections. They headed for a wooded strand. Shortly, they felt the keel grind on a shallow bottom.

"What now?" the lad asked when he descended. "We can't drag this heavy thing through that thicket."

"There's an old portage trail, paved before there were locks. Only brush will impede us." He sent Teress ashore to seek the trail. Benadek would have preferred his master to send him. The pure-human (as he often caught himself thinking of her, momentarily forgetting that he shared her distinction) would miss the trail, and they'd still be floating here like a fat balloon-toad when the sun drove off the fog.

Teress came splashing back with good news. She'd

found the old trail, and would warp the boat thither if Master Achibol's otherwise useless servant-boy could be ordered to assist her.

Achibol gave him a conspiratorial grin. "Humor her." He jerked his head toward the bow. Rather than taking the painter and pulling with Teress, Benadek tied on a second line before descending into the water. The boat rose as his weight left it, and drifted free of the bottom. They spread out in a "Y" with the boat as its trailing leg. "This way I can tell if that lazy wood-runner is pulling her share of the load," he whispered in Achibol's direction. Though the mage gave no indication he'd heard, Teress's flush, and the way she bit her lower lip, were reward enough for Benadek.

The boy was appalled by what he saw when they grounded at the portage. For the first fifty feet, there were old wooden rollers, rotted and imbedded half their diameters in the sod. Beyond that were stepped ramps separated by short stretches of flat, stone-paved path. Though only a few woody shrubs had grown through the cobbles, he saw no way they'd get the heavy boat out of the water, let alone down those slopes. Far below, hundreds of feet ahead, he heard the roar of the lake dashing through the sluices into the lower channel.

Achibol was undaunted. "Tie this ring securely to that far tree," he said, handing Benadek one end of a complicated arrangement of ropes and pulleys, "and this other to the painter—the rope you were pulling," he explained to Teress. "Sylfie, push at the stern, at my command." The three young people did as they were bade. Teress and Benadek had to pull back toward the lake, the way the ropes ran through the pulleys. Achibol climbed aboard and groped in the cockpit, retrieving his staff. "I'll lift the boat."

Lift it? Benadek raised a skeptical eyebrow at Teress, who gave an exaggerated shrug. It was the first communication between them that did not arise from mutual hostility.

Achibol affected not to notice. He fiddled with the staff, muttering. Benadek strained to catch his words, but they were in an odd singsong and made no sense. The boat, however, seemed to understand, for it rose until its chines were barely wetted. "That's all I dare for now," the sorcerer said. "I don't have the power to keep it all the way up. Pull now. Sylfie, push as hard as you can."

Slowly, the massive craft began to move ashore. Benadek expected it to grind to a halt on the first punky log rollers, but instead of digging in, its stem glided over, squeezing stinking water out as it pressed on them. The boat moved as though through thin mud—but it moved.

"Shouldn't we remove the spars, Master?" Benadek queried. "If we emptied the boat, it would be easier, too."

"It would—and less strain on the limited resources I can bring to bear as well. Under less pressing circumstances I'd let your strong young back bear the burden of carrying the mast, my trunks, and the rest of our impedimenta to the far end of the portage, but tonight . . . when we reach the bottom of the slope, and are no longer concealed by trees, wouldn't you prefer to float away with baggage, mast, and sails all aboard?" Teress snickered again.

Why did his master have to "educate" him when *she* was within hearing? Should he keep silent always, for fear the wood-louse would overhear his "lessons?"

The rope they pulled on had grown longer, or so it seemed. For every three steps they pulled backward, the boat advanced only one.

Achibol directed them to reattach the double pulley to a new tie-up further ahead, and to run the rope back through until the pulling-end was again short and the turns around the pulleys were snug. Again they labored. Benadek's muscles burned. He eyed Teress suspiciously. Her brow was beaded with sweat. She had done *some* work, at least.

"Until now," Achibol told them, "I've lifted the boat enough for you to pull it. The rest of the way will not be so easy."

Benadek opened his mouth to contest the mage. The rest of the way was downhill. It should be easier. Then he thought it through. He pictured several tons of wooden boat on one end of a rope, and he on the other. He glanced at steep ramps broken by short level stretches, and imagined the boat careering down, with him running and bouncing behind. It would be harder to keep the boat from moving down the ramps than it had been to move it across level ground. Further, there would be a time at the head of each ramp when the tackle was fixed to the stern to descend, but the boat still had to be dragged or pushed forward. Could they move it without the advantage the gear gave them?

Achibol sensed his unspoken question. "When the vessel is poised at the brink, I'll expend extra energy to hold it up while you push the stern, then run to your rope. If we're lucky, my staff won't be exhausted before we're all the way down."

"What if it fails before that?" Teress asked.

"Then the vessel will remain on land either whole or in splinters, depending on what moment the energies choose to fade."

Why, Benadek wondered peevishly, does he give her straightforward answers, yet mock me? He consoled himself that he was the magician's apprentice, and she only a hanger-on who could not be expected to understand his master's subtleties, and that Achibol had no commitment to her learning anything. His master's acid remarks, reserved for Benadek alone, were proof of the old man's concern that he learn well what he was taught, proof of his importance.

Lightening his burden with that clever rationalization, Benadek pulled his share of the load, or a bit more.

The "steps" down the slope passed swiftly. When Achibol signalled a rest they left the boat poised with its bow over the next brink. Benadek compared the distance up-slope and down, and estimated they were more than halfway, but they would have to hurry, to be in the water before dawn.

He cut his break short. "I'm going back up to brush out the marks of our passage. The rut we left will be like a waving flag." Achibol nodded approval. "Ten minutes," he said.

Benadek was amazed how quickly he reached the top, scraped and brushed over the disturbed beach, and returned. Alone, it was only a short dash; straining at the end of a rope, it had seemed miles.

When the boy returned, the others were ready to resume their toil. Benadek's muscles screamed protest as they pulled against even the magically reduced weight of the hull. Teress's grunts told him she also suffered. Sylfie labored between them in utter silence.

Dawn caught them short of their goal. They would be in shadow a while longer, but ahead the trees thinned, and they would have to cross the final slope to the water in daylight, exposed to view from the far end of the natural dam. Luckily, the roar of water rushing down stone-faced channels would mask any sound they made.

They reversed the tackle and tugged the boat ahead, repositioned the ropes and lowered once more. And so it went. They reached the final level and the edge of the trees. Beyond was a bare cobble path to the water, still sixty feet away and twenty down.

Benadek's eyes strayed to the far side of the rushing water, expecting at any minute to see black-clad figures scurrying toward them.

"Be ready!" Achibol admonished. "This is the last pull, and we must move fast. Once they see us, we'll have two minutes to reach the water." Two minutes? It would take the old man that to walk to the water's edge. The sixty feet seemed an uncrossable distance, but the rope was ready, and Benadek took his place at it. The boat began to move. He continued to watch the far side.

Finally, less than two boat-lengths below, the water seethed and boiled, drowning their voices, sending spray and fine mist into the air, where it clung to rope-hairs, eyelashes, and hair. Achibol gesticulated wildly, and Benadek followed the motion of his arm.

Upslope were honches. Four, no five of them. Six. Ten. They swarmed like black beetles, bristling with glittering armaments. A puff of steam gushed from their vessel's planking. Paintwork blistered and whitened, but the steam released from the well-soaked planks diffused it. That deadly light would blister skin, char flesh, and boil body fluids.

They were out of time. The rope lay slack in his hands. His eyes met Achibol's. He made a pushing motion with his hands, palms out, and the mage nodded vigorously, his words lost in the tumult.

Benadek grabbed Teress and Sylfie each by an arm, and rapidly pantomimed what he wanted them to do. Both nodded, and begun to pull again. The boat teetered forward, bow-down, and Teress pulled herself over the stern, which settled back again. She reached a hand down to Sylfie, who with Benadek gave one last tug. Sylfie jumped, and was pulled aboard. Achibol, amidships, gripped the mast and his staff. Benadek pulled, but the boat did not move. Sweating, swearing, dripping with spray that nearly blinded him, he thrust himself under the hull next to the rudder and heaved upward.

Grinding cobbles beneath it, the flat keel began to slide down-slope. He got behind, and pushed on the transom, felt it first resist and then pull away from him. He pulled his belly over the stern. Half-aboard, he saw Teress and Sylfie sprawled in the cockpit, and Achibol clinging to the mast, his staff still upright.

The transom-rail pounded his chest and arms as the heavy craft plunged downward, and he almost lost his grip. Then, still half over the stern, his feet dragging in water that tugged and pulled, he grimaced in pain as he slid into the cockpit, sure his ribs were broken.

With a groan, he lurched to his duty post as Achibol had taught him on the lake. In spite of knife pains in his chest, he pulled in the sheet, stabilizing the wildly swinging boom as Teress and Sylfie raised sail. Achibol, his staff forgotten, took the tiller. The ramp receded behind. Honches gathered ankle-deep in the foaming water. The sail filled with a dull snap.

He saw boats on the far shore, hitherto concealed in spray, but none had sails up. Honches swarmed on the short piers, but none attempted to pursue, not knowing how to sail. Neither did Benadek, but Achibol did. With cursive hand-motions the mage signalled what he wanted done and, clumsily, his crew obeyed.

The roaring sluices were lost to sight as the channel curved, their sounds diminishing until Benadek could hear the chuckle of ripples breaking on their craft's chines, the murmur of bubbles beneath their feet. Their path opened onto a wide stream where the current slowed, and Achibol steered them toward one of many channels that emptied it. Soon, they glided silently in water little wider than the boat. Great-boled trees lined both sides, higher than the mast. A faint breeze kept the sail distended. A leaf floating on the glassy surface moved alongside, and then was left behind.

INTERLUDE
The Great School, Midicor IV

Saphooth, Kaledrin observed, had become more withdrawn than ever after the output of Chapter Eight. Following the release of Chapter Nine, the Director sequestered himself in his cubicle with no company except his AI research assistant, and refused contact with MYTHIC staff-beings, visitors, even potential benefactors. Saphooth had never before missed an opportunity to garner funds.

Days went by. The biocybes silently mulled over their next contribution. Kaledrin became more and more interested in his superior's mysterious line of research. All he could tell was that Saphooth was incurring heavy communication and library database charges. Some were offworld calls.

"It shouldn't be hard to break into his files," Abrovid said thoughtfully.

"I didn't know you had such dark talents."

"I'm a programmer, that's all. And what of your criminal tendencies? I don't hear you refusing my offer. But I have a price."

"Oh? What?"

"Only that you explain to me what you think Saphooth's doing that concerns you so."

"Of course. But not until I see if I'm right. It wouldn't be the first time the old monkey has made me look foolish."

CHAPTER TEN,

how Teress the Earth-bond and the demon Achibol betray Benadek and steal his treasure.

The Scholarium of Ummsu contends that Benadek is the divinely inspired apposition to the evil Achibol. But who, in this presentation, is good, who evil, who merely uninformed? Clearly at odds with the classical version, it only exacerbates the disputes.

This pared-down, cybernetically reconciled Achibol story is no myth. Repetition, variation, and elaboration upon themes and subthemes (themselves elements of other cycles, in other cultures) is entirely missing. Appositions, moral lessons, and supernatural elements are gone, leaving a simple (no pun intended) narrative of events in the lives of odd human beings.

Past mythic reconciliations yielded "cultural blueprints"—underlying principles that provided insight into the cultures that created them. Invariably, fragmentary "historic" memories were discarded as bastardized by generations of faulty remembrance, transmission, and translation.

Suspicions that this narrative was artifactual were laid to rest when the processing of the raw data was reviewed. Gathered not from one cultural tradition but from many, no one set of values could apply, so the biocybes removed such "taints." Freed of culture-specific references, the reconciliation could not but proceed along an entirely different path: a "historic" narrative whose cultural attributes required only internal consistency.

Truth is elusive. This rendering is consistent to the limits of cybernetic error checking. But is it *real*? Was Achibol in fact an old brown-skinned biped? Was he immortal, as he seems to claim? Was Sylfie really so good-natured and Benadek so quick-witted, insensitive, and abysmally ignorant?

Perhaps future reconciliations will yield a map of Achibol's heavens or the coordinates of his forgotten homeworld. The neuro-credits you have spent to purchase this volume will be applied to the distilling of just such information. Additional financial aid is urgently needed. Gauge your contribution not by your credit balance but by the depth of your curiosity. At this point you have read perhaps half the translation. Whether more follows is entirely up to you.

(Kaledrin, Senior Editor)

Unlike the last swamp, this one was almost all water instead of soggy ground. Great, stubby trees lined interwoven channels, their roots covered with water from a few inches to twenty feet in depth. Reptilian creatures shyly retired as the sailboat approached.

Breezes upon the topmost portion of the large triangular sail seldom filled it completely. Benadek fidgeted and fumed, but Achibol assured him the honches could not gain the swamp's far terminus ahead of them by land or boat, so he relaxed into the slow pace of their travel.

Sylfie was the least content, though not obtrusive about it. She found a spot on the pulpit atop the bowsprit, wide enough to sit with her legs dangling. No one could come alongside her, or see her face. When she came aft for a drink, Teress attributed the redness of her eyes to the glare off the water.

"There are eyeshades below," she said. "You've been staring into the sun all afternoon."

"I don't need anything." Sylfie gulped water, then went forward again.

Achibol kept his hand on the tiller, having eyes only for their course.

"Something's wrong," Teress said, forcing him to notice her. "Sylfie's been crying."

"I suspect so," the sorcerer replied without expression. "She didn't want to be here."

"I know. She had it all planned, and then that stupid . . ." She cut herself short. Benadek was stretched on the bunk below, his cracked ribs tightly bound. Achibol had dosed him with a nostrum. He seemed to be dozing, but she was not sure, and did not want him to overhear, to resume their quarrel in such close quarters. "What's wrong with her?"

"She's a poot. She has fewer options than you, and rage isn't one of them. Her creators considered only mild pettishness feminine and desirable. Some of her melancholia could be assuaged by any simple male who'd bed her, but none are here. That, too, is innate."

"That's disgusting! She needs a good *fuck*? Doesn't she have any self-respect?"

"She isn't suffering from a dearth of sexual activity," Achibol replied with a sad shake of his head.

"You mean Benadek's no good that way? I should have known . . ."

"Lay your peevishness aside, girl!" Achibol snapped. "Sylfie is a poot, and Benadek is pure-human. *That* is the root of their pain. She cannot conceive—by him. Were you taught nothing of the world in your village?"

Chastened, Teress bowed her head. Achibol, satisfied by her contrition, leaned forward to speak in low, confidential tones, his face a wrinkled, tragic mask. "There is one more thing, which you must not repeat. She may die before we quit these waterways. She knows, but the lad does not. She will soon become ill. Once that happens, death is inevitable."

"Why protect *him*? He should suffer right along with her, because if it weren't for him . . ."

"No! It must not be." The mage's eyes narrowed and the dark skin of his face darkened further. "He's foolish and selfish, impetuous, shortsighted, an egoist, and immature—much as was I at his age. He's a child of what passes for a *ghetto* and a *slum* in this age. Did your village teacher include those words in your lessons?" Without waiting for her nod, he went on. "He's the best tool I have. I don't want him ruined by guilt. Will you honor my confidences?"

"There's no one better than him?"

"Not on this continent, in this generation. None I could smoke out in this decade or the next. A century ago, there was another, who failed me, and others before that . . ."

"I won't tell him anything, then. But you must explain it to me."

Achibol nodded. "Come closer. He must not overhear."

Teress bent her head toward him. Eventually, she leaned back. Her cynical smile did nothing for her pretty face. " 'Dispucket,' huh?" she murmured. "Well, just so Benadek *really* suffers. You're sure he will?"

"Even if he makes the right choice, his suffering may never end."

"Not even in death?"

"If he chooses wrongly, even that escape will be denied him."

"You, Master Achibol, are a cold, nasty man . . . and I love you for it."

"You hate *him*, you mean."

Teress turned her face away.

"Aren't you hot?" Teress asked. "It's shady in the cockpit. Won't you come back?"

"No. Thank you. I like to listen to the water." Teress heard croaking, buzzing, small splashes, and the continuous lapping of wind-ripples and wake on the tangled roots and trunks.

"Would you rather I left you alone?"

"Stay, if you want to." Sylfie's words wafted back like leaves on the water, slowly. Teress fought with her frustration. Sylfie was not curt or impolite, just disinterested. Teress tried several approaches to get her to talk. "In my village we had two teachers. Who taught you?"

"A boffin. And other poots."

"What could poots teach?"

"To make fires and cook things."

"You cook better than my mother, even without all the pots, or a hearth."

"Thank you." Sylfie accepted the compliment without pleasure.

"What will you do when we get out of here? Will you have to find work somewhere?"

"I'll buy new clothes, and I'll find a . . . *man*." She

used the pure-human word with bitter emphasis. "A boffin or a cozie, that is. Not a honch."

"And then?"

"A house, if I'm lucky. Children."

"Don't you want anything else?"

"What else is there?"

"This. Adventuring. Won't you miss it?"

"I suppose. It doesn't matter. What matters is that I'm a poot. I don't have to like anything."

"How can you say that? Where's your self-respect?"

"None of this matters, anyway—I'm not leaving this swamp. Master Achibol knows it, and so do you. Only Benadek doesn't, because he doesn't want to." For the first time, she turned to look at Teress as she spoke. "You'll never understand about poots. Do you know what I regret most?" Teress shook her head, her black hair swaying gently. "Babies. What I was *designed* for." She spat the word hatefully.

Benadek awakened. The voices wafting through the open foredeck hatch were unintelligible, but he recognized Sylfie's anger. He eased forward until he was below the hatch.

" . . . you can't give up," Teress protested. "If . . . when . . . won't you teach your own babies to read?"

"What for? If they're boffins, others will teach them. Otherwise, they'll be happier being what they're intended to be. My own 'father' was cruel to think otherwise."

Teress got up. "You're right—I'll never understand." She saw Benadek's head and shoulders in the hatchway.

"You know why you'll never understand her? " he said vehemently, rage welling up from unplumbed depths, "She's *normal*, that's why. Millions of poots are satisfied to fuck and cook and have babies . . . and then there's you. What do you want to be? A sorcerer? Or are you satisfied just to be a . . . a catamount?"

Teress froze, her mouth half-open for a retort that stuck like cold grease in her mouth. Benadek, oblivious to the pain he caused Sylfie, whom he thought he was defending, was equally blind to Teress's confounded silence. "She's pretty and normal, and you're a pervert. You only act like you're special."

Teress knew how his insults to her must drive into Sylfie like hot irons. "You disgust me. I could vomit on you!" She launched a vicious kick at his head.

He ducked back in the hatch. "Ow! My ribs!"

"I hope they puncture your lungs!" she muttered, kicking the hatch shut and sitting atop it, her chin pressed into her hands.

Achibol caught Teress's eye, and shook his head sadly. She looked away.

The foursome made their way ashore on the first patch of solid ground they found. There was no practical reason for the excursion, but all four craved the semblance of freedom that a few acres of dry land afforded, the impression that they could walk away from each other and the intolerable stresses that had built up on the boat.

Sylfie made tea. Teress collected clean yellow sand and scrubbed insect specks, footprints, and leaf-stains from the boat's deck and cockpit. Benadek set up the tent, brought the sorcerer's trunks ashore, then found a grassy spot to watch late afternoon clouds float slowly overhead.

Achibol gave him an hour of solitude, then sat beside him. The mage pulled a stem of sweetgrass and nibbled it thoughtfully. "I'll bet you liked it better when you and Teress weren't speaking," he mused.

"It was easier," Benadek replied. Sun and clouds had done their work—he was calmer than in days, in a mood to forgive not only Teress, but more importantly, himself. "I don't mean what I say, most of the time, it just comes out nasty. I guess it's because she hates me."

"Ummh," Achibol replied.

"I thought she was picking on Sylfie—I guess I didn't hear enough before I opened my mouth. I hurt Sylfie's feelings, didn't I?"

"Mmmph," Achibol answered.

"What really bothers me is why Teress hates me so much. If Sylfie and I could fall in love, and we're not even the same kind—we can't breed together—then why isn't it better with Teress, since we're both pure-humans?"

"Sylfie is simple," Achibol replied. "Her choices are limited, and thus her expectations. And there was that potion I gave you. I suppose that was a mistake, but I didn't expect it to last more than a night."

"Did you know it would end like this?"

"I knew it wouldn't last forever. I thought 'what does it matter? They're happy now, and happiness is rare. They'll at least have memories to savor.' "

"I still don't understand Teress."

"She's pure-human," Achibol murmured. "Like you, she has complex motivations. Unlike Sylfie, you and Teress can believe in a better world, where no honches pillage, where children grow up with families and mothers never starve. Teress can imagine a kinder, more perceptive, thoughtful you. Thus, imagining, you and she can rage at what is."

"A better me?" Benadek sat up suddenly. "Who is she to . . ."

"Sylfie spoiled you. You—and Teress—were chosen by millions of years of natural selection to struggle. Simples were created in decades by shortsighted men." The mage turned to meet his apprentice's eyes. "It's why I've gone on year after year, century after century like this—to restore strife and bickering and unreasonable expectations to the world." *

Benadek nodded, chin bumping his drawn-up knees. "How do pure-humans put their expectations aside long enough to breed? How could my mother and father have stayed together long enough to . . ."

Achibol's chuckle interrupted him. "Common upbringing helps. Most pure-humans don't have as hard a time as you and Teress. But nothing is as straightforward as for simples. The best and worst about being pure-human is the capacity to dream better things and to choose one's own path to them."

Benadek slept in the tent with his master that night. Teress and Sylfie shared the boat's cabin.

Achibol awakened to the first diurnal creatures stirring. Cold dew on leaves and grass left nowhere dry to sit. He took a rolled map from his trunk, and wandered to the opposite side of the small island, where he'd seen a good-sized flat rock.

He spread the map. It was hand-drawn and stained, a trader's map of the channels and islands. He marked their location with one brown index finger, and traced a route with the other. "Not far," he thought. "Maybe not too far. But the choice of routes isn't mine alone." Twice he rolled up the map, shaking his head. Twice more he unrolled it and pondered, in an agony of indecision, before he rolled it a final time, and with a decisive tread strode to the boat. He waded out to awaken Sylfie.

They walked the narrow strand away from the

---

* This sentence, which the biocybes have retained in its most widely known form, is central to all myths that portray Achibol as the Trickster, and Evil. Herein Achibol speaks not of *creating* all mankind's ills, but of restoring the vital evolutionary stimulus of competition to a failing race.

moored boat and the tent. Teress peered indifferently from the boat. Benadek watched from the tent door, intensely curious. Neither thought to interrupt the old man and the poot, or to eavesdrop.

"I may be wrong to speak of this."

"Whatever it is, Master Achibol, I'll share it with you if I can."

"I know you will, and that grieves me. Once spoken, it can't be recalled."

"I may not have much time," Sylfie said matter-of-factly. That sent pains through Achibol's heart that were not entirely figurative. He was, after all, very old.

"That's the substance of the weight I bear," he replied.

"Tell me."

"You're not the only one running out of time. Benadek . . . I don't think he'll make it to Sufawlz in time to save him from . . . from . . ."

"Master Achibol, you must not try to spare me pain."

"You understand, don't you? Of all the women* I've known, pure-human and poot, you're . . ." He squeezed a bright tear from his eye, angrily wiping it with the back of his hand. "You're right. I must be callous and say my piece. Less would cheat you of your freedom of choice. Sit here, and I'll begin." They had reached the flat rock, sun-warmed now. Man and poot dangled their feet over the water.

"I had another apprentice before Benadek," Achibol began, "a boy much like he is today. Too much like him . . ."

---

* Here, for once, the meaning seems clear. "Women" is clearly a collective term for both pure human females and poots. Perhaps the previous uses of "woman" and "girl" for domestic and wild beasts implies that only the females of certain species are domesticable or edible.

✧ ✧ ✧

When they returned to camp, Sylfie looked happy. Contrary to Achibol's fears, a heavy weight had been removed from her. She kissed Teress affectionately, then kissed Benadek in a more sensual fashion. Achibol, however, now bore the burden of her suffering, or so it seemed. He growled at Teress and refused to eat breakfast.

"What's happened?" Benadek asked, drawing Sylfie aside.

"We had an argument," she said lightly. "And I won. Master Achibol is unused to having a poot—or anyone—dictate to him." Benadek could not draw her out further.

"Have you noticed how much you've grown?" she asked him. "You're taller than me now. And this . . ." She ran her palm over fine, dark hairs on his cheek and upper lip. "You'll have a fine, black beard someday. Look at your reflection sometime." She hugged him before wading out to the boat, where she went forward to her spot in the bow, alone.

Teress glanced from Achibol to Sylfie and back. What had the old fart told her? Obviously, not what he had promised Teress. Sylfie was too *nice* to be that happy, if she knew that tomorrow was going to be the worst day of Benadek's life.

INTERLUDE
The Great School, Midicor IV

"I was right!" Kaledrin exulted. "Here and here." His manipulators spread across the hard copy of the sources Saphooth had drawn upon. "No wonder old sticks-and-skin is upset. Serves him right!"

"Forgive my ignorance, Scholar," Abrovid interrupted with broad sarcasm, "but these documents are about reproduction among simian-forms. 'Mating patterns of the Tree-dwarves of Alnak Five,'" he read. "'Genetic Anomalies in Palantian Land Apes.' What, precisely, is Saphooth upset about?"

Kaledrin gave a mean-spirited chuckle. "He's afraid that because he can't *change*, he's not descended from pure-human stock, that he's like . . . like . . ."

Kaledrin's outburst of laughter had little effect upon Abrovid. He waited until it ran its course, then asked, "Like what?"

"Saphooth now suspects he is a . . . a . . ." Again laughter overcame Kaledrin. Resisting a strong urge to kick him, Abrovid was finally rewarded by two final words almost lost among Kaledrin's giggles and snorts. ". . . a simple!"

At that very moment, with Kaledrin's exoskeleton in disarray, his spiracles half-choked with mirth-induced mucus, his nether tentacles entwined about himself like twine around a child's handmade ball, a shadow cast itself across the open doorway, followed by . . . Saphooth!

"Enlightening One," Kaledrin burbled, frantically untangling himself and attempting to rise from his cluttered floor. "Wha . . . What brings you here at this late hour?"

Saphooth ignored him, addressing Abrovid instead. "Is he sick? I've long suspected this demanding work would take its toll."

Abrovid, whose thoughts were deep and complex, was no quick thinker. "Uh," he said, and, "Uhhh . . ." again.

Saphooth spun on a bare, bony heel to face Kaledrin, now erect on his still-rubbery motational extremities. "When was your last vacation? Perhaps you should explore the riverbanks and sun-wallows this Institution provides for your somatoforms. Your work surely suffers from . . . instability . . . as you demonstrate here."

"But Perceptive One, Chapter Eleven is due any day."

"Never mind!" Saphooth said. "I'll write the chapter introduction and collate the reference list. Your continued participation in this project hinges more upon pulling yourself together."

Unable to correct Saphooth's error without explaining what had been so uproariously funny, Kaledrin let his eyestalks droop in acquiescence. What harm could it do? He could take a few days to enjoy warm riverbanks, gentle breezes, and sun-wallows where lethargic females lay, too full of fresh, unfertilized ova to flee his advances. The idea had more and more appeal as he thought about it.

Saphooth snapped up Kaledrin's access-module on his way out. Now Kaledrin had no choice: the office's facilities, databases, and AIs were henceforth closed to him. He could not even read Chapter Eleven until he returned from his enforced sabbatical.

Abrovid said nothing, afraid that Saphooth, for all his bluster, had not misinterpreted anything.

---

* *Journal of Developmental Psychology*, Vol. XIV, pp. 470–492, Karamfis Professional Publications, Esab IV. Midicor Cat. 1334987.

CHAPTER ELEVEN,

an encounter with Dispucket, queerest of creatures.

Psychologists cite this episode as archetypal of human drives, desires, and fears. For the late Korbuth Aggadhi, Benadek's struggle echoes primal human fear of *becoming*, the disinclination of Youth to submit to adult responsibility; Hars Kregulo * postulates inborn reluctance to assume responsibility in any form; others, concentrating on the mystery of why most humans *become* while some merely *are*, perceive an ancient conflict between the shape-bound and the mutable, a conflict buried for a million civilized generations, but still within us.

Achibol, in the classic tale, is instigator and facilitator—a kindly deity who leads Benadek to the threshold of understanding, unable himself to cross it. In others, he is Evil incarnate, thrusting unready Benadek into the abyss of premature *change*.

Biocybernetic reconstruction provides details hitherto unremarked. Experts at the Great School are working to unravel these mysterious revelations.* We have an exquisitely detailed description of the "veins" of a "leaf," a vegetal solar accumulator. We now know the superficial morphology of a small quadruped who may once have fed among or upon these "leaves." Such odd details emerge, unrelated to the tale itself. Perhaps we will never fully understand such graphic vignettes, but should we ever stand on a world where "squirrels" and "oak trees" exist in gentle symbiosis, we will know beyond doubt that the soil beneath our feet is that of Achibol's Home.

(Saphooth, Project Director)

"What's a 'dispucket,' Master—and why do you want me to meet one?" The ground they trod was relatively dry, except for dew. Squirrels chattered in broad-leaved white oaks. Silver thorn bushes tinkled sweetly. They had followed the narrow game trail for almost an hour now, and Benadek became petulant at the old man's air of mystery.

"There is only one Dispucket, boy, and when you learn what he has to teach, you'll know why I wanted you to meet him. And now . . . the moment is at hand. Stand aside." He pulled Benadek off the trail, and . . .

---

* See *Achibol's Homeworld*, a travelogue by Bann Astophal of the Department of Comparative Mythology, Midicor IV, Vol. MCXI, Issue 7, *Journal of Comparative Mythology*.

This compendium describes a mythical homeworld near the Betelgeuse supernova. Little can be verified by physical investigation, as the supernova and the consequent chain of stellar immolations have made of that entire area an impenetrable cloud of high-energy particles and deadly dusts.

The ground where Benadek had stood moments earlier bulged like a swelling boil. Sod cracked radially from the growing tumulus's center to its indistinct edges. As the ground rose, chunks fell aside in a ring several paces across.

From a distance Achibol assured him was safe, the boy watched the . . . thing . . . rise to man-height and higher. Its surface was convoluted, wrinkled, folded in a radiating pattern. It was dirty pink like old meat, streaked with dendritic markings that bulged and flattened in slow, regular cycles. Veins! Veins and pulsing arteries! Its pustules stank of carrion and ammonia.

Benadek pinched a dirty finger and thumb over his nostrils and reached for a stone. Eyes never leaving the hideous sight, revulsion twisting his visage, he drew his arm back to throw.

"Wait." Achibol's grip on his wrist was so tight the stone itself seemed to throb in time with the dispucket's undulations. "Does it offend you so?"

"It looks like a puckered asshole and smells worse."

"For that you'd injure it?" Achibol shook the stone from the boy's numb fingers. "Now, should I cast a spell that makes boils of your eyes, and your nose a crushed toadstool?"

Benadek quailed inwardly, realizing that his error must have been grave, but stubborn adolescent pride permitted him to show no fear. Achibol sighed. "Should I make your breath stink of gut-gas and hog-puckey, so every man will reach for stones to cast?" The sorcerer shook his head. "Benadek, Benadek."

Head down, Benadek mumbled, "I don't understand."

"I can't teach you what it feels like to be a dispucket. But were you as repugnant to others as it is to you, you might be less eager to throw stones."

"But it's only a *thing*, Master." Benadek was truly

afraid. Would Achibol do that? Could he? This was no gentle chiding: the sorcerer wanted some enlightened response, but the creature disgusted him. He could not claim otherwise. "I'm sorry, Master," he said miserably. "I beg enlightenment."

"Enlighten you! Hmmph. If the cost of understanding is high, will you pay it?"

Benadek held his hands tightly at his sides. His thoughts raced like leaves in a wind-devil, and he waited until one leaf spun out from the flutter to land before him. "If the learning is needful, Master, and the cost not too great for me to bear, I'll pay it."

Achibol smiled broadly, his face all brown wrinkles and big, yellow teeth. "Clever lad! You throw my words back at me and wriggle away. Should I make such a slippery one into a worm, or reward his astuteness?" He continued to grin. "Should I reward you, boy?"

"If you judge me worthy, Master."

"See? Again you squirm away. Very well. I'll give you both enlightenment and reward. Dispucket awaits you. Spread wide your arms and hug him as you might your long-lost mother."

The cruel simile jolted Benadek, who was used to gentler teaching. He looked from Achibol to the dispucket and back. His boyish face wrinkled like the old man's, silently pleading. He looked again at the dispucket, purple-veined and suppurating, wrinkled and throbbing. "Go, boy," Achibol prompted. "Embrace him."

Slowly, as if his feet were mired in mud, Benadek began walking. Like a marionette jerked along by a clumsy child, he forced himself closer, unwilling brain struggling with recalcitrant legs, step after dragging step. The fetor of dead things clung to his nostril-hairs and made his gorge rise.

Not swallowing his own polluted spit or smearing away his tears, he spread his arms. The dispucket, seeming to divine his intent, stretched upward, an elongate mushroom, a phallus whose veins swelled and shrank in obscene desire.

Caught between embracing that foul perversion and facing his master's burning, yellow-rimmed eyes, Benadek yielded to the fear he knew best: in one rough motion he threw his arms around the dispucket.

As if a nightmare had just ended in bright, warm sunlight, the stink and corruption were gone! The dispucket was gone too. Disoriented, Benadek looked upon an unfamiliar scene. From beneath a leaf the size of a cartwheel he peered through giant grasses. His tiny eyes darted from one wind-moved blade to another, seeking danger. His tiny heart hummed too fast to feel individual beats. Then everything twisted crazily, and the scene was gone.

With reptile-eyes that gauged, focused, and tracked without thought, he watched the darting motions of a sting-fly, and felt his long, sticky tongue uncoil and dart from his lipless mouth. With tongue-tip chemosensors he caught a brief taste of the struggling insect even as the world lurched again.

Benadek saw his mincing white paws through fox-eyes. Then he had kaleidoscopic insect-visions of flower stalks glimpsed from the air. Through turtle-eyes he peered through muddy pond water. Each time reality shifted, he saw something new, from a viewpoint unimagined seconds before.

Benadek's vision-voyage took him skyward, where he perceived the air as a matrix of insect movements through a white-barred nighthawk's hunting eyes. Moments later, he understood water in three dimensions, being himself a fat trout moving beneath a rippling, mirrored sky. He saw. He understood.

✧ ✧ ✧

One vision followed another, each clear and distinct. Vision was an inadequate word; sight was only the slightest part of his experiences. For a brief moment, he *was* each creature. He saw, felt, heard, and smelled the world through the senses of a hunting cat, a song-snake humming between tree branches, a fish-eating bird, and a fish being eaten. He knew senses no human possessed, and savored each one. He took life and he died. He mated, shifted, and lived again in form after form . . .

Abruptly, the visions ended. He saw his own shod feet, toes pointing skyward as he sat atop the disrupted soil where the dispucket had been. It had withdrawn, leaving only soft, churned humus.

"Boy?" He felt a hand on his shoulder. "Night approaches, and we must return to our vessel."

With legs that felt hardly his own, with downcast eyes, Benadek followed Achibol's dirty robe-hem. Later, while the sorcerer puttered and lit fire, he stared inwardly, seeing again the visions of his mind's eye. He ate with hands far away on arms that stretched distant and unfeeling to a platter that was a white blur on his lap.

When night enshrouded all but those few embers still reflected in Achibol's eyes, Benadek ventured speech. "I am enlightened, Master," he said, bemused.

"And rewarded?" Achibol prompted gently. "You are recompensed for the stink and the fear you endured?"

Benadek nodded gravely, then raised his head and blurted, "Master? What happened to me?"

"You saw what you saw through all the eyes of this small patch of forest. Isn't that so? I'm glad Dispucket was so kind to you," he said, "after what you did to him."

"But Master Achibol!" Benadek protested, "I did nothing! I only thought about throwing the rock."

"Ah! The cobble. I'd forgotten it. No, your offense was greater than that."

"Pardon, Master. I'm ignorant."

"Eyes, Benadek, eyes!" the sorcerer urged. "Think not about what you saw, but how."

Benadek put his chin on his knee and stared into the coals. "Let me think," he mused. "I saw through mouse eyes, and fishes', and a fox's. I saw through birds' and song-snakes' eyes, and I saw flowers as through a child's toy viewing-glass, in broken images—bugs' eyes, I think." He pondered the strange visions, then shook his head. "I saw only what the creatures saw."

"Why? Will you credit it to wild forest magic and dismiss it?" Achibol twisted his beard with impatient fingers.

"I . . . I assume the dispucket was responsible for the visions, Master. They began only when I touched it. Was I perhaps seeing as the eyeless monster sees?"

"Perhaps? Is the universe so vague and phantasmic? When you swim, do you only suspect the water is wet?"

Benadek frowned in angry frustration. Achibol was unfair. "I'm your apprentice, Master. If mules talk, and talismans fell honches, can anything be what it seems? I doubt everything."

"Indeed. I see now that your doubt is not stupidity—I forget the hard lessons of my own youth, long past. Assume then that Dispucket sees as you saw, through other eyes. Consider next what larger creature's eyes he might have used, there in the glade." Achibol's stare was bright and beady.

Benadek reviewed the scene. Sylfie had hung back, and Teress. Had the creature seen through their eyes, it would have seen only Achibol's back, and the forest trail. Using Achibol's, Benadek's own back would have loomed large . . . The boy's expression displayed sudden understanding. "Me! Ah, Master! The dispucket used my eyes. It saw . . . itself! Benadek hesitated, unsure of the implications of his revelation. Achibol's now-placid visage encouraged him. "Is it intelligent, Master? Could it comprehend what I saw? Could it sense the disgust behind my eyes?" His brow furrowed. "To be offended, mustn't it be a thinking being?"

Achibol merely gazed at him. "What is it, Master? What sort of thing is Dispucket?" Benadek now knew that "Dispucket" was no mere descriptor, but a proper name.

"Life, Benadek. Like you, me, and our sleeping companions. Life, and thus sacred."

"Intelligent life, Master?" the boy pressed on. "As intelligent as you or me?"

"I can't speak for you, boy. Answer yourself. As for me—no, I think Dispucket is less clever, surely less discerning, than old Achibol, for I am a human being, and it is not."

"Does humanity define intelligence, then?" Benadek challenged. "Can no other being qualify?"

"I know of none. Perhaps whales. Perhaps their shape-shifted, mutated descendants. But they don't converse with me. But between you and Dispucket, would an intelligent being choose to be the latter?"

"I would have been sure this morning," Benadek said, "but no longer. If not for the revulsion I feel, I might choose to be Dispucket for the depth and breadth of its vision. And after all, at most times, no being looks upon itself . . ."

The boy was thinking so hard that his crinkling forehead made dark lines by waning ember-glow. After many breaths, having reviewed what he had been told and what he had deduced, he spoke. "I'm sorry that I looked upon Dispucket with such disgust. I hope that his suffering was only aesthetic, and that he didn't partake of my judgments as well." He paused. Achibol refrained from interrupting his thoughts, which were deep, and which raced like stream water.

Long moments later, Benadek asked his question. "*Who* was Dispucket, Master, before he became what he is?"

"He was a boy," Achibol answered in a tone like sepulchral bells, "much like you." Was that gleam a tear? Was the old man crying, or were the fire's last fumes irritating his eyes?

"What was he to you, Master?" the boy asked softly. Petulance, condescension, and irritability were Achibol's everyday repertoire. His apprentice was cautious.

"Dispucket, son of Egdappit and Mulgay, was my last apprentice but one. He used to be a handsome boy, not a mushroom, but I failed to teach him patience, obedience, and discretion along with knowledge. He was a smart boy, or so I thought . . . but I wonder, now, don't you?"

Benadek's tongue seemed swollen like a pond-leech, preventing speech. His head spun and Achibol's form blurred. What had he gotten himself into, that fateful day when he had tried to rob a helpless old drunk? The boy's mind was incapable of translating the fear that overwhelmed it into trembling, screaming terror. He should have done that long ago, in the alley where he had first seen the mage, or in that first temple where he had thought him a demon. Now it was too late. He, Benadek, had no choice to make. No choice at all.

Achibol wrapped Benadek's blanket around him. Benadek slept on, hearing the drone of voices only as secure sounds.

"Was it only fatigue?" one murmured.

"Fatigue, and fear. His reaction to the news that

Dispucket was once a boy like him was merely a terminal event, not a radical one."

"Your words leave something to be desired, old man—clarity, for example."

"Radical, you mean?"

"It makes no sense, as you used it."

"Words change. In an ancient tongue, it was *radix*, a root. From that root—the root which is 'root' . . ." He chuckled, and Benadek stirred uneasily. For a while all was silent. Then: "From 'radix' came radish—the same radish Sylfie uses so skillfully in stews. Radical meant at the root of things. In the mouths of know-nothings it twisted itself to mean first 'extreme,' then 'politically unreliable.' You see?"

"I see that you are a foolish old man. Why was Benadek so put off by Dispucket? For that matter, why was I? He's no uglier than a trash-eating hog."

"We fear not what is different but familiar, but what is like us, yet unfamiliar. Dispucket's semblance is human, in part, but grotesquely sized and without referent."

"I know what he looked like, but I suspect there's more to it."

"I wonder if your pure-human teachers have prepared you to learn it?"

"Try me."

"Very well. Recognition pheromones—airborne hormones coded by histocompatibility genes that signal another being's relationship to you—species, tribe, family. The closer the ties, the stronger the signal. Such subtle messages attract mates if they are only species-close, but mute the tides of desire between siblings."

"My mother's sisters said as much—though I have yet to experience it."

"You'll only infer the signals after the fact. The chemistry can't be directly sensed. The first you may know is when your brain moves you to action or emotion. But have we forgotten Dispucket? Why does he raise such unlovely emotion in all of us?"

"Even you, his Master?"

"His erstwhile master. Dispucket has gone far beyond me, though for my own purposes he failed. But can you answer my question?"

"I need one more fact. Are Dispucket's 'signals' close to our own, or as distant as his appearance? Are they human or beast?"

"They have not changed since he was a human boy."

"Then Dispucket repels us not by his appearance alone, which is no worse than some things we eat with relish—bright mushrooms and organ meats—but because his messages are not those of mushrooms or meat, but of a boy. That contradiction repels us."

"Just so. I hope my present apprentice can understand as much, and come to terms with it."

"Why did you bring Benadek here? What good did it do?"

"He's proud, arrogant, and selfish, and he has too few fears. He doesn't look deeply enough into others or himself. I hope this encounter will change that. And another thing," he said, raising his hands in a fatalistic gesture, "though the boy importuned me to become my apprentice, and no words of mine would dissuade him, I've discovered in him qualities and abilities I once sought but had despaired of finding, since Dispucket went his own way. Now, in fairness to Benadek, I'll give him a final opportunity to back out. For his sake, I hope he does. For the world's sake, I pray he does not."

"Is being apprenticed to you so horrible? And what can he offer the world, anyway?"

"Ask Dispucket. He failed when the lessons were simple. Benadek has yet to begin. The *change* may destroy him—as was Dispucket, he is as far evolved beyond you and other pure-humans as you are beyond the ancients. Beyond me."

"I hadn't considered the *change* an advancement," Teress said.

"It is. Survival in a mutable world requires mutability—but intelligence cries out for control. You have only minimal control over your *changing*, but it won't destroy you. Benadek has the potential for absolute control over his, but failure at a single, critical moment may leave him like Dispucket. And Dispucket was lucky. Everything has its price."

The *change*. Teress avoided thinking about that. Begging off from Achibol, she retired to her blanket and tried to sleep, only then realizing that Achibol had only answered half of her last question.

Sleep was no escape. The *change*. She could not keep it out of her thoughts awake, and even less when she fell into uneasy, exhausted slumber . . .

. . . I hide in the thick brush, watching men in black swarm in and out of our caves. They call to each other in hoarse voices. Nobody's screaming. Nobody's alive. Mother is dead. I saw her. I trip over Father. He has a red hole in him, black on the edges. He stinks of roast meat. I recite the mantras the old women taught me, to still my pounding heart. I flee into the trees, the *change* upon me.

My blood boils with strange essences. My sweat is brown. The stink of burning granaries, hanging like fog among the branches, masks my stench from the killers. I think I'm going to be sick.

I run, leaving my last meal on the ground, my last happy meal with my dead brothers. Fear, anger, and helplessness slough off along with dead cells and unspeakable waste. I tear off my befouled clothing. It shreds like spiderweb, because I am becoming strong. Naked, I slink further into the darkness.

The fine, black hair on my arms has thickened, and

no pale skin shows through. I look down at my breasts, expecting pink nipples erect in the chill of my nakedness, but my chest is flat. Tiny black teats hide in cowlick-twisted fur. I flee again, fleeing myself and what I am becoming. I lurk behind trees and in patches of tall ferns, hiding from shadows, among shadows. I am no longer me.

I climb rough tree bark, my curved, thickened nails biting deep. I sit in a crotch and try to cry. Instead, I squall like a wild hunting-cat. I can't cry any more.

I'm hungry. I hunt. I pounce. A fat water-billy squeals, wriggling desperately. It is a sensuous struggle, and I prolong it until hunger goads me too strongly. I disembowel it with a swipe of my toes, and bury my face in the delicious stink of immediate death.

I back away from the dead thing and squall in frustration and anger. My teeth are small and weak, my face too short. I try again, smothering myself in slick meat. My stubby nose plugs with offal and my breath comes in gasps.

A strange thought penetrates my rage: I have hands, odd long-toed paws, black-furred and blood-flecked. I reach inside my prey, digging under ribs for a dark treasure. My sharp claws shred soft liver that keeps slipping from my clumsy, raking digits. I yowl again, and the forest becomes an absolute silence. *Hands*. A *thumb* and *fingers*. Slowly, carefully, I perform strange half-remembered motions. I *grip*. Fingers and thumb come together over a pink gobbet of lung. I lick food from between my fingers. My tiny teeth tear bits from the morsel and my narrow gullet swallows them. Remembering, I *reach* for more—liver this time. I feed, and am soon sated.

I course the deep swamp on thick foot-pads. I hunt often, because my gut is small, and fasting even a day weakens me. Small things surprise me: cat-sight is not gray but red. Shades of red and pink, and a palest rose sky. Crimson darkness, not black. I remember other colors, but see only one.

I am lean and sleek-furred, cat and not-cat. I sleep in daylight. At night I hunt. I cup my hands because I cannot lap. A woods-cat comes to drink, upwind and unaware. It is male. My anus twitches. I hunch down on my elbows and lift my behind experimentally, but have no tail to raise over my back. I smell cat scent, strong and sharp, but am not aroused. I am ashamed. I back away, unseen.

I encounter no more cats. They have fled my hunting-ground, for I am strange. I mark my boundaries—I want nothing to do with them. I'm not content. I'm not all cat.

Day by day my hunting shifts eastward, but I don't know it. Each day I am closer to . . . A hunger not-in-my-gut grows. I move toward the dawn.

The stench of old burning awakens a memory. It awakens Teress. I cringe and cower, unwilling to be me. Fire and death are now ashes and rotten meat. I remember a cave.

There is danger downwind. I smell dead skins and strange stone. *Leather* and *metal*, I say in my head. I remember the mother-killers, father-killers. I scrabble up crumbling rock to safety, to darkness. Heavy hard-soled feet vibrate the ground. Noisy pebbles rattle down-slope.

It knows I am here. I watch the cave-mouth, red brightness, white-pink intensity. I look away as if it were sun. I crouch, I wait. Crimson shadow blocks the brightness. I smell man-fear.

I hear a new noise. Warm emotion suffuses my blood. I hear voices, words, a rhythm of hooves. I remember happy excitement at the sound of such hooves. My muscles tense to propel me forth, but fear holds me back.

Shadow darkens the hole into daylight. I don't move,

I don't breathe. Round eyes dart about, unseeing, but I see them. I pounce. My mouth is wide, squalling. My hands/nails/claws rip hard leather and soft, white skin. I snarl, remembering death and fear. I yowl anger and sudden hunger. The twitching thing screams, then gurgles. I tear into it, pushing aside tasteless gut, seeking dark, rich meat, soft meat for my small teeth, my skinny throat. I eat one handful, then another. The liver is pale and sour, and I want no more. I hide again, licking my lips and fingers.

My prey drags itself away, into the brightness. I hear a warm-familiar voice. I move forward, but not far. I wait. I wait. The brightness fades, pink to red to crimson-dark. Night. I'll slip away soon.

A low voice is crooning. I edge closer, but another voice intrudes. I freeze, angry, afraid, but it carries a good new scent. Tea, and cooked meat with roots. A word: *stew*.

Something breaks in my head. Words rush through it, tumbling. Father mother door house person girl honch fire love death fear want hate see man cat woman old man know I know I know old man I know the old man I know him . . . I shake my head, overwhelmed. I move my mouth and twist my tongue and contort my lips. I make a word in my head. In my head, it is a word, but the sound is a mewling growl in my ears.

"Don't fear," the old soft voice murmurs. "Remain calm. I don't know who you are, but you know me, don't you? I'm Achibol, a friend. You remember Achibol. You remember me."

I remember an old brown man who laughs and bickers with my father. My mother feeds him and I sit on his lap. He finds bright beads in my ears and nose, and pulls a string from my hair. He lets me keep them all, and I string the beads and return proudly to show him. I wet my finger and rub it on the back of his brown hand, perplexed.

"It won't come off, Teress," he tells me. "No matter how hard you rub." I rub harder, but he is right. I laugh.

I laugh out loud. "That's better," Achibol says. "You remember how to laugh." Yes. I remember. I remember Achibol, and Teress. I feel wet on my cheek and I rub it away with the back of my paw, my hand. I lick the wetness and spit out fur. On my hand is a patch of pink skin. I rub one hand with the other and more fur comes loose. There is more pink skin.

"Come out," Achibol croons. "You're safe with me."

I want to obey. Achibol is warm. Achibol is my friend. But fur clogs my mouth and I itch everywhere. I brush myself with my hands, I scratch with my claws, and fur comes loose. Beneath it, I'm pink. I rub my flat chest, and fur rolls into balls and drops from me. I peer at my nipples, still tiny and dark, like little mouse-eyes. I remember clothes.

I remember nakedness. I remember Teress, and being shy. "Aaachiiibol," I croak, "wooooait."

"I'll wait," comes the low, pleasant voice. "When you are ready, come out."

"I'm not . . . not huuu-maaan." I am naked and ugly, covered with dead fur. My sweat is dark and foul. I'll be days in the change.

"You are human, a pure-human," Achibol says. "You're not a beast. You have a name."

"T'ressss," I say, and then more clearly, "Teress."

"Teress. Come to me, little girl—or are you a big girl now? Come sit on my lap and I'll find a pretty blue bead in your ear."

Achibol brushes fur from me, sticky with sweat. I shiver. "Wait while I fetch clothing. You're cold." I wait. Achibol goes in the cave. A red glow from his eye lights the wall beyond him. He rummages about. The glow dies, and he comes out. He wraps me in cloth that scratches, and raises a hood over my head.

"My companions must not see your face yet, Teress. It's our secret."

I'm grateful. I hold the hood closed, peering from my small new cave. I curl my fingers to conceal my long fingernails, my claws. I must hide until I am me again. Tomorrow I will bathe. Tomorrow and the next day and the next . . .

Benadek awoke slowly when the dawn-sounds of birds and insects aroused him, an old man's awakening, not the sudden leap into awareness of an urchin-child. With great show of unconcern, Achibol greeted his bestirral with a gesture toward the teapot on the rejuvenated fire.

Sylfie handed him tea. The warm, earthenware cup drew the grave-deep cold from his hands. The bitter brew seemed to course through his veins immediately, enlivening the rest of him. He felt almost human. (Human? Like Dispucket?) Benadek shook his head to clear it of what he wanted desperately to believe was a dream. He ate breakfast—crusts and berries—in silence. While he ate, the others broke camp. No one, not even Teress, asked him to get up and help.

While Sylfie and Teress restowed their gear on the boat, Achibol squatted beside the boy. "How do you feel about Dispucket today?"

"Master," Benadek answered, "I'm no wiser, only more fearful. Today, I have no desire to become as Dispucket, though I now appreciate that all beings make such compromises—his human appearance for extended vision and perhaps other benefits."

"Yet being my apprentice subjects you to the risk of becoming like him, or becoming something infinitely more different. I can't hold you to your expressions of desire to follow me, so consider the subject of your apprenticeship once again open."

"I'll think on that, Master," Benadek replied

carefully. The same thought had crossed his own mind. With the tricks he had picked up from Achibol—with his new, innovative mind-set—he could succeed on his own, telling fortunes and perform charlatan's tricks. He could travel, and explore new towns and villages. But did he want that? For the first time in his conscious memory, he felt that he belonged. He had adapted to the cantankerous old man's moods and vagaries, and he felt they understood each other. Of course there was danger, and not only from the honches hunting them—the old man and his unpredictable lessons were more dangerous than any honch. But where wasn't there risk?

Sylfie would not stay with him, either with or without Achibol, though Benadek still denied the implications of her depression, her desperation to be templed—thus denying his own responsibility for her predicament. Of course, staying with Achibol meant putting up with the insufferable Teress. That, strangely enough, gave him the most difficulty. The fear of becoming another Dispucket was so abstract as to hardly bother him, in the light of day.

He dismissed speculation, in favor of present reality, when they boarded the boat. He had learned to handle the sheet and tiller skillfully in the narrow channels. Achibol sat next to him, tucking his tattered robe-hem between his knees. "Well? What will you do?"

Benadek's reply surprised even himself: "I have many unanswered questions, Master. I know I must answer them myself, but alone I'll never learn to ask them properly. I must stay with you, or remain ignorant forever."

Achibol might have been pleased by Benadek's answer, or might not. His face reflected only stony acceptance. "Then let us begin teaching you to question. First, tell me what you know, and what you suspect to be true, in light of what Dispucket has taught you." He settled on the narrow cockpit seat, with his arm over the low coaming.

"I know that Dispucket was . . . is . . . human. I was disgusted because he was different, and because he stunk. I suspect such hatred is inborn, and I couldn't help myself."

"Ah! You hated him because he was different! As you no doubt hate song-snakes and birds and the very bench you sit upon?"

"No, Master," Benadek replied seriously. "He was human and, through some sense or magic, I knew it all along. But because he was not as I am, I hated and feared him."

"I see. Does that same hatred move you to pursue poots? Yes, much is explained—your disgust with the female difference compels you to seek to dominate them in undignified manners."

"Please, Master!" Benadek said, blushing hotly. Neither Sylfie or Teress seemed to be paying the slightest attention. "I meant only differences from what is usual or expectable."

"And such disgust and hatred seems innately human?"

"I suspect so," Benadek admitted reluctantly, fearing further disparaging commentary.

"You're right," the sorcerer said unexpectedly. "You sense differentness in many ways, and you define them in even more ways. But what is innate? Just the facility to hate, or the definition of what is to be hated?"

"Perhaps some of each, Master. I don't know what sense told me Dispucket was human enough for me to hate him, but once recognized, his semblance to . . . to isolated body parts . . . disgusted me. And it must be natural to hate the stink of death and corruption, though some people love ripe fish-cheese, which is foul. I don't know, Master. There's too much to be learned."

"You think swiftly, apprentice," Achibol said in a rare burst of generosity. "Perhaps you can learn it. With me for your teacher . . . After all, Teress's people, even in their rude caves, taught their children the rudiments of genetics and microbiology."

"I don't even know what those arts are, Master," Benadek replied with an air of dejection.

Achibol raised his hands helplessly. "When I think of poor Dispucket," he said sadly, "I begin to doubt that any man not raised in the Age of Knowledge could comprehend my mysteries. I tell myself that my teaching is doomed to produce results like him and not the successor I seek." A tear crept down the sorcerer's withered, brown cheek. "But then," he said, brightening, "you are not Dispucket. Where he was headstrong and sure you, with potential that exceeds his, go forward in doubt and trepidation, but are still willing to see things in new ways. Only in social matters are you utterly blind and without virtue. You underrate yourself."

Heartened by his master's praise—such as it was—Benadek declared that he was ready to forge ahead . . . with proper doubt and trepidation, of course. As for social virtues, such things would sort themselves out. After all, he meant no harm, and wished no one ill. But it was time to eat. The sun was high, so they moored the boat, angled so the sail would provide shade.

"And what of Dispucket?" Achibol asked later. "What would you do if he reared up from the water before us?"

Benadek took a long time to reply. "Knowing now the source of my fear and revulsion, I would conquer them, or if that proved beyond me, I'd look away to the shore or the sky, and not let him see himself through my eyes. I wouldn't hurt him with my flawed vision because someday I'll meet him again, and I'll look at him differently."

"You wish that to be?"

"I know it. My desire doesn't matter."

"Is it a true knowing? Are you sure?" Achibol, despite the skeptical attitudes of one trained in ancient sciences had, over many centuries, cultivated an open-mindedness about things paranatural. He himself could not read the future—his fortune-telling was an amalgam of careful listening, distraction, and circumlocution—but he had witnessed preternatural ability among the most unlikely simples. Perhaps precognition, telepathy, and the ability to twitch dice were artifacts of simples' design, or had been there all along, masked by ancient men's brilliant intellects and power over the material world. Plan or no plan, humans were still a grab bag. All the planners had really done was to make the bags' contents constant, not understood.

"I'm as sure as I can be," Benadek mused thoughtfully. "I must learn to see beyond my eyes, and feel beyond my deceptive senses."

"Oh? Why?"

"I think it's destiny—and why I must follow you. I must cease to be an ignorant boy, and must become a man." Achibol had no further questions. He took the tiller from Benadek, who settled in his master's vacated place, and promptly dozed.

"So I've an apprentice who makes me seem a fool," Achibol whispered to the trees, the water, and the wind. "His vision surpasses my own." The water made no reply, nor did the feathery breeze in the branches of channel-side trees. They only seemed to snicker when wavelets washed over protruding roots, when leaves and branches moved.

CHAPTER TWELVE,

in which Sylfie becomes ill, and Benadek feels the effects of his dangerous apprenticeship.

Psychologists and theologians make much of Benadek's unwitting *becoming*. Moralists delight in his discomforts and vacillations, as he struggles to remain *unbecome*. Does man truly desire to be not man, but a beast? Are the *unbecome* beasts? Bigots insist so, but Benadek and Achibol, herein, are no mere symbols—they are human beings. Humans, yet *unbecome*.

Perhaps Achibol's attitude provides a key: the issue is not *becoming*, but when to *become*, how to prepare for it and, remembering Dispucket, what not to *become*. Achibol provides the boy with Images of Stability* much as a mother might for an infant in the throes of early metamorphosis—a holding action until Mind has caught up with Body. But Achibol, Earth-tied as Wandag** herself, is a poor guide, and no mother, and cannot himself change . . .

(Saphooth, Project Director)

INTERLUDE
The Great School, Midicor IV

"End dictation," Saphooth told his AI. "Provide a printout and hold the soft copy pending my final approval."

Should he have said more? The whole issue of *becoming* was distasteful. It was difficult to keep his feelings from showing, even in two short paragraphs. No, it's enough. I'll put my speculations elsewhere and if there are greater revelations, I'll be ready to exploit them . . .

"Dictation," he ordered. "File name, 'Reflections of a Mythographer,' personal access only. Begin.

Despite renewed interest in the one-world hypothesis of human origins stimulated by the biocybes' tales, its proponents must overcome one seemingly insuperable hurdle. For every "human" somatotype there is an "origin world" with a fossil sequence from slime, sulfur springs, or sun-warmed shallows, through nonsentient forms, and culminating in literate, technological, and finally star-faring sentients.

---

* See Pserko, H., "Icons of Rightness" in *Occasional Publications on Infant Development*, University of Sagitarrn, Vol. XLVII.

** See below.

He paused for breath. "Display," he commanded the AI. Glowing letters formed against a blank wall, and his eyes darted rapidly across them. Where did those quotation marks come from? he wondered. The AI was remarkably sensitive to inflections. What *do* I consider "human"? Shall I delete the marks? No, this isn't for publication—at least not now. Let them stand.

> No longer so unsophisticated that we can explain away fossil shells in mountaintop rocks as traps laid by trivial-minded deities, we must consider all the evidence: the fossils, and these new "myths" that seem to contradict them.
>
> Most one-worlders come from religious backgrounds. I, however, am constrained by the ancient methodology of science. A workable hypothesis must encompass all data and contradict none.
>
> Fact: the biocybes imply a single origin-world and a single somatic expression not unlike my own. No! Delete that last phrase, after "expression."
>
> Fact: incontrovertible fossil evidence shows humanity to be a melding of many evolutions, a melding presumably brought about by the independent evolution of the ability to *become*.
>
> Is there a way to unify these opposites besides the "official" position of MYTHIC*? The intuition of a lifetime spent among these myths and

---

* Saphooth—personal notes: MYTHIC's official position is that the biocybes' tales are literary, and that historic inferences from them are irrelevant or misleading. See the open letter that fool Kaledrin sent out with Chapter Eight. But can anyone read the tales, ponder the details and their consistency, and not accept that they contain more than a grain or two of truth?

stories tells me there must be. It is a frightening intuition, spurred by a poem I learned as a child, a variation on the Wandag tale . . ."

WANDAG
A Myth of Achibol

One day Achibol was walking in the forest
The dark Lomba-eh forest.
He crossed a small stream,
And Wandag of the stream clutched his feet;
Mud grasped Achibol's feet and said
"Give me what you have, that is mine!"

Achibol became angry,
But Wandag did not hear his curses;
Wandag of moving water quenched Achibol's
  curses;
Wandag of the wet forest quenched them with
  leaves and moss,
And Achibol's feet remained in her grip,
For he would not give Wandag what he had,
  that was hers.

In the forest walked Benadek;
Benadek walked in the Lomba-eh forest
And the Sun followed him;
Dena-afa the Sun rode on his shoulder
In the forest by the stream Wandag.
Benadek saw Achibol;
He saw Achibol's feet in Wandag's mouth
And he asked Wandag
"Why do you hold this stick man?"
And Wandag said "I am mud, and this
  one is mine."

Then Benadek addressed Achibol.
"What do you have that is Wandag's?

What will you give Wandag to please her?
What do you hold that is of her?"

Achibol held out a coin, and said
"From mud came this bright gold.
To mud I will return it."
Achibol threw down the yellow gold,
And Wandag let go his feet.

Benadek took the stick man's hand
And pulled him away.
Thus Achibol was freed of Mud and Water,
But his wet, dirty shoes shamed him,
And he was angered by his empty purse.
Achibol in his pride caused the coin to rise;
From mud to his outstretched hand came the
  bright gold,
And Wandag was angered,
But Mud and Water could not rise to take
  it back.
Achibol had cheated Wandag.
He held in his hand that which was Mud's.
Benadek saw that and he rebuked the stick
  man, saying
"Did I pull you from Mud's grasp?
"Did you give her the golden coin?"
And Achibol pushed him into the stream.

Benadek, blessed and pure, became a
  water-bug
And came ashore still dry.
Then Achibol knew he was Benadek, first
  of men,
And bowed down and said "What must I do?"

Benadek commanded him "Return to
  Wandag what is hers:
Give Mud's child to Mud.

Give the child of Water to Water.
And spit water into Mud."
This Achibol did;
The round of gold threw he,
And he spit in the stream.

But Achibol was still angry.
As Wandag swallowed what was hers,
Achibol took Vine, rooted in Earth
And bound Benadek with it.
He again caused Water to give up the coin,
And it gleamed bright in his hand.
Then Achibol the stick-man cut Benadek's
member from him
And mocked the Pure One with it,
And cast it down into Mud.
Benadek's member became a small snake;
It crossed Wandag's face and crawled over
Earth.
The snake that was Benadek's Member bit
Achibol's foot
And caused Achibol to fall down.
Benadek became a greater snake,
And he crawled free of Vine.

Unbound, Benadek gathered the stick-man in
his coils
And crushed him,
And Achibol died.
Benadek became a stick-man then.
He picked up his member in one hand;
He picked up Mud in the other hand
And he made fast his member with Mud.
Then Benadek went into the forest.
Then Benadek left Achibol,
And Dena-afa rode with him;
Dena-afa, Sun, followed Benadek,
And Achibol's curses were not heard.

In Mud lay Achibol,
And Mud took him,
And Benadek the stick-man walked away.

from *Salist'efen Myths in Translation*
Midicor IV
Vol. 234a unit 38887,
Database ref. XCd 3992

The next day brought them to the southernmost edge of the swampy valley, where they filled their water barrel at a spring splashing from a rocky outcrop. Benadek lugged the wooden container up the slope, and immersed it in the pool at the spring's source. He saw his distorted image in the water. Remembering Sylfie's remarks about his incipient beard, he withdrew the cask and waited for the ripples to die.

He expected changes, but the face that peered from the water was no stranger's. The dark fuzz on his chin and upper lip was a sinister shadow. His eyes were dark, deeper-set than he remembered. His cheekbones flared, giving him a gaunt air. With a bit more beard and darker skin he might have been a young version of . . . Achibol himself. His appearance shocked him. I'm going to look like *him*? At least his face was a man's, not a boy's. If only the rest of him would catch up.

He related his discovery to Achibol, who said there were few others Benadek could have modeled himself after for better effect. The way he said it, though, seemed to imply that Benadek had *chosen* to pattern his visage after his master.

"That's the subject of your next lesson," Achibol said. "Your earlier changing led me to suspect you shared Dispucket's talent." That sent chills up and down Benadek's ribs. "It's no chance resemblance—you're patterning yourself after me because you haven't learned control. To survive, you must learn it."

"Why now, Master? If this . . . talent . . . has lain in me since birth, why only now does it plague me?"

Achibol recognized accusation in the lad's words. "You think I've triggered it? Think, boy. How long before we met did you find yourself becoming obsessed with poots? One change presaged the other. Besides, how do you know what changes you may have effected within yourself, unknowingly? Do you remember your father's aspect? Your mother's? How like them were you, or how like other urchins?" He shrugged. "No matter. Change is upon you, and you must deal with it. Shall we begin?"

They had gone half the length of the morass, and had an equal distance to travel—more or perhaps less depending on the routes they chose, on the wind's force and direction.

Benadek had been at his lessons for three days, with no impression of progress. He missed Sylfie. She had retired to the boat's cramped, humid cabin, and allowed no one but Teress to see her. Benadek knew she was ill, but Achibol would not speak of it, and the lad refused to ask anything of Teress. She darted evil glances at him when she thought he was not looking, and ostentatiously ignored him when she thought he was.

"Put Sylfie out of your mind," Achibol told him. "There's no time for distractions."

Some lessons were academic. Achibol had produced a real book with tiny printed characters and little paintings called photographs. Some pictures were flat and gray, others were colored. Some were magical and did not stay on the page, but popped out at him. All were of people.

There had been many kinds of ancient man, including dark-skinned ones like Achibol. "There,

Master. Bantu Chieftain, Kah One-eight-nine-seven. Master, you must be a Bantu."

"*Circa* eighteen ninety-seven," Achibol said. "It's an abbreviation."

"But it says here Bantu."

"No. 'Ca.' is 'Circa,' not 'Kah.' And I'm no Bantu. I'm pure all-American black. My ancestors were Yoruba, Cherokee, Irish, Ashanti, Scotch, Chaldean, Korean, Ibo, Mandingo, and Dutch. Maybe I have a little Bantu blood way back, though."

"I haven't seen Allamerkan in here. Maybe you're a Hausa?"

"Enough, boy! Have you measured your hand today?"

"This morning, Master. My fingers are no longer than they were, but my thumb has grown two millimeters. Or maybe it's my thumbnail."

"I'd be content with a thumbnail. Are you sure?" Visualization, concentrated effort to make predetermined changes, was the second facet of the lessons. Benadek felt foolish willing his hand to grow, but Dispucket was an ever-present reminder of the consequences of failure.

"I measured it from the ink-spot on my knuckle."

"Keep visualizing. Feel it growing. Feel the bone, muscle, and skin cells multiplying."

"What should that feel like? How can I visualize something that has always just happened?"

"They're your cells, not mine," the old man snapped. "Find out for yourself. It's all symbolic, anyway. At Sufawlz I'll show you pictures of cells—pictures of anything you want—but the sensations must be your own. Now: your hair? Can you feel it grow? Have you concentrated on its color?"

"Grow! It's not growing, it's dying. Look at this." Benadek ran a hand over his scalp. It came away with a thin handful of lank, black hair.

"Hmm. What have you done?"

"I pictured it pushing up through those little holes in my skin."

"Follicles."

"Yes, those. I tried to picture them making yellow hair like Sylfie's, but it's just falling out."

"Bend over here." Achibol parted the thinning strands of the apprentice's hair and peered at his scalp. "You've done it, boy! They're there. Little blond hairs. You've done it." He grasped Benadek's hands and danced with him around the cockpit, rocking the boat fiercely.

"What's happening?" Teress demanded, poking her head from the companionway.

"He's done it!" Achibol shouted. "Tell Sylfie! Benadek's changed."

"She's sick," Teress snapped. "She's sleeping." Her head disappeared abruptly.

Benadek worked at his lessons in earnest once he had demonstrated bodily change by will alone. His enthusiasm grew with his mastery. Over two days his eyes became brilliant blue-green. He pondered the opportunities, could he duplicate mayors, chiefs, and rich merchants. He considered the windfalls he could claim should he come to resemble the husband of a poot whose loveliness had lodged in his memory.

Not all his speculations were base. "Why wouldn't it have been easier to have stored the old human patterns for a thousand years, and have done away with the complications of poots, boffins, cozies, and honches?"

"And have had the new humanity awake to a world with no towns, roads, mills, ferryboats, bridges, or comfy inns? Think of simples as caretakers." Achibol shrugged. "Besides, living wombs are required. Patterns can be preserved, but mothers with breasts, cozies with hands to build cradles and grow crops?"

"I see," said Benadek.

His dark hair thinned and his blond stubble grew apace, a halo of pale gold. He learned to make cuts and scratches heal in minutes, and to make himself distasteful to voracious insects. "Clever tricks," Achibol muttered uneasily, "but he'll need much more to keep from becoming another Dispucket. Sooner or later, his new skills will be tested to his limits, perhaps beyond." He shuddered.

Though Benadek did not realize precisely whom he was patterning his new being after, he could have been Sylfie's brother (though simples were often denied blood resemblances by the temples). Achibol recognized the subconscious desire that guided the boy, the pain and concern under his bravado and self-involvement.

Benadek had not seen Sylfie. Teress became like a vixen in her den whenever he approached the companionway. Sylfie herself, behind the insect-cloth over the hatch, bade him stay away. "I don't want you to see me looking sick."

At the far end of the swamp the valley narrowed to a distant point marked by rising hills. Mooring out of the final channel, Achibol sent Benadek ahead over soggy hummocks and shallows. He returned wet and disheveled, and reported that their way was blocked. "They've strung logs across the river, and there are scores of tents on both sides. I've never seen so many honches."

"I feared as much," Achibol replied. A careful observer would have seen the sag in his narrow shoulders, the yellowing of his walnut skin. "There's another way out. We passed it a few days back. We'll have to abandon the boat and much of our baggage, but once on the level plains, we'll make it to Sufawlz almost as quickly as if we stayed on the river.

Three of them would make it, he thought dismally,

but not Sylfie. It was too late to get her to a temple. They'd have to wait in the swamp until she died. It would not be long.

CHAPTER THIRTEEN,

the travelers' flight, and the fatal consequence of Benadek's disobedience.

Little is said of Sylfie in most Achibol tales. Many never even name her, but the biocybes have given her real existence. Having chosen to ignore the moral content of the myths, Sylfie had either to be treated as real or be deleted. Perhaps her demise provides an easy way out.

Benadek's unreadiness to assume human responsibility is apparent. He is demonstrably able to *become*, but the *who* and the *what* of his "change"* are unknown.

"Changing" herein is to be feared, an attitude foreign to the polymorphic over-species we call *sapiens*. An absolute superiority of one form over others has never been considered. Are the biocybes trying to tell us that, in our remote past, it was?

We have accepted that evolution convergent toward mutability is inevitable. *Becoming*, we claim, is to the development of sapience as puberty is to an individual—painful but inevitable.

Have we unfairly ignored other hypotheses? Could there be an explanation for *becoming* besides convergence? It is not the place of this editor, a mythographer not a paleontologist, to propose them, but it is every sentient's duty to wonder . . .

(Saphooth, Project Director)

INTERLUDE
The Great School, Midicor IV

"That does it!" Abrovid decided, pulling the datacube from his terminal. "Old Saphooth's up to something. It's time to find Kaledrin and bring him back."

Midicor was a blue-white star. Unmodified simianforms like Saphooth could not remain exposed to its actinic light without damaging their delicate tissues. For Abrovid the barrage of radiation was life itself, and it took all his willpower not to forsake his quest, not to claim a plot of poolside sand and bask in it, leaving Kaledrin to his own mindless ecstasies.

---

* The biocybes' use the neutral "to change" in place of the accepted "to become." If *becoming* was indeed new and frightening in this "mythical" past, that makes sense. The verb *to become* would create an air of ease and familiarity false to the spirit of the tale.

Happily, his energy levels were not as depleted as Kaledrin's had been. He was able to resist sun, sand, and soft-chitined females beckoning from every pool, every mud-bank and sun-heated rock. Hopefully Kaledrin, when he found him, would have passed beyond the mindless stage and could leave of his own volition

"Where are you, Kal? I've got to bring you back before it's too late."

Achibol, bitterly silent, blamed himself for Sylfie's plight. He hoped one moment that a miracle would happen, and prayed the next that she would die, ending her suffering—if not his own.

Teress passed from one day to the next in the numb state of one who lingers overlong beside death-beds. She drank water and ate, but her circumscribed world had no room for sunlight or chatter.

Sylfie would not allow Achibol or Benadek to see her. She was no complainer, nor demanding; Teress wondered how anyone could be so damned nice. Then she spat disgustedly. Sylfie was a poot, she reminded herself, and poots were always nice. They even died nicely.

No one would tell Benadek anything. He ground his teeth in frustration. Sylfie had to beg him, through concealing screen or shuttered hatch, to stay away. He maintained his equilibrium by pushing himself to his limits. He taught himself to turn as dark as Achibol, then light again in an hour's time. He learned to make his hair grow inches in a day, the new growth any color he wanted. He shrank himself by half a head, then forced his spine and legs to lengthen until he towered over Achibol.

During each change his copious sweat discolored. His urine was yellow, rust, brown, and stunk of ammonia and corruption, much as Dispucket had smelled. Even his involuntary tears were tainted, and left his cheeks crusty and stained. He ached. Each change required careful visualization, and flawed imagery resulted in parts that failed to work properly together. He paid for mistakes with burning cramps, nagging pains in his joints, headaches, a knotted stomach, and foul, watery stools. He became quite knowledgeable of human anatomy.

His companions were marginally less uncomfortable. There was little breeze, so they had to pole the clumsy hull. The lack of breeze accentuated heat and humidity, so sweat did not cool them. Their skins became oily. They bathed often, though the water was currentless and undrinkable, a breeding ground for vicious insects. Achibol and Teress, badly stung, sickened from accumulated poisons. Benadek grew daily more concerned. The swamp had to end sometime, somewhere, didn't it?

Supplies spoiled in the dense, hot air. Benadek's changes required nourishment in great quantities; he would have consumed their last crumbs, had Achibol not acerbically suggested he learn to eat leaves, snails, and batrachian creatures snatched from water and overhanging vegetation.

Benadek complied. His internal organs seemed to know what they needed, and synthesized it from his crude diet. He learned to pay attention to cravings. Sucking the rusty iron tip of a boathook relieved him when meat was scarce; without conscious effort, his saliva became acidic, etching away red-brown and deep maroon oxides. He ate fur and bones, and consumed netted minnows whole.

He was not even disgusted. He visualized his body as a complex of organic reactions, and created symbolic visions of its processes. Food was mass, chemical structures to be broken down by the raging furnace within, then converted into . . . Benadek.

Yet for all his fine resolve, in the aftermath of meeting Dispucket, Benadek was not yet the man he wished to become, and whenever he ate something particularly strange—something that wiggled or squeaked when he crunched it between his strong, young teeth—he tried to make sure Teress noticed, and drew satisfaction in direct proportion to her disgust.

Days passed. Benadek ate and thrived while the others languished, until one morning . . .

An hour after sunup, the heat was oppressive. Benadek cracked open gritty eyes. Nothing moved. The swamp did not awaken with the sun, but with its setting. He stumbled to where Achibol had sprawled, feverish, as much unconscious as asleep. He felt the old man's forehead, and was relieved to find it dewed with sweat and cooler than the night before.

Teress did not answer his croaked inquiry, nor did Sylfie. He scooped greenish water and gulped it untasted. He paced the small cockpit, and tried to make out figures in the gloom below. Teress lay spread-eagled on the cabin sole. Sylfie was a shadow on the bunk, a dark convolution too small to be full-grown.

He grabbed handsful of leaves and stuffed them in his mouth, chewing noisily. He unfastened the mooring line, pushed the boat away, and poled it along a narrow channel, glancing frequently at Achibol and at the companionway.

Finally, his uneasiness became too great. He let the boat drift, then dropped into the cabin. He felt Teress's forehead, and snatched his hand away from its heat. Near at hand was a bowl of water and a rag. He wrung it damp and spread it over her forehead, then turned to Sylfie. As his eyes adapted further to the shadows, her still form became clear. Horrifyingly clear.

His breath caught in his throat. His trembling hand pulled back the sheet that almost covered her face.

It was not Sylfie. Sylfie was no ancient crone with skin like old paper over jutting bones, with white hair falling out on her pillow, and wrinkled, liver-spotted hands. Her dull, cloudy eyes stared, unseeing.

Her voice brought him back from the edge of madness—Sylfie's inflections, but an old voice that cracked and grated on his ears. "Is that you, Teress? I can't see you." Benadek trickled water over her dry, hot forehead. "That feels good," she murmured.

He took her withered hand. His tears fell on it. He willed her to *change*, to heal herself. He was not so mad with grief that he thought it would happen, but there was nothing else he could do except let his tears fall on her hands as he held them.

"Don't cry, Teress," she said, feeling his tears dotting her skin. "I chose this. I know you hate Benadek, but it isn't his fault." Her words were breathy and slow. Her mind had not failed, only everything else. "I mean that, Teress," she continued. "If you hate Benadek, you must hate me too. I've said that before." She panted softly. "If he succeeds, he'll change everything. There won't be any more poots like me, only . . . people." Her voice faded. Her weak, steady breathing indicated sleep.

Benadek climbed jerkily to the cockpit. He soaked his shirt in water and bathed Achibol's face and naked, bony chest, a chest that for all its years was no more shrunken than Sylfie's. He tapped a meager half-cup of potable water from the cask, and held Achibol's head for him to drink. The old man's eyes were clear. "You know," he stated. "You've seen her." Benadek nodded. "But . . . do you understand?"

Benadek said nothing. He laid Achibol's head back. Without emotion, he bathed Teress too. Without lust or anger, he cooled her body with the water-soaked rag. Her fever lessened. She opened her eyes, and looked up with vague comprehension, with what might have been reproach.

Sylfie was again awake. "It's Benadek," he said, not able to deceive her further.

"Benadek. I'm sorry. I didn't want you to see me . . . I wanted you to think of me as a pretty young poot forever." Her wrinkled brow furrowed. "Why did you come?"

"I had to," he choked. "I couldn't stand it any more, I missed you so much. I should have been here, taking care of you, but I didn't know."

"Take me up on deck. I don't have to hide any more. I want to die with the sun on my face."

"You can't die!"

"I want to. If there's anything after . . . then maybe I'll have a better chance. If you succeed . . . a better world. Real people, not simples. No more . . . handicaps."

"Handicaps?"

"Master Achibol's word. For people like me. You can change that."

"I don't know what to do! He hasn't told me anything."

"He doesn't know. At Sufawlz, you'll learn. Then you'll have to tell him what to do. And do it. For me."

"I don't want you to die."

"Benadek, my love," she said so softly he heard no trace of the wreck her voice had become, "there's no chance for us. There never was. Take me up into the sun, now?" He put his head on her emaciated breasts, the breasts he had taken joy in, a lifetime ago, and he wept. Her hand lifted to stroke the back of his head. All too soon it stopped.

Benadek stayed there, denying what he already knew from the absence of breathing and heartbeat. Then, in a feverish blur, he got up to check on the others. Teress was sweating freely. Achibol slept easily. Both were out of danger.

Kaleidoscopic visions rushed through Benadek's

tormented mind. He remembered Bassidon, where he had written "poots can't read." He visualized Sylfie playing the coquette on stage while Achibol performed. He saw himself ignoring her, walking with Achibol while she lead the mules. He remembered her silent sadness when she forgot things she had learned. He remembered making love, and soft, huddled nights. Sickened and ashamed, he recalled forcing her after Teress had shamed him, her silence thereafter, and her forgiveness. He saw the temple square in Lacedemon, and heard her magical tablet clatter across the cobbles, and he cringed at the look in her eyes: she had known she was going to die. "We'll have a little more time," she had said, later. More time—and he wasted it, letting her sit alone in the bow of the boat, unwilling to pass the hated Teress to go to her, absorbed in his own lessons, his own cares . . .

Even now he realized his latest selfishness: Sylfie lay in the dark cabin, her eyes staring, unclosed. He had ignored her last request: "I want to die with the sun on my face." He had wept, and she had comforted him, as if his grief over her passing were more important than her death itself.

That last revelation was too much. It was too late. Too late for anything. She could not even die in the sunlight, now.

Benadek could no longer endure her dead presence. He could no longer endure . . . himself. He leaped from the boat to a hummock, and half-ran, half-waded to the next rise, splashed through shallows, ran over stretches of ground, tripping and sprawling, then proceeding on all fours. Batrachian croaks, ophidian hisses, and the swish and rattle of small creatures unseen swelled to fill the disturbance of his passage. He could not stop, or his wretched thoughts would catch up with him. He plunged deeper into vast, trackless swamp.

Hours passed. He was safely, securely lost. At another time, he might have panicked—there were no sounds but the gurgles and croaks of small lizards and the booming calls of reptilian beasts, long-snouted and thick-tailed, that no longer tried to elude him. He named them crocodiles after mythical beasts.

Water, brush, and thick tree boles hid the signs of his passage. No echoing calls followed him. If the others knew he was gone, if they cared, they were far away. Sighing branches, lapping wavelets, and dense brush would snatch the sounds of their cries from the air.

Benadek stopped running. Slinking creatures with no names scuttled across his feet, unafraid. Uncaring and cold, they warmed themselves in the sun, ignoring him. One beast emerged from the water a few yards away. He watched it approach, impassive, uncaring. It could have killed him, but merely passed by, as uninterested as its small brethren. Benadek was no longer a stranger to the denizens of the morass. He belonged. The others knew. Their behavior showed it.

Immensely weary, he sank to the ground. He did not notice the sweat that beaded his forehead and ran down his sides, dark as dried blood. His skin took on a yellow-green hue. His hair was falling out. While he slept his testicles withdrew like a baby's. His penis pulled back, like a turtle's wrinkled neck into its shell.

Benadek awakened to terrible thirst. He dragged himself toward water, his stubby arms out at his sides and his body slung between like a sack. His belly dragged, and his legs cramped tightly against his sides. His coccyx uncurled, elongating into a tail. His anus was an invisible slit at its base.

The water was green and full of life. In it, he saw his face. Only then did he experience brief psychic agony. Now it's all gone: Sylfie and I, and all the dreams. He was doomed, like Dispucket, but to a worse fate. There would be no visions, no creatures to share their sight with him. He would be alone amidst others of his kind—cold, unfeeling reptiles without the spark of vivacious intelligence of the birds and mammals Dispucket knew. It was only fair. Someday he would die, and if he had a spirit, as Sylfie believed, it would perhaps join hers in some unimaginable place where poots could all read, and where urchins learned to care for their fellows more than for their own survival.

Benadek saw his snout reflected in the water, and peered into the wavery image of his reptilian eyes. His vision blurred. Tears? No, merely nictitating membranes, not fully formed yet. He lowered his snout to the water, scooped a mouthful, and tilted his head back for it to trickle down his throat. Already he was learning what he needed to know in this new life. He looked down at his gnarled, knotty hands, his splayed fingers fast becoming sharp, pointed toes, and wished he could weep. He remembered something Achibol had said: "crocodile tears" were not tears of grief.

CHAPTER FOURTEEN,

wherein Benadek is rescued from himself.

It becomes difficult to regard this account as "myth." Even holy Grandfather—myth within myth—is shorn of his supernatural aura. He could be a cracked pot instead of an ancestral calvarium. The computers themselves have ceased to "believe" in magic, and report only the tangible and prosaic.

But second-guessing biocybernetic minds has its own perils. Take Achibol's statement that Benadek might be "the last of his kind" (in this context, the sole ancestor of modern humanity). While lending credence to the one-world theory on one hand and adding suspense to the narrative on the other, the notion itself seems preposterous.

Even dedicated one-worlders do not claim that the whole human gene pool sprang from the unimpressive loins of one lone individual whose futile striving for reproductive success gives the tale comic relief.

What tenuous but immutable logic has forced the biocybes to retain this? Is the answer buried in the dim past, or within the tumorlike memories of the computers themselves? It is as inaccessible as a trip to yesterday or the heart of a star. We can only trust that logical bonds do exist, and hope that further "feedings" of newly unearthed myths will add to the tale.

On a hundred worlds, scholars delve in ancient archives for more legends, "food for thought" for the biocybes, but progress is slow. Future input will only be found in village temple attics, in translations of Karbic medicine-runes, Emboth rock writings, and oral histories narrated by shamans on backwater worlds.

A thousand scholars would be too few—and scholars must eat, must buy oil for the crude lamps that light their way through ancient passageways and illumine their notetaking by peasant firesides. They must buy, often with their savings, baubles and trinkets for their informants.

Another volume like this depends not only on their dedication, but on your generosity. Have you enjoyed this as much as a night in a synthisense pavilion, an afternoon excursion to your family burial plot? Your sacrifice of one ephemeral pleasure might make a crucial difference—for who knows from what source revelation may come? Perhaps from a hungry myth collector debating whether to miss one more meal to buy a fresh holocorder powerpack, or from a reluctant medicine-priest whose lips are loosened by the sight of glassite beads on a string . . .

(Saphooth, Project Director)

Teress found Sylfie's body. Maintaining control of her emotions lest stress and sickness bring on the *change*, she awakened Achibol. They brought the frail remains on deck. At that moment, Benadek's absence registered on the old man's recovering brain.

They scoured the boat for a note or other indication of his whereabouts. Teress noticed that the rag she had used to cool Sylfie's fevers was not where she had left it. From that small clue they guessed with surprising accuracy what had transpired while they had lain in fevered sleep.

"We must find him. He'll *change*, and won't be able to stop."

It might do him good, Teress thought cruelly. He would make a fine flying toad, or a . . . Aloud, she said "Can't we wait? He'll come back sooner or later—I did."

"The boy holds no monopoly on arrogance," Achibol growled. "Had I not come for you, you'd be yowling, eating guts, and pissing from trees. You'd have remained half-cat until some hunter killed you." He paused for breath, and bridled his anger. "Benadek's ability to *change*, like Dispucket's, is far beyond yours. Untrained, he'll become so different we'll never know him, nor he us. As you became physically half-cat, your mind changed. Wasn't your father's last kill a cat? I saw its rotting hide on the curing-frame."

Teress nodded. "It was fresh in my mind."

"What will Benadek become? A fish? A songtoad? A great lizard, most likely. He'll complete the physical *change*, and the mental one. He'll *be* a lizard, with no human mind to bring him back."

Teress felt sorry for the old man. He, at least, would miss Benadek. "The swamp goes on forever—how will we find him?"

"I'll ask Grandfather," the sorcerer said mysteriously. "Help me drag my trunk up here."

Had fever affected the old man's brain? The trunk? Achibol motioned her to sit, and drew forth . . . Grandfather.

Their helpmate was a brown, misshapen skull, and a matching heavy jawbone with no chin. Teress knew little anatomy, but those bones would not have fit beneath the skin of anyone she knew. The low cranium bulged rearward where normal heads were flat. It was flat above the eyebrows, where ordinary foreheads rose, and had a heavy ridge over the eye sockets. Its owner must have been remarkably ugly.

Achibol lifted the calvarium from its resting place, closed the trunk, and set his burden on it, facing him. "Grandfather," Achibol addressed it, "I need your help."

<Light, boy!> the skull replied, its words hollow as the ancient cranium. <A candle! These old eyes see but dimly by the light of such a feeble moon.> The sun was shining.

"Of course, Grandfather. A candle, Teress." She went along with the charade, and snatched one from the running light nearest her. Achibol lit it with a flourish, a trick the pure-human had tried without success to fathom. "Careful, girl," he cautioned. "Drip no wax on Grandfather's fine old gourd. Have you no respect for the old, the infirm?" Placing a gnarled hand alongside his mouth, he addressed her in a conspiratorial aside: "In his day, the sun and moon were as big as apples, not these small, dim coins we see—or so he claims." The sun seemed ordinarily bright to Teress.

"He's a bit deaf, too," Achibol whispered, "deafened by cannon at the battle of Shiloh." Teress had been exposed to Achibol's tricks from early childhood. She raised a quizzical eyebrow and awaited his further whimsy, not long in coming.

"Grandfather! Old fellow, are you awake?" Aside, to Teress, he said, "It's hard to tell, isn't it? If he had eyelids . . ." Grandfather said nothing. "It's Umry's boy Achibol, Gramps. Wake up, won't you? I have a question."

Teress grew impatient. "Why all the hoko-tonko? It's only an old bone."

"An old bone? This is my ancestor, my most ancient relation. Those eyesockets have gazed upon times beyond imagining. Tell her, Grandpa," he pleaded.

<Cold and damp,> the skull echoed. <Long-dead flowers' crushed petals graced my grave-pit. I lay bound and ochered, my spirit trapped by those mortal remains.>

"Wake up, old gourd, you're not in your grave. This is the future, and I'm your grandson Achibol. You remember me, Achibol."

<Who sneezes?> the skull asked, annoyed. <Who keeps sneezing? What passes, here?>

"Time passes, Grandsire. Awaken and aid me."

<Awake, I am, and cruel it is. This is neither my grave nor my snug glass showcase. Has the museum been robbed? Am I in thieves' hands?>

"There are no thieves. I am Achibol."

<A sneeze! I heard it again. Achoo! Achoo! Ah! That silly name. I remember you now. You're Archie Scribner, Umry's brat. Runny nose, sniffles, sneezes. What do you want, boy?> The skull sounded petulant. Teress barely suppressed a giggle. Achibol glared fiercely at her. <My back hurts,> Grandfather complained. <You're supposed to oil it, and rub it for me.>

"You have no back anymore, Grandfather." How young Achibol sounded. How incongruous the voice of a small boy piping from between ancient, shrivelled lips. It was as funny as hearing *his* voice coming from . . . Grandfather. It was hard not to laugh aloud. "There's been only your poor old squash for . . . oh, it's been centuries. Don't you remember the fire? When you lost your last remaining femur? I barely saved what you have left now, and a few finger-bones."

<Ah! I knew it! I knew you took those fingers. Sold them to those priests. Don't think I don't know whose fingers you *claimed* they were, either.>

"Enough, Grandpa. I need to find a lost boy."

<Lost? Achibol, you say? Young Umry's son? Are you lost, boy?>

"Not me, old bone. Benadek, my apprentice, is lost." To Teress, Achibol whispered "I hate it when he's like this. He's not really senile, just mean and stubborn. *I'll* never be like that when I'm his age." That time, Teress did laugh out loud. Achibol's glare silenced her.

<Well, what then?> Grandfather sputtered petulantly. <If you can't just ask, then put me back in my box. Drafts! I hate drafts.> The candle flame danced momentarily and the sail cover's light fabric fluttered ever so slightly. <Archie? How can I find this apprentice if you play silly games? Get me a map.>

Achibol gestured briskly to the girl, then toward the companionway and the chart rack. "Quickly! Before he forgets." Teress found the fabric map, and unfolded it next to the skull. "Hold it where *he* can see it," the mage said. "No, never mind." He turned Grandfather instead, and held a finger to the chart. "We're here, Grandfather. Where is he?"

<Of course we're here, Archie. Where else would we be? If we were *there*, then there would be here. The boy's south and west of us. There's a sandy spot, and trees, and open water . . . >

"Trees are everywhere. Be more specific."

<Bossy, impudent child! South first, then west. Yes, like that.> Achibol's eyes narrowed as if a scene were painted on his eyelids. His finger moved a tiny distance.

<Further west. No, not so far. He's a boy, not a

fish? Then he hasn't gone that far.> Again, the sorcerer's long, brown finger moved a short distance. <There! A lovely beach of soft, white sand. He lies asleep. But wait! A boy, you said? A green boy? And that snout! He's not yours, Archie. Not with that long nose.>

"Tell me more," Achibol demanded in a quiet, deadly tone.

<What's to tell? You're here, he's there. You know how to find him. Now put me back in the box. This air is damp as my grave.>

"Grandfather?" Achibol prompted. He waited without reward. "It's no use," he told Teress. "I hate it when he's stubborn. It would be easier if he still had flesh to pinch." His words might have been intended to be funny, but they fell flat on Teress's ears. "Ah, well," he said as he lifted the trunk lid, "we know how to find Benadek . . . But what we'll find . . . "

Teress remained silent. Such absurd showmanship was best confined to a magic show, or performed with a small girl on his lap. The matter at hand was far too serious for mummery. She became more comfortable moments later when Achibol stood, all business again, and issued directions to ready the boat.

Unable to bury Sylfie among the tangled roots and watery muck, they laid her remains at the base of a large tree and covered them with brush. Neither cried or said words over her. Soon Achibol was wielding the pole with steady hands, snaking them along the winding, narrow waterway, away from Sylfie's grave.

He *does* know where Benadek is, Teress realized. But how? Surely not because that old headbone told him. But he's carried it with him all this time. Could it serve some real purpose? She would ask him later, and not accept any of his nonsense for an answer.

They came to open water about mid-afternoon, and raised mast and sail. The sun was hot, the sky unrelieved by a single cloud, and they were soon moving at a good clip. Achibol's hands were easy on sheet and tiller, and he seemed unconcerned about snags or sandbars, so she gratefully let her fever-weakened mind and body slip into sleep.

Once, while Teress slept, Achibol luffed the sail and drifted for a quarter hour. He lifted the ancient skull from his trunk, and held it in front of him, staring into its empty orbits, seeing within those shadowed holes . . . what? It was a short interlude, and after a brief perusal of the map, the sorcerer put the skull away. He worked the craft back into the wind and sailed straight until the sky reddened in the west, then steered toward the edge of the open water, which only in places warranted being called "shore." He raised both leeboards and coasted onto a muddy beach.

"Is this it?" Teress asked sleepily. "Where is he?"

"Not yet. This is no sandy beach, but clay—and slippery. Watch your step. We've sailed to the far side of this lake, but we've been blown further along than I'd have wished. In the morning the wind will shift, and we'll sail directly to him. At any rate, it will get dark soon, and the wind's dying."

"Will we be too late?"

"Possibly. But we mustn't give up."

They slept on the boat, mostly free of mud-bred insects. Teress asked questions about Grandfather, but Achibol dismissed them unanswered. "Later, girl. That seeking is the only true magic I know, and I can't explain it. Even discussing it, I might begin to doubt—and there's no time for that."

In the morning, after a skimpy breakfast of soggy crackers, they set sail again. The wind alternated between the port forequarter and abeam, so they were either close-hauled or reaching all the time. Teress liked it best when the sail was sheeted in tightly and the hull leaned against the rushing water. Then, it seemed they would reach their destination in no time. She did not ponder her eagerness to find Benadek; perhaps it was only the contagion of Achibol's desire, but whenever the wind shifted and the mage eased out the sail, she fidgeted. The easy wallowing motion of a beam reach seemed to get them nowhere, and she urged Achibol to make them go faster.

"We're moving toward our destination faster now than when we were close to the wind," he explained, "though with less splashing and rushing. Our speed before was an illusion, a better one than I could ever create. See! There's the beach. Take the helm, and I'll guide us closer." Their speed fell off as he climbed the mast and guided Teress with gestures. From the height of his vantage he saw that the shore they approached was more apparent than real. The gritty strand was an old sandbar that divided clear water from swamp. "He's close. I can feel it. Slack the sail and run us up on the sand—there."

After they beached, everything seemed quieter, but Teress realized they'd only traded one kind of sound for another. Beyond the brush that divided the sandy side of the bar from the swamp rose all the croaking, squeaking, and chittering they'd left behind for the brief day's sail. The heat and humidity of the morass struck her with greater force than before.

"Listen," Achibol bade her. "Do you hear it?" Teress heard only the gruntings of beasts, the sunset chattering of smaller creatures. "There. That one. That's no beast." It was possible, she admitted, that the groaning of one beast was a few tones higher than the others, that it resembled—ever so slightly—human agony, but without Achibol she would never have singled it out.

They pushed through tangled willow-brush, following the sound, seeing nothing but leaves, stems, and the sky overhead. As Teress broke through the final barrier, there was a hissing, grunting moan almost at her feet. She backed up, stumbling on springy willows. Achibol's words paralyzed her further: "That's him. That's Benadek."

It was once Benadek, perhaps, though she could not accept it. Though she too had known the *change*, she had seldom seen herself then, or been conscious of her murky reflected image as she drank. Somehow, she pictured herself as still human during that period, though she knew it had not been so. What she saw now was not human.

The lizard lay half-submerged in swamp water turned opaque with its exudations. Only its stubby snout, its back, and its bowed front legs were exposed. Its clawed feet might once have been hands—they still had five digits, though the outermost ones were tiny and useless. It reeked. The stink of carrion, ammonia, and vinegar inundated her. Scent-memory, primeval and intense, threatened to drag her back to the last time she had smelled it—as she had *changed*.

She forced herself to focus not on her fear but on the thing sprawled before her. Its skin was mottled yellow-green and brown, nubbed and bumpy, crusted with drying residue of the *change*. Its eyes, even by dusky light, were black slits with yellow irises. Milky nictitating membranes flickered up-down-up. Wrinkled lids drooped and then opened wide, as if they disbelieved what they saw. She looked in vain for intelligence in those eyes. "We're too late, aren't we?"

"I don't know. Here, help me pull him out of the water."

Teress bent to grasp a rough, reptilian limb. "It's . . . he's so heavy!"

"Yes. Better this than lost mass, though. He's absorbed nutrients from the muck. He'll need them if . . . when he *changes* again." Achibol knelt beside the lumpy shape. Teress observed that its legs were more human than the rest of it, though drawn up in cramped rigor near its ribs.

"Ah, boy, what have I brought you to?" the sorcerer moaned. "Can you understand me? Do you remember words?"

The thing that had been Benadek opened its mouth in a laborious, foul-smelling hiss. "Good! Excellent! Then listen well. You must remember you are a boy, a man. You are Benadek, my apprentice, who walks on two legs. Do you remember?" There was no response from the distorted lizard. Achibol's face twisted in despair. Teress shrugged sympathetically.

"Benadek, Benadek, you must try, you must remember yourself in order to . . ." Achibol murmured on and on, reminding the inert beast of all that he had been, describing the boy Benadek over and over, remembering detail after detail and recounting each aloud. But there was no response. The lizard might have been dead but for the yellow gleam of its eyes.

Teress felt useless. She stared at the darkening ugliness of the swamp, swatting tiny night-flies more annoying than painful. She went back and forth between the far end of the strand and the place where Achibol knelt, crooning and murmuring without success.

"Shit!" Teress said aloud. "I must be crazy." Achibol raised his face to look at her. It was too dark to read her expression. "I'll try it for a while."

"You have no obligation to . . ."

"Just shut up," she said disgustedly. "I'll do it. You're not getting anywhere."

"That is so." He moved aside to make room for her.

"Leave me with him. Go on back to the boat and rest."

Reluctantly, the mage rose. Helplessly, with no spring in his step, he pushed aside the tangles and worked his way to the sandy side. He checked the line from the boat. He lowered the sail and wrapped it. After that, there was nothing to do. He tried to study the stars, but his eyes kept blurring.

He never knew how far he went up the beach, but he must have been gone for several hours. Feeling guilty at having left Teress so long, he pushed back along the path.

At first he saw nothing, then objects took on a dim, reddish glow—the same red glow that had illumined pursuing honches on the far side of Vilbursiton, when he had unthinkingly steered the murderous band to Teress's camp; the same glow that had lit the doors into temples' inner rooms, and the cave where Teress had lurked. By that odd light he saw Benadek as an indistinct crimson shadow. A reptile, he thought dejectedly. Not much heat in it at night. Teress, by contrast, was like a torch, glowing lava radiating intense heat.

The pure-human girl had removed her clothes, and was parading proudly, nakedly before the reptilian form. Achibol remained still, listening.

"You remember *this*, don't you?" Her voice dripped scorn. Achibol cringed, afraid that she would drive Benadek even further away. He cursed himself for underestimating the depth of her hatred for the boy. "Of course you remember," Teress snarled. "*This* is the very last thing you'd forget, isn't it?"

The reptile hissed. It grunted, and struggled to pull itself up on its malformed forelegs. "Oh, yes!" she spat. "You're still Benadek under that snake-skin. I'll bet you're really pissed, but you can't say a word. All this time you wanted me, and now here I am, and you can't do a thing! Just think about all the times you wished you could fuck me. What will you do now, if I get on top of you? Hiss at me? Bite me?" She laughed malignantly. Benadek let out a high-pitched hoot unlike any lizard sound. To Achibol, it did sound angry.

Teress, grown impatient with crooning and

reminding Benadek what a nice boy he had once been, had tried a different tack, and . . . it seemed to be working. The boy was responding.

Achibol retreated, and paced back and forth in front of the boat, never more than a few steps from the path through the willows. He occasionally heard a loud hiss, and that strange, unlizardlike hooting.

The sun was coming up. Teress sat on the sand, still nude, and Benadek lay on his back, his head on her lap. He looked like a very dead lizard—his belly flaccid and white, his arms/forelegs lifeless, the baggy skin of his neck wrinkled and still. His snout seemed oddly different. Was he *changing* again? Achibol could not tell, but Teress seemed content. He could hear her crooning, though he could not make out her words. Too tired to pace further, the old man climbed back on the boat and stumbled below. He fell asleep on the narrow bunk where Sylfie had died.

"Master Achibol, come here!" Groaning, the mage swung his thin shanks over the edge of the bunk and wiped sweat from his eyes. Full, bright daylight glared through the companionway. How long had he slept? He pulled himself out of the cabin, dropped over the rail, and set off at a lope.

He found Teress washing Benadek with swamp water, which soaked into the sand beneath him, leaving a dark, odiferous stain. Her thighs and belly were smeared with the same stuff, but she did not seem to notice. Benadek looked horrible, though obviously almost human. His warty hide was scaling off like peeling sunburn, and underneath was pale pink skin. His eyes, alert and intelligent, were blue where they had been yellow, framed by a face that (though not recognizably the mage's apprentice) was unquestionably the same species.

"He's still changing, Master Achibol, but it was a

mistake for me to remain with him so long. Look." She pointed to the juncture of Benadek's thighs. Achibol stared. Where crinkled reptilian skin had so recently been, the flesh had folded, forming a new structure. New, but not entirely unfamiliar to the old man. Not entirely.

"At least she's human," he said with the faintest hint of a chuckle. "I wonder if she'll be as pretty as you?"

Teress frowned. "Can't you do something?"

"You, of all people, should see the irony of it, Teress. What could be more humbling for the boy?" As her frown intensified, he hurriedly assured her that he would try. "He may be patterning himself on you or, considering his new blue eyes, on his memories of Sylfie. If the latter, my presence will make little difference. We'll have to see. Either would be preferable to another Achibol." He knelt next to the silent figure and whispered in its ear. Teress, utterly exhausted, stiff from hours kneeling and sitting with Benadek, stretched out on the sand and fell immediately asleep.

Thus went the day, with Achibol and Teress alternately talking to Benadek, forcing him to respond first with gestures and grunts, then finally with words. Once small, perfect breasts formed on his chest—a grotesque parody of femininity, because Benadek had already reformed his genitalia on Achibol's impressive scale. "You must be a man," Teress whispered. "I want you to have a smooth, hard chest. Then you can have me, if you want. Be a man for me." Achibol snorted, his skin darkening in what may have been a blush. Teress glared at him.

"Sylfie," Benadek muttered.

"I'm not Sylfie," she replied. "I'm Teress."

"Sylfie," Benadek persisted, "Sylfie's dead. I . . . my fault. Better I died."

"Sylfie wanted you to live. She said she wanted us to . . . to be . . ."

"Benadek," Achibol interrupted, "Sylfie asked Teress to take her place when she was gone. She loved you, and wanted you to go on. She expected it. You must, for her."

"Teress?" Benadek said softly. "You? Sylfie?"

Understanding what he was trying to say, she nodded. "You must become Benadek again, for Sylfie and me."

"Yes," he agreed, "Benadek. Me." His eyelids drooped.

Achibol squeezed his shoulder. "Have you stabilized, boy? Do you dare sleep now?"

Benadek blinked. His eyes and his face were entirely human. He had no hair yet, but his next words assured Achibol and Teress that he soon would: "I can sleep. The . . . *change* will continue."

"I'll bring blankets from the boat," Achibol said. "Then we can all rest."

"You knew!" Teress accused the mage when he returned. "How could you know?"

"I guessed," the oldster half-admitted. "It wasn't hard, knowing Sylfie—and you. You came to care very much for her, and she loved Benadek, for all his faults. How could you have refused *her*?"

Achibol and Teress alternated watching Benadek through dusk and darkness. When morning came, they lit a small fire on the sand and brewed tea. The strong aroma aroused Benadek, who sat up, and then stood. Achibol and Teress both stared at his nude form. He was taller than Achibol, more mature than before, with broad shoulders and heavy bones, but thin to the point of emaciation. His hair stuck up straight and fuzzy, a dark bronze. He poured his own tea, then sat.

"Will you swim with me?" he asked Teress. "I promise not to sit on your clothes." She looked sharply at him, then grinned. She set down her cup and tossed off her blanket. Beneath it, she too was nude. "That's an easy promise to keep."

He grinned, and took her hand. Achibol rolled his eyeballs at both of them. They went through the brush to the fresher water near the boat, but returned sooner than the oldster expected, clean and pink from the cool water. There had been no time for more than swimming. Was he disappointed?

"Are you stabilized, boy?" he asked sharply. "Is that form enough to your liking for you to keep it a while?"

"For now," Benadek answered seriously, "but there'll be others later on."

"No hurry, you understand? I'm too old to be learning new faces all the time—and your last one . . . ach!" Benadek and Teress laughed. Achibol drank the last of the tea while the two young people readied the boat.

"You don't have to keep any promises you made when . . . during the *change*," Benadek told her. "I know what you said, when I needed it, but you don't have to."

Teress smiled. "Thank you. I'm glad you feel that way. No promises, then. But that doesn't mean you can't ask, sometime."

"I will," he said with a broad grin, "and I'm sorry for everything, before. I just didn't understand. All I'd ever known was poots. And you're not like a poot—you're more like a boy, in a way."

"A boy! I think I liked you better when you wanted to rape me! A boy?"

"I'm sorry! I can't say what I mean. I never knew anyone like you, that's all."

"Never mind," she replied with a shake of her head. "We're both learning things. We both acted as best we knew." A boy, indeed!

INTERLUDE
The Great School, Midicor IV

Kaledrin pushed himself from the terminal. "I'm glad you came for me. Do you understand where he's heading with this?"

"Saphooth? Not really," Abrovid admitted, "but he's obviously onto something everyone else is missing. I'd hoped you could explain it."

"'Another explanation for *becoming* besides convergence,'" Kaledrin quoted. "He's fishing, hoping someone else will come forth with an idea he's already had, that he's afraid to take responsibility for. He's awfully gentle on the one-world idea, but he can't be thinking of that—it's been too well discredited. If we toss out that, and convergence, what's left? What possible evolutionary mechanism?" Kaledrin entwined his eyestalks and his motile mouth-tendrils in a gesture of puzzled exasperation. "Hmmph. When is Chapter Fifteen expected, Ab? I'd like to see it before Saphooth has a chance to think about it."

"Too late," Abrovid said, holding up a second datacube. "Here it is, along with his introduction to it—he already submitted them to the net."

---

* This episode prompted sanity tests during which the biocybes were determined to be wholly in possession of their wits, as it were. The tale has been certified by the respected biocyberneticist, Dr. Abrovid, as a rational result of their programmatic deliberations.

CHAPTER FIFTEEN,

wherein safe harboring is found in a nest of bodiless souls.

No longer content to strip the legends of everything mystic and supernatural, the biocybes proceed to rid this myth of even the natural aspects of *becoming*, substituting elaborate machinery and fabricated biochemicals.

RNA transfer of molecular memory is not only "natural" and "human," but is the basis for the biocybes' own thinking processes. Have the Great School's computers, inundated with conflicting data, developed quirks?*

But let us not doubt. Instead, let us ask what must follow from literal acceptance of this tale. One is forced not only to accept the one-world hypothesis, but to carry it further by throwing population genetics and paleontology aside and postulating a single common ancestor for all humanity, and another explanation for *becoming* besides convergence. Then, credulity already stretched to breaking, one must accept that our hypothetical ancestor arose not in a planetary paradise, but as an evolutionary response to the mutagenic cesspool his own ancestors had made of his world. It is neither elevating nor flattering. It may even be ominous.

(Saphooth, Project Director)

INTERLUDE
The Great School, Midicor IV

"Most Sapient One," Kaledrin addressed Saphooth, suppressing his anger. He did not venture beyond the open door to the latter's office.

"Ah! Kaledrin," Saphooth replied jauntily. "I trust you enjoyed your rest? Your body-plates gleam, and your eyestalks no longer droop."

"I'm quite well, thank you," Kaledrin answered. "But I'm puzzled by the direction this project has taken in my absence."

"Ah? Of course you are. As am I. Is that new? From the very first, the biocybes have taken us by surprise again and again."

"I refer to your commentary, not the text," Kaledrin spat, committing himself. "It goes beyond the bounds of our study. What, exactly, are you leading to? Either these tales are—as you state on one hand—a farce and a fantasy, or they are not—as you equally fervently avow elsewhere."

"I state nothing. I avow nothing. My words are meant only to illuminate the pitfalls of simplism and linear thought."

Saphooth was always quick to smooth his path with equivocal words. Nevertheless, Kaledrin pressed on. "You have an agenda, Elevating One, and the editorial commentaries on these installments are not the place for it. The Board of Trustees will surely agree. Publish your speculations in the popular media, not under MYTHIC's aegis."

Saphooth was taken aback. Perhaps, he thought, I'd have been wiser to have let him collapse from overwork. But he remained quick on his mental feet. "Very well then," he said with hardly a pause. "Be as noncommittal as you wish. Others will speculate, and you'll know nothing about it until it hits you right in your sensorium." Saphooth drew himself up to full height, towering over Kaledrin's bulk. "There is," he said with oratorical majesty, "nothing like heated controversy, even notoriety, to advance an otherwise stodgy and undistinguished career."

He spun upon one heel, an action particularly well suited to his spindly simian form. The door irised shut behind him. It was an eloquent gesture, one Kaledrin was sure he had long rehearsed.

The confrontation was over. It was just as well, Kaledrin admitted, because he had nothing further to say. He had gotten what he wanted, at any rate. What he thought he wanted. The project was once again under his control. The threat that the mere mention of the Board of Trustees represented had been the key. But Saphooth, as usual, had the last word. Kaledrin uneasily wondered if he would have the last laugh, too.

Ten days later—thin, haggard, brown as nuts—three exhausted travelers drew their algae-stained, battered boat ashore in a tiny cove. Above and around them steep talus slopes gave way to steeper black cliffs, so high that the midmorning sun had yet to shine directly on the valley floor. Achibol was optimistic about finding a way to the top, and thus out of the morass.

They scuttled the boat offshore, weighted with blocks of frost-broken basalt. They laid Achibol's trunks on a travois of light poles and distributed a few tools and belongings between three rude knapsacks sewn from an old sail.

The winding animal paths to the top of the cliff were the most arduous part of their ensuing journey, and once behind them, the going was easy. Open grasslands stretched to the north, with a hint of purple-gray hills on the horizon. Game was plentiful; they dined on great-rabbit and ground-pig stews thickened with oystery primrose root, flavored with sage and salt. Benadek and Teress began to fill out healthily. Achibol gained no weight, but regained the wiry bounce in his stride, and only occasionally became gray and waxy-skinned when their daily trek stretched on close to sunset. He assured his companions that his "malfunction" was minor.

They walked for seven days. Achibol was pleased to confirm that the truce between his companions was holding. A casual observer might have called it friendship. They walked together much of the time, or in a rank of three with the old man.

Perhaps, indeed, Benadek was maturing, Achibol thought. Perhaps, indeed, he will become a man, and less obnoxious. But whenever the sorcerer entertained such hopes Benadek the boy, the urchin, surfaced again, farting noisily and obnoxiously while walking ahead of the others, or pulling a six-legged toad from a pocket when they stopped to rest, and . . .

Occasional streams caused them to break their stride, but those were slow and shallow. There were no signs of habitation. That, Achibol told them, was not much different than in ancient times, when the land had been used to graze beasts. Ruins of farmsteads and small towns were now grassy mounds and jutting artificial stones.

They saw Sufawlz's ruins from a distance. Their true destination was on the outskirts, a discrete settlement once pent within high metal fences, now no different from other mounds and irregularities.

The mage drew out his talisman, the universal interface, and tapped several keys. He turned in a full circle, watching the readout. "This way." He headed southwest. Whenever he wavered, the talisman gave a chirp, and he corrected his course. He had only gone a few hundred yards when he stopped. "It's right here," he said.

There was grass aplenty, and sky, but nothing else. Seeing Benadek's and Teress's expressions, Achibol said "The ancients were like squirrels—they buried everything valuable." He tapped other keys. Underneath his feet, Benadek felt the earth shudder. Teress grabbed his arm. "Whoo!" the mage exclaimed, "I don't think there's much soil over it. I hope there's enough juice."

"His devices need sunlight," Benadek explained to Teress, "from which they squeeze the juice. Like tiny cider-presses."

Teress, who had been taught about such things, said, "It's called electricity." She refrained from telling him that the "juice" Achibol was concerned about was that in the facility below. Benadek was nicer now, and she was careful not to bruise his fragile ego and chance causing him to revert. She need not have been concerned; the changes in Benadek went beyond appearance. He was different for his traumatic experience, though all that could be observed was that he was quieter and less inclined to make wisecracks.

"What's happening, Master Achibol?" she asked tremulously.

"Beneath us, the 'gate' into the Sioux Falls Experimental Complex—Biopsych Three—is pushing against the soil that's blown over it. It's a miracle it's functioning at all, a thousand years beyond its designers' intentions . . . but then, I'm surprised anything has survived—not least myself. Temples, satellites . . . I must force myself not to believe in some god overseeing all that we petty mortals strive for, and aiding us, perchance."

Benadek sprung back. The ground bulged upward. With sudden déjà vu, he expected some kin of the unfortunate Dispucket, but what emerged was a dull metal cylinder, eight feet high and of equal diameter. Its top remained heaped with soil but its sides looked brushed clean. With a ratchety groan, part of its surface slid aside.

"Good," Achibol said. "The door needs lubricating, though. Well? Let's go." He stepped inside the cylinder. Benadek followed. Teress clung to his arm. The inside chamber was small and they had to squeeze together. "Now we go down," Achibol explained. The far wall, Benadek observed, was transparent like glass, but without bubbles or flaws. It looked out on metal patched with whitish efflorescence, a wall that suddenly began to move.

Achibol seemed relaxed—though their strange conveyance rumbled and shuddered ferociously—so Benadek and Teress remained outwardly calm also. The metal wall beyond the window disappeared at the top of the clear pane, replaced by progressive layers of gray and dark reddish rock. They were dropping below the surface of the earth. At least it was not dark; the very walls seemed to glow. The ride went on and on.

"What part of the plan was served here?" Benadek asked, to take his own mind off the vibrating floor. "And why is it no longer?"

"The idea was to reconstruct ancient humanity via the temples and the simples, and then pack them with the memories stored here—all the skills to rebuild the world. Some hoped to restore themselves with their personalities intact. Immortality, of a sort."

"You mean they planned to take over the ones who took on their memories? And you expect me to do it? What'll happen to me?"

"They never solved the problems of personality transfer. There was no way to get rid of the original personality. Electric erasure proved temporary, while chemical means left residues that resulted in madness; brain-burn destroyed too much, too indiscriminately. There's little danger to anyone with a strong self-image—unless more than one or two 'memories' are taken. Then there's no telling what might happen. There are horror stories . . ."

"What's it like down there—down here?" Benadek was not ready for horror stories. Maintaining a superficial calm was hard enough in the groaning, shuddering little room. He didn't even want to guess how far down they had come.

"It's probably no different than the inside of a temple, but on a grand scale."

A new view rose in the window, contradicting him. Their tiny room was dropping slowly past a great, open chamber dimly lit by scattered points of light, reflected from crystal windowpanes and glittering balcony-rails. Silvery footbridges stretched like spiderwebs between brick, stone, and textured metal towers that reached from unimaginable depths to the cavern roof they had come through. There were arched loggias, crenelated walkways, stepped corbels carved with ornate swirls, and cantilevered platforms that jutted wildly and defied conviction that they must surely bend beneath their own weight.

"What are they?" Benadek asked in a hoarse murmur.

"Living quarters, I imagine," Achibol replied emotionlessly, though his own fixed stare belied his tone. "See how the cavern roof has been smoothed and painted blue? From below, with proper lighting, it must look like the sky."

Already, the sky-ceiling was dim grayness far above. Balconies, fenestrations, and rococo buildings rose past them and out of sight. The cavern floor rose toward them. "I wonder if those trees are dead, or merely dormant," Achibol asked, pointing. "I can't conceive of their remaining alive all this time. The planners must have intended to live here themselves, but there's no sign that any of this was ever used."

Their conveyance dropped below the city floor. Intervals of dull stone passed before their window, broken by openings onto white, utilitarian rooms and corridors, irregularly lit by glowing patches in the ceilings. Benadek thought he saw something move—a floor-hugging shape no larger than his head. He might have been fooled by shifting perspectives.

He counted eighteen levels. At the nineteenth, the elevator screeched shrilly, and ground to a halt. Outside, white walls glared shinily in bright, diffuse light. A blue panel with white lettering flashed monotonously: INCOMING PERSONNEL.

The door opened. The air that wafted in was fresh and forest-scented. "Good!" Achibol said, sniffing noisily. "That means domestic services are functioning." He went immediately to a panel much like the face of his talisman, and punched keys in rapid sequence. "My codes are valid here. The system's accepting me. Teress, put your thumb on that sensor-pad—the shiny spot. Push on it. Good. Look into the eyepiece. There'll be a flash of light, but don't be alarmed." As she pressed and peered, Benadek saw words appear on the talismanlike screen: [Surname?] Achibol typed "FELIX." Then: [First Name?] "TERESA." [Rank?] "CAPTAIN." Captain Teresa Felix? What was a "Captain," and a "Felix"? Benadek had never heard of a surname, except that Achibol was "the sorcerer," and others were called "the miller," "the scribe," "the . . ."

"Now you, Benadek," Achibol commanded. The boy uneasily pressed his thumb on the shiny rectangle, and peered into the "eyepiece." Thus he could not seek what mysterious characters appeared on the screen, or what responses Achibol typed.

"What's happening?" Benadek muttered.

"I'll explain fingerprints and retinal IDs later," Achibol said. "We're cleared for the entire facility. Let's see what happens." He spoke, but not to Benadek or Teress. "Query: location of dormitory facilities and refectory."

Benadek heard a faint susurrus, like a breeze over dry stones. A mellow voice came from nowhere. "Welcome to Biopsych Three, Commander Scribner. It's not necessary to use comspeech with this command-level interface. English, or any recognized dialect, will do." Teress, already close to the apprentice, drew closer.

Who was "Commander Scribner"? Couldn't the voice's owner see who they were, through its spy-hole? Benadek could not find the hole. Perhaps it was among the rusty water-spots that marred the otherwise perfect white walls . . .

"Your suite will be activated in forty-five minutes," the voice continued. "Follow the green guideline. The Incoming Personnel cafeteria is on permanent standby."

"Ah . . ." Benadek said.

"You have a question, Lieutenant Benedict?" The voice was female. Lieutenant *Benadek*? The pronunciation had been odd, but . . . "Ah . . . No question." Achibol seemed to enjoy his discomfiture.

"Shall we find the cafeteria?" the mage asked. A thought struck him. "Wait," he told his companions, raising a finger for silence. "Query: what is your monitor status?"

"I am in full interactive mode. As base commander pro tem, you may order me to shift to record-only mode with keyword access. Full privacy mode is restricted to conference rooms and general officers' suites."

"Hmm," Achibol mused. "We're field officers, used to our working personas. Will it confuse you if we continue to use them?"

"Not at all. I am programmed to respond to alternate names and nicknames, and to ignore persona-generated anomalies. Just state your full name, and the alternate you wish to be recognized, and I will voiceprint it. May I suggest that I assume record-only mode to eliminate possible confusion? Such records are stored unedited and unreviewed unless recalled by a grade seven security officer or general staff."

"Please do," Achibol said, "but not quite yet . . ."

"Do you have a specific keyword you wish me to respond to?"

"How about 'Circe'?"

"An excellent choice, Commander. It creates multiple resonances in my integrative nodes."

"A good pun?"

"An excellent one."

"Very well, Circe. Please recognize me as Achibol the Scrivener, an itinerant charlatan. Lieutenant Charles Benedict is Benadek, my apprentice, and Captain Teresa Felix is Teress, our sometime companion. Assume record-only mode at this time." Benadek felt as if a presence left the room "You may both speak freely, " Achibol said. "Our resident sorceress won't interfere. But shall we eat? Who knows, there may be wine, if it's not all gone bad."

True to Circe's words, a green line glowed in the center of the hallway floor, leading around a corner. Parts of the line were missing where the light sources had failed, but there were enough to follow. As they walked, the green telltale behind them faded. A door ahead was bordered with the same shade. It opened by itself, causing Benadek to jump back. "Food," Achibol said.

Over a substantial if bland meal of pasty meats and unrecognizable vegetables, Benadek and Teress began the long process of attaching real significance to words he had never known and she had known only as dead history: fluorescent light, freeze-dried, terrazzo, Salisbury steak, rubber chicken, paper napkin, pop, and instant Liptons®. Achibol explained Circe—the legend and the cybernetic device to which he had given the name. It was hard to believe no human mind lay behind the disembodied voice.

Benadek's eyes roved across the fifty-odd white (formica) tables, the two hundred glittery-slick (chrome and vinyl) chairs. There was no more than the thinnest film of dust on anything. "Cleaning robots," the mage explained. "You'll probably see them now and again—small canisters like fat, geometrical rats." Benadek, remembering the moving thing seen from the elevator, nodded knowledgeably.

While Achibol lingered happily over his third glass of wine, Benadek directed his attention to the machinery that had delivered their food. He studied pushbuttons, holo-pictures, florid descriptions and flapper-doored slots. His favorite was the wall cabinet with a spigot that flowed with bubbly, fruit-flavored drinks. He experimented with its simple keyboard and sipped the products it produced until he hit upon a combination of keys that produced a water-clear beverage like bitter pine sap. He spat explosively.

Achibol chuckled. "You have to develop a taste for gin." Benadek's fascination with the machinery waned rapidly, as had his interest in temple gimmickry. There, his function had been only to hand Achibol tools. Here, he reminded himself, it was to eat. He punched for "cherry pie," and later vowed he would never forget that particular button.

Teress was content that Benadek, even with "cherry pie" all over his face, was less obnoxious than he had been. Perhaps it was only because there were no juicy bugs or six-legged toads in this underground place. Or perhaps he really was trying to be mature, and just did not know how. After all, he had only her and Achibol for role models, and neither of them were . . . suitable.

Benadek grew impatient once his physical appetite was satisfied. At the root of his restlessness was a mental picture of a room with buttons like the food machines, but with pictures of ancient men, and descriptions of the talents and abilities he would gain from draughts of their memories

Achibol's eyes drooped from fatigue and wine. At his request, Circe provided a new green line to guide them to the "Commander's" suite. Benadek was too tired to marvel at the great soft bed that lowered itself from the wall of his room, adjacent to Achibol's. The bedding had a dry, unpleasant odor, but looked soft and inviting. He stripped off his dusty clothes and lay down.

Before he could fall asleep, Achibol entered with a tray of odd things. First was a metal-mesh hat like the honches had worn. "Put it on," he ordered. "It will help you learn while you sleep." When Benadek hesitated, he said, "Do you want to drink gin the rest of your time here? Put it on. Tonight, you'll learn the layout of the complex, and how to work things." He gave the lad a tiny cup of something sweet and flavorless. "That will make you receptive to the learning."

He went out, quietly shut the door, and opened another. "And you?" he asked Teress. "You'll need to know your way around, too." Reluctantly, she repeated Benadek's actions.

The old man could not fall asleep. Was he doing

the right thing? Benadek did not take his admonitions seriously. Whenever augmented memory was mentioned, the boy's eyes brightened with avid desire. Achibol knew him too well to misinterpret it. By morning, Benadek would be able to operate the facility by himself. It was tempting to slip over to the boy's bed, shut off the sleep-teacher, and pretend that the machinery would no longer work. He scolded himself for those thoughts. He had been in control too long, and had not had to trust anyone else. The boy would justify his trust. The alternatives were unthinkable.

In the morning there were minor marvels to satisfy Benadek and Teress as they tested the extent of their new knowledge. The white ceramic toilet whisked waste away, beds and tables folded themselves from the walls with a whine of servomotors and only an occasional creak, and doors opened to the touch of a palm on glassy surface-mounted plates. "Limit your experimentation to a few tries," Achibol admonished. "Everything here is as old as I am, and less durable. The doors could fail, and then where would we be?"

The sleep-teaching program left strange gaps. Ordinary folk of the old times had already known the meanings of the "H" and "C" on plumbing fixtures. Benadek and Teress had learned more about Biopsych Three's innovations, like waterless toilets and housekeeping automatons, than about its basics, like light switches.

They decided to explore, with Circe's help. "I'll see to the reactivation of the laboratories," Achibol said, pleading off from a long, tiring tramp through corridors all alike but for differing corrosion and water damage. "Don't touch anything you don't understand," he cautioned them.

They wanted to see the "crystal city." Following

Circe's guidelines, they reached it in an hour, after several elevator rides. Emerging at the edge of a great square, they peered upward at towers that disappeared into dim twilight. Obligingly, the command interface showed them what it would have looked like occupied. One by one and in clusters, lights came on. Faint echoes of unfamiliar music filled the air, and a fountain splashed merrily, its jets and sprays dancing in ever-changing patterns, lit from the pool below with shifting color. A few patches of windows remained dark, a few pools silent.

As they explored luxurious suites, plush even by the ancients' elevated standards, and leaned from crystal bridges that turned out to be polished metal, they became used to Circe's cooperative presence. "There are five hundred and twenty residential units in the 'city' complex," she told them. "It was designed to provide the illusion of greater population, believed necessary for the mental health of its residents."

"How large is the rest of the facility?" Benadek asked, consciously adopting the precise inflections he believed "Lieutenant Charles Benedict" might use. "It seems to have been made for more than five hundred."

"The entire complex has slightly over twenty square miles of accessible floor area, on seventy levels of a million square feet each. The design population is eleven thousand four hundred and eighty, including transients."

After several minutes of thoughtful silence, Teress raised a question. "Then nine or ten thousand people were to live in the rest of the complex, and about two thousand here?"

"That's roughly correct," Circe replied. "The design workforce is nine thousand two hundred ninety-six."

"What about their families?" Teress pressed. "The workforce, I mean?"

"The workforce was intended to be military

personnel whose families would live elsewhere." Was it Teress's imagination, or did Circe sound defensive? As well she might, Teress thought. It was another example of the planners' callous elitism. The "crystal city" was only for the powerful. She probed deeper. "How were residents of this . . . residential complex . . . to be chosen?"

"That information is not in my records. Do you wish me to speculate, based on available data?"

"Please do."

"Many names on the roster are prefaced with political titles like Senator, Congressman, and Judge, or military ones of equivalent rank. Most refer to adult males. Others with the same names may have been wives and children. I speculate that reservations were awarded based on potential value to the community that this facility was to become."

Teress saw Benadek's face grow livid, and heard his intake of breath. She quickly said "Circe: assume record-only mode at once."

"Why did you do that?" Benadek spat. "I was going to tell her why they were *really* chosen!"

"That's why I did it! Now whatever we say will be unavailable to her unless she's ordered to examine her recordings. There's no sense confusing her. She's got enough troubles already."

"But she thinks those corrupt . . ."

"She doesn't 'think.' She was programmed—the way the ones you were going to criticize wanted her to be. What if she decided that 'Lieutenant Charles Benedict' was disloyal?"

"I never thought about that."

"What were you doing last night? Didn't you learn anything?"

"Not the same things you did, I guess."

They compared notes. Beyond the basic orientation module, Achibol had indeed given them different knowledge. Teress had a better overview of the facility's history, systems, and purposes, while Benadek knew more about the labs and information centers. Hers was a supervisor's view and his a technician's.

"What did you mean 'she's got enough troubles'?" he asked.

"This place is falling apart, and I don't think Circe can do anything about it. I think she's failing too. See how that light is flickering? And the dust everywhere? I saw one of those little metal scurriers lying in the street. I think it wore out."

"What makes you think Circe herself is failing?"

"That humming when she's in interactive mode. And coming here, she led us the long way around, when there was a straight hallway leading here."

"I heard you ask about that. She said there was no information about it."

"She knew nothing about a whole block of offices and labs she's supposed to be maintaining. There are blanks in her memory."

"I suppose we should let Achibol know," he said. Teress agreed.

When they were at the edge of the great cavern, she told Circe to turn everything back to standby. "There's no sense keeping it lit."

They found Achibol in the cafeteria, sampling wines. His eyes would not come into focus, but his voice was unblurred. He agreed that Biopsych Three was deteriorating, and that they'd best hurry to accomplish what they must. "We must give you the memory-tools you'll need to understand, and thus control, your mutability," he told Benadek. "Though you've made great strides, stress or shock could send you the way you were going in the swamp, the way Dispucket went. Only when you fully understand your own workings will you be able to visualize and control your *changing*."

"How do we go about it? When?"

Benadek was a little too eager, his master thought.

"The files for stored memories are separate from the Circe system," the mage said. "We'll have to go to the laboratory and examine the listings. You're not afraid?"

"It wouldn't matter if I was, would it? I *am* afraid of *changing* again, and being out of control of it." In truth, Benadek felt no fear. He felt burning eagerness to begin, to know not only himself and his workings, but everything.

His blood surged with the excitement he had felt when first he fantasized becoming Achibol's apprentice—but now, having lived and traveled with the old charlatan, he understood that Achibol's "powers" were trickery and technology. The true power was superior knowledge.

Benadek wanted that power, though not for the base reasons he once had wanted to be a sorcerer. He wanted to avenge his dead parents, Teress's village, and Achibol's melancholy solitude as the last of his race—and Sylfie. Above all, Sylfie. It was one with the rage he had felt in the crystal city at the fat, powerful ancients in glittery palaces, their slaves doomed to the bleak, white corridors of Biopsych Three. It was one also with his disgust that the best of the ancients had become mere memories, packets of skills to be fed to a new generation of slaves, while the powerful were to have come back entire, their personalities intact, to impose their corruption on the fresh, clean world that was his, Benadek's inheritance. But of that, he said nothing to the mage.

Achibol led him to the lab—white, antiseptic, and bleakly lit. An anteroom had once served as a lounge. Chairs were dried and cracked with age, and a sideboard with utensils and cups was dusty and cluttered with crumbling, ancient refuse. Within the lounge was another door. A sign above it lit when Achibol opened it, and stayed lit as long as one of them was in the room the door gave upon:

EXPERIMENT IN PROGRESS

The laboratory air was dry and stale, colder than midwinter. Metal tables supported keyboards and screens, wired together with a chaos of colored strands taped, tied, and twisted to the table legs, wires which ran in seemingly careless fashion across the floor. The back wall was all doors—small, thick doors with heavy, shiny hinges and latches. When humid air from the outside hit them, their shiny finishes dulled with frost—the source of the chill, he realized, and guessed that whatever was behind them was colder still. The other walls were lined with gray metal shelves of electronic equipment encrusted with dials, readouts, and lights. Unlike the carefully mounted devices in temple rooms, these were piled helter-skelter, wired together carelessly, and covered with dust.

Benadek began to be scared. The machinery had a temporary look; he was not about to be exposed to tried and proven technology, but something that, to the ancients, had been dangerously new.

The most frightening article was the padded chair in the middle of the room. It was connected to peripheral equipment and computer terminals by more wires, but what caught his eyes and held them were the straps, positioned to restrain arms, wrists, thighs and ankles. Hanging above the seat was a globular helmet with its own collection of spidery filaments. Sharp needles lined the inside.

Resisting a strong desire to sidle from the room in search of a safe place to urinate, Benadek walked directly to the terrifying throne.

The mage opened a frost-covered door. With what seemed an evil chuckle, he said, "Sit, and we'll begin."

✧ ✧ ✧

His eyes were encrusted as if he had slept for days. Achibol's face swam into view as the helmet rose from Benadek's head. His scalp felt as if thousands of tiny fleas had bitten it. His hands and feet tingled. As he regained the ability to focus, he glimpsed the tubes taped to his bare arms and thighs, now filled with dark redness like blood. Other tubes rattled at his neck as he twisted his head to watch Achibol. The sorcerer flicked switches and twisted dials. Glowing lights and readouts faded. The tubes connecting him to the chair paled, then ran clear. Hot flashes coursed along his nerves. Why should he be more afraid now than before?

Achibol's voice sounded loud but fuzzy. "It's done, boy. You have the memories. Now you must integrate them." The oldster spread a curved, metallic screen before his face. "This will show images as fast as your eyes can register them. Through your earphones, you'll hear words for what you see, speeded up but intelligible. Don't try to memorize them."

Achibol peered at a monitoring device on the chair. "Do you remember what I told you? The fear you're feeling is adrenaline injected into your blood, a chemical of fear that will fix your new memories firmly. We remember best what we experience when we are afraid." The screen in front of his eyes lit up, and meaningless sounds murmured in his ears.

Benadek remembered. He remembered DNA and RNA. He recalled how memory is bound not only in brain cells, in neural connections, but how its pathways are mapped on chromosomes. Genes coded for life and the memory of life past, the chemical trickeries that made him what he was. He remembered instincts and race memory (dark forests, deep caves, raw, charred meat, and the screams of great beasts).

If Benadek had been an ancient, he would have recognized Achibol's brisk, artificially cheeriness, a doctor's bedside manner. As it was, it only made him uneasy. "How do you feel, lad? Look around and tell me what you see."

He saw an EKG, a blood sampler, the induction helmet now suspended over his head. In an orgy of naming, he called out CRT, IV, catheter, light switch, and return air grille. He even knew, after a fashion, what they were.

He remembered Teress and Achibol half-carrying him from the laboratory. He remembered foreign stuff surging in his blood and brain, and understood what it was doing: no false memories were imposed on his own, only patterns. New connections were made among his own cells, fabricating "memories" where none had been before, using the raw stuff of his own thinking to create knowledge where before had been randomness.

He remembered thumbprint-ID locks and electroluminescent panels. Finally, he remembered falling asleep, and waking to see Teress asleep in a chair with her head against the wall.

Days passed. Teress continued to learn via sleep induction. They wandered the depths of Biocybe Three with Circe as guide, cementing abstract knowledge with continuing exposure to the solid realities it represented.

Then one morning, as Teress sipped coffee and Benadek ate cherry pie (Achibol had finished his meal, and had departed), Benadek told her how he had spent the night.

"You did what?" she exclaimed.

"I took another memory dose last night. By myself." He looked as if he had not slept in days. "I had to. The first one helped—I can understand myself and my body better now. I can visualize what I need to stave off or even control the *change*." He shrugged. "But those were the memories of a biochemist, not a computer specialist. I'm trying to work my way through the data banks, but they're hiding things I need to know."

Teress gave him a skeptical look. "They? Who?"

"Circe. And the military computers on the lowest level."

"They're just machines. Just because Circe can talk . . ."

"They were programmed by clever, secretive men. I'm trying to find out about the honches, and what's behind them."

"Somebody named Jorssh. We know that."

"Who's behind him? Where are his troops getting lasers? Even those mesh headpieces are electronic mind-screens, not just little fences that keep out emissions from Achibol's gadgets. There's a storeroom in the armory, with hundreds of them. Does Jorssh have access to a place like this, with data banks and a command interface like Circe? Did someone actually succeed with complete-personality transplants? Perhaps that's what Jorssh is. Are there ancient planners in new bodies, preparing to take over? I have to know, and Achibol won't help. He wants to go back to business as usual as soon as I'm 'stabilized.' "

Teress eyed him uneasily. This new—admittedly more "mature"—Benadek was an unknown quantity. Was it the infusions he had taken, the new words that rolled off his tongue as if he had used them all his life, or was he really growing up? If so . . . what was he growing into? "Master Achibol believes that pure-humans like us—like you, really—will be enough," she said cautiously. "That we're evolving into an adaptable human species that will take over naturally."

"The ancients didn't plan us. Do you think they'll let us continue to evolve? They were callous monsters, and their honch tools still are. I've got memories of two burnt villages to prove that."

"I've got some too, you know."

Seeing the pain in her eyes, Benadek put his arm around her. "It doesn't get any easier, does it? I'm sorry."

"It's not too bad. It's like it happened to somebody else." She shrugged.

"Teress? Will you tell me what happened to you before we found you?"

"I suppose it's only fair, isn't it? After all, I saw what happened to you . . ."

"It was the *change*, wasn't it? The hooded robe, the baths . . . You were changing back from . . . from a cat."

Teress spun around at him, her eyes blazing. "You knew!" she spat. "How?"

"I knew something right away. I even told Sylfie. I had dreams, nightmares, about you, and about hunting-cats."

It took a moment or two, but she calmed herself. "Resonance!" she exclaimed. "I should have known. But I didn't know you were a pure-human then, so I thought my secret was safe."

"Resonance?"

"That's Achibol's word for it. Most pure-humans can't just *change*. We have to resonate with something, identify with it, like you were doing with the swamp reptiles." She shuddered. "Like I did with the wild cats—and like you did, with me. But none of us did it completely. We only made superficial changes. The genes are all there, Achibol says, whole coils of extra, mutable ones that radiation and chemicals can't touch, that can change us back, if we're damaged, or into something else . . . . We should be able to change like you can, by visualizing, superimposing cat genes or whatever upon them, but there isn't enough resonance."

"There's nothing in my adopted memories about that, and Achibol won't talk about *changing*. He tells me I have all the answers, and I just have to find them in myself. Sylfie said that too, when she was . . . before she . . ." He shut his own eyes tightly, squeezing back tears. Teress hugged him.

"Tell me more," he asked when he recovered his composure.

"Achibol calls it telepathy. Not mind reading. It's more like getting on the same level as another mind so when it thinks something, you think it too. When that mind reads its own genes—don't ask me how—*your* mind reads them too, and changes yours to match."

"I'm going to need more memory-doses, I can tell."

"You can't! Two are all anyone can take. The ancients proved that. I've seen recordings of the ones who went mad."

Benadek's knowing smile frightened her. "That may be—for the ancients. But I know things they never could. I could take on a dozen 'souls,' or a hundred, and know more than any living being has ever known."

CHAPTER SIXTEEN,

in which Benadek is consumed by the Trickster's demon kin, and is brought back by One Born of Earth.

The primary sources for this tale are chants of the Te'hen of the Arafan Cluster. They recount the adventures of Bhena-d'kha and Ta-rossa, a star-sprite and the servant-girl he created from the dust of a dead moon.

But herein, demons have become "memories." Valdak, Bostak and the devil-sibs Sod'vha, Ahn'hva and Jahn'hfra are transmuted into less-mystical but no less intriguing forms. The latter half of this episode finds the Demon-King Ahk'hvol split in two: one aspect becomes Achibol, drunk and pathetic, and the other aspect, vague and mysterious, has overtones of a distant, familiar Evil. *

(Kaledrin, Senior Editor)

INTERLUDE
The Great School, Midicor IV

"There!" Kaledrin sighed. "A quiet, literary reflection on the new chapter. With Saphooth minding his own business, things seem almost normal around here. Even the flood of indignant letters has peaked."

"The quiet before the storm," Abrovid muttered ominously.

"What do you mean?" Kaledrin's eyestalks rotated swiftly and his chitin-plates tightened over his soft parts.

"The flood of *supportive* letters from fanatical one-worlders hasn't peaked yet," Abrovid replied.

"Fringe cultists and fundamentalists. They'll lose interest soon enough. This is a literary project, remember. The biocybes have no instructions about religious matters." He relaxed again, like a bud opening in the sunlight of noon.

"Seems to me you can't separate them from what the biocybes are coming up with, though. Saphooth doesn't even try."

"Eh? What have you heard?" Again, Kaledrin shrunk against himself.

"I've gotten a listing of his calls. Would you like to look at it?" He held up a data-cube that seemed,

---

* See Distant Evil, Chapter 5 editorial commentary, and the relevant chapter in the K. V. text.

to Kaledrin, to gleam with bright, Evil light, not distant at all.

"Give me that!" the scholar snapped, lurching with all seven free tentacles outstretched.

Benadek drew Teress close. He was going to have to explain everything, and it would not be easy.

There had been more to the first dose of memories than rusty skills and terminology, as Benadek had his first inkling when he had tried to sleep. He had tossed and turned, unable to get comfortable, sprawling across his wide bed in vulnerable, exposed positions no urchin would adopt. Just as baby tree-men never let go of their mothers' fur even in sleep, just as sloths and bats clung upside down, urchins never sprawled; they wedged in dark crevices or huddled foetally in places too small for their enemies. They never snored. But Benadek had wakened sprawling and snoring.

A day or so later he had started drinking coffee, and liking it. He had not even realized that his finger had pushed the COFFEE BLACK button instead of the LIPTONS® one until he had drunk most of a cup, and enjoyed it.

"That was when I discovered that Dr. Vladek Sovoda, the biochemist, wasn't completely dead," he told Teress. "He snored, and liked coffee. And he was inside me."

"What did you do?"

"I hunted him down inside my brain and nerves and cells," Benadek said with an indecipherable shake of his head and the faintest of sly grins, "and I killed him." Teress's hissing indrawn breath warned him he had gone too far. "It wasn't like that, not really," he explained hurriedly. "He wasn't a real personality. But behavioral memories like his preference for coffee were influencing me without my consent, even my knowledge."

It had been extermination, not murder. The

Sovoda-thoughts had only begun to congeal in Benadek's brain, to form synaptic trails that would become memories and action-patterns. Most still floated free in his bloodstream and cells, strands of ribonucleic acid coded for the production of specialized neurotransmitters, complex proteinlike molecules that would determine new connections in the gray shadows of his brain. The differences between such Sovoda-thoughts and Benadek's own body-chemicals were as slight as the reversal of a loosely bonded hydroxyl on a primitive amine. A lone enzyme might act as a neurotransmitter, causing the firing of first one synapse, then another and another, their characteristic pattern resulting in a flash of memory or an action, or both. Such subtle, weakly bonded differences identified them as Sovoda-mind. The developers of the memory-transplant techniques had not known there were differences—after all, there were hundreds of neurotransmitters, perhaps thousands, if one counted dual-purpose enzymes whose neural functions were masked by more obvious body-regulating uses. Only a handful were fully understood. But Benadek knew them all. . . .

Extermination. As Sovoda-memories drifted to his brain, he "imagined" antigens—their ID tags bumps of bonding-energy. In the rapid shuttling of energies of his own thinking, in structures like tiny glands, antibodies formed. Ironically, Sovoda's own understanding of the complex relationship between brain, glands, and the immune system betrayed him. He could not have used that understanding directly, but Benadek could. So Benadek, lymphocyte-borne, hunted and killed.

"When I'd wiped out his individuality, leaving only the memories I wanted to keep, I wished I hadn't. He wasn't a bad person, even though he was an ancient . . ."

"Achibol's an ancient too," Teress interrupted.

"Of course—though he may be as different from *them* as we are. But that's another story. I shouldn't have been so thorough. I was scared. It would have been harder to have kept all of him, isolated from the 'command network' I call 'me.' This next time, I will."

"You should talk to Achibol before there's a 'next time.' "

"He'll get angry and refuse, then watch me more carefully. Besides, he's been drinking too much. I only saw him drunk once, before we came here—when I first . . ." Benadek grinned at a secret memory, " . . . when I first met him. I've got to get to work fast, and get him out of here."

"He's idle and frustrated," she agreed. "But are you sure you can handle more memories? What about last night? Is that one trying to take over?"

"Not yet. I've been able to recognize him and channel what's left of his personality into a safe place, bound up in chemical form. Will you help with the next one? I can do it alone, but it would be easier with you to monitor things."

Teress reluctantly agreed. "But if things get out of hand . . . if I even think they are . . . I'm going to get Achibol. All right?"

They started that night, after the sorcerer was asleep. Benadek still thought of him as the "sorcerer" even though his doses of ancient memory gave him a fair understanding of what the old man really was. Even his averred long life was not that mysterious any more. Sovoda, the biochemist, had known several experiments that might have led to Achibol's kind of immortality. Most required sophisticated equipment for blood filtering, ion-flushing, electrochemical stimulation and so forth. One technique, developed in Europe, used a viruslike "nanomachine." Injected into a host, it checked cells' chromosomal DNA for errors by comparison with its own codes and stimulated genes that harmlessly destroyed erring cells. It could not repair cells, but as long as the host had others that could divide without error, he could function without symptoms of aging.

That report dated to the decade before the Plan was put into effect. A lot might have been done in those ten years.

The apprentice pushed speculation aside. Teress eyed the equipment and the big chair with its wires, cables, tubes, and straps, and shuddered. "Is that where the frozen memories are kept?" she asked, pointing to the freezer doors. Benadek nodded. She watched him punch in strings of characters. Her sleep-taught familiarity helped her understand what he did.

The data he called up was presented as lists. The main one catalogued occupational skills in broad, general categories—more occupations than she had ever imagined. "What are those?" she asked, pointing at the final category: <MISC>. She reached over Benadek's shoulder and shifted the cursor. She read downward from Astronomy past Agronomy, Library Science, Musicology, Psychology . . . and stopped at Philosophy.

"What kind of doctor is that?" Benadek asked, scanning the single record that appeared.

"Someone who thinks about things out on the edges of what's known. See? *The Ethics of Technological Power*. That sounds interesting."

"What?"

"A book, I suppose. Try that one."

"Huh? You mean his memories?" At Teress's emphatic nod, he shook his head. "I need to know about computers and military security and . . ."

"Later. Choose him this time." She spoke with such cool conviction that there was no need for her to state the obvious: if Benadek gainsaid her, he would have to proceed without her. He shrugged, then typed in a string of code.

<BOSTWICK, James Wold;
374-46-6390-1318; Access 4D;>
<RETRIEVAL IN PROCESS>
<RETRIEVAL COMPLETED. SPECIMEN ACCESS CHUTE 4D.>
<IS SUBJECT PROCESSED?>

"That's me," Benadek said. "I've got to get in the chair. Four-dee. That's the fourth door over and the fourth one down—see the green light?" Teress examined the storage wall while Benadek seated himself. He showed her how to strap him in, and told her where to place monitoring pickups. Gritting her teeth, she slid the intravenous taps into his wrists and neck and taped them down. "You'll have to use those padded tongs to pick up your philosopher," he told her. "He's about seventy degrees Kelvin right now." Having no experience with anything colder than the iron hoops on a frozen bucket, Teress had to imagine how her skin might stick to the frosted, fuming metallic canister she found behind door four-dee. She slid it into a machined receptacle and dogged its insulated cover down.

"You'll have to do the rest from the terminal," Benadek said.

"How did you ever . . ." she began.

"I had to run back and forth a lot, and I wasn't strapped in. I had a lot of trouble with the IVs."

"I can imagine," she murmured, marveling at his determination. She typed [Y] to indicate that the "subject" was indeed "processed," and followed a series of prompts that caused one piece of equipment after another to light up, hum, whir, or otherwise indicate readiness to precede.

✧ ✧ ✧

"Another?" Teress protested. "But you haven't slept since the last one." Six days, six steaming, frost-covered vials containing the essences of men's lives. Benadek's body fluids swam with foreign substances. His mind was aswarm with vivid, conflicting life-images of scientists, a philosopher, an Inuit shaman (again Teress's choice).

"I've done fine so far, haven't I? When all this stuff comes together, I'll have everything I need."

"And what will that be? I don't see why . . ."

"I want to know who's controlling the honches, what they're trying to do, how to fight them, if I must and . . . and what's the right thing to do."

"I was right, wasn't I?" she stated. "About the philosopher?" She knew that Benadek's last "want" was a reflection of the scholar Bostwick's careful, pondering manner. Had Benadek's behavior and thought-patterns not shown signs of the philosopher's effect, Teress had been prepared to take a fire axe to the computer terminal, the restraint chair, and the memory-storage compartments. She still paid close attention to Benadek's utterances, especially after his assimilation of the army security chief and the Air Force astronaut. Like honches, military men were too fearsome to be allowed to run freely within the mind and body of whatever Benadek eventually became.

No memories could furnish the answers he sought, she realized. They were all long dead before the first honch was born, but they "knew" the systems the honch-creators had used, and their thought-patterns were more appropriate than hers or Benadek's.

"Trust me?" he had pleaded. She had little choice.

The Benadek who stood before her was not the obnoxious boy she had first met. He answered questions with polysyllabic words or paraphrased equations that probably held no meaning for anyone alive besides himself. Sometimes, when he realized what he had said, the lost boy would surface in a rueful, mischievous grin. "I didn't know that a minute ago," he would say. "I wonder what I mean?"

More and more often, he knew exactly what he meant, though no one of the individuals he had greedily consumed could have assembled the thoughts and concepts he wove. "I'm a catalyst," he told her. "I allow them to 'talk' with each other, but I'm not one of them, and they're not me. I'm an arena where their ideas fight. I skim off what I want, and let them go on—and on and on."

"How did you avoid the madness the ancients suffered?"

"I'm different—as are you. It has to do with *changing*."

"Then I could do it too?" she asked cautiously, her expression halfway between fear and feral eagerness. "I feel so ignorant. If I could learn . . ."

He shook his head slowly. "Achibol was more right than he knew when he called the transfers murder. I could show you how to kill the relict personalities, as I did my first one, but unless . . . until . . . you can control your own *changes*, I can't teach you how to shunt them safely aside, and still let them live."

"I'll pass," she said, sighing with the release of tension that had built up without her awareness. "One more time, you said? Promise?"

"Just once, and I'm done. I promise."

The door swung open with enough force to set wires in motion, and slammed against its stop. "No more!" Achibol bellowed. "I've heard every despicable word." He staggered, his robe aswirl about his skinny legs. He was drunk. Teress backed away, frightened less by his anger than by his glazed, unfocused eyes.

"I was afraid of your intemperance," he snarled. "You were too eager. From the first time I told you of this place, you planned to rape it, didn't you? As you'd have raped Teress? Sylfie?" Benadek flinched, and pain invaded his eyes. "How many?" Achibol pressed, swaying as he stood. "How many have you destroyed in your unholy, wanton quest?"

"None, Master," Benadek replied, regaining his composure and rising to face Achibol squarely. "Or . . . only one, the very first. The rest are more alive than they could hope to be in another host. I have them all."

"Impossible—you'd be driven mad! Your body and mind would be a battlefield. You've learned how to choose a tidbit here, a dab there, and destroy the rest. No man could survive what you say you've done."

"Then I am either mad, Master, or—as I've long suspected—I'm no man, but something different." He drew himself up to his full height, and looked the old man straight in his hazed, fiery eyes. "I refuse to discuss it until you're sober."

"Are you the master here, and I the apprentice?"

"I'm apprentice to Achibol, not wine." Benadek feared the old man would strike him with his staff, or down him with its emanations. But Achibol spun unsteadily on his heel and reeled out. Teress followed him.

Benadek's shoulders slumped. He squeezed his eyelids together to ease their burning, swung the heavy door shut and bolted it from the inside. The red sign glowed brightly:

EXPERIMENT IN PROGRESS

Perhaps Teress could make the old man see reason, or at least sober him up so Benadek could explain. In the meantime, he would have to do the procedure by himself this last time, else Achibol might, even in his drunkenness, find some way to thwart him.

Memories roiled and swirled in his blood, prototypic vestiges of thought not yet mapped in synapses, little more than molecular codes for the living connections they would become, if he let them. His visualizations were clearer now, thanks to those sequences he had chosen to integrate into the vast complexity of his brain . . .

Each strand of foreign RNA-analogue was attached to a similar strand that had originated in the ancients' laboratories as a retrovirus. Its own code was carried not on the double strands of deoxyribonucleic acid but on more primitive, single-stranded RNA. Encapsulated in sheaths of viral protein, they pierced cellular membranes, then synthesized enzymes that cut his own stranded, coiled, and twisted genetic molecules with an accuracy no surgeon could duplicate. Viral RNA drew cellular nucleosides to it and created DNA versions of its foreign codes. Spliced into the host's own genome, they programmed his brain to make new connections in a manner similar to, but subtly different from, what his own embryonic cells had used to create brain connections in the first place. They created spurious thoughts and memories he could hardly distinguish from his own.

There was haunting similarity to the *change*, but the memory-codes merely governed the configurations of synapses, and regulated the kind and the numbers of neurotransmitter molecules—dopamine, norepinephrine, serotonin, and a host of others—that would determine the intensity and "color" of the impulses that passed from one neuron to another. What was a memory or a thought? Was it no more than a specification for what cells are activated at one time, a subset of all the possible internal connections that many billions of neurons could make? The foreign memories were no longer matter, but connections of synapses physiologically no different than those that grew out of his own experiences and actions. His brain was like any other, but more connected. The memories of others did not occupy the parallel pathways that they, as individuals, had strived to create; he was not one man with many brains. He was one man with one brain, one seat of his being. But he was more "intelligent" than any man before.

That had been the mistake previous subjects had made, for which they had paid with internal war that began in insanity and ended when molecular warriors stormed the final strongholds of the brain stem and the autonomic functions. The new memories could not be compartmentalized. Too many synaptic pathways were the same for each memory-set, indeed were identical for every human being, and the war for the use of those vast but limited superhighways could not, among more than two minds, ever be settled. Instead the battles spread to secondary routes, byways, and finally paths and country lanes, into the thrumming caves of the heart, the gateway sphincters of gut and glands, the fingers and vocal cords. They led not to wisdom but to spastic death.

Benadek alone had visualized another way, a template for processes he could never truly see. Just as an ignorant man could picture his lymphocytes as tiny octopi eating invading bacterial sharks, thereby autostimulating his immune response, so Benadek created, out of the stuff of his own brain cells, new tags that identified neurotransmitter molecules as his own, or as James Wold Bostwick's, or Paula Race Farr's.

He did not, as might a conventionally educated man, distinguish between cholecystokinin molecules digesting food in his gut and the same substance regulating synaptic firings in his brain. He saw how such enzymes served dual functions, separated only by the length of an artery, the threadlike path of a nerve. He did not distinguish synapses' recognition-shapes from identical antigen-receptors on certain very specific "memory" immune cells. Those were subtle convolutions, shaped by molecular charges pulling against each other in infinitely varying but individually constant ways, far too complex for his still-crude resolution. On the level of his body's protein structures, Benadek saw no real difference between a memory, a hormone, or a disease.

How could he keep the foreign bodies, neither destroying nor succumbing to them? Where could he save them, ready for his call, to be integrated as convenient bits and pieces according to his need of them? Benadek considered his brain a massive, diversified gland, his glands as scattered brains, and his immune cells—that remembered the shapes of thousands, even millions, of antigens—as disenfranchised thoughts. Such chemical thoughts were no different from cerebral ones, only slower. They depended for transmittal on the pulse and flow of blood from one part of him to another, from glandular emitter to distant neuronic receptor.

As each rush of foreign information was forced into him by the pumps and micropistons of the restraint chair, Benadek called upon his B-lymphocytes and his tiny neural "endocrine glands." He forced the twisting coils of bases and sugars, the loose- and tightly bound hydroxyls, hydrogen atoms, oxygen and phosphate ions, in the cells of his roiling, surging gut, to accept them. To accept and subtly change them. No longer would antibodylike motes in his blood tag them for ingestion by hungry macrophages, or mark them for subtler destruction by T-cells, for neutralization in a hundred devious ways; instead, the visitors were tagged for delivery to sites far from his vulnerable brain, where they happily penetrated his lesser cells and became part of them.

Love was a vagrant memory. Its ultimate source, said the American entomologist, Anna Reschke, his fourth assimilation, was the heart. He understood that it was not literally so; the part of Dr. Reschke that was now Benadek admitted there was no silly valentine-shaped organ where "love" resided, that the notion was a childish fancy with no basis in fact.

Love—according to Jean-Francois Ailloud, a French naturalist of Vietnamese, European and North African ancestry, Benadek's eighth acquisition—was seated in the liver (or so his emotions insisted). Of course the rational Frenchman Benadek hosted insisted that there was truly no specific seat for any emotion. They resided no more in liver than in bowels or, as the foolish American woman proclaimed, in the heart.

Benadek knew both were right and wrong. No emotion or thought resided in isolated purity within the brain. Heart, liver, gut, and hot, working muscles all supported the vast chemical process of mentation. As his clever cells and raw, unsheathed enzymes routed intruding memories not to his brain but to tiny subcellular glands in his heart-muscle, to dark, mysterious cells in his liver and spleen, to all the slow, secretory parts of his body, they would discover the verity of his visions.

Dispersed and fragmented, the thoughts of his new companions were safe from each other and from Benadek's immune system. While Benadek-thoughts leaped swiftly between tight-woven brain cells, across synaptic gaps so tiny the space between tightly pinched fingers would seem vast, other-thoughts followed the course of blood vessels, their speed regulated by the beat of his heart, and politely queued in bumbling, molecular fashion in his thalamus, hippocampus, and amygdala, to be assimilated, translated and integrated (or rejected) at his discretion. Within him a dozen others lived on, thought, wondered, and partook of the taste of his own thoughts, the aroma of his food, and the contentment of his evacuations. It was a slow life, and placid, but none saw fit to complain, for it was life, not the frozen suspension they had endured unknowingly for two thousand years.

✧ ✧ ✧

When Benadek staggered from the memory lab, Teress waited outside, despairing, after almost twenty hours. She flung herself in his arms. "I thought you died," she wailed, looking up into his fatigue-reddened eyes. Even as a deeply buried part of her muttered acerbic, disgusted comments concerning her prideless, undignified performance, its complaints were washed away by relief. Tears flooded her eyes as she realized how much the ill-mannered boy had come to mean to her. As he wrapped her in his arms, she accepted unquestioningly that he was taller than she, that his arms were thicker and sheathed with muscle that she had never noticed before, and that rank maleness replaced the sweet, boyish scent she had come to associate with him.

"When you didn't come out, I thought . . . are you still Benadek?"

"I'm still me," he murmured in her ear, "perhaps more so than ever before."

"Achibol was here twice," she told him. "He's terribly worried."

"Worried, or angry?" he asked, his grin making deep grooves beside his mouth, where before only boyish crinkles would have formed.

"With Master Achibol, who can tell?" she joked as adrenaline dissipated.

"I'll see him soon, but I doubt he'll be happier. I want to talk with him out on the surface, not here."

"Up above? But why?"

"Because it's neutral ground. Down here . . . " Benadek waved his hand lethargically, not wanting to let go of Teress or let her move away. " . . . surrounded by all this, I'm a soul-consuming monster. Up there in the 'real' world he'll be able to see me as Benadek again, and berate me as he always has, instead of fearing what I've become."

"I've never thought of Master Achibol as being afraid. But you're right—he *is* terrified. I hope your plan works."

"It will," Benadek assured her.

"Are you sure you're all right?" she asked again. "You seem different."

"I am different," he agreed, drawing her closer, "and much more than just all right." His hand crept up behind her neck.

Her face was already close, her eyes joined with his, as she rose on tiptoe to meet his lips. "Shut the door," she murmured.

Later, when she awakened entangled limb for limb with him, warm and limp in the aftermath of her failed resolutions, the door was closed. For once, the tiny, critical voice within had nothing to say. Had she still been a cat, she would have purred.

When Benadek awoke, he rediscovered her, and more time passed before they began planning his escape from the underground facility.

During the long periods when Benadek had struggled with the computers, the foreign memories, and himself, Teress had been above ground several times. Ostensibly she checked their back trail to assure that no honches had found it and followed them. In reality, she got out from under the oppressive mass of earth and let her body rhythms adjust once more to sun and moon and stars overhead. She felt the wind and reassured herself that she was not soul-dead as well as buried. When the time came, she would go most of the way with Benadek, then return to fetch Achibol.

He dressed quietly, then kissed her more awkwardly than before. Her shoulders felt cold where he had held her, and she felt suddenly bereft and alone. The small, contemptuous voice inside was no comfort.

Firelight licked at the rudely woven wall of sticks and brush. The wind was flat and steady from the southwest. Achibol approached carefully; the shadow cast by the fire seemed larger than Benadek's should be. Had he grown? The sorcerer swallowed dryly, though physical changes were trivial, compared with what he feared Benadek might have become. But he would soon know. Benadek was unique. If his personality were no longer his own, he could not hide it.

"Master Achibol? Come out of the wind. I've brewed tea." Benadek's familiar inflections were reassuring—there was no trace of ancient accents. The mage circled the windbreak and approached the fire.

Brushwood flames flared and crackled briskly. Benadek's eyes sparkled in the vermilion and gold light. They were not dark and beady, as when he had first met the boy—but then, they had not been like that since the first time he had *changed*, in the swamp. Let him speak. If ancient minds commanded him, they'd not be able to hide. Their arrogance would give them away.

"Well, boy," he assayed, "have you survived intact, as Teress tries endlessly to assure me?"

"I'm still Benadek, Master. But I'm hardly the same. I understand things that were mysteries before."

"Tell me," Achibol commanded quietly, his heart fluttering less fiercely than a moment before.

"I understand what I am, and I know what we must do next,"

"It's still 'we,' is it? I was afraid you'd have no use for me any more." Achibol's gruff sarcasm was transparent. Benadek grinned. More of Achibol's doubts fell away before that wide, sunny smile. "Well?" he prompted.

"Well, what?"

"What are you, now that you know all these things? And what must we do?"

"I'm the ultimate adaptation to a mutagenic environment—heredity under the control of mind. I'm what the pure-humans were evolving toward. Mind is the only island of stability in the shifting waters of shape and chemistry."

"*Were* evolving? Aren't you proof that they still progress?"

"The crisis that forced our evolution is past. Atmospheric ozone is back to normal. Radiation levels are low, and most heavy metals are locked as oxides at the bottom of the seas. The atmosphere is as pure as before man discovered coal. The human race is as stable as it ever has been, and pure-human genes have no selective value. They'll gradually be lost—if they're not wiped out by our enemy."

"Indeed, you've learned much," Achibol said, nodding emphatically and pulling on his goatee. "I hadn't thought things through that far. But what enemy? The honches?"

"Honches are symptoms of the planners' failures. Living ancients are orchestrating the campaign of extermination against the pure-humans—and against a certain old brown man who's managed to stay alive since nineteen-ninety-three." The grin on Benadek's fire-lit countenance stretched all the way across his narrow face as his master's astonishment grew.

"Even that? You understand that too?" Achibol whispered.

"Not directly, not the pain of it. There were no black men's memories in the lab. I can't know the alienation of being the last of my kind, of seeing the others die, one by one. How could I? But for me, for the pure-humans, there's still hope. If we succeed, such small differences will fade next to the changes I anticipate."

Achibol drew breath to question further, but Benadek forestalled him. "Unless we succeed here, there'll be no future. But your race isn't necessarily more extinct than the 'white' one. Being an 'American' prejudiced you. When's the last time you heard from Africa?"

"That thought has occurred to me," the old man agreed, first nodding, then angrily shaking his head to clear the blur of undignified tears. "But I doubt the white militarists who took over the plan considered black simples worth designing. What if the only blacks to survive are like you and Teress—pure-humans, in danger of extinction?" He shrugged. "At any rate, I am, or was, an American, and my assigned place is here. But you haven't said what you plan for us, right now."

"The ancients must be found," Benadek replied. "They've had two millennia to dig in, so it won't be easy. And then, we've got to neutralize them."

"How will we find them?"

"Through Circe, and the military data banks. That's one reason I took the memories. I had to know enough to ask the right questions. Between me, you, and my 'silent partners,' they can't hide forever."

"I wish I could believe those 'silent partners' are truly better off now than frozen," Achibol said pensively. "Not that I don't accept your belief, mind you."

"Can you accept that I needed them? Even if you think of them only as soldiers who must die for a cause? You told me I'd have to ask my own questions here, and answer them."

"It will have to be enough."

"One more thing . . ."

"Yes?"

"Circe—all Biopsych Three—is failing. Sooner or later, those memories still stored will decay."

"You're right. Perhaps those you've taken are better off than the rest." Achibol got stiffly to his feet. "Well, boy? You can't sit here stargazing forever when there's work to be done."

INTERLUDE
The Great School, Midicor IV

"The Archmandrite of Vestivol? The Senior Prior of the Reformed Gathering of the One Beginning? The Guardians? The Rite of the Old Believers? Ab, those are fringe cultists and archconservatives. Saphooth is mad even to acknowledge them. What's he thinking of? We've got to put a stop to this." Kaledrin rose to full motator height and in his rush slid directly over his static-free work surface instead of going around it.

The two men glided down empty halls, hesitating at Saphooth's door. It was partly open, which was against the secretive old man's custom. Only the glow of monitor-lights on his ancient printer gave notice that it was not an abandoned storeroom. The shadowed, boxy forms of his simian-adapted furniture loomed like so many crates.

"Of course," Kaledrin thought, an uncomfortable suspicion already forming. A sheet of printed material projected from the machine. "Light," he commanded. As the lights came up, he snatched the sheet free. "He did it again," Kaledrin muttered. With a rattle-plated air of dejection, he handed the paper to Abrovid. "He outflanked us. Old bones has resigned—and he didn't even have the grace to appoint me his successor."

"Resigned?"

"Read it for yourself. I should have seen it coming."

"What's SOMA—the 'Society of Man, Absolute'?" Abrovid murmured.

"Pan-ecumenical fundamentalists. It's recently become MYTHIC's chief financial backer." He shuddered. "What a fool I've been. I thought it was just Saphooth's greed."

"Saphooth's working for them?" Abrovid asked with a gesture of amazed negation.

"For them? No. Read on. He's their new director. And considering SOMA's financial backing, he's probably still our boss!"

"But what does this mean for MYTHIC? Will they shut us down?"

"Oh, no. They'll fire me and appoint someone more 'flexible.' The Board of Trustees will resist, but Saphooth wouldn't have resigned unless he knew he could still control MYTHIC, perhaps more firmly than ever."

"What will you do now?"

Kaledrin tightened his body-plates into a suit of faintly iridescent armor. "I'll fight him."

---

* Of particular interest is Achibol's response to the boy's mention of reaching for the stars, the only concession the biocybes make to popular myth. It is Achibol, earthbound, who understands that aspiration, and where mutable humanity fits into it, not Benadek, our archetypic "ancestor."

CHAPTER SEVENTEEN,

in which Benadek casts a Spell of Age and Dissolution upon the Trickster, and takes his rightful place as First Among Men.

The Benadek of this episode is a familiar figure—the innocent whose clear sight illumines the Path of Salvation. Benadek's discovery of ancient Evil that binds mankind's feet in clay, his Quest for the Darkness at World's End, and his final victory, are culminant events in the orthodox Ksentos Venimentum text. In many culturally specific myths, the Pure Boy's confrontation with the Trickster replaces the KV text's formless, generic Evil. Other variants substitute Wandag, an Earth-spirit, for Teress.

Long accepted (in its traditional form) as an allegorical account of man's early forays into interstellar space *, this episode must now be viewed in a different light.

> Here Benadek's inspiration is not divine vision, but memories lingering in ancient molecules. Gods and demons have been demoted to computing devices inferior to even rudimentary biocybes.
>
> (Kaledrin, Senior Editor)

"Circe—voice mode please," Benadek said with a yawn, thrusting his castered chair back from the keyboard console. He shook his head to clear it and sighed gustily.

"Done, Lieutenant Benedict. Shall I complete the tabulations you requested, verbally?"

"Ah, no thanks. Printouts would be better. I'm too sleepy to listen right now. I'll read them after I've rested."

"Very well, Lieutenant. A printout is being assembled in niche five, with your other material."

"Thank you, Circe."

"You're welcome, Lieutenant."

Benadek slid the thick stack from the bin, being careful not to bend the corners of the sheets. Like many details at Biopsych Three, longevity had been overlooked for commonplace things like printout paper—or perhaps even the best could not survive twenty centuries undecayed. It was yellow-brown and brittle. Sometimes he had to open the printer to pull out crumbled sheets.

Even with expert memories, it had been a difficult and boring search, complicated by time-wasting security requirements. The Circe-interface could not always be used, and Benadek was unused to sitting for hours at a time, day after day. The highest-clearance information was screen-access-only. He had to scribble voluminous notes. Mistakes led to data-lockups, and he had to reapproach particular files by circuitous routes; sometimes he never found his way back to the data he wanted.

Cradling the printouts on his forearms, he fumbled with the door. Teress, waking from a doze in the lounge beyond, raised her head sleepily, then brightened as she noticed the look of satisfaction on Benadek's exhausted face. "You have it? You're done?"

"Almost," he said. "It's in here somewhere—every military or government installation, every university facility in use from 2005 on. There's a pattern I can almost feel. There are ancients hiding in this paper . . ." He reddened as she lifted the top sheet and peered under it. " . . . who're being supplied from the outside. I have records of computer accesses to eight installations similar to this one, all as recent as seven years ago. And two of them are completely off-line now! They're probably stripped and empty, or destroyed."

One significant discovery was satellite, radio, and land-line communication between centers of ancient activity. Another was that Circe, though not privy to all the data-transfers that had taken place between them, had handled all Biopsych Three's inputs and outputs, and had kept records. "No wonder she's befuddled," Benadek thought. "She's shuffled data into every nook and cranny of memory and she still can't contain it all." No one had foreseen that over two thousand years, even at low activity levels, her massive storage arrays would be overwhelmed with routine transactions. While the computers had continued to function, the humdrum data had continued to be exchanged.

"What's left to do?" Teress asked.

"I'm going to read through all this, and sleep on it," he told her, shifting his burden to his left arm and rubbing his eyes with his right.

"Do you want company?" she asked, batting her eyelashes mock-suggestively. "Never mind," she added quickly when she saw his expression. "I know you're too tired." He was always too tired. Her nagging, internal critic never ceased to remind her that after her fling (when she had allowed her body to have its way, ignoring all the lessons she should have learned about involvement with Benadek) he had never had time, energy, or interest to approach her again.

Rationally, she made apologies for him: he drove himself and was totally involved in his search; he was so tired he hardly slept (she had to wave food under his nose to get him to eat). But it did not help her feel better. She wanted him to say "Let the ancients have the world—all I want is you," but Benadek was not one for grand gestures. Besides, if he approached her now, after ignoring her, she knew she would snap at him in her nastiest way.

"Here," she said, "let me carry some of those." He nodded gratefully, and pushed the latch-pad. The door had been sticking lately, and he had to shoulder it open. They took the papers to his room, and she waited hesitantly. Setting down his papers, Benadek put his hands on her shoulders and looked into her eyes. She twisted free. "Shall I wake you, or will you have Circe do it?" she asked from the doorway.

"You're much nicer to wake up to," he said. He intended to go over the printouts, but as soon as he sat to remove his boots, he knew he was not going to get up for several hours.

The sound of his door opening awakened him. Urchin-habits died hard, overriding the deepest sleep. Expecting Teress, he was surprised to recognize Achibol's dark face. "We must talk," the old man stated quietly. "Are you awake?"

"I am, now," Benadek replied grumpily. "It couldn't have waited until morning?" He swung his bare legs over the edge of the bed and motioned Achibol to sit down.

"It *is* morning. For that matter, it's always morning

down here—or night, or afternoon. You lost track. Consider it morning, and wake up. You've overslept again." Achibol laughed. It could have been a sneeze, thought Benadek.

"What do you want to talk about?"

"Teress—and you. That's a problem." Benadek only raised a mildly curious, noncommittal eyebrow. "You slept with her, didn't you?" Achibol accused.

Benadek did not know how to react. There had only been one night with Teress, after he had absorbed the last ancient's memories. He hardly felt accountable. Jack Van Duinen, engineer and construction boss for NearSpace Industries' orbital operations, had been a vital, hormone-dominated man. It was as much he as Benadek who had swept the vulnerable Teress off her feet and bedded her when she was bored and lonely, in the aftermath of fear for Benadek's survival. Big Jack had been so intense, so life-loving that Benadek had even unconsciously began to *change* physically to match the man's dominant self-concept. But he could not admit to Achibol that he had lost control. "Yes," he admitted. "One night."

"And then?" Achibol was not mollified.

"Then nothing. It was an accident. I'm sorry if I displeased you."

Achibol had not become accustomed to his apprentice's new clarity and facility, absorbed from his secondary personalities. "It's not me who's displeased," the mage said limply. "It's Teress."

"What's she got to complain about?" The old, belligerent Benadek overpowered his adjuncts. "I didn't rape her. It was mutual." Very mutual, he remembered warmly. "And I haven't bothered her since."

"That's the problem. You haven't."

"Huh?"

"She's no more casual with her love than her disdain, which you've experienced." Benadek stared uncomprehendingly. "She's in love with you, boy! You should be grateful, but you spurn and torment her."

"She is? I do? I mean, I like her a lot. It was good, that time. Almost as good as with . . ." He shied from that still-painful line of thought. No matter what the future held, he affirmed with boyish loyalty, no one would ever replace Sylfie.

"That's another problem," Achibol snapped. "A living girl can't compete with a dead poot! Forget Sylfie!" Achibol immediately wished he had bitten his tongue. "No, I don't mean that," he said gently, his dark, deep-set eyes apologizing, "but you must put her out of your mind when you're with Teress. She too loved Sylfie but she can never *be* her. Nor would you want that."

Benadek nodded. He was more at ease with Achibol as advisor and confidant than Achibol, protector of female innocence. "You're right," he agreed. "But I don't know what to do! We're running out of time. I think I love her, but I need every moment, or there'll never be time for love."

"How is that? You're both young, and have lifetimes ahead." Running out of time. For Achibol the concept had suffered centuries of disuse. Only in his haste to get Benadek to Biopsych Three when his first *changing* had been imminent had he shown any sense of urgency. Now there were far too many reminders of time—some of them, internal ones, he did not want to think about, because there was nothing he could do about them. He was not really immortal, only old. Too damned old.

"It's a multiple crisis." Benadek interrupted the old man's reflection. "I discovered it through the data banks. Equipment failure is the most material problem. You've seen often enough how things are running down, decaying, both from observing the condition of the temples, and from your failure to contact Gibraltar."

"What?" Achibol snapped. "What did you just say?"

"Gibraltar?" Benadek asked, toying with the old man and masking a sly smile, "A second-rate military base co-opted by idealistic scientists to combat the planners' schemes. I discovered a lot of things in the data banks.

"Dr. Archibald Scribner," he said in a synthetic-voice monotone, "BA, University of Michigan, Medieval Literature; MS, Columbia, Genetics and Microbiology; PhD, Michigan State."

"You got that from Circe? If the planners knew about Headquarters . . ."

"They may not. I figured it out from your remarks and the raw data—including my memories. That combination of information wouldn't occur elsewhere. No, I think the secret of your headquarters, and the immortality process that's kept you alive, is still secure. The planners never knew there were watchdogs like you until recently. You felt their reaction via the honches." Benadek paused to yawn and stretch.

"Well?" Achibol urged impatiently.

"As I said, equipment failure—first peripheral stuff like computer paper and lighting, then hardware, and finally software and data. In twenty years, whole systems will fail, and there'll be no chance of using the temples to revive ancient man—the gene-records will be trashed."

"That's bad," the mage agreed, frowning, "but do we really want to bring them back? Between simples and the pure-humans, things will go on. Who needs the honky bast—"

"Not so!" Benadek interrupted. "Without the temples, simples will degenerate. Even if not, with the most stable genomes ancient science could create, and low levels of pollution and radiation, they'll remain simple forever. In a thousand thousand years they may accumulate enough genetic errors to begin evolving, but why would they evolve *upward*? They'll never reach for the stars."

"The stars? An interesting vanity," Achibol mused. "In all these earthbound years I've forgotten them except as guiding lights in the sky. Yet once man dreamed of visiting the suns they represent. Have you revived their dream? Hmmm . . . Pure-humans scattered across the void, *changing* to fit one environment or the next . . ."

"Unless we act soon, there'll be no dreams to revive," Benadek interrupted. "The ancients' extermination of pure-humans will succeed."

"Impossible! They'll never hunt down every last one."

"They don't have to," Benadek insisted. "Honches' programming will outlast the machinery that supported them. They'll continue to hunt down anyone that's different. They've already succeeded in bringing about the crisis: the surviving pure-humans are in hiding, scattered so widely they can't interbreed. When a gene pool falls below five hundred individuals, it fails."

"But the conditions—genetic drift within small gene pools, and occasional exogamy producing hybrid vigor—would be no different than those that caused their evolution in the first place . . ." Achibol began, then stopped himself, as a key thought surfaced, "except for the mutation rate. Without selective pressures and constant mutations . . ." His face fell. "How long before they'll be gone?"

"Five to seven generations. A hundred and fifty years, at the outside."

Achibol's eyes reflected every year of his two millennia. "What can we do?"

"In the long run, we should reestablish genetic communication between the remaining pure-humans."

"And if the honches prevent them from gathering in villages . . ."

"Exactly. The honches must be stopped. Their masters must be found and neutralized, and the honches reprogrammed."

Achibol saw the bright intensity of his apprentice's gaze. "You have a plan?"

"A plan and a destination. I'll show you and Teress after breakfast."

"Teress . . . we've forgotten about her, about . . ."

"I haven't forgotten, Master. Give me a while alone, and I'll solve that problem, at least for now. Then we can discuss the larger one, and how to deal with it."

"Two hours, then," Achibol said, slowly getting to his feet. "I hope you know what you're doing," he said emphatically, "for I surely don't."

Benadek, through his alter egos, had mastered the conference room's sophisticated holo-systems. A shimmery, immaterial image formed at the far end of a darkly polished table littered with the remains of breakfast. In response to his subvocalized command, beams of light visible in the ubiquitous dust converged into a solid-seeming sphere. Blue, beige, and startling white swirls flowed across its surface, and it resolved into a side-lit globe.

It seemed to Achibol that the Earth itself hung poised before him. The projection drew his attention away from Benadek, from the boy's solution to the problem of his relationship with Teress. Benadek had surprised him, indeed. He had taken the easy way out of his dilemma. "He could have had the grace to *change* into an inexhaustible satyr, instead of back to his old self, but even younger," the oldster had muttered to the girl when they first saw him. "I can't remember if he was really that ugly or not."

Teress was not distraught by Benadek's choice. His narrow head with its shock of unruly black hair, his beady, black rodent-eyes darting quickly, never resting a full second on anything, his skinny arms and prominent ribs visible under his knit military-issue undershirt, all seemed to appeal to her in some perverse way. "He's terribly cute," she told Achibol, "and he's changed his pheromones."

"Cute? Where did you hear that? Old movies?"

"Teevee, daddy. I 've been watching beach flicks on the tube."

"Arrghh! Spare me the worst of the old times. Beach flicks! Can't you watch war movies?"

Teress laughed. "Omaha, Iowa, Gold, Juno . . . Normandy beach flicks. History tapes." Achibol could not help grinning, but returned his attention to Benadek and the globe.

" . . . The temple malfunctions, up until seventy years ago, were random. The only consistent change was this . . ." Black dots, functioning temples, were thick over the inhabited parts of the globe. Blinking red ones represented malfunctions. Suddenly a green one appeared. As Achibol watched, several nearby temples, red and black alike, turned green. Steadily, the number of green dots spread. A few reverted to red, but only a few. "Do you recognize that, Master?"

The mage stared at the holo-image for several seconds before he understood the pattern. "You've traced my route over the last century. How?"

"The error-checking codes in the temples' satellite uplinks. They're stored on a first-in first-out basis. Since Circe's memory is at capacity, earlier ones have been wiped. I can't chart anything after the uplinks failed, either, but many of the temples you repaired and modified are still active. I'm surprised you didn't try using the satlinks to contact Gibraltar."

"I did, boy," Achibol muttered, "but I gave up. I'd gotten no response in two hundred and seventy years of trying. You see," he explained in response to Benadek's incredulous look, "there weren't that many of us to begin with. The immortality process had . . . drawbacks . . . and we were volunteers. Five hundred years ago, Yasha, the only surviving field agent besides me, reported in for the last time. I kept in contact with Gibraltar for almost fifty years, but after that—pffft! Nothing more. No answers. I never knew if equipment failures were at fault, or if the others just shut the base down and walked away. But go on . . ."

Benadek nodded. "All right. Seventy years ago, the pattern changed. Like this." Achibol caught a hint of his subvocal utterance to Circe. Red flashes lit the globe in increasing numbers. At first they clustered near several points. One was in central Asia, another in sub-Saharan Africa, and the last a few hundred miles north of the old United States border with Canada. "The yellow dot there is Biopsych Three," Benadek said, confirming the mage's guess. "Now watch." The infecting glow of red spots, malfunctions, spread patch by patch until the room was lit with the ruddy glow.

"That's a future projection, then," Achibol surmised. "How long do we have?"

"That was ten years ago," Benadek said.

"How can that be?" Achibol quavered in confused dismay. "What of the temples I've visited since then? There have been hundreds! You—you were with me some of the time. You know they were functioning. Why aren't those still green?"

"I wondered too. That's what led me to suspect the nature of our enemy—that, and the honches' anomalous equipment. Did you see how the 'infections' spread?" He took the brief jerk of Achibol's head for a "yes." "They aren't infections. The temples haven't really failed either—we know that because we've been there—so the dearth of signals, the red on the globe, had to have another explanation. They're being jammed."

He explained. "The communication channels are

being overridden. Look, I'll run it back a few years. See how it all happened at once, within each locus? Now it's holding steady. Now here's another 'growth spurt,' and another, and . . ." He spread his empty palms.

"Transmissions!" Achibol exclaimed, his mind rapidly assimilating the significance of what he had seen. "Ground-based signals overloading the intertemple nets and the uplinks themselves. As they knocked out the uplinks, it spread faster, shutting down whole areas. Does the timing of the later bursts correspond with the 'deaths' of the other facilities your records show?" Benadek stated that the facilities' computer systems had been accessed in February, and that they were silenced in mid-March. "Then the purpose of the raids was to obtain transmission equipment. Hmmm . . . The necessary antenna arrays might well be visible in satellite cameras."

"I must not have made myself clear, Master. That final 'growth spurt' is inferred from the fact that all Biopsych Three has received since then is high-strength noise. None of what I've shown incorporates current data. All communication with the satellites ceased ten years ago, and what rudimentary contact remains with other facilities is via underground cables, relics of a fiber-optic system."

"So for ten years the temples have been operating independently," Achibol said, quickly recovering from his momentary dismay. "But why? What purpose is served?"

Benadek laughed dryly. It was strange, Achibol thought, to hear an adult laugh issue from the boy's now-prepubescent throat. "They've countered *you*, Master. Don't you see?"

"Me? But what reason . . . ah, of course. If we assume that their purpose is not to destroy the planners' 'simple' world, but to maintain it indefinitely, then all is lucent. As long as pure-humans were 'templed' on a statistically regular basis, the planners' central computers put off the renaissance of ancient genes. But when I reprogrammed temples to reject pure-human data instead of incorporating it into the database, the day of reckoning, the revival of ancient humanity, drew nearer. It makes sense, but it doesn't explain why our nameless enemy wants it that way. Is there an answer to that?"

"There is, but not here in outdated computer memories. The answer is there!" Benadek stabbed an accusing finger at the red-pocked globe, indicating the Rocky Mountains north of what had once been the Canadian border. "The Columbia Icefields. Does that stimulate your memory, Master?"

"Indeed it does, it does," Achibol confirmed. "I've been there . . . On my honeymoon." He shook his head sadly, and let old memories flow. "Jasper Park. We took the train out of Edmonton. The Icefields are a remnant of the glaciers that covered much of the country, a long time ago. There was a lodge, and campgrounds. What would we find now?"

"I don't know. What we seek was created in accord with the Continental Defense Treaty of 2013. What would that signify?"

"A command center! A cave complex like this, but under the ice—a perfect ablative shield against thermonuclear attack." Feral light gleamed in his dark eyes. "The last refuge of the generals who perpetrated the 'simple' atrocity . . . and alive! Still alive. Yes, boy, the answers will be there. But the generals have had two thousand years to develop their horrors. I wonder what we'll find?"

CHAPTER EIGHTEEN,

Messages from the Black House, where dwell the Dead.

The Eater of Souls belongs to a separate mythic tradition from Achibol and Benadek, but the biocybes have cited it as source material.

Romantics may be disappointed, because the story of Gaddo and Ameling, dear to young females galaxywide, is presented unconventionally. The biocybes have deleted the lovely Ameling entirely and replaced her with . . . but see for yourselves. Just remember the inherent flexibility of myth: one people's god may be another's demon.

Debate rages, exacerbated by the precipitous resignation of Director Saphooth, and his acceptance of a position with SOMA*, a consortium of archconservative one-worlders. SOMA, through various front organizations, controls a significant share of MYTHIC's financing—and the influence that goes with it. The director's position is still unfilled, and SOMA is pressing for a sympathetic replacement.

This must not happen. A research project, no matter how it catches the public interest, must not be influenced by beliefs. Beliefs and convictions inspire the collection of facts that support them, but facts, even in the greatest numbers, are only data. They may inspire confidence, but they *prove* nothing. Skepticism, on the other hand, is vital to scientific inquiry. In science, there is no *proof*. Hypotheses (not beliefs) can only be *disproved*—and one contradictory datum is all it takes.

MYTHIC straddles the border between science and belief. Its data base is myth, its goal neither to prove nor to disprove, but to understand the processes underlying myths' creation.

It is vital that the new director understand the project's philosophy and goals. He should have specific qualifications as well:

1) An extensive background in comparative mythology.
2) Experience applying rigorous scientific methodology in his own field.
3) The capability to set aside personal convictions. He must be a monument to probity and impartiality.

Neither SOMA, the GSHP ** nor any other "interested" party should decide MYTHIC's strategies or edit its publications. That task must remain in the hands of literary scholars.

If you, the reader, have been stimulated by these tales and wish them to continue to unfold

---

* Society of Man, Absolute.

** Galactic Society of Human Paleontology.

in an unbiased manner, exactly as the biocybes have produced them, then make your voices heard. Though SOMA currently provides 40% of MYTHIC's operating expenses, you, subscribers and supporters furnish 55%. The Board of Trustees will listen to you.

(Kaledrin, Senior Editor)

INTERLUDE
The Great School, Midicor IV

"Will it make a difference?"

"I hope so, Ab. Our original subscribers aren't fundamentalists."

"They won't vote as a bloc like SOMA. You'll be lucky to get an equal showing."

"If twenty percent write in, the Board will pick me, or someone like me. They weren't appointed by SOMA. They don't want priests, magisters, and medicine men standing behind their desks dictating to them."

"Why didn't you say that? All that 'rigorous scientific' stuff leaves me cold."

"You want me to be as bad as SOMA? 'If my opponent wins, every geologist will have a priest holding his hammer! Every surgeon will operate beneath the eye of a shaman in grease and feathers!' That sort of thing? No, they'll understand."

"I hope so. I really like working here."

The days following Benadek's revelation of dangers unforeseen flew by, free of the stresses that had driven the threesome. Benadek's *change* relieved sexual tension between him and Teress, though it was far from a perfect solution, as Achibol frequently reminded him with snorts of exasperation and disgust not entirely feigned. Benadek's relationship with the pure-human girl was amicable. His barely adolescent body's innocuous chemical signals neither threatened nor enticed. Apart from an occasional nostalgic look she treated him like a well-loved younger brother.

"Whatever he has in mind," she explained to Achibol, not for the first time, "he'll be in great danger. That kind of bond might distract him."

"He told you that? The boy's tight as a clam, with me."

"He hasn't told me a thing," she reassured him obliquely, patting his hand, which he indignantly snatched away.

"Don't *do* that! I'm not your old grandpappy, remember?"

"My what?"

"Never mind. Did you find the storerooms?"

"Circe did. Everything we need is here—and lots of things I don't recognize. You'll have to come with me, next time. I took three canvas packs with lots of pockets, and some cook-pots that fit inside each other."

"There should be tents, heaters, ration packs . . ."

"There probably are."

The outfits they put together were as light and compact as late-twenty-first-century science and industry could make them. They gathered throwaway lights, shelters that collapsed to fit Teress's palm, ration-packs that heated themselves and tasted no worse than Circe's fare.

Teress found wristwatch-sized communicators that worked fine in the hallways of Biopsych Three, but were useless on the surface. "It's the jamming," Benadek said. "Just as well—we might alert the ones I want to sneak up on. I'm hoping those honches have reported us dead in the swamp, by now."

"Do you think they have?"

"We almost did die, didn't we?"

"Now that you mention it . . ."

To Achibol's and Teress's surprise, Benadek began acting like the boy he purported to be. Preparing to depart, free of the most grueling work, he took time to discover some of the ancients' entertainments, as Teress had been doing for several weeks. She became his enthusiastic guide through the esoterica of "the movies." Benadek watched cube after cube of fictional adventures and documentaries. He soon stabilized on a diet of twentieth-century naval stories and on fantasies about far-future civilizations and the exploration of the galaxy. The slow, protesting murmurs of the other residents in his body did not faze him. Their staid denunciations of instantaneous travel, paranormal powers, time machines, and faster-than-light spaceships flowed through his blood and impinged on his brain with no more lasting effect on his addiction than did Achibol's all-too-frequent diatribes against "filling your narrow head with the accumulated trash of the ages."

He dutifully watched romantic comedies with Teress. Her grasp of the nature of the ancients' ordinary folk, their lives and desires, was more useful, she insisted, than either fantasies or the dark, somber drama Achibol indulged in. But the oldster grew petulant if they did not join him in his viewing. "At least the ones I watch are supposed to be funny," Teress protested, "and though I don't laugh at all the same things those ancient people did, I've probably learned more than you have from that awful *Macbeth*."

"The Scottish Play is great drama," the mage said pompously.

"So are *we*," she countered.

Achibol raised his eyes to hers. "You may be right," he said after much deliberation, "but I hope our outcome is less . . . tragic."

✧ ✧ ✧

The first few days' journey traversed terrain like that surrounding Sufawlz. Further north, it became rougher and rockier, but the hills remained small, and they had a well-preserved ancient vehicle. The "Tin Mule" ran on stabilized hydrogen. It electrolyzed fresh fuel from spring water, using power from solar collectors on its roof. Its fuel tanks held enough for thirty hours of continuous operation.

The Tin Mule was a hybrid, a ground-effect machine on smooth surfaces and unruffled waters, wheel-driven on steeper terrain. The first days were mostly over the latter, but shortly after crossing the old Canadian border they turned westward, and now slid smoothly over rolling grassy plains that stretched from horizon to horizon, relieved only by deep-cut river valleys. Nothing rose above the endless grass; even the blessed, shade-giving cottonwoods that crowded the riverbanks did not project much higher than the high banks that sheltered them.

For four days, they saw no trace of human activity. On the fifth, a column of smoke rose straight into the pristine blue afternoon sky. Not wildfire, it was concentrated in one narrow shaft and erupted from ground level in puffs and small clouds instead of a steady stream, only blending into a uniform haze where high-altitude winds feathered it south and eastward.

After all their time alone, first in the morass, then in Biopsych Three, now in the wilderness again, the very idea of other living beings seemed eerie. Nonetheless, they steered north of their former course and headed toward the slowly twisting, segmented black pillar.

"How far is it?" Benadek wondered after they'd pursued the column for several hours. Sunset was not far off.

"Still more than twenty miles," the old man

estimated when they stopped to stretch and relieve themselves. "I've noted its direction on the auto-compass. We'll be there tomorrow." They traveled another hour before night fell, preceded by a rose and crimson sunset that decorated even the eastern-most wisps of cloud with color. They made a simple camp under the open sky.

"There's a little black house ahead," Teress reported when she returned from her scouting mission. Seeds of late-blooming grasses clung in her tight-bound hair. "I saw wagon tracks, but no people. They must have moved on before dawn."

"Hmmm," Achibol pondered. "Perhaps we should examine what traces they left. Are they simples, I wonder, or closer kin?"

"How will you tell that from wagon tracks?" Benadek asked skeptically.

"You'd be surprised what can be deduced."

Assured by Teress that no one lingered around the odd, small building, the Tin Mule's infrared scope confirmed it. Trampled grass and grown-over ruts mingled around the unadorned stonelike cube. Its walls were five paces in length, unmarred by joints, slightly weather-rounded at the corners. The east wall held a gray metal door, of a kind Benadek had seen before. Achibol's exclamation confirmed his speculation. "A temple! I haven't seen one like this, uncluttered with outbuildings and additions in . . . let me see now . . . it must be twelve, no, fifteen hundred years. How small and strange it looks, here in the midst of this grassy sea! Already I'm learning much about the people who visit it."

"You are?" Benadek considered the barren cube unrevealing. Tracks and trampling told him only that recent visitors used carts or wagons, and had beasts to draw them—oxen, to judge by the cloven hoofprints, though of the four-, six-, or eight-legged types he could not tell.

Achibol noted the boy's tone and manner with well-disguised pleasure. Their return to the world of sunlight, weather, and fresh air was having effects besides sunburn. Away from the computers and frozen memories of Biopsych Three, Benadek was losing the mannerisms of his secondary personalities. Whether merely dormant, as the boy claimed, or fading entirely away, Achibol was happy for the return to their old, comfortable relationship. He could be as condescending and irascible as he wished. Benadek, too, seemed to welcome it, and played the "ignorant apprentice" broadly, a knowing caricature of the boy he had been in their easy, carefree days.

"Observe, apprentice. Absence often says much. The barrenness of the structure declares that there is no priestly caste—people visit here without cultish impedances and tolls. The deep ruts, all the same width apart, state that such visitors are one people, who make their conveyances to a standard. The old sod in the ruts informs me that they are nomadic, passing by only infrequently, perhaps as one of several temples on their annual round. Further, lightly trampled grasses, undisturbed growth roundabout, and the dearth of ruts off the main track assure me that travelers arrive here only one wagon or so at a time, and never linger—or there would be other ruts, where latecomers and early departees could pass by the rest. You see?"

"They're nomads with no love for temples, then," Benadek observed, "simples who dislike the necessity of having to visit them—and there are no honches among them."

"How do you figure that?" Teress asked.

"They travel in small groups. Honches need people to dominate. I think there's some critical number necessary to hold a honch in a particular place."

"An interesting speculation," Achibol commented. "It's not beyond the planners' capabilities to have arranged. It makes sense that police—which honches were, before their natures were perverted—would linger with groups large enough to need policing. That would ensure that the least productive simples didn't impose unduly on the resources of others. Large gatherings of honches, quasi-military organizations, may be aberrant results of the secondary geas placed on them to eliminate pure-humans . . .

"But what now, boy? We could overtake them by noon." Benadek and Teress agreed it made sense to gain information about what lay ahead, and that an innocuous family would be less risky than a settlement or a larger gathering.

Before they departed, Achibol wished to examine the temple, though it might not matter much longer if he repaired it or reprogrammed its computer. Using his "talisman" key, he entered alone, and a scant half hour later emerged with a puzzled frown and a small greenish component board.

"What's that?" Benadek asked.

"I'm not sure," the mage muttered, his frown deepening. "It's not a standard replacement unit. I had trouble reprogramming the system until I found this and pulled it out. It overrode the euthanasia chamber, lowering the microwave intensity and cutting the duration in half. I can't understand that. Who would have wanted anomalies—pure-humans—to be *half* killed, then expelled? Who, and why?" Neither Benadek nor Teress offered suggestions.

They climbed aboard the Tin Mule. Teress drove. Benadek sat silently, envisioning a big, bearded man emerging, screaming, from a wide-swung temple door, his clothes crackling and smoking, his skin reddened, his hair smoking, and his eyes blistered blind. A pure-human. His father . . . Half killed and then expelled . . . His father's suffering had not been a fluke. Benadek's knuckles whitened. He clutched his knees and stared unseeing at the flat prairie that slowly, all too slowly, moved by.

The sorcerer, meantime, held the microchip card, turning it over and over in his gnarled hands as if it would yield its secrets to the intensity of his gaze.

The large-wheeled wagon rested hub-deep in yellow grass, its two oxen grazing on coarse stems. The Tin Mule drew abreast, thirty paces distant. Achibol aimed the IR scanner toward the wagon. "They're hiding under it," he concluded from the screen display.

Teress lowered herself to the ground. "What do you think you're doing?" Benadek demanded.

"They'll be less threatened by me."

Achibol stilled Benadek's protest. "I'll have my staff close at hand," he said, "and this too." He held out the talisman. "If you sense trouble, fall to the ground, and I'll activate the unconsciousness field."

Benadek reached for a laser pistol to plug it into the dashboard. Achibol restrained him with a casually outstretched arm. "Unnecessary," he murmured. "If they've seen such weapons in the hands of honches, they'll be cowed, but we'll never gain their trust. Teress is in no danger."

So it proved. Too far away to hear speech over wind-rattled grasses, they saw a man emerge, then a female—a poot of the red-hair-and-freckles variety—and three smaller figures. The poot looked too young to be mother to the children, one of whom was only a head shorter than she.

Teress motioned Benadek and the mage to come forward. She introduced Gaddo, a short, muscular man—pure-human?—clad in soft-tanned hides, and Jilleth, his companion, whose smoke-stained full-length skirt and blouse reminded Benadek of "Western" garments from Biopsych Three's drama collections.

The children were shy waifs who nodded silently as their names were spoken. "They lost a sister an' their ma to honches last winter," Gaddo confided in soft, slurred tones. "They've never seen many strangers."

"What business do honches have with women and children?" Achibol asked.

Gaddo snorted derision. "You mock me, old man. How could you live to grow that beard, an' not know honches? Or don't you or yours need the damned temples, where honches lurk?"

"I don't mock you, Gaddo," Achibol replied mildly. "In our far home, honches behave differently. Answer me truthfully, that we may prepare ourselves." Gaddo replied that he would explain all he could, but over hot brew by a fire, not standing exposed to hostile eyes. He gestured to a low copse where dry wood and concealment would be at hand. He expressed a desire to ride the Tin Mule there. "I've seen the hulks of such things on the prairie, but never alive and moving," he explained. He was unable to say who might have driven the abandoned vehicles, or how long ago. Achibol motioned him aboard.

While the four adults waited for weed tea to boil, Jilleth and the children kept watch from the tallest tree in the copse. They watched less for distant enemies or friends, Gaddo explained, than for the puffs of smoke that served as distant early warning of honch raiders, a kind of prairie radio network. The very smoke that had led them to the temple had been Gaddo's contribution to the net, when he had determined that no honches lay in ambush. Though one might ride for days without seeing another family or band, he told them, scarcely a day went by without at least one such signal being seen, oftener several.

Benadek, the dutiful apprentice, carefully noted the smoke-codes as Gaddo enumerated them. It was a simple system, albeit slow, but honches had yet to demonstrate that they'd deciphered it. Meanings of phrases changed with the seasons and the time of day. Even Circe would have been hard put to decrypt them.

Gaddo filled out their knowledge of the prairie folk. Nomads traveled in search of bounteous but seasonal resources; they fished, hunted, and gathered roots in season, never overburdening the fragile balance with large groups or too-consistent patterns in their roving. In Gaddo's mother's mother's time there had been gatherings at the weirs on the river called Center of the World, but the coming of the honches had changed that. "Ma's ma was young when the first honches came," he explained, "an' she saw whole families killed at the weirs. They took only the untempled, then, but killed others who fought them."

"The untempled?" Benadek and his master blurted simultaneously.

"Ones who never feel the craving. They're who the black ones seek."

"Pure-humans!" Benadek exclaimed.

"So it must be, boy. Let Gaddo continue without further outbursts."

Plainly disapproving of impertinent boys, the plainsman did so. Honch strategy emerged, clearer for the outsider's knowledge. They hid near temples, and watched the comings and goings of nomad families, observing who went within and who did not. (As a rule, Gaddo explained, regular temple-goers entered the shrines as opportunity presented, rather than risking debilitation later should such opportunity be denied them.) When honches took note of people who remained outside, they attacked. They did not kill untempled ones outright; they forced them to enter the temples. When the victims were ejected kicking and screaming in blind agony, the honches dragged them away. None were ever seen again, not alive.

"Honches put the devices there, then," Benadek

blurted, earning a further disapproving glare from Gaddo.

"I suspect you're right, boy," Achibol agreed, ignoring the plainsman's displeasure. "Making the cremation-cycle merely disabling, they identify pure-humans without destroying them, and satisfy their innate cruelty at the same time. But why save them at all? That seems in conflict with the planners' intent."

Gaddo had listened silently to the old man's talk of devices and purposes. Now he silenced the mage with a slashing motion of his hand. Like a bear awakening in midwinter, he stretched and swelled as he spoke, his face a mask of bright, bitter anger. "Such questions form too readily on your well-spoken tongue. You've asked nothing of the fate of the untempled. You ask, 'what winds will blow tomorrow' when you don't know the time of the day, the season, or even where on the face of the world you stand."

Achibol was taken aback by his intensity and the salience of his speech. What, indeed, did they know of the captives' fate? The mage reprimanded himself for his blindness: the uneducated nomad understood more than appearances suggested.

Teress took the opportunity at hand. "What follows their capture, Gaddo? What do you know of their fates?"

The plainsman acknowledged her with a nod, less upset that a female should ask than that a boy should interrupt the speech of men. "They're taken into the Great Lodge of He-Who-Eats-Souls, fodder for the Nameless One. Their husks are sucked like spiders' prey and cast out again." Nomads, they were to discover, often employed the odd, staccato inflection of "speaking in capital letters" when referring to things Spiritual, Mysterious, or of great emotional impact.

"You've seen them?" Teress asked.

"I've carried away the empty shells of my Rosalie and my child. I made the Long Journey to the Vale of the Dead. In the second moon of Winter, I found Rosalie, and in the third, the girl, Shabeth."

Silence followed, broken only by the harsh rale of Gaddo's breathing. He hid his eyes behind lank hair that hung from his bowed head. When his breathing evened, he again took up his tale. "I knew the husk had been Rosalie by her red hair and the scars of childhood pox. Otherwise all I'd loved was gone. There was no moisture in it, no weight but bones."

He paused, defiant, as if expecting them to contest his tale or mock him with casual words. Teress's hand crept out to cover his where it rested on his knee. None spoke, but questions still lingered in their eyes. Gaddo nodded. "There's little more to tell. In the days after Rosalie was Made Ashes and Returned to Wind, madness consumed me. I found Shabeth later, the worse for having lain untended while my mind was fled. Rain had filled her husk with moisture and it wouldn't burn, so I took her and another of my tribe to the hills beyond sight of the Vale, where I cut wood for a great pyre, and sent them On." Spreading his hands wide, he shrugged. "That's the end of my tale. It's little different than what any man might tell—the path to the Vale of the Dead is well-worn by the wain-wheels and feet of my people."

While they'd talked, the sun had sunk low and the fire seemed to burn the more brightly for it. Now Gaddo removed stick after stick, smothering each one, allowing no smoke to rise. Teress helped him cover the fire-pit with earth. Gaddo strode to the side of the clearing nearest his wagon, then turned back as if a further thought had struck him. "I know nothing of your customs, men from beyond the Edge of the World. I would not offend you, but . . ."

"Say what you will," Achibol urged him. "No offense will be taken where none is intended."

Gaddo looked toward Teress. "It's been two seasons since I returned from the Vale, fifteen moons since Rosalie was lost. Jilleth is but a child, and for long, I wanted no woman over my wheels, but now . . ."

Achibol shook his head slowly, not even glancing at Teress. "It is not our custom to . . ."

"Not custom, but still my right to choose," Teress interrupted him. "I'll visit your wain, plainsman—for a single night only, and you'll not ask me to linger when my companions are ready to depart. Is that agreeable?"

"More than I would have hoped for," Gaddo replied with quiet intensity. He glanced cautiously toward the mage and the apprentice, whose expressions were uniformly unreadable. Then, with a curt nod, he spun on his heel. Teress remained long enough to fix her companions with a stern gaze that brooked no protest, and followed Gaddo.

Benadek turned to his master, his mouth ajar, words he had been too stunned to voice moments earlier now ready to spill forth. Achibol forestalled him. "Serves you right, boy," he said with a malicious snigger. "Had we not been an old man and a hairless boy, that wagoner would never have considered asking. Had you been a virile warrior, Teress would never have followed him. Have I reminded you lately of your cowardly choice? Need I do so tonight?"

As the sense of Achibol's comments penetrated his hurt and surprise, Benadek realized the truth. Having abdicated adult sexuality, he had no valid claim on Teress's. Only on one count was the old man in error—Benadek knew full well that Teress's decision was based less in attraction to the plainsman than in compassion.

Had Benadek been fully adult, she might still have risked his hormone-driven rage out of that gentle concern. As it was, the most Benadek was capable of feeling was petulant frustration. That, he reminded himself, was one reason he had assumed his current state; he had been afraid to take on hormones and intellect at once, when the fate of his world hung in the balance.

That situation had not changed: the plainsman's story confirmed what he had suspected. The denizens of the command center beneath the ice were diabolical; they had lost all claim to humanity, but they still controlled mankind's fate. The boy was more anxious than ever to move on in the morning.

Teress had been specific. Her cool bargaining with the nomad had at first bothered him as much as her acquiescence: she had been as matter-of-fact as a whore. But was that wrong? Gaddo had not been offended. Teress could not replace his Rosalie, but could for one brief night give him happiness without fear of importunements and demands on the morrow. She had protected her own interests, Gaddo's, Benadek's, and Achibol's as well.

"Incredible!" he reflected, considering the tenor of his thoughts. "Is this really me? Is jealousy no more than chemistry?" He wanted to explore that avenue, to poll the other minds dormant within but, as from a great distance, he heard Achibol address him.

"Well, boy? Put your jealousies aside, for we must talk."

"I'm not jealous, Master. What Teress did was right—and kind."

"You're not . . . it is? I mean . . . well then, fine." Achibol recovered quickly. "Let's discuss what the plainsman's told us. A remarkable adaptation to difficult conditions, wouldn't you say?"

"Truly, Master. And not only to the ordinary hardships of the prairie, but to being a mixed society of simples and pure-humans, and to honch predation as well. A less kind people might have driven the pure-humans from their midst."

"Just so. But why do these honches want pure-humans alive, when elsewhere they kill them outright? That's the meaning of the added circuit board, of course—to identify, disable, and take them alive."

"Gaddo gave us the answer."

"His talk of 'dried husks,' you mean? I've hardly speculated as to why the bodies of the dead are returned in that manner, or why returned at all."

"Immortality, Master. The ancients maintain themselves at the expense of pure-human lives. The 'husks,' drained of blood and fluids, are what's left after they're 'processed.' I came across the technique in Circe's files. It was considered impractical, because every eight or ten weeks of extended life required sacrificing the life of another. Even the ancients hadn't stooped that low."

"Hmmph. They hadn't stooped that low, or they couldn't cover the disappearances, in their well-regulated society? They developed the technique. They're using it now, when no one can stop them. But how is it done?"

"A recombinant virus infects the 'immortal,' cleansing his body fluids of mutagens. His cellular reproductive codes are thus less prone to replication errors and degeneration. But there's a problem."

"Obviously. What?"

"When the virus runs out of consumables to attach to its surface receptors, it begins collecting similar-shaped neurotransmitters. Those it modifies, if only so slightly. Their function is changed: the host is killed by the disruption of his own synaptic transmissions—his brain malfunctions. In fact, it can blow up."

"Oh? How can a brain, a soggy mass of fluids held together by flimsy membranes, burst?"

"Perhaps I misspoke myself. Do you happen to know the electrical potential across a neuron's membrane?"

"The sodium and potassium ion-charge differential? About seventy millivolts, I believe."

"Exactly. And the strength of the electric field created?" Achibol shrugged, obviously neither knowing nor caring, wishing the boy would stop playing *his* role and get on with it. Benadek continued: "Almost two hundred kilovolts per square centimeter. And that, across all the synaptic surfaces of all the neurons in the entire brain . . . ? All released at once, or near enough so as to make no difference? In the close confines of the cranium, the brain itself becomes a steam bomb."

"Horribly impressive, I should think," Achibol responded laconically, "but what of the pure-humans, boy? Where do they fit in?"

"I already told you. But you want to know the process, I suppose. Periodically, the host's blood is pumped through a tank of modified kidney tissue, whose cellular membranes permit the flow of virus, with its cargo of undesirable elements, in one direction only. The other side of the kidney tissue is connected to the victim, who must be genetically similar to the host—and to the kidney tissue itself—to be made compatible with simple MHC*-suppressor drugs. The pure-human is given a drug which stimulates the production of 2AIII Pentaphosphorylase, an enzyme. Under the stimulus of ever-increasing quantities of it, the virus, now in the victim's blood, enters its shedding phase—it reproduces. The victim dies. His body fluids are filtered of the virus, now free of aging products and enzymes. It is reintroduced into the host."

Achibol was as much impressed by Benadek's delivery of the information as he was by the hideous nature of the facts. "Whoo-eee, boy! Is that you

---

* MHC: Major Histocompatibility Complex, the genes that define "self" and "non-self." They are most similar in close relatives.

talking, or one of your companions? I think I understand it, but do you?"

"Completely, Master—just as well as I've come to understand the workings of my own cells. I'm less clear about the external facets of the ice-dwellers' activities. I can't answer your other question."

"Oh? What other question? With all this talk of enzymes and viruses, it's slipped my mind."

"You wondered why the 'husks' are returned to their relatives in the vale of the dead, didn't you?"

"Ah, so I did. So I did. That's all quite clear now."

"It is? Then will you enlighten me, Master?" Even now, Benadek felt a faint twinge at the remembrance of past "enlightenments."

"Of course! Have I ever failed to fulfill my obligations? Are you not more sage—or at least more erudite—than any apprentice sorcerer before you? I'll enlighten you."

"Please do, Master."

"What? Oh, yes, the 'husks.' It's been seventy years or so since the raid on the fish weirs. That marked the collapse of the ancients' breeding pool; until then, victims came from their own lower-class population—but that population could never have been large, and as only the best and healthiest were chosen to be living filters, the gene pool must have degenerated rapidly, especially at the last. The resulting defectives may not have been compatible. So there you have it."

"Master?"

"What?"

"The husks, Master. You were about to explain . . ."

"Weren't you paying attention, boy? Must I belabor every nuance? The surviving ancients needed a source of fully human bodies, and the widespread plains cultures, having integrated pure-humans and simples, were the obvious source. But they abandoned the weirs and other gathering-places. Ask Gaddo tomorrow—he'll tell you there used to be trade fairs, communal hunts, and other excuses for getting together to mingle and mate. The ancients are modifying plains culture to their own ends. The husks could be incinerated, but instead, the 'Vale of the Dead' has become tradition, a reinforcement of the power of 'He-Who-Eats-Souls.' Just you wait—the stage is set for the next phase, when the plains folk will select their own sacrifices from among their pure-human numbers, and truck them to the Vale personally. They'll bargain with the 'gods' in the traditional manner—with the living flesh of their best and most beautiful."

"A repellent idea, Master. Surely these folk are above such things."

"Right now, perhaps, but such sacrifices are as old as humankind—and for the first time, perhaps, there really will be a 'god' to bargain with. It will happen. Unless, of course, the remaining ancients can be stopped. Have you given thought to that?"

"We must go to the Vale of the Dead. There must be an entrance to the redoubt."

"And then?"

"Let's see what develops." Benadek knew what he intended, but it would not be easy for Achibol or Teress to accept. He would reveal his plan only when it was too late for argument.

Achibol rose. He mumbled something about lonely beds and stupid apprentices who deserved them. Benadek lingered by the dead fire, wistfully wondering whether Gaddo and Teress were yet asleep.

INTERLUDE
The Great School, Midicor IV

Abrovid peered over the clutter that surrounded Kaledrin. "When will the Board decide?"

The overworked editor did not look up. "Soon, I hope. I'm doing my job and Saphooth's, too. I can't keep on like this." Kaledrin's chitin was once again dull, edged with rough, fibrous delaminations that should have been polished away. His eyestalks were scaly, the orbs atop them clouded.

"Speaking of Saphooth," the programmer asked, "what's he been up to?"

"He's having his own troubles. SOMA's split."

"Split? You mean gone? Pffft?"

"A fine thought! But no, they've divided into two groups. Saphooth is now the leader of the smaller, extreme faction. Financial power lies with the majority, leaving Saphooth without influence. But he still has the public's attention, if only because he's controversial.

"That's good news. What did they split over?"

Kaledrin's laugh sounded to Abrovid like scrap-metal being thrown on a pile. "SOMA was begun by fundamentalists and know-nothings of a dozen beliefs. All they had in common was the one-world conviction and a hatred of universities and 'freethinkers.'" Kaledrin raised two eyestalks and swivelled them so their orbs stared at each other. "What wasn't obvious was that there was a strong subgroup in SOMA that cut right across sect lines. A group that was a natural for old Saphooth to discover . . ."

"Go on," Abrovid urged impatiently.

"The fixed-forms! There are more of them than you can imagine, Ab! We don't notice them because they don't advertise their infirmities, and they stay on the worlds they're born to. They have to, of course—most couldn't live anywhere else. Their attitudes are shaped by their restrictions; they gravitate toward provincial and conservative sects, that insist *their* origin-world and ancestral form are 'original.' But since none of them can agree on which one . . ." He made the same mocking eye-to-eye gesture again. "Saphooth found something they could all agree on—he teaches that they're all 'original' species, and that only one race ever evolved *becoming.*"

"Which one? Boneyforms like him, I suppose?"

"Only because MYTHIC's output seems to support it. But that's not the point. Would you say that being a fixed-form makes someone a minority?"

"Huh? Is that the point?"

"No, no! Not yet. But would you say that?"

"If there are less of them than us normal people, I would. QED."

"I mean a persecuted minority—an underclass."

"I don't know about that. They're just . . . challenged, that's all. Nothing to make a fuss about."

"Well, Saphooth thinks there is. He's telling them they're the true inheritors of their homeworlds, and that every normal . . . every mutable human . . . is of an entirely different race, a race of imitators and conquerors that has stolen not only their worlds, but their very forms. Our race, and . . . Benadek's. And worse, he's calling for a war of liberation against mutables everywhere."

"War?" Abrovid was aghast, though skeptical. "War? Nobody fights wars. Not since they got interstellar travel, and can go somewhere else and *become* . . . Oh." He stopped, trapped by his own words. "But wars are unnatural," he essayed again. "They're sub-human . . ." Again, he stopped. Kaledrin let him ponder, his posture conveying expectant neutrality. "War?" Abrovid finally asked, as if pleading for Kaledrin to contradict him.

"Riots, at least," Kaledrin replied. "Political action groups, pressure tactics, lawsuits—and guilt. I doubt they even know what they really want. But we know what Saphooth wants, don't we."

"We do?"

"To be like us! To *become*, like we do. But he can't. Not if his hypothesis represents reality—and I must admit, it seems to satisfy the facts, and I'm so agitated I can't even imagine a disproof."

"What should we do?"

"I don't know. We can hope the biocybes don't make things worse, that MYTHIC's output doesn't add more fuel to their fire—but that's a forlorn hope. I try to keep up the pretense that it's just a literary production, but . . . have you seen Chapter Nineteen? No? I suppose not. I've been sitting on it." Reaching beneath himself, Kaledrin drew forth a data-cube and proffered it to Abrovid. In truth, Kaledrin had been sitting on Chapter Nineteen.

Abrovid knew he would get no more explanations now. He had to read the output, fail to understand its significance, and then stroke Kaledrin's ego by asking enlightenment. It was, he reflected, not that much different—or better—than dealing with Saphooth.

---

* For a Glestuungo, little more substantial than swamp-water itself, the specter of earth or soil, of dry land in any form, is a symbol for all evil.

CHAPTER NINETEEN,

wherein the stick-man's flesh is become water, and Madness rises from Dirt.

The flexibility of myth is fully exposed in this episode, demonstrating the ease with which archetypal characters fission or fuse from one culture to another.

The primary source-myth arose among the Glestuung water-men whose colloidal bodies flow with the streams they live in. Ameling, rudely deleted from her role of quintessential lover one chapter ago, becomes a tragic figure of major proportion. For the Glestuungo, she is a symbolic victim of that Evil which springs from Earth, Dirt, Rock and Soil.*

Here, the Achibol of the Wandag cycles is split in two. Stick-man and Madman meet face-to-face, erstwhile colleagues but distinct and separate. Benadek alone remains One, the Pure

Boy of classical myth, as yet *unbecome*. But soon, the tale promises . . .

(Kaledrin, Senior editor)

The full moon came and went, tracing silvery fingers the length of the Tin Mule's back trail and beyond, from the plains and rounded eastern ridges to the gray line of jagged peaks below the western horizon ahead. Gaddo and his broken family were hundreds of miles behind.

Achibol had considered asking the plainsman to guide them to the mountains and the Vale, but Teress insisted they push on alone. Benadek wondered if her dalliance with the nomad had displeased her or if, to the contrary, she feared that his presence would have led to complexities. Knowing her, it was the latter, but either way, it pleased him. The complexities would have centered around himself. His present mild attitude would evaporate when he *changed* again. He would curse himself if he had lost Teress for good in the meantime.

They proceeded north parallel to the distant foothills, and the trail curved westward. The terrain roughened into rounded hills and rolling valleys, grassland broken by roadless tracts of dark, dense forest. Entering higher latitudes, days lengthened until the sun seemed to rise almost before sunset's glow died. They took turns driving, stopping for hot food and sleep only when fatigue overcame all three of them. The Mule's detectors provided their night watch.

On the first leg of their journey they had seen few others, but had read frequent smoke-messages. Now they saw no messages—contrary winds over hills and down the length of valleys made them possible only on calm days. Nor did they see other humans, though the trail was deeply rutted. When it angled west, another joined it from the easterly plains, and then, finally, they saw other wagons. One was far ahead, visible only as it crested hills, and one entered the trail behind. They would overtake the wagon ahead before sunset; the Tin Mule was little faster than a horse cart on level ground, but it gained on the hills. "I wonder what they'll think of our Mule?" Teress asked.

"Yeah! Should we just pass 'em as fast as we can, or pull 'em over? Where's the siren?"

"Was he watching 'cop' shows?" Achibol grumbled to no one in particular. "If they hide in the grass, we'll continue on our way—but I wouldn't mind talking with others who've undertaken a pilgrimage similar to our own."

"You think they're going to the Icefields too?" Benadek was skeptical. "Maybe they're just traveling."

"Hmmph! Once, people 'just traveled,' but in this age, no one goes a step further than he must. Even the prairie nomads only cover the distance between seasonal food sources. What's ahead but rocks and ice?"

"I wonder," Benadek said thoughtfully.

They shared a campfire with four gaunt men. Barl, the eldest, was a cozie, having the round head and bland, regular features of that breed, but the others were heterogeneous. Ambo's face was almost as dark as Achibol's—though his neck, when he loosened his jacket, was pale. Dennet was skinny as Benadek, but taller and blond. He had a sparse beard, and six fingers on each hand. Willer had brown hair like a cozie, but his face was sharp and lean as a hatchet, and he was a full head taller than anyone Benadek had ever seen. The latter three were pure-humans beyond doubt.

The grim foursome had been incurious about the Tin Mule, and were no more interested in those they now shared a fire with. They spoke only in response to direct questions, and then only with great effort of will.

Six pure-humans together around a fire with a single cozie. A reversal of the usual order of things; the normal ratio, Achibol estimated, was more like sixty thousand simples for every pure-human. The conclusion could not be avoided: the plains were a breeding-range for the genetic types the planners had tried to destroy, now allowed to survive by a coven of depraved ancients who used them to maintain their own unnaturally preserved selves. Elsewhere the failed plan continued haltingly as honches wiped out pure-human families and tribes, but here the "gods" merely culled their herds, and others, like these four grim men, traveled long and far to pick up drained corpses, to bury them or cremate them.

Gaddo had said women were taken more often than men; children of both sexes were also claimed—adolescents, for the most part. That discrimination had not gone unnoticed. "Brides of the Dead, " Dennet growled. "No matter some are boys. The young an' the fair. When I was a boy, y'saw old women, but now? Only old men. A woman's lucky to have two babes ere she's taken. Soon there won't be enough of our kind to carry on, only Barl's sort."

Benadek's eyes moved meaningfully from Achibol to Teress, projecting an unspoken question.

"It makes no sense," Teress commented aloud. "What will happen when our kind's gone?"

"It's poor eugenics," Achibol replied. "Better to cull only males and the very old." The strangers, uncomprehending, unused to Achibol's blunt speech, glared suspiciously. "If you hunted only bulls, not cows, and left the sick and weak alive, how long would the herds last?" the mage clarified.

"Gods and spirits need not make sense," Willer stated flatly.

"Is that what you consider them? Gods?" Achibol snapped. "Then what hope is there for your kind?"

"None," Willer snapped back. He spat into the fire.

The four men had lost seven loved ones between them, and hoped only that their remains would shortly be found, laid out neatly on the rocky ice flow of the Vale of the Dead. That alone would lay their agonies to rest, for their conviction was absolute that the "brides" were as ill-used in captivity as their bodies were in death. Only the recovery of their desiccated flesh would prove their mortal suffering had ended.

"Autopsies," Achibol suggested the next day, as the Tin Mule moved out ahead of the wagon. "If there are unclaimed bodies, we can discover more of what we're facing."

Benadek and Teress disagreed. "We need to know how to *stop* them," the boy said. "The details are irrelevant. We already know the process."

"Besides," Teress added, "what would we do with the ones we cut open? We couldn't leave them for their relatives to find, and it would be wrong to hide them. Why add to the suffering of men like those?" She gestured behind them, though the wagon was no longer in sight.

"Of course," the sorcerer agreed. "I grasp at straws." The subject was dropped. The trail narrowed until they could pass oncoming wagons only at the widest places. Silent nods passed between themselves and the occupants of the wagons. Some carts were well-laden with large, light bundles: the unburned dead.

Ahead were jagged processions of higher and higher hills, bordered by cloud-tipped, snow-covered peaks. Spruces and delicate aspens clung to the rocky slopes, mixed with odd leafless trees like giant mosses—far removed, Achibol suspected, from their unmutated ancestors.

✧ ✧ ✧

"Wagons," Teress exclaimed. "There must be a hundred of them."

"Looking for bodies," Benadek speculated.

"So many? All together? There can't be that many kidnap victims . . . can there?" Teress shook her head in wishful denial.

"You underestimate the population of the prairie and forests." Achibol's head swayed sadly. "Because nomads walk lightly and no longer gather together, they seem few, but there are tens, even hundreds of thousands scattered out of sight of us and of each other."

"And the ancients' need for fresh victims grows as they age," Benadek commented. "A hundred years from now there'll be ten times as many wagons down there. It'll be a city, unless . . ." He left his hopes unspoken.

"Shall we join the unhappy throng, apprentice? Or have you decided upon another course?"

"No. I mean, yes, let's go down there." They engaged the Tin Mule's wheels and crept down the muddy, rock-strewn, rutted trail.

It was a cheerless gathering. They edged the Mule between irregular rows of wagons identical except in color and minor accouterments. Incurious faces observed their progress past one fireside gathering and then another. "There," Teress said, pointing at an open space. Achibol guided the Tin Mule into place. Faces turned from the nearest fire, but no one greeted them or sent them off again. It was almost dark, and the wind from the icefields cascaded down the valley, cold and damp. The ground itself, deposition of recent receding glaciation, was soggy and rilled with melt-water from the ice beyond, ice held by the saw-toothed arête as the chipped brim of a much-used bowl might hold thick porridge.

A ripple of moving shoulders and shuffling bodies

opened places for them at the fire. Achibol sat next to a burly leather-clad fellow who smelled of wood smoke and grease. Benadek lowered himself beside a woman of indeterminate years whose blond or white hair was thick with yellow smoke-residue, her coarse-woven skirt stained with ashes and pinholed with tiny burns. Teress wedged herself between her companions. A wooden cup was passed, and Achibol drank cautiously, inclining his head ever so slightly as he passed it to Teress. Warned by the mage's hand on her knee, she took only a sip. Bitter, with a flavor of evergreens, one sip was enough—an appropriate brew for a gathering of lost souls.

"Gin." Benadek's lips formed the syllable without voicing it. The distillation of fermented juniper berries made his tongue dry, but this time he neither spat it out nor expostulated. Fiery warmth grew in his gut, driving out the chill that swept down from the icefields. Shuddering, he took another swallow.

"Who seek you?" a burly plainsman rumbled from across the fire. "Perhaps your search will be short, if your kin are as dark as you."

Achibol responded with a slow shake of his head. "We seek no kin. Rather, we would find those who take yours."

"You're seeking grain in an apple tree." The other laughed dryly. "The honches are down there." He gestured in the direction of the plains far away. "Here, there are only the dead, and we who await them."

"They must be brought here by some means," Achibol persisted. "And where do the captives go, between their taking and their reappearance in this sad place?"

"Beneath the ice are the caverns of Endless Life, the Soul-Eaters' realm. Would you go *there*?" The nomad laughed louder than before.

"If there's a door, I'd consider it. Do you know of one? From whence do the remains emerge?"

"You're mad, dark one. The passage to Endless Life is through Death's door. Are you so old you'd pass through willingly?"

Though the intellectual parts of Achibol's mind sparked with the desire to explore Life and Death in the new theology the plainsman's words hinted at, he stuck to his immediate objective. "Perhaps my madness surpasses even your speculations. Perhaps I would converse face-to-face with the ones who so misuse our kin. Is there a door?"

The man's expression showed pity and scorn. "The husks of Those Who Return appear among the rocks. If there are tracks of booted feet, of wagons like yours, then rains, melting ice, and our own footprints, erase them. If there are lights in the nighttime dark, we don't see them, but look instead to the warmth of our fires, and await the day. If sounds are heard over the whisper of Nightwind, we don't hear them, for they are out of the Depth, and we are dwellers on the surface of this Sphere." His words, delivered in a singsong chant, were obviously not new. In a generation they would be no longer a nomad's chant but a somber hymn. Long silence ensued, broken only by breathing, sniffling, and the creak of leather and stiff limbs.

"There's the Immortal Fool," a soft, feminine voice broke the quietness, "in the small valley by the ice's verge." Of she who spoke, Benadek could see only a shadowed blotch in the darkness.

"There is that," the plainsman agreed, though all could hear the disapproval in his tones. "And would you lead them there, Ameling?"

"I've brought the Ancient Fool his offerings three times," the unseen voice replied without hesitation, "and spoken with him, and shared his rude bed. I'd go there with this one if he asks. These three aren't like us. Their quest surpasses ours."

"As this old one claims!" the nomad snapped.

"Believe it, and you'll die there on the verge. You'll lie unrotted, shunned by the very ground."

"I'm already dead, Jask. I merely linger—and now I know why. My fate is to guide these seekers." The newcomers' eyes turned to the rustle of cloth as the woman Ameling came into the light, throwing back her hood. With ill-concealed horror, they recognized what had befallen her in the valley near the ice. Ameling was bald. Her face, neck, and scalp shone with crimson scarring. Burns. Swatches of skin had burned, scabbed over, and curled loose again under the assault of the cool, deadly fire that now raged within her bones. Ameling spoke truthfully: she was already dead. Achibol recognized radiation poisoning. He gave her a week to live. Benadek, with the benefit of medically trained memories, allowed her a further month of living death.

Teress, once the initial shock was banished, saw beyond the pain and the scarring to the delicate bone structure, the patches of pale, clear skin, and the lovely, intense blue eyes, lashless and mostly lidless. Tears blurred her vision as she recognized what she hoped Benadek would not: Ameling, unlike most others here, was a simple, a poot. A very specific kind of poot. Had some kind god given Ameling back her long, blond hair, her gently arching brows and her long, dark lashes, she would have been identical in every respect to . . . Sylfie.

This moment had been bound to occur, Teress told herself. Only their long isolation from simple humankind had prevented them from coming across such a poot before. There were, after all, only a limited number of templates. Hopefully Benadek would not notice, right away. Teress had no idea how he would react. He might even *change* again.

"Well?" Ameling demanded abruptly, standing over Achibol, her back to the fire, her face fortuitously in shadow, "Will you risk *this* for a chat with an old madman who claims to have lived for thousands of years? Three nights with him has done this to me." When Achibol did not answer immediately, she covered her head with the hood once again.

Achibol was struck dumb by the connotations of her words: ".. lived thousands of years . . . an old madman . . . " Ameling could have been describing . . . him. Hope, and its companion, fear, raced through his stony thoughts like a mountain deer and a pursuing wolf.

Benadek, recovering, dwelt upon the physical implications of Ameling's condition. Three times she had been exposed, three nights she had spent "in the old man's bed," intimately close to him. Three exposures, with weeks between them, in which some healing had occurred. Six, even eight weeks or so later, she was still alive. Facts and figures about radiation, about therapies and dosages, welled up from his liver and marched across the surface of his brain. "The radiation level isn't too high. If the exposure is brief, it won't kill me. A gate. It has to be a gate to the redoubt below, with a radiation-barrier gone awry. And if I need to, if there's cell damage, I can *change* just a little . . ."

Achibol's silence grew to awkward length. Only when a heavyset plainsman snorted derisively, mistaking silence for terror, did the mage recall his wandering thoughts. "Will you guide us? I have medicines that will ease your pain—though no remedy will cure you."

"You're kind," Ameling replied, "and honest as well. Until tomorrow, then. I have little strength, and must ration it." With a curt nod, mostly hidden in her hood, she made her way from the fire.

"I suppose that's all the fun for tonight," the woman next to Benadek muttered snidely, getting to her feet. "I've pyres to build in the morning."

"Pyres?" Benadek asked.

"We aren't all here seeking kinfolk," an elderly man commented. "This fire belongs to those of us who dwell here in the vale, eking a living from the seekers, who come and go."

"You mean you don't have to be here?"

The old man, who was missing several teeth, laughed unpleasantly. "Have to be? No one has to be here, or anywhere, but for some of us, there's no reason to depart, and nowhere to go. Jask, for instance . . ." Jask, the burly fellow, scowled. "He's lost his whole band. When he left them to seek the husk of a sister taken in the spring, he came here and what did he find? The rest of them, wives, sisters, and daughters, had preceded him, and he gave them all to wind, on one great pyre. Here he's stayed, to build pyres for others who have something to trade. Why would he depart?

"And Ameling?" He shook his head and wiped spittle with his sleeve. "At least there's work—husks to be located, pyres to be built at the valley mouth, and guidance for seekers. But don't sleep soundly, boy. Some here like the taste of smoke and sweat less than others, and live by easier means. You understand?"

"Thieves," Benadek stated flatly.

"Mind it well." He struggled to get his feet beneath him, and tottered off among the irregular ranks of wagons. One by one the others departed, leaving the fire to glow, not bothering to cover it.

"You see?" Achibol said, "It's begun already."

"What has?" Teress asked.

"The priestly cult—these pyre-builders and corpse-finders. Now they merely serve the seekers, but how long before they build tollhouses on the valley path, and crematoriums, and sell cemetery patches of forest soil to grieving kinfolk? In time, they may collect the husks themselves, and innocents from the plains will pay them for remains lined up like sides of meat in the market. What stately mortuaries they'll build!"

Neither of the mage's companions commented on his gloomy predictions. If they failed, it might indeed come about just so. A City of the Dead might rise here at the entrance to the Vale—but it was idle speculation; much could happen in the days ahead, and morning was not far off.

Benadek had never imagined so much ice. Its depth was suggested by the chuckle and gurgle of running water deep within, which found its way up through tortuous cracks and melt-holes. On either side of the glacial tongue, jagged rock walls confined the ice to a path hundreds of yards wide, the Vale of the Dead. In front, still higher, the glacial remnant ended in a cirque, a steep amphitheater cut into the spine of the mountain.

They walked half the day up the rising valley, and hours more up the rotten slickness of the stagnant glacier, picking their way over cracks and silt-heavy rivulets that wove across the ice and beneath it, carrying its substance away. "When I was young," Achibol reminisced, "the glacier still grew. There was a lovely stone lodge, well back from the advancing ice, with a good asphalt road. Vehicles like our Mule carried tourists as far as we've come, in minutes. The trails and crevasses were well-marked, and the way safe. Still, when the glacier moved, cracks like these could snap shut like snakes' mouths."

"Why don't they do it now?" Benadek asked skeptically.

"Because the ice no longer grows. For centuries it's melted a few feet a year. If we were to wait long enough, even the command center beneath the great ice sheet above, this small glacier's rich relation, would be exposed."

"Where, exactly, is the redoubt?"

"Ahead, beyond the rim of crags up there where the blown snow hangs like roof-eaves. Dug into rock that has seen no sunlight in a hundred times my own life's span. As for the entrance, ask Ameling."

The maimed plainswoman had said little all day, merely cautioning them about weak ice, where glassy patches of luminous blue-green marked immense hollows below—from whose slick, cold embrace no one could escape if he broke through their treacherous crusts. Now, she pointed to the valley wall, just below the low-hanging afternoon sun. "We must climb. There's a trail, and spikes driven into the wall. We can be atop the ridge by nightfall."

"And then?" Achibol asked. "How far will we be from the hermit and his cave?"

"We'll be there."

"Then we'll camp below tonight, and climb in the morning."

"There's no dry place! Our blankets will become dank, and we'll freeze."

Achibol waved his talisman. "I've been monitoring the radiation," he said. "The hidden fires which burned you emanate from a place on the cliff top. My companions and I have to pass through them, but there's no reason to sleep among the invisible flames. For that matter, there's no reason for you to make the climb—another dose will kill you."

"Do I care? My fate is in my hands, not yours, and I don't expect to return to the valley floor again."

Knowing the constant suffering she endured, the pain and nausea that never waned, the mage made no effort to change her mind. "Then we'll camp below for our own sakes, and perhaps avoid your fate."

Ameling approved his callous decision. "Your mission is of great import to all men, even beyond the Edge of the World."

"What do you know of our quest, Ameling?"

"What my heart tells me. You're much like the Immortal Fool, though neither mad nor immortal yourself, I suspect."

"Tell me about him," Achibol urged.

"He's smaller than you, like a child, but with no hair atop his head—though he's not lost his eyebrows as I have. His brows are as white as fresh snow and as bushy as the beard that covers his chest. And . . . he has a magical box like yours, though his is dead."

"Then he's Yasha!" Achibol's eyes went wide, and his talisman dangled unnoticed, scant inches above the snow.

"He calls himself that," Ameling cried. "I knew you were the ones—his reinforcements!

Achibol's hand rose to clutch at his chest. "A seat, boy! Set your pack beneath me, for I must rest." Benadek hurried to comply, his face registering his concern. "Master? Are you ill? What must I do?"

"Nothing, boy, nothing." Achibol's face was several shades lighter than usual, an ugly ocherous color, and he shook as if in the grip of a terrible ague. Sweat glistened on his wrinkled brow in spite of the damp wind off the ice above. His breathing echoed with a high, metallic whine. "It's the shock of hearing that my colleague still lives. I'll recover enough to go on, never fear."

Benadek seemed not to hear, as if listening to sounds beyond the range of ordinary human ears. Kneeling on the slick ice before his master, he laid his hands on the old man's. "You have many secrets, Master Achibol, Sorcerer, Scrivener, and Charlatan. I, as your apprentice, have been privy to some. But before we go one step further, there must be one less secret between us." Though his features were as boyish as ever, Benadek's expression was as stern and old as Achibol's at its most severe. The boy's dark irises thinned and his pupils expanded in spite of glaring ice all about. They seemed ready to absorb every nuance read from the oldster's eyes, locked now to his own. "What are you, Master?" Benadek asked, unblinking. "You're less human than Dispucket. Are you a machine like Circe?"

Achibol did not answer immediately. Slowly, blood suffused his face and his yellowed skin darkened toward its normal shade. His breath came more easily, without the eerie whine of moments before. He grinned, a prankish, sinister expression that Benadek remembered all too well . . . It seemed so very long ago that the mage had stood in an alley, grinning just like that, blocking his escape and holding a shining gold coin in his outstretched hand.

He remembered, too, mischief in Achibol's eye as he drew a tiny vial from his voluminous trunk. "Androsterone Five," he had said. "Just the thing for a night on the town."

"I'll give you enlightenment," the mage had said on still another occasion, "Dispucket awaits you . . . Spread wide your arms and hug him . . ." Oh yes. Benadek remembered. That chill wind from the depths of his own memory made him shudder spastically.

"You know what I am, boy. You discovered it in Circe's archives . . . but now I'll show you." Never taking his eyes from his apprentice, Achibol lifted his hand to his face and laid a gnarled finger just below his right eye. "See now how I look at the world, apprentice," he rasped, and Benadek stared. Slowly, as if drawn aside by some vision of infinite attractiveness, Achibol's eye turned to the outside. Further and further it rotated, while his left one remained fixed on Benadek's face. Red blood vessels appeared on the nasal margin as the dark iris buried itself on the other side . . . and the eye rotated further.

The sorcerer's eye seemed about to reverse itself in the socket, to reveal the tattered, twitching ends of muscles ripped free by the unnatural movement, but . . . beyond the white surface, past the red-veined perimeter, Benadek saw a sharply defined, metallic edge! As Achibol's human eye disappeared entirely into the folds of his face, the reverse surface was revealed, a steely orb which stopped with its tiny red-glowing pinhole aligned with the bridge of Benadek's nose.

"You've seen the red glow of my eye before, haven't you? Though I've tried to conceal it? Was it magic, did you think, that you failed to investigate further? How long since you ceased believing in magic, boy? And how long since you thrust this particular mystery aside, unanswered? What have I failed to teach you that you discover only now, through one mechanical system's momentary failure, that such systems exist?" Achibol's eyes, flesh and metal, remained fixed on Benadek.

"You've accepted my immortality, haven't you? You even discovered the techniques—but didn't you wonder where the precipitators and filters were? Did you suspect I 'plugged in' when I slipped inside the temples without you, and thus pacified yourself to seek no further for my secrets? Did you assume falsely that the odd bits and pieces stored in my trunk would assemble into my machinery of life? Shame, boy! It's a tradition from time immemorable, an apprentice's duty, to ferret out his master's secrets. Ah well. You're slow and late, but at least you've arrived. You know now where my devices are hidden?"

Benadek nodded, focusing on Achibol's chest. "Of course," the mage chuckled, even though his lengthy speech seemed to have weakened him again. "Everything is inside. Miniaturized, to be sure, but still too bulky to fit in a human body, with all its wet machinery. Do you begin to understand?"

Benadek forced his lips to open, sucked breath through his throat, and forced it back across his vocal cords. "How much of you is human?"

Again Achibol chuckled. "Not my balls or their impressive companion, nor my guts or my other eye. Not even most of my muscles. My skin is still my own, though modified, and I've retained a few shreds of contractile tissue beneath it—my smile, thus, is my own. What else?"

"Your brain, Master."

"Excellent, boy—and why so little else? Come now, use the facilities you were born with—and those you stole from Circe's cryo-vaults. Why am I no more than a brain and a bag of skin hiding a tin-and-plastic imitation body? What purpose is served?"

Benadek, faced with Achibol's barrage of questions, delivered in a manner he was uncomfortably familiar with, replied more easily than before. "For the filters and such that sustain you to be carried within, other functions had to be sacrificed, leaving room only for your brain and the glands that support it."

"Exactly, lad. I'm proud of you once more. What else?"

"You must have an atomic-decay battery for energy. Your bones? I don't know."

"Silicon, apatite, and gold," Achibol told him. "Interwoven lattices with organic carbon-fiber reinforcing. I don't break legs easily." His face relaxed slightly. He smiled benignly. Benadek relaxed too, realizing that this . . . man . . . was still the Achibol he had known.

"Anything else, boy?"

"The eyes, Master. Infrared—projector and scanner both—in the right. What's in the other one?"

"Rangefinder, short focal-length organic-lensed and mirrored catadioptric telescope, a microscope and several low-discrimination pickups for the rest of the electromagnetic spectrum. My microwave radar used to be in the right one."

"Do your bones have other functions too?"

"Ah—you're still thinking. Good. Of course they do—what a waste of good space, otherwise. There are biochips and nonmagnetic ROM for my autonomic functions, and protected storage for those bits and pieces of gland and organ that keep my brain happy and sane. And now you have it all. So . . . speculate, boy. Generalize a bit, if you will."

"Master, I know now that you are only as immortal as your fabricated systems, and that some of them are failing."

"Failing? Hmmph. Many failed so long ago I've entirely forgotten the habits of dependence on them. Here, under my fingernails, were microprobes—generalized chip pinouts—and chemical injectors for nasty compounds. I had to remove those myself, at no little discomfort, for fear the only one poisoned would be me. Unfortunately, other functions had to be sacrificed with them, and the 'talisman' is only a poor substitute. Even my self-diagnostics are casualties of entropy, so I can't tell you just how much of me still functions. Did you hear the noises in my chest?"

"I did, Master."

"You heard my heart fail. I don't need diagnostics to know that. It stopped several minutes ago, I'd guess, though my clock-functions are erratic."

"How do you remain alive now? Your organic brain must still need blood."

"I have two hearts. Now I'm at the mercy of the primary one, shut down centuries ago when it became unreliable. It was the backup unit that just failed."

Benadek hesitated to ask the obvious question, but Achibol anticipated it. "How long? An hour or a year—a decade if I'm lucky." He drew himself up, preparing to rise. "So, succeed or fail, we must hurry, if I'm to see the end of this mission of ours."

"We'll succeed, Master. You'll live. Surely there must be some way to repair you. We'll find that too." Benadek's brave words belied the knot of feelings bound tightly inside him.

"If Gibraltar Base survives, and if we succeed here, I have half a mind to attempt the trip. There are spare parts, and equipment to maintain my brain functions during major repairs. But that's an ocean away, and no ships have crossed it in eighteen hundred years. We'll cross that water if we come to it, but now—help me up. I fear to strain this worn-out pump."

Benadek and Teress helped Achibol regain his feet. Ameling observed, not understanding what had transpired, but knowing that a crisis had arisen and passed. Her brief glimpse of the steely eye confirmed that the sorcerer was unique, and that she had chosen rightly to exert herself for his cause.

Both Achibol's eyes looked normal now, as the four of them trudged carefully over the wet, slippery ice to the edge of the stagnant glacier. They made camp at the foot of the ascending trail. Benadek pulled portable shelters from his pack, and when they were expanded and joined together, Ameling saw that no one would have to sleep in wet blankets. She was glad, then, that their ascent had been postponed, for though she knew she would soon die, she no longer wished to hasten it—to the contrary, she wanted to live, if only to see what great events the strange threesome might bring about.

The climb was less difficult than it seemed from below. Though there were switchbacks and places where the weakened Achibol had to be hauled up on braided leather rope, the grade was otherwise gentle. At the top, they waded through deep snow. Yasha's cave was visible as they neared the ridge.

Not until they came within a few dozen paces of the cave-mouth did the talisman indicated the radiation hazard was severe. Benadek insisted that he go on alone. Achibol protested. "Yasha won't know you, boy. If he's truly deranged, I may have a chance of getting through to him."

"How many heavy particles can your hardware sustain? Teress and Ameling will hold you here if you try to follow." The mage saw the women nod.

"Go on then!" Achibol said. "Bring him out here." Benadek pushed off through the snow.

The first indication that Benadek had found the "Immortal Fool" was a high-pitched scream. The second was a tiny, white-haired figure leaping and bounding across the snow. "That's him!" Achibol and Ameling declared as one.

"The Fool," Ameling said.

"Yasha, you runt," the mage hooted.

"Keep away from me!" Yasha squalled.

"Yasha!" Achibol shouted. "Calm down. Look at me."

"What's to look at, old man?" Yasha spat. "There're prettier faces than yours—even that one, marked as she is." Ameling flinched.

"Stuff it, Yosh!" Achibol yelled back. "I'm Archie. You remember me!"

"Archie? Archie? Naw—Archie's that black kid they gave the East Coast to. You're not Archie."

"But I am, Yosh. I'm Archie Scribner, and I'm no younger than you are. Now look at me."

Yasha looked. For a moment, a gleam of comprehension lightened his face, but it quickly faded. "Archie's old, Archie's dead, and you're a liar. You're one of *them*." He looked around, seeing threats in every direction. "You can't fool me!" The tiny man leaped away with surprising agility, and dashed back through the disturbed snow. He dove between Benadek's outstretched arms and slid belly-down to the black cave-mouth.

Benadek shrugged. "He's crazy as a tree-pig in springtime," he called back, peering into the cave. "There's nothing here but soggy bedding, rotten potatoes, and a pile of corroded instruments that can't have worked in years. He's talking to one of them."

"Poor Yasha," the sorcerer said sadly. "he's the other

side of the coin—his mechanical systems function, radiation or not, but his mind has flown.

An hour later, Benadek trudged back through the snow. Achibol raised his head. "What else did you find?"

"There's a metal door with no handles. Yasha spies upon honches who go in and out, and 'reports' with his broken talisman. He knows of ancients who live beyond the door, but believes them trapped within. He awaits 'reinforcements' from Gibraltar. I think he's inverted the situation—the honches, or their masters, watch him."

"How so?"

"I had a feeling that I was being watched all the while I was in sight of the door. I think the level of radiation is controlled too, and diminishes when he is alone in there."

"How does he live? Do they feed him?"

"We do," Ameling interjected. "He lives on the gifts I, and others, bring. The honches may feed him too—I'm sure they tease and torment him."

"He's been here a long time?" Achibol asked her.

"I've heard he was here when the first seekers came—fifty years ago."

"Fifty or five hundred, it's been long enough. We must capture him and, if there's a kernel of sense left in his head, perhaps it can be brought forth."

"How, Master Achibol?" Teress wondered. "If we force this metal door and seek the ancients within, we can't bring him with us."

"He may know something useful to us, if it can be gotten at," Achibol replied, "and besides, he and I may be the last of our kind. I won't abandon him."

Benadek silently agreed with the mage's intent, for his own dark reasons: were the components in the small madman's body identical to Achibol's? If his mind were truly gone, could Achibol use his . . . spare parts? "It won't come to that, Master," Benadek said quietly, "because from here, I have to go on alone. You and Teress and Ameling can take him back to camp with you."

"What do you mean?" asked the mage. "You're only a boy . . . only one man, I mean. How can you face the ancients alone?"

"I'm less a child than any of you—even you, Master—and I'm more than an ordinary man. I can get inside, because the door will only open to those who are wanted inside."

"They'll want you?"

"Honches come and go. I'll be the next honch."

"They'll see through any disguise."

"It won't be a disguise, Master. I'll *become* the honch."

"It's too dangerous," Teress cried. "What if the *change* goes too far, as it did—"

"Everything's been building to this. Dispucket, the *change* in the swamp, Sufawlz and the memories . . . as if the world forced me out of its womb unfinished, in desperate need. I had to learn as I went along—as I still must."

"You had friends, boy. You weren't alone."

"Am I ever alone? I have Jim Bostwick, Jean-Francois, Jack, Anna . . . bits and pieces of poor Vlad Sovoda even surface once in a while—and there's really no choice. Not only can you not get in, but none of you could survive the radiation for long. That wash of deadly particles would have killed me if I hadn't *changed* even as I started to die. Those within obviously tolerate the old Fool, or he would be dead."

"What must be done?"

"I'll catch Yasha. Take him with you to the camp, and if I succeed I'll look for you there. You should be safe enough."

"Safe from what? Honches? Perhaps we should hide in the woods."

"Perhaps—though honches aren't my worst fear. I don't want you hurt if the redoubt is destroyed. There'll be more radiation."

"The reactor! You're planning a meltdown!"

"It's a magnetic-containment fusion reactor. It won't melt down, but it can be overloaded. Superheated steam could be dangerous."

"And you?" Teress asked. "How will you survive it?"

"I'll try to find a way, of course, but if I don't . . ." He shrugged. After all, it was not as if this were the first time he had thought about death. There were worse things.

INTERLUDE
The Great School, Midicor IV

"So?" Abrovid asked reluctantly, fulfilling his own prophesy. "What exactly does it mean. To Saphooth, I mean."

"Benadek's going to *become* a honch, right?"

"That much I understood," Abrovid muttered irritably. "So what?"

"What's he going to do with the original honch?"

"Tie him up? Surely not kill him?"

"Exactly!" Kaledrin beamed as if Abrovid were his star pupil. "Kill him. Just as Saphooth claims that we—descendants of Benadek—did to his 'original' races. Except their fixed-form remnants, of course. The ongoing tale supports his paranoia."

"That's bad, then. What will you do?"

"I had hoped you'd have a new approach."

"Me? I'm a systems programmer. What do I know about myths . . . or wars?"

"So be systematic about it!" Kaledrin snapped.

Abrovid brightened internally, but kept his feelings concealed. Kaledrin really did need his help. "Let me think a minute," he said. And he did.

"Well," Abrovid began, breaking the silence that had continued not for one minute but a score. "It *is* a systems problem. Even if Saphooth's partly right—if we mutables are Benadek's descendants and he isn't." He paused, enjoying waiting for Kaledrin to beg him to explain . . .

"Well?" Kaledrin snapped. "You have an idea, not an egg! You don't have to hatch it!"

That was not the response Abrovid had fished for. Ah, well. He was still Abrovid, and Kaledrin was . . . Kaledrin. "Assuming it's true that we normal people . . . we mutables . . . are a race apart, then the others are like applications programs. They do different things, and are adapted to different circumstances, and have different talents. Right?" Kaledrin bobbed his eyestalks impatiently. "There has to be an operating system to tie them all together and keep everything running smoothly. That's us. Without us norm—mutables—nobody could understand what it's like to be not only an Arkendhi vacuum-dweller, but a Saritan mudworm, a simian-form forester, and . . . and you name it. Without us, they couldn't even communicate with each other. Then there'd be wars. Galactic society, trade, everything—would crash, and . . ."

"Magnificent, Ab! You've said it! All this time, it's been there, lurking in a dark corner of my mind, and it took you—of all people—to give me just the prod I needed. Yes—a system in which we mutables are the reticulum, the over-program. Perhaps I can defuse Saphooth yet. Oh, how I wish he were here right now! I'd make him see it!"

Abrovid moved quietly toward the door. Kaledrin

was so involved with "his" new idea he did not even notice Abrovid leave. Abrovid did not wish Saphooth back. In his opinion Kaledrin had replaced him all too well.

CHAPTER TWENTY,

Wherein Benadek enters the Weaver's nest, and himself *becomes* Evil.

The Weavers' Song

Weaver, what do I see on your loom?
What threads do you weave?
I weave the events on the warp of men's
lives
And beat the wefts of destiny
Each one against the ones I wove
before.

Weaver, how do you choose the threads,
The colors you use?
I pick from my basket the bright threads
and black.
According to the Pattern they lie

Each one against the ones I wove
before.

Weaver blind, in darkness bound,
How do you choose?
Threads choose themselves; the pattern
rules
The way they come to lie
Each one against the ones I wove
before.*

In its entirety, this work chant of the Arkendhi orbital spiders** recounts the destruction of the primal Pattern of their weavings by the demideity Bheh-a-ghe, and their subsequent banishment from the security of planetary surfaces to their orbital habitat.

"The Weavers' Song" is a late adoption from some other culture, for the actual process by which they "spin" and "weave" is like insect trap-building. "Warp" and "weft" have no counterpart in their constructions.

The biocybes claim that Arkendhi tales contribute to this episode, but they seem to lack the requisite continuity. Perhaps theirs is a philosophical gift, or a mood. Still, the "husks" can be equated with the cocooned prey of

---

* From *Worksongs of the Lesser Cloud* by Amahl Pero Dih, Sevar Institute of the Arts, Anthology VI, Vol. III.

** Among humans the Arkendhi are unique. Having regularized the orbits of their native star's satellites and strung them together with a great web, they have adapted to life in high vacuum. Their ancestral species, those who chose to remain forever *unbecome* and planetbound, still subsist among the trees and cliffs of their world, a source of both pride and humility for their human kin.

Arkendhi planetary ancestors. Future episodes may clarify this.

Former Director Saphooth's notions are not borne out in this episode. Indeed Benadek, purported progenitor of this conquering race, is reduced to a helpless mote within a honch, Gorb, equally a victim of circumstance. Benadek teeters on the brink of *becoming*, but does not *become*.

The Arkendhi did not spurn the risk of *becoming* a new entity in the universe. Breaking their Pattern, they kicked dirt from their feet and joined the interstellar community. And so with us all, and with Benadek, the test of a Man is to *become*. Short of that, there can be no true understanding, no resolution of our differences. All humans, fixed and mutable, depend upon those of us who *become*, who give up the comforts of homeworld and form to serve mankind. We are the threads that weave our differences into the vast tapestry of Mind, the greater Pattern that is Mankind.

(Kaledrin, Senior Editor)

INTERLUDE
The Great School, Midicor IV

"Oh, come on, Kal. You're stalling, aren't you?"

"What do you mean?"

"This episode *does* support old boneyform's thesis. Benadek is an invader. What are you trying to pull?"

Kaledrin shrank inwardly. Was it that obvious? "It's

only one episode, Ab. I'm not going to make a one-eighty turn based on it. It's the body of work that counts. This could be an aberration, a simple plot twist."

"Sure it could. And the sky could turn blue, too."

"The sky's bright red, as always."

"Uh huh."

Capturing Yasha was easy. When Benadek confiscated his corroded, useless equipment and lowered it by rope, the tiny man scrambled frantically after. Benadek kept it dangling just out of reach until the others had all climbed down too. Except himself, of course.

Benadek hated living in the cave. Not only was it damp, but his fire filled the entire cavity with smoke.

Radiation was a problem at first, but after several days, out of sheer boredom, he began to "go within" himself, browsing in his subcellular environment like a Sunday-afternoon book shopper (Anna's memory). Proteins bumbled and flowed, squeezed through double-walled lipid membranes *here*, were rejected *there*. He sensed DNA molecules not as distinct entities in each cell but as dark, heavy concentrations of potential that only rarely, as cellular reactions went, burst into the frenzied activities of synthesis and replication. Such events were spectacular enough, on the tiny scale of his perceptions, to warrant observation.

In the first weeks of his hermitage he only observed the events and mechanisms of RNA formation and protein-building, but he eventually became interested in the codes themselves. It was only a step from interest, to understanding, to total comprehension. Benadek conceptualized his entire genome. Just as temple computers maintained exacting templates of simples' genes, he held in conscious memory, engraved in synaptic paths, an immutable, unmutable record of his genetic makeup, a single over-copy he could compare his trillions of cellular copies against: the true key to the pure-human adaptation.

From there, it was easy to modify a hindbrain error-checking routine for damage control. Massive quasi-lymphocytes gravitated toward DNA-active cells and read their exposed genetic material prior to mitosis, meiosis, or protein-synthesis. If the lymphocyte-copy disagreed with the cell-copy, both cells fused, and were devoured by macrophages. Benadek consequently ran a constant low-grade fever, and his appetite increased.

He could eat almost anything—pine-seeds, tough grasses, moss, and lichen—but the "offerings" left for him at the cliff top made it unnecessary. He knew Teress was bringing them, but he only went forth to pick up his supplies at night. Should he see her, his resolve would weaken.

He searched for the massive door's sensors. Failing to find them, he plastered the entire rear wall of the cave with wet ashes, and the radiation level dropped. Perhaps the watchers feared that the deadly emanations would kill their own returning compatriots, now that they could no longer ascertain who was in the cave. The spindly boy must have seemed no threat, no match for honches who might return at any time. They probably judged him half-dead already.

It troubled him that he did not know when they might appear, or if they would. How long would he have to wait? He gave it a month. But when that month came to an end, he resolved to stay just one more day, then another . . .

Teress left notes. They had locked Yasha's treasures in the Tin Mule's storage compartment, and Yasha slept on the rear seat from then on, sending his "reports" through a heater grille. Achibol reluctantly concluded that Yasha's mind was irreparably damaged. Ameling still lived, thanks to the mage's medications, but did not improve. Achibol sat by the fire day and night, a taciturn shadow wrapped in ashy blankets.

"Where you at, old Fool?" The harsh voice bounced off the mud-smoothed wall, disorienting the cave's occupant. "Why'd you hide the door? Come out. I got something good to eat."

Honch! Only one voice. Benadek huddled within his moldy blankets, and groped for Achibol's talisman . . .

"Benadek! Benadek!" Teress's voice reverberated as had the honch's. "Are you all right? We saw someone on the cliff edge, coming this way. Benadek? Benad . . ." Her voice stopped as if strangled on her own terror. The hand that emerged from cave-darkness gripped her wrist like a steel clamp. It was huge and hairy, and it stretched outward from a bulky, black leather sleeve. She struggled silently, but there was no escape from that crushing grip. Inexorably, she was pulled into the gloom of the cave.

Her eyes darted from the craggy honch face to one, then another pool of shadow, hoping against hope that she could catch a gleam from Benadek's eyes or a chance reflection from the talisman, held in his hand. But there was no gleam, no telltale motion. What she saw was a boot. A black, fit-all military boot, still shiny after months of abusive wear. Benadek's boot. Her eyes widened and her stomach churned as she forced herself to recognize what lay beyond.

The frail, naked body sprawled awkwardly on blood-spattered blankets. The gray-green cast of death was unmistakable. Benadek was dead, blotched with black smears of already-drying blood. A calloused hand covered her face from eyes to mouth, stifling her outcry before it began. But it did not conceal the boy's mutilated image in her mind. A rumbling basso voice reverberated in her ear. Hot breath pushed out words that made no sense. Her name. How did the honch know her name? "Teress!" the honch murmured softly, as if afraid he would be overheard. "Teress, it's me, Benadek. I'm here. I'm inside this honch. I've *become* him!"

That was inaccurate but it did not matter to Benadek. Only Teress mattered. She should not have come. She should not have seen—it was not meant for her. He felt with his meaty honch-hand as she swallowed her screams unvoiced, as she twisted to free her covered eyes. Slowly, he released her. "It's true," he whispered.

Her eyes sought his, seeking some sign that behind that brutally handsome honch-face was Benadek. "I'm here," he repeated. "What you saw in the cave was a trick meant for other eyes."

The talisman had worked fine. As the honch stumbled and fell, Benadek eased him to the ground. Then he lay down naked and shivering next to the unconscious figure. If he *changed*, he would be far too large for his own clothing. He would be skin and bones, with half the mass of the honch, but tall enough to shred his own garments.

Later he understood why the *change* had failed. There was too much difference in size. He felt it soon after the *change* began—a dizzying weakness, muscles attenuating, stretching, then a deadly lethargy. As he began the plunge into unconsciousness that could only end in death, he desperately fought his way back to his own form, concentrating the vital energies, the precious elements and compounds that made up his physical being.

Even as he groped for dank blankets to warm himself, he understood what had gone wrong. In the swamp—it seemed years ago, in another life entirely—he had absorbed mass and appropriate body chemicals from the foul marsh water as he changed. But here in the cave, there was no nutrient-rich slime. Had he thought it through more carefully, he could have *changed* before, added mass to his own body, reserved kilo after kilo of proteins, lipids, bone-calcium, and blood-iron. But he had not. He was physically himself, but mentally still entwined with his enemy, weak and deathly cold. And the honch was stirring.

Benadek panicked, suspended somewhere between skinny boy and hypertrophic honch. Fear drove him where reason could not. In one immense mental heave, he concentrated everything that was uniquely Benadek into new, fluid molecules, complex RNA-like strands barely slim enough to squeeze through his capillaries, and he flowed into the honch. His hands swelled and reddened where they clutched that thick, muscular honch neck. Tiny blood vessels ruptured as dermal cells parted and questing molecules of Benadek made their way to the surface of his skin. Like corkscrews the tight helical forms crossed the minuscule chasms between Benadek-skin and honch-skin and, once across, they reburied themselves in flesh. . . .

The twisting, contorting protein-chains that were now Benadek rode honch-blood. Unstable, their tiny, complex electrochemical charges yearning for completion, for merger and stability, they tumbled through honch-capillaries seeking his brain.

The nodes of Ranvier were minuscule interruptions in the axons of nerve and brain cells, the only breaks in the myelin sheaths that isolated the seat of consciousness from the body that supported it. Most chemicals in blood never made it past that armor, but the brain still needed nutrients, so some molecules were allowed to pass. And the Benadek-molecules were clever. They possessed, as part of their structure and repertoire, shape-and-charge codes that said "I belong." Wholly or in fragments that rejoined on the far side of the myelin barriers, they invaded the honch's brain.

Other Benadek-proteins, polypeptide neurotransmitter-analogues, edged between synaptic gaps from the outside and formed shapes and charge-patterns that tickled receptor-sites into accepting them. Neurons fired. Weak neural pathways were reinforced with strong, repeated seventy-millivolt signals—tens, hundreds of times each second. Stimulated by nerve-firing and hormone-flooding, neurons put forth new dendrites, microscopic branching tendrils that connected to axons, to other dendrites, and to the bodies of brain cells. They shaped new pathways, new thoughts, in the dull honch-brain. Benadek-pathways. Benadek-thoughts.

Fever raged in the honch body as blood shunted brain-fires away, cooling the skull now swarming with microbial invaders. Honch resistance was fierce but futile—like enchanted soldiers the occupation forces were not only untouchable, but held the keys to the honch's own defenses, the codes and passwords of life. Meningitis, brain-fever, gradually cooled. Captured synapses shaped Benadek-thoughts, cool thoughts. Quisling brain cells synthesized new messengers and sent them down axons or through capillaries. The war is over, they said. The invasion has succeeded. Surrender, now, and rest.

Even as the honch-body was surrendering piecemeal, the Benadek-body began to die. But as Benadek's sentience faded from it, other silent, molecular voices sang out. Wait for us! they cried. Don't let go of him! Even as Benadek's brain function ceased, a new flood of complex polypeptides, enzymes, and RNA-analogues freed themselves from resting places in muscle and liver and gut. They flowed outward in blood that his heart still remembered to pump, to hands that still clutched the honch's neck in a grip that did not loosen even in death.

Through the ruptured capillaries of those hands, across the sweat-pools that joined them to the honch's neck, flowed the fragments that were Jean-Francois Ailloud, the motes that were Anna Reschke and James Wold Bostwick, and the molecular remnants of the others. Through skin pores and barrier membranes they swarmed, following the path that Benadek had made. Into the honch's bloodstream they plunged. Tumbling, contorting, cavorting with unsatisfied energies, they were pumped through his limbs, gut, and brain. One by one and thousand after thousand they found places in the cells of honch-heart, liver, muscle, and cancellous bone.

Later, sweat-soaked and stinking, Benadek arose. Huge, hairy Benadek-hands pushed the pale corpse of once-Benadek from him, then wiped foul sweat from his ice-blue eyes. Stripping off soggy leather clothes and wet cotton undergarments, he waded naked into the crusty snow and scrubbed himself with cold, gritty crystals.

Steam rose from golden Benadek-skin, from dense mats of white-blond body hair, from immense, dangling Benadek-genitals. Grinning broadly, Benadek the honch took his thick member in his right hand and watched his urine tunnel hotly into the fresh, clean snow.

Later still, tired but much refreshed, he reentered the cave to set up the horror scene Teress had accidentally stumbled into. He had planned to leave her a note at the cliff-edge, telling her what had transpired.

"Benadek?" Teress blinked tears from her eyes and rubbed her sore lips and jaw with both hands.

"I'm sorry," the honch rumbled. "I hope I didn't bruise you badly. I haven't gotten used to this body's strength. I had to get you out of the cave before you warned the listeners beyond the door."

"It's you. It really is you! But then . . . who's that?"

She nodded sickly in the direction of the cave-mouth and the crumpled corpse within.

"Just what's left of . . . of the honch. I had to use most of his mass to *become* like him," Benadek lied. He did not know how she would react if she knew the truth, that the creature who stood before her was mostly honch, and only a tiny bit Benadek, but he did not have time to explain. "The listeners have to believe I killed the boy, that I am one of them." His eyes narrowed anxiously. "But why did you come? Is something wrong below? Achibol?"

"Nothing's wrong," she reassured him. "I just wanted to warn you. You could have been sleeping when the honch came."

"As a matter of fact," he said with a broad grin, "I was. But that didn't help him much." The corners of his eyes and mouth crinkled in a warm, unhonchlike way. "Oops! I'll have to watch my expressions. Gorb can't be seen smiling when he goes in there, can he?"

"Gorb?"

"Me. This body, that is."

"Oh." She did not really understand.

"I have to go," he said. "They'll wonder why I'm taking so long to identify myself."

"I suppose so," she conceded reluctantly.

"A hug first?" he asked, almost shyly. "Before you go?"

Teress felt strange, being hugged by the huge, entirely male body, nothing like her Benadek, nor like wiry Gaddo, the plainsman. But she let herself be enfolded in those knot-muscled, leather-clad arms anyway. It felt good to be hugged by someone so big, like being a little girl again.

It felt strange for Benadek too. For one thing, his body was fully adult, and he was more male than ever before. His impressive member swelled tightly against his thick, leather trousers.

Honch reaction? he wondered, momentarily alarmed. No. Benadek. Benadek and Jim Bostwick and Jack Van Duinen and . . . Anna? Oh. I didn't know you were . . . no, it's not a problem, not at all. It's probably easier for all of us.

They did not make love, even though Teress found herself responding to Benadek's maleness, though he (and the others) wanted her. There was no time, and no place there in the snow, only the cave where the boy-corpse lay cooling. Benadek walked her to the edge of the scarp.

"Right now," she told him as she lowered herself over the edge, "for the first time, I really think we might have had a chance, you and me."

"Me too," he agreed. "And we will, when I'm through with all this." He felt like he was lying.

Benadek trudged back through the trampled snow to the uninviting cave. "Gorb," someone said as he approached it. "I heard you before. Why'd you go away?" The naked honch stood in the open portal, his pale blue eyes examining Benadek/Gorb with paranoid care. "Why'd you take so long? An' where's that boy?"

"Over there." Benadek/Gorb thumbed casually at the corpse.

"He dead?"

"Uh-huh."

Benadek/Gorb gestured at the open door. "I'm hungry."

"Hey, wait! What're you doing? Stop!" The honch lurched toward Benadek/Gorb, who stepped through the doorway before the other could reach him.

Pain! Agony like fire in his veins! His muscles knotted in deathlike spasms and his spine creaked with the strain of them. He was falling! He screamed. He bellowed until his throat was raw and his cries diminished to croaks in an emptiness like the void between the Earth and the Moon. Every nerve pulsed with unendurable pain. Gorb seemed to know what was happening, but Benadek did not.

Benadek did not know what or why. After a while he could not feel the pain any more, though he knew it was there. He could not see either. He struggled to grab something to break his endless fall, but there was nothing to grip, nothing to struggle against. He could not even feel the wind of his passage. There was only the unbearable, endless agony of the Gorb-body, far away.

"What happened to Gorb?"

"Dumbfuck left his metal stuff on in the empty. I stripped him."

"'He dead?"

"Nah. Gimme a hand. Gotta send him along. Here. Shove him through the door."

Again, the disorientation, the falling. Benadek screamed silently. He had just begun to regain control when the honches bundled him through the second nightmare door. Now Gorb was shrieking again. The other honches had removed everything metallic from his body and clothing, so there was no more pain, but still he screamed. The empty was always like that.

It must be some kind of screening device, Benadek thought, that won't let metal through.

It's just the empty, Gorb said.

What? Benadek asked.

Empty, Gorb repeated impatiently.

Yes, Benadek thought, It's empty. Everything is. I can't feel a thing.

"Gorb. Get up."

"Huh?"

"Get out of the door. Somebody else's coming through, dumbfuck."

"'Kay. " Gorb struggled to his feet and stood, teetering. He took two steps into a well-lit, laboratory-white room and looked back over his shoulder at the doorway. Another honch stood where he had just been standing—but it was only a metal-lined closet, with no other way in or out. How had the honch gotten there? For that matter, how had he?

"Hey Gorb! You sick? Get out of here."

"I'm going." The exit opened onto a barren corridor lined with other doors. Gorb knew where he was, and where he would go from there. That's a funny thought. 'Course I know how to get to my barracks. Gonna stop at the mess hall first, though. His thoughts were marginally clearer than his speech.

Benadek was less coherent. He thumped and pounded against the metaphorical walls of his prison with imaginary fists. He shouted with incorporeal lungs and vocal cords and struggled with figurative muscles to free himself, but to no avail. Gorb was in control of the body.

Gorb picked up a tray and thrust it at the messman. "Gimme a lot. I'm hungry."

"Sure, Gorb. You been back long?"

"Jus' got here. Wish I was back outside."

"Me too. Ya do anything?"

"Killed freaks. Caught a boy outside the empty. He died, though."

There were no tables. Honches ate with trays balanced on their knees. Honches did not use spoons or forks, either. Just knives, sometimes. When Gorb left his bench, he methodically washed his greasy hands at the wall sink.

Benadek continued to scream and pound. Gorb put a hand to his temple. Headache, he thought. Need a pill.

Gorb pushed through the door into the dim

hallway, moving faster as his coordination returned, burning the nervous energy that bubbled up inside him in his confusion. He did not understand why he had gotten in the empty with his metal on. He was not that dumb. He could not remember killing that boy, either, though he obviously had, because he was dead, and no one else had been there. Why couldn't he remember that? Maybe he was really sick. Nonetheless, he jogged toward his barracks, not sick bay. Maybe I'll get better by myself. Honches always jog. Beyond many open doorways others slept, lulled anew by the familiar, comfortable sound of pounding, booted feet.

Number five-oh-seven. The numbers were meaningless to Gorb, but he recognized their familiar shapes. Inside, he went straight to his bunk, removed his leather garments, folded them neatly, and placed them on his single shelf. Removing his undergarments, he placed them atop the rest. Shaking out his single thin blanket, he lay down on his stiff pad. Gorb slept.

Benadek did not sleep, but he finally stopped screaming. He thought he understood, now. The "empty" had done it. Not empty; Em Tee. Matter-transmitter. The "doors" were not to other rooms, tunnels, or hallways. They were protective covers over fields of forces that twisted space. Matter-transmitters had been proven possible—Arnie Sonnenfield, the astronaut, could quote the equations—but they had proved fatal to living things. Not even a marigold had survived. If our emtees had worked, we'd have had the stardrive, Arnie told the rest of them, and we'd have left the polluted, UV-burned Earth behind. There wouldn't be any honches. I wouldn't be having this nightmare. Like Benadek's other companions, Arnie was appalled by the boy's world. It bore little resemblance to the one they had left behind in death, or the one they had hoped to awaken in.

But you are having it, Anna thought back at him. I want to know what can we do about it.

Not a damn thing, Benadek interjected miserably. We're trapped. When we went through the M.T., it rearranged things.

But how? We—or you—had control of him. The Gorb-personality was suppressed. That was Jim's thought. Benadek recognized its calm strength.

The machine is programmed to honch parameters. It doesn't just "send" something, it knocks it apart and rebuilds something similar—not necessarily identical—at the receiver location.

We abandoned that approach, Arnie reflected. The space research teams weren't looking for a system that required a receiver.

This can wait, Anna sent. How can we regain control of Gorb?

I don't know, Benadek admitted. I'm less used to this than any of you. I haven't even figured out where I am, yet.

By the "taste" of your signals, you're still in Gorb's brain, Arnie answered him. I've concentrated in the spleen.

I'm in smooth muscle tissue, Jim Bostwick said. His intestine, maybe?

Is there muscle in intestines? Benadek asked.

How should I know? Bostwick responded irritably. I'm a philosopher, for God's sake!

Shut up, all of you, said Anna. He's waking up.

"Hey Gorb! You got a hard on. Didn't you get any, outside?" Honches had little or no privacy, even in sleep. Honches did not crave aloneness. Gorb woke immediately, without grogginess.

"No such luck." Gorb had not been dreaming of sex. He had been listening. There had been people talking . . . three or four of them . . . only he had not understood what they said. It was like listening to boffins. Most words were ordinary, but with enough strange ones to render them meaningless. They had been talking about him, though, and about empties. He had that headache again. Gotta take a pill, he reminded himself.

"C'mon, Gorb," the other prodded him, "get your butt up. Platoon's got Executive Guard tomorrow."

Executive Guard. Gorb had only had that duty once before. He reviewed his memories. Though honch mentation might be weak, honch memory was superior. Gorb remembered Executive Guard duty with precision that would have surprised a boffin. The platoon, fifty strong, would be scattered about Central, two men at each weak point, one at each strong one. It was a shiny-boot sinecure, and the platoon had earned it, outside. Gorb, a rear guard, had returned empty-handed, but the main body of the troop had captured forty-two pervs and deevs. Now they had two weeks of easy duty ahead. But no goof-ups. The General himself might be watching. Gorb tossed off his blanket, folded it neatly and stowed it, then pulled on his clothing.

In the interminable, indistinguishable days that followed, Benadek learned many things through Gorb's eyes. He learned that honch lives were regular and circumscribed. Honches slept on schedule, ate on schedule, even defecated within closely defined time frames.

Honches played twenty-card Jimmy and watched the "tube." Gorb conceived of that as a real tube, a glass-faced window into the poot-pens below, where honches sported with new captives. They were not really poots, of course. They were muties and deevs, smart ones. It was vaguely satisfying to see them get normal, as time went on. As honch after honch used them, their speech became slow and comprehensible and their eyes dulled. Gorb felt good about that. It was good to be normal.

But now, when he watched the tube, his headaches got worse. It was his duty to report his condition, but the boffins might take him off duty, and that was unthinkable. He just stopped watching the tube. As a consequence, his bunk was always perfect, his weapons shiny. He had to do something with the time on his hands.

Duty. Authority. Dominance and submission, all according to rank. Honch lives were, to Benadek, uniformly dull.

During off-duty hours the call bell rang once or twice. Sleeping honches never stirred unless it was their ring, their particular call signal. Those could mean anything—sick call, temple call, or a randomly generated trip to the poot-pens, like the one Gorb got, the week after Executive Guard.

There were no "pens," really. Just a hallway like all the others, with doorways but no doors. Females stood in some—deevs who were almost "cured." Empty doorways signified that the rooms' occupants were busy inside on their rumpled cots with the honches who had chosen them.

Gorb peered into each room. That was not impolite—some empty doorways belonged to the newest pervs, still unadjusted. They hid in corners or under their cots, and it was a honch's duty to use those rather than the ones who were almost better. Of course it was not as satisfying, but then, no deev was as nice as a real poot. Real poots liked honches.

Gorb's assigned rutting was over in minutes, a simple matter of a grunt and a gesture, three steps to the cot, and a moment's fumbling with his trousers' fastenings. Besides, Gorb had a terrible headache. Almost, he wished he had gone to the infirmary instead. He picked the first dull-faced female whose door he came upon, after passing up a young one with fear-bright eyes. He would have had to force her, and she would have cried aloud.

Regulated internally by habit and phlegmatic nature, externally by bells, grunted orders, and rules, Gorb seldom thought about abstractions like time. Those others who rode within him did, though. Benadek was less enured than his companions to the syrupy-slow pace of molecular existence. He missed the flash and sparkle of cerebral thought. They only "talked" while Gorb slept. When he was awake, the rush and surge of signals flooding his bloodstream was like the roar of a waterfall, or pounding waves. Quickly (as time goes for nonsynaptic minds) they evolved a "shorthand" that squeezed the equivalent of several thousand discrete words into one of Gorb's seven-hour sleep periods. The rest of the time, they pondered in gut-rumbling, blood-pumping solitude.

Benadek no longer hated Gorb. Like a force of nature, like waves or weather, Gorb simply was, neither malicious nor consciously cruel, the simplest of simples, controlled almost entirely by his rigid nature and training. Where Evil is understood, there can be no hate, only regret.

Benadek now understood, with his access to scattered Gorb-memories, how honches became what they were. From infancy, they sought consistency. Rules were to honches as sparkly baubles to poots. Rules lessened confusion (uncomfortable) and simplified decisions (painful). Rules were made by anyone more forceful. Military units were paradise for young honches, but most had to make do with the less structured, less satisfactory rules of cities, villages, even employers. Every honch was a catalogue of rules, stronger superimposed upon weaker, broader upon narrower, in a tightly organized mental hierarchy that used a good part of every honch's limited capacity to maintain.

As Benadek grew to understand the futility of hating Gorb, he no longer hated any honches, for one was much like another. His bitter hatred now focused upon the honches' long-dead creators, the perpetrators of horrors like the poot-pens. And one of them was still here, still very much alive: honches called him "the General." He had been human once, responsible for his actions and choices, and was thus culpable and a worthy object of Benadek's revulsion. Benadek imagined him as the honch of all honches—tall, broad-shouldered, blond, wearing a black uniform bright with braid.

One day Gorb was assigned to Processing. He reported to a boffin in the laboratory anteroom, and having received his orders, traced the familiar path to the poot-pens. The hallways were thronged with boffins and cozies, less coordinated than honches, so he walked, not jogged. Usually, Gorb had to restrain himself consciously, but today his footsteps dragged and it was easy to keep his pace slow.

The white-coated boffin shifted impatiently from foot to foot, his wizened face twisted in displeasure. "There you are! The order went out hours ago." Gorb stolidly awaited instructions. Boffin anxiety had no effect on him. He was ordered, he came, and when ordered to do something else, he would do it, unquestioningly. But the boffin had ordered nothing, yet. Boffins' time sense, Gorb realized, was as different from honches' as . . . As what? What strange kind of thought is that?

"Follow me," the boffin said. "Hurry, now—there are two to process today." Skinny and birdlike, he strutted off, glancing back over his shoulder to make sure that Gorb followed. Gorb did not hurry. He took one step for each of the boffin's two, and kept up easily.

"This one goes," the boffin said, gesturing at an open doorway. Gorb peered within. The female was young, but her eyes were old, windows onto a dying soul. Gorb drew breath to order her out, then grasped her arm instead. Down the hall and around the corner, the boffin indicated another room. The pure-human woman inside was older, her eyes dull and expressionless—until she saw that Gorb was not alone. Then she stood up. "Come," the boffin snapped. "Processing."

Yes, come, Benadek called silently to her, suddenly aware what Gorb's mission was, and what was to be the woman's fate. This is the last day of your torment. Tomorrow, you'll be a husk on the hillside and free of your suffering. As if she had heard, the woman followed Gorb. Behind fatigue-swollen eyelids, something gleamed, alive for now. The threesome moved off, the boffin circling like an eager sparrow, twittering, "Hurry! Hurry! One of these is for the General himself."

Benadek and his companions felt growing excitement. They were finally going to see something of the underground redoubt besides troop quarters and utilitarian passageways. Were they going to confront, even for a moment, the evil force behind its continued existence?

Processing. First came scanning—a process Benadek suspected was related to the emtee. Two boffins operated unfamiliar equipment with wristpad data-units, tapping notes and numbers with quick, bird-like pecks. Huge glassy tubes of colorful fluids lined an entire wall of the white-tiled room. A cart stood by the door, stacked with bulky, shapeless objects. Because Gorb did not look directly at them, Benadek and the others were unable to see them through his eyes.

"Process this one first," said the elder boffin, selecting the older specimen. The woman was strapped into a freestanding frame. The boffins tapped away, then the body shuddered with what must have been intense pain, though only a grunt showed it. Pain, for the mind-dead and dying, was only another sensation.

The boffin dithered over verniers, switches and readouts. Twitching with excess cerebral energy, he adjusted and muttered until he was entirely satisfied. "There," he sighed, and flipped a red-painted toggle.

"Hmmm . . ." went the processor-field, and the pure-human slumped in her bonds. "Glug . . . gurgle . . ." went one of the fluid-filled containers along the wall. In Gorb's peripheral vision, Benadek saw ripples roil the transparent-pink liquid within.

"Hmmmmm . . ." continued the invisible, perspective-distorting energy-field, and further glugs, bubblings, and plashings came from the direction of the glassy cylinders, just out of sight.

Gorb watched. The female's skin no longer shone with sweat. It was dry and dull. Her eyes, wide open, staring, no longer glittered with unvoiced pain, but were dry, shrunken in their sockets. The humming went on. The fluids went out. Tube after tube glugged, blupped, and trickled.

"Done! Remove her!" Gorb hastened to obey. He lifted the remains from the frame. Error! He had overcompensated. One of her upper limbs, snagged in its shackle, had pulled from its shoulder socket and remained attached to the frame, bone-dry and bloodless, a bundle of mummified fiber. Gorb silently reprimanded himself. I knew she'd be light. What's wrong with me? He disengaged the arm, and stacked the dry husk on the cart, on top of several others already there.

The boffins led the other female to a couch festooned with tubing and metering devices. Huh? Gorb thought. Meedering 'vices? Musta heard the boffins say it. Got another headache.

The girl was placid. Death, in whatever form, with

whatever suffering it entailed, was fulfillment and release. Her remains would be laid in the Vale beyond, and her husband, or lover, or sons, would find peace in the sure knowledge that her soul had fled. Gorb shook his head muzzily, discomfited by ill-understood thoughts. His head throbbed.

"Prepare the General for the procedure," a boffin ordered. He sniffed, and wiped his dribbling nose on his stained white sleeve, blinking grit from congenitally red eyes.

A faint carillon-chime echoed across white tiles. "He's ready," the other boffin replied, stepping to the far wall. A panel hitherto unnoticed hissed aside, revealing two honches and another boffin. Between the honches was a white-shrouded cart. From the shroud poked a head of grayed yellow hair atop a wrinkled, ancient face.

"Easy there! Easy. Watch the door frame," the cart's occupant squawked. "You there! Boffin. Have you picked a good one this time? My last treatment faded in days."

"She . . . she's young and healthy, General," the boffin replied, trying to suppress a fearful tremble. "The interval between treatments must inevitably decrease, and these specimens mutate further and further from the old norms."

"I know your tricks," the General croaked. "You'd give me old worn-out whores if I weren't careful. I want fresh, red meat. Let's see her."

"Certainly, General," the boffin quavered, all the more frightened because he knew that the horrible old man's accusations were true. His everyday task was to see to the health of the poot-pens' denizens, and this process conflicted with his mindset. Perhaps a faint echo of genuine human sentiment lingered in his pared-down genes as well. He motioned to the honches to bring their charge alongside the pure-human. "See?" he addressed the

General. "She's lovely, isn't she? And her blood tests out optimally."

"Shitcan your tests. Let me *see*!" The General sat up. His white surgical drape fell away to reveal a skinny, shallow chest with sparse white hairs.

"You wish to see the test results, General?" said the boffin, reluctantly playing out a familiar ritual.

"No, you simple fool! The blood! Show me her blood!"

"Certainly. I'll just finish connecting her and then I'll tap off a sample . . ."

"I want a scalpel! I'll see for myself!" The third boffin had anticipated the demand. He scurried forward with a glittering instrument in hand. Snatching it, the General leaned toward the nude, silent female and with a flick of his wrist opened a two-inch gash in her drooping breast. Red blood welled up, masking the sight of yellowish tissue. The pure-human flinched reflexively, but otherwise lay motionless. The scalpel clattered on the floor and the General stretched greedy, talonlike fingers to probe the wound, coming away dark with blood. "It's old blood," he shrieked. "Not red enough!"

"But General," the eldest honch protested, "according to the tests . . ."

"There's only one test," the General snarled, and sucked his fingers, making wet, popping noises. "It's weak and salty," he whined. "It won't last a week. Find me better blood."

"There is no better, General," the boffin mewled. "This one's the best we have—she's young and ripe, not a day over twenty."

The General eyed his victim with fresh interest. "So she is!" he cackled. "Ripe." His damp fingers traced a circle around a flaccid nipple, avoiding the bleeding wound. His other hand disappeared beneath his drape and sought his crotch. He grinned broadly. "I'm becoming interested in her," he crowed. "Go now! Leave us! Perhaps this time I'll sire an heir. Then we'll let her live a while."

"Of course, General," the head boffin assented. "When you're ready for the treatment . . ."

"I'll ring, I'll ring," the old horror snapped, climbing down from his cart, his drape forgotten. "Go, before I become distracted and lose this monstrous . . ." The door slid shut on his words, on the evidence of his obscene passion.

CHAPTER TWENTY-ONE,

wherein the Pure Boy dons Wandag's Mantle of Remembrance, and knows his soul's past.

The Arkendhi "Weavers' Song" depicts the merger of souls, the creation of the Ksentos Venimentum text's Mantle of Remembrance. In this tale not Benadek but Gorb seems like the kindly god Benakh, who shelters children beneath his magical robe. Meanings entwine, coalesce, and confuse: the Old Arkendhi word for "robe" is "gorban." Does Gorb then symbolize Remembrance?

But what of Benadek, subsumed in a collective identity? Will we hear no more of him? A status check of the biocybes' input buffers indicates that there are few tales left to be integrated. Does the final chapter of this experiment draw near?

On another level, does this episode hint that the ability to *become* is no more than a contagious microorganism, a germ or virus carried from star to star by early explorers? Is that original organism, now integrated into mutable genes, like some super-mitochondrium? Then the fury of the one-worlders and parallel-evolutionists has been wasted, and the true tale should offend none: species evolved separately, as all but fundamentalists have long known, but *becoming* appeared only once, on a long vanished planet that may indeed have been called Earth.

If this quasi-organism exists, can we afford not to find it, and pass it to the unfortunate "immunes" among us, the fixed-form humans?

(Kaledrin, Senior Editor)

INTERLUDE
The Great School, Midicor IV

"Aw, come on, Kal! You can't publish that. Benedek is a disease?"

"I can too. Look, Ab, a few chapters ago Saphooth and his crowd were calling us mutables body stealers. If it's just a few transferred genes that came in on a virus, they can spend their energy curing the immutables' immunity, and we'll all be happy."

"Yeah," Abrovid admitted uneasily.

"You don't sound convinced."

"Yeah, well, I was just thinking . . ."

"Thinking what?"

"Well, what if instead of trying to catch our disease, they develop a vaccine instead?"

The boffins dismissed Gorb. He returned to his bunk to await further orders. The premature termination of his task got him back long before his bunk-mates, so the barracks was empty. Gorb was not sleepy, but with his headache worsening, he decided to try a nap. Surprisingly, he dozed almost at once.

Benadek did not sleep. For all his former hatred of the General, he felt only disgust and scorn, now. His sworn enemy was no towering honch, no godlike or devilish being, only a warped old man. He was not as evil as he was senile.

Don't underestimate him, said Nimbuk, the Inuit medicine man. Age does not diminish Evil, it refines it. Nimbuk "spoke" so seldom that Benadek hardly recognized his chemical "voice." Among my people, age is the essence of Evil, and death our salvation from it. This creature has clung to life so long that all goodness has sweated away.

No wonder Nimbuk has been so quiet, Benadek thought privately. What must he think of Achibol, and even 'memories' like himself?

I agree with Nimbuk, Jack Van Duinen said. The General makes Gorb seem like an innocent babe.

Gorb *is* innocent, Benadek replied. Men like the General created him. Gorb only follows his programming, jumbled as it is by the afterthoughts they tacked on. But what have you come up with? Can we regain control?

If he uses the matter transmitter, Sonnenfield, the astronaut, speculated, maybe we could reverse the changes. At least we wouldn't be taken by surprise again.

We could wait a long time. His platoon's assigned to inside duty indefinitely.

Can't be helped, can it? At least we should be prepared.

I don't know if I can stand it! Anna communicated so vehemently that Gorb twitched in his sleep. That girl the General mutilated . . . in a week, there'll be another, and then another. I can't just sit by and watch that. I'll go mad.

Can you do that? the philosopher, Bowers, asked reflectively. Or are all of us trapped in our dubious sanity? I suspect we'd all have to make that choice together.

<Choice?> Anna sent bitter-acid and sharp-metallic ions afloat. Since when is sanity a matter of choice?

Excepting organic disfunction, disease, or genetic flaws, madness is a choice, Bowers answered coolly, an option all minds have. But wouldn't you feel some obligation to us? Should you escape in that manner, the rest of us would still have to . . . to live with you.

Did you notice what happened? Benadek interjected with a burst of peptide-chains. A responding trickle of small, tightly bound molecules of neutral charge indicated the others' incomprehension. Anna, when you first 'spoke up'—as upset as you are—Gorb twitched. We can influence him!

A little jerk here or there? That's not control, Arnie Sonnenfield derided. We've been giving him headaches for months.

It's a foothold, Benadek replied.

You're locked out of his hypothalamus and other critical brain areas, Anna protested, and you don't dare push. If he starts making antibodies against us, we could be destroyed like any infection. The antibody problem had been discovered after Gorb's self-assertion. Because Benadek had not merely changed himself, then killed the honch, but had invaded him, the takeover was vulnerable, like any invasion, to organized internal resistance. Initially, Gorb's immune system had been overwhelmed. Had Benadek and the others been a viral or bacterial onslaught, Gorb would have died, but because he did not, his own defenses still had a belated chance to fight them off. Their protective mimicry of Gorb's identifying codes was incomplete. Immune systems possessed enormous "libraries" of identified infections and seemed to create new entries as fast as invasions occurred. Even attacks on the immune system could be overcome, if the victim could be kept alive long enough.

A belated chance, but not a winning one. Benadek's desperate plunge into the Gorb-body, and the systemic chaos it caused, might well have killed that body. Both forces might have been decimated and the battlefield left a ruin. Neither side could have won quickly enough, decisively enough.

The matter-transmitter had actually saved them all: incorporating elements similar to the temples' gene-scanners in its error-checking systems, it simultaneously reinforced Gorb's normal honch patterns and edited identified disease-causing lifeforms from the transmission. All else was transmitted exactly as scanned: Gorb's weight and electrolytic balance remained the same, his stomach and intestinal content, even the dirt under his fingernails, were left intact.

Random bits of Gorb-tissue were sampled and subjected to more extensive testing—and everything so tested was destroyed in the process. Ordinarily, such sampling had no deleterious effects. After all, what loss to Gorb were a few cubic millimeters of his last meal—half-cooked rabbit and wild turnips? What matter if he lost a few brain cells, a bit of muscle even, or twenty milliliters of blood? But when the material tested included Benadek and his companions, so soon after their takeover, there was no redundancy. What was lost in the emtee's processing and sampling was lost forever. Even the memory of it, the recognition of loss, was obliterated—for what was Benadek now but the memory of himself? The sampling had broken the invaders' hastily constructed control.

Gorb's conductive buckles and studs and weapons had created eddy currents that broke tenuous chemical bonds and shattered blood proteins. While Gorb experienced the pain of misfiring nerves, he lost nothing that could not be replaced by his own DNA-coded protein factories. The invaders' losses were final, and their control could not be regained.

But the eddy currents that destroyed their coherence had muddled the scanner's readings of their foreignness. Obviously, only the M.T. to and from the outside had such screening, or the foreigners would have been eliminated in the later transmission. But even if Benadek regained control, he would have to avoid the outside transmitters, and find another way to leave the underground installation, when and if the time for that came. Nevertheless, he did not hope to control Gorb again . . . not exactly.

If Gorb knew about us, if we could somehow introduce ourselves to him, could we convince him to share this body with us? What benefits could we offer him? Day and night, in his slow, chemical thinking, Benadek pondered that question. He was less bitter in his imprisonment than he might have been without that task and the slim possibilities it offered. Anything was better than outright destruction.

A honch? Share with us? One silent voice scoffed.

He's hardly more than a mindless beast, a programmed engine of destruction, another voice protested.

Even if we revealed ourselves, and didn't drive him mad, why would he do us any favors?

Benadek let them have their say. He let them fume, protest, and deny. He waited as patiently as a seed awaits the melting snow, the cessation of winter's blasts. When the last protesting wisps of protein-thought broke down amid the mute whisper of Gorb's ordinary enzymes and simple lipids, when the last chained word-codes were silenced by free-radical combination and macrophage-ingestion, Benadek released the story he wanted them to know.

It was a brief tale of a poot, a simple girl who wanted to be more than her inborn limitations decreed. A girl, little more than a child, who struggled against her nature—was it pseudohuman? Less than human? No, he said. She was simply human. A pun? Chemical speech had no sly inflections or raised eyebrows—and no laughter. No one as much as chuckled. Benadek told of a soul reaching beyond the frontiers of its imprisoning brain and flesh in search of a dream, and dying there.

Benadek recounted meeting Sylfie—his mockery, lust, and ignorant cruelty—without explanations, apologies, or perverse pride. He described her agony, and the hope she held to the last, for generations to come, generations that would never spring from her own womb.

He told them, finally, of the last effort she made to send that hope onward beyond her own death: himself. He told them of Benadek, whose survival was Sylfie's final cry of defiance, echoing down the myriad branching corridors of future time.

When he finished, only the white noise of Gorb-processes swirled around the invaders in their scattered hiding places. Between the pulses of Gorb-blood driven by Gorb-heart and the silent stretching of encircling capillary walls, amid the bumping and thumping of platelets, the slip and slop of dead cells being consumed and carried away, there was silence. For the duration of a hundred heartbeats, a thousand, through the sucking meioses and mitoses of a hundred thousand cells, the flabby collapses of as many others, the thoughtless, mindless silence was sustained.

Benadek waited. Meaning must create itself. His

initiative must be followed not by the thrust-and-push of his will, but from without. He waited.

When the silence had endured a hundred, five hundred, a thousand heartbeats more, when a million, a hundred million nerve impulses had passed from sleeping Gorb-brain to beating heart and rolling intestine-wave, a trickle of thought rewarded Benadek's patience.

What does a honch hope for? someone asked.

What pain lies in the deepest, most hidden cells of a honch's poor brain? he replied. And what might ease it?

Even as these questions flowed, seeking their own answers, new ones were raised. They were phrased in glutamine linked to aspartic acid and lysine in specific order—protein chains, transparent to Gorb's bodily processes, that linked with others of their own kind wherever the dangling question marks of receptor shape and electromolecular charge allowed. They formed new questions and commands: neurotransmitter commands that made their way from blood to unsheathed olfactory nerves to brain, where they caused synapses to fire in specific, concerted ways.

As each question arrived, each by its own unique path, so Gorb's limited brain answered them with more conventional but no less wondrous firings of neurons. For the first time in his life—for eighteen or twenty-two years, he guessed, never having wondered before—Gorb opened his eyes and really saw.

As Benadek before him had awakened in the laboratory chair in Sufawlz, knowing not only what light switches and cathode-ray tubes were, but how they functioned and why, so Gorb opened his eyes and saw, for the first time, that the call box above the barracks door had a wire that ran down the jamb, to the baseboard, and into a hole.

He understood more: from the hole the wire ran through a conduit to the central command computers.

Other wires ran to boffin quarters, to the emtees, even to the General's own bedroom. Gorb, who had never made an analogy before, who only now knew what a simile was, said clearly and succinctly, "Like nerves, those wires," and he grinned proudly.

Could Benadek have grinned, he would have responded like a proud father to his offspring's first words. But even as Gorb reveled in the new capabilities of his rapid-firing synapses, he was flooded with new realization. Within the matrix of his expanding world was a very special being whose name was . . . Gorb. Awash in a tumult of concepts never contemplated—love, responsibility, the sharing of joy and pain, self-sacrifice and noblesse oblige—Gorb saw himself not only for what he was, but what he had been. For the first time since he was a greedy, cranky infant pulling with tiny, pearl-white teeth at his mother's swollen nipple, Gorb wept.

He wept for himself, and the depth of ignorance that had allowed him to do all that he had done—the suffering he had caused, the poor pervs, deevs, and muties, the mothers, fathers, siblings, and children. He wept for dull-eyed rape victims, callous honches still ignorant, indifferent boffins locked in clever impotence, poots, bland cozies, and above all for the willful cruelty and arrogance of the intellects that had created them. He even wept for the General, the last pitiable ancient clinging to life long after it should rightfully have faded away.

"You wanted to know," he chided himself as huge sobs racked his massive frame. "You wanted to know what was behind your headaches. Maybe you didn't want to know so much, but it all came in the one package. Now take it like a soldier.

"No," he corrected himself. "Like a man."

The human mind—honch, pure-human, ancient—had only so much room for understanding, or for grief. Gorb absorbed the naked concept of guilt, and his mind rebelled. Unable to absorb more, horrified by what he understood, he escaped in the only way he could. His head slumped back on his pillowless pad and his eyes, beneath shuttering lids, rolled up.

In the backwash of Gorb's thudding heart, the chemical chaos of a bloodstream flooded with molecular snags and the tumbling wreckage of Gorb's emotion, the minds responsible for his enlightenment and torment waited in isolation, unable to call out above the tumult. As Gorb fell deeper into unconsciousness, they sent tentative messages afloat—short notes in fragile bottles that more often than not were smashed on the molecular logs, rocks, and flood-wreckage that swirled beyond their refuges.

When words and concepts could finally flow unbroken, when Gorb's breathing slowed and became regular and his murky blood cleared, someone asked, What was that? What happened?

I found something Gorb wanted, Anna replied contritely, and I nudged an answer his way. A tumbling, twisted DNA segment, topped off with a partly phosphorylated kinase—a meaningless molecule soon dissipated—was her equivalent of a shrug. He only wanted to know if something was really wrong with him—his headaches, you know. But it didn't stop there. The answer wasn't simple. The neurotransmitter surpluses we created allowed him to think it all through, and with their help, he . . . we lost control.

He raided us, Benadek interjected. And now, when he wakes up and integrates what he took, he'll know we're here.

Who's in control? demanded a panicky, negatively-charged flood of tiny proteins. Us or him?

He is, Benadek replied. For now, anyway.

For now?

If he wants us, he'll keep us. Otherwise . . . a few

days' fever, and we'll be sweated out, a stain on his mattress.

What can we do? Arnie asked anxiously.

Wait, Anna answered him, and hope.

Benadek's wordless agreement followed her passive, quiet-flowing thought. Gorb's heart had beaten twenty-one thousand times since his overburdened mind had rebelled. He was awakening. Wait, Benadek cautioned the others. Just hope he likes us.

QUERY: WHO ARE YOU? Gorb's question resounded with power and confidence.

I'm the boy you thought you killed by the emtee, Benadek answered.

QUERY: THOUGHT?

Benadek created a scintillant image of himself lying next to Gorb. He showed himself flowing into Gorb. Gorb-now saw Gorb-then arrange the limp body, watched himself cut it and smear it with blood. Gorb-now shuddered. The killing hadn't been real? He could not find a word for what he felt. Before, he would not have needed one. Relief was too simple a concept.

QUERY: YOU ARE ALIVE? Gorb's questions, Benadek thought, were like hearing one of Circe's defective speakers turned up too loud. The not-sound of those questions—part bioelectric, nervous, and tight; part chemical, molecular, and loose—unnerved him.

I'm alive, Benadek volunteered. You can destroy me, if you want. There was no risk in saying that—Gorb could discover it for himself. Better to reassure him and give him time for thought. Benadek was glad Gorb was communicating, not just taking what he wanted. That mental shudder over Benadek's fraudulent "death" demonstrated Gorb's repugnance for his ignorant honch-acts, and the killing he had not actually committed.

It took Benadek a while to realize just what emotion was steering the big honch. The ex-honch, he corrected himself. He remembered something Achibol had told him long ago. "The honch template is derived from military policemen, a retired Los Angeles police lieutenant, and several sheriff's deputies. Cops." And that, Benadek knew, was what honches had been created to be. Cops. Not the twisted warriors that patchwork modifications later made of them, but simple small-town cops: peacemakers, rule-keepers and protectors. That revelation was the source of Gorb's remorse. He had been, as Achibol might have put it, a rogue, a bad cop.

QUERY: WHY DESTROY YOU? Even as he "spoke," Gorb plucked the answer from his own cells and his visitors', his demand so intense that Benadek could no longer distinguish question from answer. The thoughts that Gorb plucked from Benadek's essence, from Anna's, Jim's, and the others' coalesced as further questions, which in turn became demands . . . Finally it stopped. For a hundred heartbeats Gorb was silent, mulling what he had gathered. Then . . .

WE ARE GORB/BENADEK/ANNA/JIM/ARNIE . . . ONE. NOT MANY.

If Gorb was suggesting what Benadek thought, what he hoped. . . .

THERE MUST BE ONLY ONE. It was not a statement, it was a command.

One being, one mind? Benadek asked. If we merge, you may not be the dominant one. Have you considered that?

NO MATTER. ONE. NOT SIMPLE. HUMAN.

Benadek saw what Gorb saw, and understood the sacrifice the honch was willing to make—and why. Gorb's sacrifice, and Jim's, and the others'. Not his, not Benadek's. At least, not much. Even now, fragmented, the Benadek-personality was the most complete. When they merged that personality would dominate the rest and integrate them. Gorb, Anna . . . all the memories would be Benadek's, perhaps confused by the parallel time lines of shared lives, or suppressed, to be drawn upon only in time of need. Benadek hoped they would remain, if only as poignant, contradictory memories, like the recollection of a dream.

It was not Benadek's choice to make. He could not kill those he shared a body with. Even if the power to decide had been his, not Gorb's, he could not have done it. Benadek withdrew. He withdrew not only his thoughts, but his aspiration to live once again with a body and a mind that responded to him alone, without contradictory voices—but with Anna's spirit, Jim's analytical wisdom, and Gorb's rules, all at his command. Benadek drew himself close, a benign tumor in a little-used part of Gorb's brain. Let them decide, he told himself. Let them decide their own fate.

INTERLUDE
The Great School, Midicor IV

"See?" Abrovid chortled. "I was right. He didn't have to kill anybody. Benadek's not a bad guy—and neither are we. Old Saphooth and his 'evil invasion' can go climb a tree."

"That last chapter is reassuring," Kaledrin admitted, "but not because it's necessarily true."

"Huh? The biocybes can't lie, Kal."

"I suppose not. But that's not what I mean. Just because Chapter Twenty—and Twenty-one—undercut Saphooth doesn't mean I believe the story. It's cobbled together from old folktales, remember?"

"Is that what you think? Am I a cobbler? I wrote

those specs. If I thought for one minute . . ." But Kaledrin had already turned away. He was dictating to his terminal.

AFTERTHOUGHTS

There is a test of the biocybes' reliability and Saphooth's contentions, if anyone dares try it. It's not proof, of course, because there is no "proof," only levels of confidence. But if there ever was a real Benadek whose mutated kin learned to *become*, and not a Benadek-virus that has infected us, wouldn't his ability to share a body with others be duplicable in his descendants?

The advantages are obvious: all the expenses of travel, entertainment, and subsistence would be halved for two. If a mutable furnished the body, and the second personality were of a fixed-form individual, the latter would gain all the advantages of mutability. There would be no cause for the jealousy that motivates MYTHIC's former director, Saphooth.

Will anyone out there volunteer to take on a passenger in his mind and body, for the sake of an increased confidence-level? A passenger like Saphooth himself, perhaps? The benefits of such a merger, as the yet-undistributed Chapter Twenty-two clearly illustrates, go both ways.

(Kaledrin, Senior Editor)

INTERLUDE
The Great School, Midicor IV

"You can't publish that, Kal! Somebody will actually try it!"

"I'm not worried. Of all the millions of species and millions of worlds, don't you think someone would already have tried? If they did, it didn't work, did it? We'd have heard something." Kaledrin waved his eyestalks gleefully. "I'm telling old boneyform to put up or shut up. Wait 'til he reads Chapter Twenty-two."

"When are you going to distribute it?" Abrovid asked. "You've been sitting on that data-cube for days."

"I'm going to sit on it a while longer. Then, when it's released, I'm going to take a vacation."

"Vacation?" Abrovid queried. "You don't need one yet."

"I'm not going to bask and rut, Ab. I'm going to *become* something else. I've wanted a change, but there's never been time. Now, whether the Board wins or loses its suit against SOMA, the pressure will be off me."

"Have you decided what somatoform you want?" Abrovid asked.

"Something different," Kaledrin replied wistfully. "I'm sick of chitin and tentacles."

Abrovid departed. The halls and corridors of the Great School echoed emptily with his passage, then were silent, half-lit in nighttime standby mode. Kaledrin remained. Despite the late hour, he was expecting someone.

Kaledrin glanced frequently at the wall clock, his tentacles coiling and uncoiling impatiently. Then at last, when he was about to give up, he heard the airy swoosh of the outer door, then the clatter of hard-soled footgear, the one-two, left-right bipedal gait of . . .

"What's this about, Kaledrin?" snapped Saphooth. "It better be good!"

"Oh, it is," Kaledrin replied in tones sweet as honeybug oil. He reached under himself, pulled out the data-cube, and proffered it to Saphooth. "Here. Chapter Twenty-two. When you've read it, you'll understand."

CHAPTER TWENTY-TWO,

wherein Distant Evil closes in, and Benadek must face his Final Choice.

In our editorial enthusiasm we have too often strayed from our primary concern, the myths of Achibol and Benadek. It is time to get back to them.

The origin of Chapter Twenty-two in myths of the Salist'efen Cycle is clear. Many of you are familiar with the story of Wandag. But there are others equally strongly represented, like Alnra'kof, Eater of Souls, who herein (and only herein) gets his just desserts.

(Kaledrin, Senior Editor)

He stretched massive, well-proportioned limbs, and absently scratched his naked, blond-furred buttocks. It was good to be alive, to be in control, and not to have to share his body and mind. It was good, too, to think clearly without his thoughts being blurred by others'. This is an astronaut's body, he thought, fine-tuned and reflex-fast, the perfect tool for the difficult task ahead of me.

This is an astronaut's brain, too, he thought further. Computer-perfect. Astronaut, philosopher, soldier . . . and these are fine hands, strong precision tools. He turned his hands palms-up and flexed his fingers. He smiled.

"Watcha doing, Gorb?" asked the honch in the next bunk, observing his odd behavior.

"Nothing," Gorb replied. He thought of himself as Gorb, right now, so the answer had come automatically. He could, if he wished, think of himself as Benadek or any of the others. It made no difference. He was himself, and he was one.

Dressing rapidly, he jogged to the mess hall. He was not on duty for six hours, and there was much to be done. It would be easy, he realized as his fine body adapted unprotestingly to his smooth, jogging pace, to forget all the details of this body, to let the cells and nerves and enzymes follow their ordinary programs and not think about them. We all do that, most of our lives. Someday, if I survive what's ahead, I'll allow myself just to exist like that again. But first . . .

He ate rapidly, tray on his knees, and rose as soon as he had finished. His next stop was a repair shop he had observed incuriously on many occasions. . . .

Boffins bent over well-lit workbenches, engaged in the intricacies of portable com units, lasers, and less familiar equipment. Gorb stood in the doorway holding a list. He had written it himself. The sources of the electronic expertise he had drawn upon were identifiable, but he did not bother putting a name to the memories. He was all one, now.

A boffin snatched the list. "Who wants this?" he snapped. "What's it for?" Gorb shrugged wordlessly.

Honches never explained their orders. "Never mind! Wait here. I'll get it."

There were many empty rooms in the underground complex, gathering dust through doors hanging open on rusted hinges, accumulating black mold and white mildew from decades and centuries of unchecked seepage and poor ventilation. Gorb hunted until he found one with a functional ceiling light and a door that still shut, and set to work. He unpacked circuit boards, microchips, pinout sockets, a spool of hair-fine wire, a soldering pen, a clip-on heat sink, and a pair of locking needle-nose pliers. Arraying tools and components on his spread-out jacket, his big hands began their delicate task.

With his completed product hidden inside his jacket, he sought an abandoned barrack with a functional call bell. Removing its cover, he wedged his small creation inside with neatly cut blocks of foam, and connected it with tiny copper alligator clips at the ends of fine leads. He replaced the bell cover. That was all, right then. His bunk-mates would be returning to the barracks to prepare for platoon assembly, where they would be given their duties for the next shift.

Gorb's platoon drew hall-duty—mopping and cleaning. A part of his mind long enured to monotonous tasks performed them no differently than the other honches. What was different was the level of bright, active thought that went on in other parts of his brain and body. Later, when the platoon returned to its bunks, only Gorb had trouble sleeping. He woke up for every call bell, no matter whose.

The next day was a repetition of the one before. The rumble of his impatient curiosity and low-level anxiety, like unheard subsonic vibrations, made it hard to keep his mind on cleaning. No wonder he had had those constant headaches before he had merged with . . . with himself.

Finally, with eight unplanned hours ahead, Gorb returned to the barrack whose bell he had modified. He removed a thumbnail-sized data-chip and wrote a brief note. The heat-pencil and flimsy paper looked incongruously delicate between his big, blond-haired fingers.

Once their annoyance at being distracted from one job and set upon another ran its course, the boffins at Data-Processing took up the new task with myopic enthusiasm, and Gorb was shortly presented with a sheaf of printouts. "I wonder who wants this stuff?" a boffin asked as he handed it to Gorb. "Never mind!" he spat, before Gorb could shrug.

Gorb took his printouts back to the empty storeroom and read page after page of cryptic data. Then he got out tools and components, and built another device. Hiding it in his jacket, he returned to his barracks.

The device he installed in his own barracks bell was simpler than the other one. The first device had recorded all the call-signals that traveled the main bus wires. It recorded time, source, and destination data for every one. The printouts put names and locations to otherwise meaningless numbers. He could have mapped most of the complex's communication system from that data, but only needed to know four codes—the identifiers for his barracks, his personal bell-call, the series of bits representing calls originating from the horrible Processing lab, and the General's personal sequence. He now had those vital codes.

The device would read bus signals traveling through the system, and occasionally modify them before they reached the bell itself. If any call requesting honch labor was routed from Processing or the General's private quarters, the bell would ring Gorb's summons only.

✧ ✧ ✧

That night Gorb—or Benadek—had second thoughts. He had no plan past the moment he confronted the General. Theoretically, since all knowledge of the *change* was extant, he should be able to use it. But this body was Gorb's, not Benadek's. If some lost secondary function of an overlooked gene was required, and Gorb's chromosomes lacked it . . . the ability might be gone. There was only one way to find out. He was not going to get much sleep. What if the call came tonight? He should have allowed more time to practice, to get to know "himself."

There were no calls. An hour before reveille, he visited the latrine. By its single, dim light, he examined his left arm's light bronze skin and sparse, white-blond hairs. Only what was missing told him he had succeeded: there were no scars, and Gorb had collected several. He had *changed*. Reassured, Benadek went back to bed, but did not sleep. If only the bell would ring right now . . .

Hall duty again. Gorb went through the motions. If he had to go through another day like this . . . That night the bell rang. He sprang to his feet, and began pulling on his trousers. "Hey Gorb! What're you getting up for? It's my call." The honch, Effred, looked long and hard at him.

Before Gorb could think of an excuse, the bell rang a second time—Gorb's code. "See?" he said. "My call."

Effred became less perturbed. Two bells, two honches. Gorb—or Benadek—was less satisfied. What duty was Effred called for? If the two of them were assigned together, why had not his, Gorb's, code been first? In fact, it should have rung the Gorb-code twice.

Perhaps Effred's call was for something else entirely. For that matter, so might his own be. The small, ironic thought that followed could have had its origin with no one but Gorb himself: if all this idle speculation is typical, no wonder we honches are efficient. Effred is dressed already. He'll be at the assignment station before I get my boots buckled.

Effred was there ahead of him, but had found out nothing. "Follow me!" a waiting boffin ordered. Benadek almost blurted "Where?" but Gorb-habit overrode his impulse. It was odd, he thought, to have one personality again, but still to have such inconsistent urges. Or was it? He could not remember.

Their route led toward Benadek's desired destination. When they passed the intersection leading to the poot-pens without changing direction, relief overrode his growing anxiety. There would be no dead-eyed girls to fetch. At the processing lab, they were ordered to take a gurney from storage.

The boffin led them from the lab to a kitchen where elaborate meals had been prepared for the underground base's elite. But the stink that assailed his nose was unlikely to appeal to the most jaded ancients. The carcasses that lay coldly on stainless-steel countertops were neither meat-beasts nor ancient, unmodified cattle. They were human. The stench alone told him they were far beyond any use in the lab.

Benadek's stomach twisted in rebellion. The nearest body was a child's. Its wide-eyed stare and twisted mouth, rigid in death, showed that it had not died wrapped in the unfeeling dullness of the broken ones, the "cured," though there were no marks on the corpse. The honches picked it up and dumped it on the cart.

The second corpse's throat was like scavenged meat mauled by an old, dull-toothed cat. Blood was everywhere. That one had been male, very much alive, and had struggled. Benadek fought the urge to gag.

The third one had been dead longest. The stink was overpowering. Effred grabbed an arm and pulled. Flesh and skin peeled off in his hand. That was too much even for a phlegmatic honch. "Acch!" Effred dropped the arm, shaking rotted meat from his palm. Benadek's head swirled. Effred's effort had rolled the body over, exposing her face. She, at least, had not gone to her death fearful and struggling. She was smiling.

With an agonized cry, Benadek averted his face. Tears blurred his vision, and his stomach revolted. Bile and the remains of his last meal splashed across the corpse. Dimly, he heard a prattling boffin voice, and an answering basso murmur from Effred. When he looked up with tear-filled eyes, the other honch was eyeing him most strangely. He opened his mouth to speak just as something pricked him sharply in the side of his neck. He staggered a step away from the mess he had made before his knees folded under him. The last thing he saw was the boffin's bright, curious stare.

He heard the gabble and screech of angry scratchbirds and the jagged, off-key clatter of an overheated bearing grinding itself apart. The annoying sounds threatened to resolve into words, but he could not quite wake up. Something foreign roiled through his blood and interfered with his awakening. He wanted to concentrate, to force his blood to cleanse itself, but it was hard to think straight. He slipped back into unconsciousness.

"Not a honch?" the cackling voice squalled. "Of course he's a honch. I'm not blind. Be careful, boffin. Don't overreach yourself." Not a honch, indeed. What's the boffin up to? A trick? Are they becoming capable of manipulating me?

The General was afraid. More afraid than ever in his two thousand years. Everything was falling apart. Once, a single deviant "pure-human" wench would have given him a month of rigorous life. Once boffins obeyed without sidelong looks, and plumbing worked properly. Once, he had been tall, commanding, and strong. His voice had boomed, and men—real men, not simples—had jumped to obey him. Now even these slavish half-men dragged their feet and told him lies.

"Explain yourself," he said, forcing his voice to remain low so he did not cackle. "What *is* this creature on the transfer-table? Why does he look like a honch?"

"We don't know, General." The boffin quivered with unconcealed terror. "He came in through the sally-port M.T. several months ago. Outwardly, he is Gorb, but his genes are anomalous."

The General's sagging face reddened, and he sucked air into his shrunken lungs. To forestall another outburst, the boffin pressed on quickly. "He has a full complement of old-human genes—and some odd ones we can't identify. His blood is as clean as a youth's—a perfect donor, far superior to the ones the troops drag in."

"A perfect donor?" A feral gleam lit the raddled, ancient face. Suspicion faded in the bright light of that wonderful news. "But if this fails—if he's not what you say . . ."

If the composite being who was Gorb, Benadek, and old memories had been awake, he would have understood. *Changing* was not just a variation in gene expression, but in the molecular codes themselves. The incorporation of ancient memories wrought no such changes, nor did the willy-nilly invasion of Gorb's body. Old memories and Benadek had existed in Gorb as entities apart. But they were all information, and information could be coded in many ways, remaining essentially the same. When those scattered souls all joined to become one being in Gorb's massive body, information merged, and the new "document" contained all the original "pages," in one integrated format.

The totality was too complex to fit within Gorb's fourfold-redundant genetic structure. Simples, unlike the fully human, had no introns, no "waste space" in their coding. The new Gorb genome, the synthesis, contained only a single copy patterned most strongly on that of the dominant one in the gestalt, Benadek. Now there was only one being, with one genetic code, optimized to partake of the best of every one of them. There was much of the original Gorb, not just Benadek and the memories of ancient genes. The final melange was closer to the old human norm than to honches or latter-day purehumans. But as the boffin had remarked, there were anomalies . . .

"Why wait? Open the valves now! Give him to me."

"But General, the sedative. There are still traces in his blood. They'll dissipate soon."

"You probably gave him too much," the old horror grumbled, but did not complain further.

It had almost been too much. The proper dosage for a honch would pacify any simple mind's coarse channels, but for the complex being Gorb had become, it was immeasurably more disruptive. Benadek/Gorb did not regain consciousness until long after the drug had dissipated to what the boffins considered safe for the General.

The first thing Benadek realized as consciousness returned was that he was dying. He was being poisoned with the breakdown products of the General's aged blood. He was growing old, cluttered with free radicals and dangerous clumps of foamy cholesterol and lipid precursors, inert leukocytes, bits and pieces of uningested dead cells.

He did not recognize what was wrong immediately.

Sovoda-memory did, but there were more pressing things on Benadek's mind. He could not see. His optic nerves and brain centers seemed to be functioning, but he could not open his eyes. He could not move either. His wrists, arms, and ankles were restrained. It was hard to think with all the junk accumulating in his bloodstream.

"It's working," a voice crowed. "I can feel it! You were right, boffin. This is a good one." It was a familiar voice, evoking uneasy feelings, but Benadek, in his enervated state, did not dig deeper. It was too hard just remaining conscious.

Headache, he thought, as Gorb. Sick. The others, those bright voices in his mind that had opened doors onto endless vistas of understanding, were silent. Gorb the honch resented the dullness that clung like a stinking, sweaty blanket, like a dirty fog between him and the brilliant sun. Part of him was dying, and Gorb did not want to die. Honch breeding dictated survival: death was not glory, but failure. And Gorb did not want to fail.

Like an antique battle-computer coming on-line after long downtime, the memory of his specialized honch-brain performed its hardwired tasks.

SELF CHECK: DATA PHASE.
- MUSCULAR DYSFUNCTION.
  ALTERNATE POSSIBILITIES:
- FATIGUE: (NO CONFIRMATION.
  DISCARD.)
- AGING: (NO CONFIRMATION.
  DISCARD.)
- DAMAGE: (PINPRICK/PUNCTURE;
  NO IMPAIRMENT. DISCARD.)

SELF-CHECK: DISFUNCTION ANALYSIS.
- IMMOBILITY; (9 DISTRIBUTED
  POINTS PHYSICAL RESTRAINT.)

Of course, Gorb was not a computer. His was a very specialized organic mind, designed not for analysis, but for . . .

ACTION: SELF-PRESERVATION.

For the milliseconds the analysis required, Gorb did absolutely nothing. In the seconds that followed, he did everything possible to correct the dysfunctional situation. He flexed powerful arm and back muscles, and his left wrist sprung free. A restraint strap and buckle clattered to the floor.

"Hey, what's going on?"

DATUM: UNIDENTIFIED VOICE.
ACTION: DISREGARD; CONTINUE
SELF-PRESERVATION.

Another clatter, another restraint released. Slipping the head strap loose, Gorb sat up. His eyes were taped shut. He ripped the tape away.

DATUM: PAIN; NO DAMAGE.
DISREGARD.

Gorb's eyes scanned everything in range, absorbing, recognizing, cataloguing. The straps holding him were designed to restrain a sedated victim—or once, too long in the past to matter, a surgical patient—not a hyperdeveloped, fully conscious honch. Perhaps, too, they had deteriorated. Gorb freed himself with little effort. He studied the clear plastic tubes that connected him to the massive circulatory equipment. He studied other tubes that ran from those paraphernalia to . . . a wizened old man, whose smug, petulant demeanor was only now giving way to fear.

Still addled with gerontogenate toxins, Gorb wanted to jerk free of the deadly bonds, but a small voice inside told him to leave them in place. He must control their output. He needed only a respite. Gorb reached toward the device that hummed and burbled, and toggled a single switch.

Silence ensued. Only the whisper of his breathing, and the harsher rale of his counterpart's, could be heard. Gorb relaxed. He visualized processes within, cleansing, purifying. Hardwired function gave way gradually to the brighter glow of rational thought.

Gorb/Benadek pondered with increasing clarity what he should do next. He observed the General peripherally. Aged, dissipated eyes continued to stare at him. Unsure that Gorb's actions were more than undocumented honch reflex, the General was afraid to stimulate him to further action.

Benadek/Gorb smiled. With a shrug, he reached back to the medical machinery and again toggled the lever. The machine resumed its hum and babble, not unlike a rock-bound mountain rivulet, the murmur of bees in warm afternoon air, and to Benadek no more threatening than those sounds. He turned at last to meet the General's eyes.

"What are you doing?" the old man croaked. "What's happening here?"

"I'm going to give you a taste of real immortality," Benadek said. "You'll feel it happening soon. Be patient. You've waited two thousand years for this." His quiet monotone, the icy intelligence in his blue, honch eyes, belied the benevolence of his utterance. "But first, I will judge you."

"Judge me? Who . . . no, what . . . are you?"

"You should know me," Benadek breathed. "I'm your creator and your victims. I'm simple, pure-human, old-human, and the next step beyond all of those. I'm uniquely fit to judge what you've done with your two thousand years of life. But first, I must know you."

While he spoke, blood-borne essences filled the

machine's selective membranes, plugging here, dissolving there, changing flows and functions almost as if he, Benadek, were inside the apparatus. Where gerontic poisons had flowed, other substances circulated. Benadek passed through the barriers that had isolated victim and oppressor, and entered the General himself. The flow was in two directions. This was no invasion, only a raid, and the booty Benadek sought was information: the memories of two thousand years. Even as microscopic soldiers blitzed through the seat of the General's identity, others carried back what they'd found. Benadek absorbed it, pondered, and eventually wept.

The General had no way of understanding what was happening, but biologically, or through some higher sense, he felt the rape of his essence. Errant memories rose to consciousness one after another, some tainted with a horror that may have been Benadek's or his own, others carrying traces of sweetness, wistful memories from a past he had long forgotten or suppressed. All, he sensed, were being weighed by the anomalous being who watched him in silence from the other side of the machine.

Benadek was less placid than he seemed. The memories he reviewed—and the reviewing was hardly different than living them—filled him with bleak horror, heartsickness, and agony that threatened to drive him into total withdrawal. Nimbuk had been right. Age did not diminish evil, but concentrated it. What had begun as petty human greed for life, natural and healthy, had transformed with time and excess into a nightmare of slaughter and debauchery.

The slaughter had come first—the sacrifice of one life after another as the General and his companions strove to maintain themselves. Depravity came later, a natural follower: having committed murder upon murder not in the heat of battle but by sucking the living essences from other bodies, the General was obligated to prove that his depravity was total, and that he thus bore no guilt for what he had done, or what he would do in the future. It was his last reasoned thought.

From that time on, a dozen centuries past, the General—and those other survivors he would later kill in the competition for scarce bodies to victimize—became self-preserving organic machines. The underground stronghold became a battleground in which the weapons of war were bodies, and coup was counted in debasement, degradation, and shame. It was a war which the General finally won, and thus lost.

With the other ancients gone, the war turned inward, its battleground the mind of the last depraved warrior, and the carnage within was as extreme as the desolation without. The General, for centuries not sane by any human standard, had gone entirely mad.

By the time Benadek revived those memories little was left of the man who had once been, little even of the twisted beast he had become. Benadek found a shell, a collection of petulant, rote responses triggered by bodily functions and feelings, by boffin words and honch actions; a hollow shell with no more function than the ancient, useless fortress beneath the ice.

"I have judged you," Benadek said, eventually. "There is nothing good that you haven't polluted beyond redemption." He did not explain. There could be no explanation.

"You can't judge me!" the hollow shell echoed.

"I can. I have."

"You'll kill me?" The General's voice was flat.

"I can't. You can die—or take the immortality I promised you."

"I don't understand. Immortality is a myth. There are only more and more years, until they're all gone."

"Your way. Mine is different. Be silent, and you'll understand." Within Benadek, strands of RNA long in the building broke loose from their ribosomal attachments and floated away. Through veins and arteries they made their uncontrolled way to the tubes in his arms and thighs, and thus to the machine. They crossed over to the shrivelled body of his pitiful archenemy. . . .

Minutes passed slowly. Boffins returned to check on their responsibilities. Strangely, their ancient master remained silent, his eyes locked with Benadek's. The broken restraint straps remained unnoticed, and when instruments showed nothing amiss, the boffins retired.

"Do you understand, now?" Benadek said at last.

"You'll take my memories, and this body will die." Curiously, the aged, dilapidated face seemed less twisted, the rheumy eyes brighter not with the light of madness but with a nuance of forgotten brilliance. "I'll be diluted by you. But in a sense, I'll be as immortal as you may choose to be. So be it. It's more than my failure warrants—or less."

Benadek then understood: this General had been no ordinary man, but the pick of his generation, his long-gone world. Memories of Arnie's surfaced, highlighting the training the General had received, the rigors of the Academy, the demands of staff and general office. Where the very best, the most highly trained, had failed so utterly, he wondered, what might have been the fate of a lesser man?

The General, the once-rational man whose traces now surfaced as Benadek manipulated and prodded, understood both his salvation and his penalty: his memories—his soul?—would live on. Immortality, (if Benadek chose it, through the *change*), was his too, but his every atrocity—cannibalism, necrophilia, and the more personal outrages of rape, murder, and degradation—would survive, testaments to the nadir of human behavior. Standing beside the cool rationality of James Wold Bostwick and the disciplined flexibility of Arnold Sonnenfield, the hard, honest passion of Jack Van Duinen and the bright spark of creativity and élan of Jean-Francois Ailloud, the debasement of General Allan Robert Kauffman would remain always, an example and an admonition.

"I accept—the opportunity and the penalty." In that moment, even before Benadek's answering nod, the General began the final step in his long dying and the first of his new life.

Benadek got up. The door to the General's quarters opened to his touch. For a quarter hour he explored, and found what he suspected he might: a closet. Uniforms.

When next the boffins inspected their patient and his intended victim, they found only a dried-out husk where Benadek had lain. Benadek stood beside it. Boffin querulousness died before his imposing figure. His antique military uniform, resplendent with ribbons and untarnished braid, was no conceit, for the man who had once earned the right to wear it resided within him. Only a slight *change* had been necessary to fit Gorb's body to the General's clothing, for the latter had once been large and impressive.

Where the General had been dusky and black-haired, his successor was fair—but boffins who might have remembered his original appearance were hundreds of generations dead. These boffins merely saw and, though without understanding, accepted his miraculous rejuvenation.

Allan Robert Kauffman had maintained his fine military figure through his dynamic years. After taking his first surrogate life, before becoming enured to such taking, he had put his uniforms away. Later, when shame ceased to have meaning, the clothes no longer fit what he had become, and he no longer cared about them. Thus the Gorb/Benadek body fit them easily.

The boffins did as he bade them. His stature, his visual and chemical signals, and his voice of command precluded their doubting his orders.

Those orders were extensive. Though boffins seldom forgot anything, they soon found it necessary to use their hand-held terminals to record the stream of directives Benadek issued. With General Kauffman's knowledge at his command, Benadek charged the boffins with the shutdown of Continental Defense Treaty Command Post Alpha. Even as his dictates were issued, boffins throughout the underground facility dithered and scooted to carry them out. Benadek gave only superficial attention to the process. Much of his mind was elsewhere, on matters he had had little opportunity to consider since the long, trapped days while the Gorb-persona had governed. Even then, helpless and impotent, he had abstained from tormenting himself with speculation and worry.

Did Achibol still live? Had his faltering heart held out through the long months above, without a word of hope or a hint that all had not been lost? Benadek instructed a boffin to search for anything that might help the old man—or rather the old machine: his human parts were not failing. He told the boffin to search the fragmented remains of the world computer net for "Gibraltar," and for records of the cyborg experiments that had been performed there. There had to be a way to save Achibol.

Was Teress there, or had she buried the old charlatan and given up on the skinny boy in his honch-body, thinking him dead or reverted entirely to what he had seemed to be?

Had Achibol's medicines kept Ameling's raddled body from expiring? Was mad Yasha still with them, or had he run off with his rusty treasures?

What would they all think when the first tattered pure-humans emerged alive from the pit of horrors? Would they hear only tales of depravity and despair? Would they welcome any change in the deadly sameness of husks appearing again and again in the bleak valley, to be carted away and burned? Would they recognize that any change was reason for hope?

Benadek considered sending boffins to find his companions, to reassure them, but there were too few boffins, too many honches to be commanded, and far too many miles of corridors and wires and fiber-optic channels to be decommissioned and prepared for a discontinuation that might be forever. There was no need to destroy the facility, even though it was within his power to do it. Instead, let it remain a hidden monument to the glory and folly of the race that had created the world he had known.

Benadek questioned honches and boffins one by one and in groups. Not surprisingly, the honches sought orders. Benadek knew that they would be more fulfilled outside in the real world than marking time on barracks-duty below. But all could not go. He intended that Command Post Alpha remain minimally functional, not succumb to the continuous onslaught of groundwater, mold, and corrosion. It might someday have a higher purpose to serve, and maintaining it required a skeleton staff.

The boffins presented no problems. Given the alternatives of continued service below, with new, challenging tasks, or emerging in the world above to struggle with the vagaries of weather, climate, animals, undisciplined, uneducated simples, and irregular pure-humans, their preference was clear: they would stay where they belonged. Benadek assigned honches to them, for they would need manpower to maintain their small world, and arranged that departing honches would periodically send young members of their ilk to the sally port in the cave, to relieve, serve, and learn.

The problem of the temples had to be solved. Boffins supplied with replacement circuitry and tools could continue the chore he and Achibol had struggled with. Perhaps the boffins, using land-lines and satellites restored to service, could reconstitute the network and begin the long-postponed rejuvenation of the human race. But Benadek had set himself another task entirely.

The braid and medals of the General's uniform had no metallic content; they passed the matter-transmitter gate without difficulty. The emtee had been reprogrammed to accept what Benadek had become. He steeled himself for the single step that would convey him forever beyond this maze under the ice. What would he find? Would there be nothing but a long-decayed Benadek-body huddled on a blanket long gone to mold? Would a gathering of dear friends greet him? Would Teress's eyes light up, knowing him even in this magnificent body? Would the grand, crotchety old sorcerer smile proudly upon his young apprentice, now grown tall?

Taking a deep breath, Benadek stepped through the door into the world.

INTERLUDE
The Great School, Midicor IV

Saphooth backed away from the console—and from Kaledrin, whom he eyed with revulsion and horror. "He did it! The little bastard really did it! Just as I suspected! Benadek the body snatcher. And you . . . you want to . . . " He backed up another step—or rather he tried to, but his feet would not move. Something tough and rubbery held his bony ankles.

"No!" Saphooth shrieked. "Let go of me!" He struggled then, but it was too late. Kaledrin had many tentacles, far more than he needed to immobilize the rickety simian-form Saphooth, and to stifle his cries.

For several minutes, anyone up or down the hall could have heard the moans and grunts of the two men struggling, molluscoid tentacles against simian-form muscle and bone—but no others heard. There were only the two of them—and then only one.

CHAPTER TWENTY-THREE,

wherein the boy sorcerer gives old Achibol a soul.

This episode's Ksentos Venimentum heading must suffice for this chapter and the next, for Benadek has more than one gift to give, and not to Achibol alone.

(Kaledrin, Senior Editor)

Benadek's clear honch-vision made out a tiny figure standing beside the tent on the ice, but he could not tell who it was until he was halfway down the cliff face.

"Teress," he cried, but his honch-voice made it a booming call. The pure-human girl looked first at him, then away, then back, as if she wished to flee, and to run toward him—but both impulses negated each other, and she stood, waiting.

"Are you . . . are you . . ."

"Benadek. Yes, I'm Benadek."

He held out both arms to her, but she stood rigidly. "How can I be sure? All the hideous stories the refugees tell . . ."

He let his arms fall to his side. "I guess you'll have to wait and see," he said, then grinned. "If it walks like a duck, and talks like a duck . . ."

"What's a duck?"

He sighed. "Never mind. If I'm Benadek . . . I mean, I am, but you don't know it. . . . You'll just have to watch me, and listen to me, until you're sure."

"I guess so," she said. "Maybe Achibol will be able to tell."

"Where is he? He's all right?"

"He's alive. He's pretty much as he was the last time . . . you . . . saw him."

"Where? Take me to him."

The wagon camp seemed deserted. It was dusk, and people had eaten, and would be preparing to sleep. Many seekers had left with their returned loved ones or their confirmed dead, thus at peace, but the constant trickle of departees from Continental Defense Treaty Command Post Alpha continued, and filled the tents and makeshift shelters left behind.

Over Teress's shoulder, Benadek saw Ameling—and was the tiny man holding her hand Yasha? His white hair and beard were neatly trimmed; he looked almost . . . human. And there, wrapped in blankets, facing the small campfire, was Achibol. The sorcerer's dark eyes were bright as ever, and they tracked Benadek's approach like the mechanical scanners they truly were, but they looked like eyes, not metal orbs, and there was no telltale red glow.

"Master," Benadek said, and hunkered down on his haunches. "You've got to come inside the stronghold with me! I think I found—"

"He's not going anywhere until I'm sure you're Benadek!" Teress snapped.

"He is," Achibol said.

"How can you tell?"

"If it walks like a duck, and talks like a . . ."

"Will someone tell me what a duck is?" Teress's face was red. Benadek grinned.

"Maybe you're right," she said to Achibol. "No one but Benadek could make me so mad! That insufferable grin! That smug—"

"Later," Achibol said. "What have you found, boy?"

"Parts, Master! I won't know for sure until we open you up and look, but there's a whole lot down there, storerooms full of prosthetics—even hearts! The boffins think they may be able to replace yours."

"This isn't Gibraltar," Teress protested. "They won't be the same! And what will happen to him while they're replacing it?"

"It's all right, child," the old man said. "One pump's pretty much like another if the capacities and voltages match. And they can replace my original heart—I'll be using the backup, just as I am now."

"I'm afraid," she said, kneeling, putting her head on his shoulder.

"Me too," he said, "but I've been afraid so long it feels normal to me."

"We'll go in the morning," he said to Benadek. "Tonight, let's just sit by the fire and . . . get reacquainted."

Will it work? Benadek asked. Then he waited. Gorb and the others were part of him now, inseparable memories that he would not ordinarily call upon from day to day, stored chemically in out-of-the-way places. They took time to fetch.

Finally a thought crossed his mind: It will work. But it requires a permanent, full-time consciousness. Which of . . . of us . . . will it be? It was not really

Paula Farr's thought, but it had a certain, recognizable "flavor."

Can we do that? Reconstitute one of your personalities then . . . then kick it out? Banishing it to . . . what?

Do you have ethical objections? Someone would have to volunteer.

But you're all me now. It would be me "volunteering" one of you.

We're you. So it would still be genuinely voluntary.

Who then? Which of me will go?

While this interim discussion went on, Achibol watched expressions dance across Benadek's face. It had been *his* idea, not the boy's, but he was far from sure that it was right, morally right.

Benadek had told him what had happened to Gorb and the once-frozen personalities, and he had immediately thought of . . . Yasha. His poor, deranged buddy had recovered somewhat, with care and kindness, but he would never get much better than he was right now. When the tiny scraps of endocrine tissue preserved within his mechanical self had died, his brain had been irreparably damaged.

Early cyborg experiments had interfaced brains and mechanisms. That worked fine as long as there was still a body attached to the brain. The "brain in a box" idea never panned out—people weren't brains, they were . . . people. Whole entities, brains, glands, bodies, in complex interaction. Saving enough glandular tissue, skin, muscle, and so forth to stimulate the boxed brain with the chemicals of stress, fear, elation, and even fatigue, kept it sane—after a fashion. Achibol was not entirely convinced he himself was sane, but he wasn't entirely nuts, like Yasha.

The essence of Benadek's other selves was chemical; endocrine secretions and byproducts . . . just what Yasha had lost when his internal tissue cultures had died. And they were—or had been—coherent personalities too, something Yasha wasn't.

But what right did Achibol have to decide whether Yasha was better off as he was now, or with an internal "partner" to regulate his flawed brain? Partner—or dictator? Who was to say? Who would speak with Yasha's voice once the transfer was made? What was the right thing to do?

He must have spoken aloud, because Benadek answered: "What was done to Yasha—and to you—was wrong. And what was done to . . . James Wold Bostwick . . . was also wrong. Two wrongs can't make a right, but maybe they can be . . . mitigated."

"Bostwick. The philosopher?"

"The ethicist. Who better to make the decision once he's inside Yasha, and can determine what's best—for Yasha, and for him too?"

"Indeed. And what about you?" Benadek's face told that tale: chemicals were chemicals. They could be duplicated, and in living bodies they were, continually. Personalities weren't static. They were constantly being recreated out of fresh materials. Only their patterns were relatively constant. And such patterns could be duplicated. Benadek would not lose his "conscience." His memories of James Wold Bostwick would remain.

"That's it, then." Achibol got to his feet. Sticking his head outside, he called to Ameling. "Get Yasha."

"We have to tell him what we intend," Achibol mused while they waited. "We have to give him the choice."

"But he's crazy! He doesn't know what's good for himself."

"We must make him understand." Benadek knew that tone of voice. Achibol's mind was made up. And there was no time for more discussion: Yasha had arrived.

"I won't go in that tent!" the little man protested.

"Your friend Archie's inside, waiting for you," Ameling said.

"Stuff Archie!"

"Yasha! I've got your new orders in here!"

"Orders? For me? You mean somebody's finally gotten through? Let me see!" He pushed the flap aside.

"Here," said Achibol, holding out his "talisman." The tiny screen of the universal interfaced glowed, and words marched down it. "Your orders."

Yasha snatched the device, peered at the screen. "What does it say? Read it to me."

"Read it yourself."

The little man's face twisted and reddened. Tears sprang into the corners of his eyes. "I can't!" he wailed. "I forgot how!"

"Poor fellow," Benadek said sympathetically, putting a hand on his shoulder. Already he felt the swarming essences of James Wold Bostwick readying themselves for transition . . . but it was not yet time. "Don't you want to remember?"

"Of course, you imbecile! My orders!"

"I can help you remember how to read again."

"You can?" The wistful look in Yasha's half-mad eyes reminded Benadek of Sylfie, struggling how to learn . . . but this was not Sylfie. "How?"

"Remember the little voice, Yasha—the one you listened for in the Tin Mule's heater? Would you like to have it inside your head—to read to you, and explain things?"

"I want it! Where is it?"

"You wouldn't mind sharing your head with the voice?"

Achibol added, "For the rest of your life?"

"As long as it's not your scratchy old voice, Archie!"

Benadek raised an eyebrow toward Achibol. Was that enough? Was that "permission" to go ahead?

Achibol nodded. Benadek's heartbeat quickened. The palm of his hand tingled, and dampened. Unseen fluids penetrated Yasha's jacket and shirt, then entered the pores of his skin . . .

He stiffened. "What are you doing?" He tried to pull away, but could not. "Let go of me!"

Ameling pushed into the tent. "Everything's fine, Yasha," she murmured, grasping his other arm firmly. "Soon you'll be well again."

"I'm not sick! I'm just . . . I'm just . . ." His face wrinkled. "I don't know what I am," he howled. "I've forgotten!"

"Just hold still, dear," Ameling urged, "and you'll soon remember."

Benedict felt the flow of complex chemicals, the departure of James Wold Bostwick—of a part of himself. It went on and on. He felt Yasha's trembling, and grew angry. The little madman couldn't understand what he was getting—what Benadek was losing.

At last it was over. The last traces of Bostwick had crossed over, and Benadek was left only with the memory of him.

Yasha stood rigidly, his eyes wild as ever. "It's done," Benadek said. "How do you feel?"

"I have a headache! My stomach hurts and I'm cold! I'm tired!"

"Here's a blanket, Yasha," Ameling said. She and Achibol wrapped him up, and settled him at the rear of the tent.

"How long?" Achibol asked

"I don't know," Benadek replied. "I didn't time things before. Just let him sleep. He'll . . . they'll sort things out." His eyes drooped. Ameling saw, brought another blanket, then guided him to a soft bed of spruce branches.

The next morning Benadek led Achibol, Ameling, and Teress up the cleft to the so-called "empty" cave, and hauled the old man's two trunks up by rope, without assistance from anyone.

Yasha alone stayed behind. "I'm remembering," he said, tossing a dry branch on the fire. "By the time you get back, I'll remember everything!"

Was it so? Were the "original" Yasha's memories intact, and no longer inaccessible? Or would the essences of James Wold Bostwick merely "fill in" where necessary? Benedict suspected he would never see an obvious trace of the philosopher in Yasha's speech or manner; true to his principles, Bostwick would remain in the background, a tiny voice even Yasha might not consciously "hear."

Teress insisted upon preceding all of them into the underground stronghold, and returning, before she let Achibol or Ameling do so—the honch spoke with Benadek's words but his voice was not a boy's, nor were his stance and strength, and she knew no more about "ducks" than the night before.

The reprogrammed matter-transmitter did not balk at Achibol's metal parts. The hallway leading to the prosthetics lab and storerooms went left, then down an elevator, but Benadek led them right, to a different place. They understood nothing of the great, transparent tubes of colored fluids, the complex piping and instrumentation, but all sensed the horror, pain, and spiritual agony that lay like oily dust over every surface.

"If this works," Benadek said in a low, anxious baritone, "this place won't feel quite so horrible." He turned to Ameling.

"There?" she asked, nodding toward the wheeled hospital stretcher at the center of the maze of tubes, pipes, and wires. Benadek nodded. He helped her to lie on the fresh, crisp sheets, and gently drew straps snug at her wrists, chest, knees, and ankles.

The ghost of Dr. Paula Race Farr, M.D. rose up to take over Benadek's big honch hands, to guide the

I.V. needles smoothly, painlessly, into Ameling's shrunken veins. Whoever then controlled the hands that switched on the multitude of mysterious pumps and devices, when those hands squeezed Ameling's shoulders reassuringly, they were Benadek's.

"Soon you'll doze," he said. "I don't think you'll dream."

"If I do, I'll dream of something quite strange," she responded.

"What?"

"The future," she said. "My future. There was none to dream of, before." Her eyelids drooped. Somewhere a monitor that had chirped busily slowed, then steadied—a quiet, regular, musical tone once every second or so.

"She's asleep," Benadek murmured. "There's nothing more we can do, until the process is finished."

"I'm not leaving," Teress said abruptly. "Not until—" she almost said "Only if"—"she wakes up."

"I thought we could start getting Achibol ready . . ."

"Not until she's awake," Teress snapped, settling stiffly to the floor and folding her arms across her chest.

Benadek caught Achibol's eye.

"There's no rush," the old man said. "I feel just fine." At least he understood the source of Benadek's anxiety—not that the "experiment" upon Ameling wasn't reason enough.

Benadek sat. Achibol squatted. Teress remained as she was, arms still folded. Occasionally one of the big flagons "glugged" or "blupped," and all three of them twitched anxiously. Benadek wanted to get up, to peer closely at Ameling, looking for . . . changes, but he refused to give Teress the satisfaction of knowing how afraid he was. Besides, she'd probably think he was going to *do* something to her . . .

Teress allowed herself no expression. Only her eyes

moved—from Benadek to Ameling to Achibol. She was thinking about . . . ducks.

Whenever Benadek looked at her, he thought about ducks too—though he had never seen one, except in pictures. "The cow says 'moo,'" he quoted from the stained, tattered book of ABC's he had left behind in his hidey-hole beneath the tailor shop. "The duck says 'quack, quack, quack,' and the rooster says 'cock-a-doodle-do.'"

It seemed years since Benadek the urchin had read those words. What had happened to that urchin-child? He must be inside me, Benadek thought, along with all the others. Maybe I'll find him again, someday . . .

Achibol squatted stoically. If he had any thoughts at all, they remained hidden behind a weathered, unreadable brown mask.

"Cheep, cheep, cheep cheep cheepcheep . . ." The heart monitor's beat quickened with Ameling's waking pulse.

Benadek leaped to his feet—with Teress only a heartbeat behind. They rushed to the stretcher. Ameling's halo of short blond hair was unstreaked by gray, and her eyes were chicory-blue, like the horizon on a bright, clear day. The angry red blotches that had marred her skin were gone: her forehead was smooth, pale, creamy, and her cheeks had just the slightest rosy blush.

"Are you okay?" Benadek asked softly, his vision blurring as he fumbled with her restraints.

"I'd forgotten how it felt to be well," Ameling said in soft, smooth tones without a hint of scratchiness. "I feel . . . young."

"You are," Teress said. "It worked. Benadek's plan worked."

Benadek hardly noticed Teress's admission of his identity. He turned aside, and his broad honch-shoulders shook with the intensity of his weeping. His throat ached with the effort to stifle sobs that nonetheless pushed forth. Teress's eyes darted from Ameling to Benadek to Ameling . . . "Go to him," the lovely blond poot commanded her. "He needs you."

Benadek sank to his knees when Teress reached out to him. He buried his face in her midriff. She held his head there, her fingers in his hair, so different from the soft, black locks she remembered—yet not so different, not really.

"Sylfie," he moaned, no longer trying to stifle his sobs. "Sylfie is . . . "

"I know," Teress murmured. "I know. It's all right. Sylfie wanted this. She wanted you to succeed, to fix what was wrong with her world—and now you have. She's happy now."

"She's dead!" Benadek wailed. "That's Ameling over there, not Sylfie."

Now he knew what Teress had known all along; after all, there were only a limited number of poot templates, and he was bound to run across someone made in Sylfie's mold sooner or later. Teress was just glad Benadek hadn't recognized Ameling before he had saved the world, and redeemed Sylfie's death—which he, stupid, selfish brat, had caused.

But her anger was gone. Tears wet her cheeks: tears for Sylfie, for Benadek, for Ameling's suffering. Such tears didn't have to be for anyone in particular. She thought of her parents, her village, pure-humans everywhere who had been slain, simples whose human potential had been denied them. Such tears just had to be.

CHAPTER TWENTY-FOUR

Benadek could look at Ameling without tears now. She wasn't really Sylfie. Identical genes had made them similar, but divergent lives had drawn them differently. Even the suffering she had endured was scribed across Ameling's features in a way unlike Sylfie's. They were no more than cousins, he thought.

Two boffins in white lab coats met them at the elevator, though no one had seen Benadek call them. "The facility is ready, General," one said.

"We found the parts you wanted," the other added.

Benadek nodded absently. Parts. A heart, even a human one, was just a "part," wasn't it? But what a terrifyingly important part! A man, even a cyborg like Achibol, couldn't just be parked and turned off like the Tin Mule. Everything had to be kept running without faltering, or the man, the mind, died.

It might have been easier if the "facility" had looked like a workshop or garage, not an operating room. The table was draped with cold, white plastic. The monitors winked red, blue, green, and yellow.

Achibol sat on the cold, hard bed. Benadek helped lift his skinny legs. There was no pillow for his head. Boffins looped wires over the old man, plugged tiny probes under his fingernails and in the corners of his eyes. One opened Achibol's black jumpsuit, then probed at his chest. It popped open.

There were no ribs, no red flesh or lungs, only shiny metal, colored wires, and pale green circuit boards like those in the temples. A boffin carefully lifted wires and tubes aside, and Benadek caught a glimpse of two shiny cylinders. Hearts. Just pumps, with bearings, lubricants, gaskets . . .

He placed his hands on Achibol's face, touching not machine, but skin: real, human skin, warm and dry.

"What are you doing?" Teress asked anxiously.

"I have to be in contact with the organic part of him. If . . . if something goes wrong, I'll try to save him another way."

"How?"

"Later, child," Achibol said softly. "I know what Benadek means to do."

Benadek had told him about Gorb and General Kauffman. If the "surgery" didn't work—if there was no other way, Benadek would "invade" the old man's remaining human flesh as he had Gorb's, and would try to guide the essence of Achibol from his dying brain . . . into himself. It was not a "life" the old man would enjoy, but . . . but there was still much to be done, and Achibol wanted to be there to see the end of what he had begun.

Another boffin came in, wheeling a cart heaped with mechanical objects. They looked—somewhat—like the dual heart-pumps in Achibol's crowded chest cavity. Somewhat, not exactly. That was the problem. But maybe one would fit in the space available.

Benadek held his breath while the boffin, with sharp-nosed pliers, tugged at a connection. "This is the primary heart," he said. He probed with a long pin at the end of a wire, and gestured at an instrument dial. "No current. It's nonfunctional. I will remove it."

Benadek's jaw ached from clenching his teeth. The boffin tugged disconnected wires aside and draped them down Achibol's sides. Then, pliers in each hand, he lifted the shiny cylinder out. "This is a sealed unit," he said. "It can't be repaired. Pass me the Gamma-205." His companion carefully lifted a similar-looking device from the cart.

The first boffin measured Achibol's burnt-out heart with calipers. "One hundred two by sixty millimeters," he muttered, sounding petulant, annoyed. "The Gamma-205 is ninety-eight by seventy-two. It won't fit." Benadek heard the hiss of Teress's indrawn breath.

"The Delta-220 is one-oh-one by one-oh-four," the second boffin said. "Let's see if it can be squeezed in."

"The original is threaded. The Delta-220 has a molecular-weld surface."

"What's that?" Achibol asked, his voice as calm as if they were puzzling out the insides of the Tin Mule or a temple's interior, not his innermost physical self.

"Molecular-weld surfaces are so finely polished that when they're pressed together and the protective coating on them is dissolved, their surfaces become as one."

"Can the fitting inside me be polished like that—ground down to fit?"

"It has to be done in a vacuum," the boffin said. "The metals have to be exactly the same alloy. "

"Never mind then. Will one of the others work?"

"The Delta-80 is small enough, but it has male threads. Fember"—the other boffin, the one with the cart—"do we have couplings with molecular-weld ends? I'll need two, female-threaded on one end."

"I'll go see." He scurried off.

Benadek had to remind himself to breathe. He forced his jaw to relax. Wasn't the storeroom right next door? What was taking so long?

Fember returned with a handful of boxes, which he opened gingerly, careful not to touch the burnished ends with their thin coatings of soft, clear, plastic. As he unwrapped each part, he handed it to his associate who spun it into place, his long spindly fingers inside Achibol's chest. He tightened each with a wrench—an ungainly tool for such vital work. Benadek's teeth ground against each other.

"Now the Delta-80," the boffin said. "I'll need a wire harness to place it."

Moments later, he lowered the pump by two loops of wire. He nudged it this way and that. He maneuvered spring clamps into place, and drew the Delta-80 tight against the new fitting. He tried to do the same with the other end, but the first clamp flew off. "I'll have to make the first weld, then pull the second joint together," he said. "Fember—the solvent."

"What if the other end won't fit?" Benadek blurted.

"I'll rotate the entire unit off and try something else." He replaced the first clamp, then carefully dribbled clear liquid from a long, thin bottle onto the joint. Misty vapor arose.

"What will that do to his insides?" Benadek asked uneasily.

"Nothing. It's already evaporating—and the protective seal with it." Benadek noticed that the boffin didn't sound flighty, nervous, or agitated. Was that because he was in his own exacting milieu, doing what he did best?

"There. Now the other joint." He struggled to pull the two halves together.

"I can't make the two ends meet," said the boffin, his face red, and his fingers white with effort. "Help me, someone."

"I will." Benedict pushed forward. He reached into . . . Achibol. Into the maw of the great wound that was not a wound. His big honch-fingers spanned the new heart. With his thumb on one end and the flange of the molecular-weld fitting pinched between his index and middle fingers, he squeezed, and the gap narrowed by two millimeters.

"More," the boffin said. "It's almost halfway there. Just a little more." Benadek squeezed. Straining tendons crackling were the loudest sounds in the room. The two vital surfaces moved ever-so-slightly closer together. "Almost. Almost," the boffin murmured between clenched teeth. Benadek's strength was at its limit, but there was no room for both his big honch-hands in Achibol's crowded interior.

Sweat poured down Benadek's face, blinding him. "How much more? I can't see it. A millimeter? More? Less?"

"Less. Keep squeezing. The joint must be absolutely tight when I apply the solvent." Benadek's muscles burned. His fingers felt as though they might snap. "Good," the boffin said. "Hold that. It will be just a minute . . . seconds." Benadek held. Seconds? How many? How long could he hold?

"You can let go now," the boffin said. "Stand aside. I have to reconnect and test it." Benadek moved back only a step. He needed to see. That was Achibol, his master, his friend, not some inanimate machine. The boffin remade connections, reinserted loose wires and tucked them neatly away. "Pass me the data-probe," he commanded Fember, who proffered a long needle on the end of a coiled wire.

The lead boffin tweaked a dial on one black box, eyed a line of tiny red lights that fluctuated back and forth across it, and nodded. Then he leaned down toward Achibol's face. "The pump appears to be interfaced with your autonomic systems," he said softly. "Are you ready to switch over?"

"Can't you get *that* out of the way first?" said Achibol, gesturing loosely at the front of his chest, which still stood out at a sharp angle from the rest of him.

"Oh. Yes. Of course. I have every confidence the pump will work just fine." He removed the probe and pressed down on Achibol's chest-plate, which latched shut with a sharp, final, click. "There now, are you ready?"

Achibol nodded. There was no outward sign of change but, seconds later, the old man smiled. "It's so smooth," he crooned delightedly. "I can hardly feel it. But I know it's there, working. I feel refreshed, as if I just had a good night's sleep. I could dance. How long has it been since I danced? Five hundred years? A thousand? Let me up."

"Master Achibol," Teress said anxiously, "shouldn't you rest?"

"Rest? I've been resting. I've been at half-speed since your great-great-great-great-great-granny was a zygote. Now I want to dance. Let me up."

She sighed, and shrugged. "There's nothing holding you down."

Achibol sat up, swinging his legs to the floor. He smiled—a great yellow-toothed grin—and reached toward her.

"What?" she asked.

"Let's dance," he said. "Benadek! Music!"

"Huh?" Then Benadek remembered the Command Center's interface. He had discovered it soon after his conquest of General Kauffman. It was not as "personable" as Circe, but he had given it a name anyway. "Ulysses! Let's have something to dance to—something . . . sprightly." Immediately, sweet notes of piccolos filtered down from the ceiling, and were joined by softly brushed drums and a mandolin.

Achibol grasped Teress's hands. The music swelled. They danced. Teress's light steps might have reminded a watching ancient, or Achibol himself, of an Irish jig. The older man's sinuous, suggestive movements evoked a different culture, one just as extinct.

Vagrant memories tugged at Benadek's awareness. Whose memories? Who remembered the way black men had once danced beneath bright, colored lights—the drumming beat, the staccato voices? Who remembered also Gaelic girls stamping, their hard-soled feet accenting the wail of penny whistles, the moan of concertinas and humming fiddles?

What survived out there, in the wild, fragmented world? Were there still Irishmen—pure-humans subsisting on moss and memories on a far green isle? Did ebon men still dance in hidden corners of the sub-Saharan wastes, or in the ruins of great Eastern cities?

Though he enjoyed the music, and the joy of his friends, Benadek grew restless. There was still much to be done, before they could be on their way. There was a big world out there, and real work still to be accomplished. His mind ranged out across that vastness, impatient to take the first steps toward some greater, still-undefined goal.

EPILOGUE,

being the conclusion of the first tome of Achibol the Sorcerer.

This conclusive chapter in what might be called the first Book of Benadek has no apparent roots in the collected mythologies. The biocybes, however, have certified it with an unprecedented level of confidence.

A more fitting conclusion would have been hard to devise—but there are loose ends. Even the unsubstantiated idea that Benadek alone might be father to the entire Race of Man demands clarification, and the introduction of a quest for Gibraltar hints that there are more tales to be told. Entire cycles of myth have been ignored herein, strong ones like "Benadek among the Cannibals of Orkenor." Have they been discarded, or can we hope that they will find a place in a future tome? Upon what yet-undiscovered legends will their telling depend?

(Kaledrin, Senior Editor)

EPILOGUE

Massive, pearly clouds gathered high above the jagged mountain barrier, and low-angled sunlight sprawling across the eastern plains tinted them with the rose blush of early morning. The Tin Mule was heaped high with trade goods and the amenities an old man would need on the long journey ahead. Achibol swung the ancient craft in a great loop around the Valley encampment, swelled now and bustling with the departing population of Continental Defence Treaty Command Post Alpha.

"That's one prophecy that may yet come to pass," he thought wryly, not unhappily. There would indubitably be a city here, a few years hence. Or would it only be a stone lodge and a campground, where sightseers could rest between forays out on the icefield nested among the Alberta mountains above? Eastward of the camp, he searched the ground for the ruins of ancient buildings, but trees had thrust up and died and grown again many times in the two thousand years since he had honeymooned there. The ice had advanced and retreated, and not even the greatest monuments of man could have withstood its grinding progress. Only the graceful northeasterly arc of the valley itself marked the route of the old road.

He proceeded slowly, savoring bracing mountain air laden with spring flower-scent and traces of everlasting ice. There was no hurry. Either his old heart—and his new, jury-rigged one—would last, or they would go out in spatters of melted bearings. He would make it to Gibraltar one way or another—on his own feet, or as a reluctant, carping, complaining passenger in the mind and body of his apprentice, who was up ahead.